Y0-AWG-495

BOLD SURRENDER

"When I saw ye standing there in the moonlight, I knew ye for an angel . . . I was but thinking I had died and gone to heaven."

Kelt swept her up in his arms and carried her to the bed.

Ashley's eyes grew heavy-lidded with passion as she watched him pull his shirt over his head. "I never thought a man could be so beautiful," she said.

"I never thought to hear a lass speak so," he said, pulling her close to him. "Ye must be a kelpie . . . or at least a witch, for I be bewitched if ever a mon was."

"You promised me a Christmas gift," she whispered throatily.

"Aye," he answered, nuzzling her neck and the curve of her breast. "And ye shall have one . . . or I shall die trying."

Other Books in
THE AVON ROMANCE Series

BELOVED ROGUE *by Penelope Williamson*
CHASE THE DAWN *by Jane Feather*
DEFIANT ANGEL *by Lisann St. Pierre*
MARISA *by Linda Lang Bartell*
PASSION FIRE *by Mallory Burgess*
RENEGADE LOVE *by Katherine Sutcliffe*
UNTAMED GLORY *by Suzannah Davis*

Coming Soon

DARK DESIRES *by Nancy Moulton*
MATTERS OF THE HEART *by Mayo Lucas*

Avon Books are available at special quantity discounts for bulk purchases for sales promotions, premiums, fund raising or educational use. Special books, or book excerpts, can also be created to fit specific needs.

For details write or telephone the office of the Director of Special Markets, Avon Books, Dept. FP, 105 Madison Avenue, New York, New York 10016, 212-481-5653.

JUDITH E. FRENCH

Best wishes!
Judith E French

AVON
PUBLISHERS OF BARD, CAMELOT, DISCUS AND FLARE BOOKS

For my friends,
Joyce A. Flaherty, Carin Cohen,
and Ellen Edwards,
with a very special thank you
to my technical advisors,
Lester F. Bennett and Keith Culver

BOLD SURRENDER is an original publication of Avon Books. This work has never before appeared in book form. This work is a novel. Any similarity to actual persons or events is purely coincidental.

AVON BOOKS
A division of
The Hearst Corporation
105 Madison Avenue
New York, New York 10016

Copyright © 1988 by Judith E. French
Published by arrangement with the author
Library of Congress Catalog Card Number: 87-91687
ISBN: 0-380-75243-3

All rights reserved, which includes the right to reproduce this book or portions thereof in any form whatsoever except as provided by the U.S. Copyright Law. For information address Joyce A. Flaherty, 816 Lynda Court, St. Louis, Missouri 63122.

First Avon Books Printing: April 1988

AVON TRADEMARK REG. U.S. PAT. OFF. AND IN OTHER COUNTRIES, MARCA REGISTRADA, HECHO EN U.S.A.

Printed in the U.S.A.

K-R 10 9 8 7 6 5 4 3 2 1

Chapter 1

Morgan's Fancy, Maryland
Autumn 1743

The storm gathered fury as it rolled eastward across the dark, turbulent waters of the Chesapeake. Thunder shook the cosmos; jagged bolts of lightning joined heaven and earth in terrifying splendor as the tempest unleashed its raw power against the land.

Sheets of driving rain assaulted the house, rattling the windows and cascading down the steep shingle roof in drenching waves. Streams of water made their way down the insides of the chimneys, causing dying fires to hiss and crackle, and sending off sparks that bounced against the wide brick hearths.

Groaning, the giant poplars that sheltered the house bent under the wind as leaves and small branches were stripped away and tumbled into the darkness. A weakened limb gave way under the strain and crashed against the house, shattering a precious multipaned window.

The sound of broken glass was followed almost immediately by a low whining and scratching at Ashley's door. "Just a minute, Jai." Ashley pulled the ledger closer and ran a finger down the neat rows of figures written first in her grandfather's bold hand and then in her own, mentally verifying the sums and subsequent balance. The dog's whining became more insistent. "All right, all right."

With a sigh, Ashley replaced the goose quill in the inkwell, stepped over a half-mended saddle, and strode across the shadowy bedchamber to throw open the door. Instantly a huge, shaggy dog bounded into the room, nearly knocking her over in his enthusiasm. A wet tongue scratched against Ashley's face, and she pushed him away. "Down. Down, Jai," she scolded, halfheartedly. "You're in, but you're not going to make a habit of it."

The dog pushed his nose under her hand, and she capitulated, kneeling on the cold floor and wrapping her arms around him. "Good dog, good Jai." She ruffled his shaggy fur. "You're not a coward, are you? Not afraid of a little old thunderstorm?"

Ashley knew she should investigate the broken glass, but Thomas or one of the servants would see to it. If anything serious was wrong, they would have been shouting for her by now. She gave the dog a final pat and returned to the plantation accounts on her cluttered desk. Jai settled onto the small rug by her chair, laying his massive head against her high leather boots.

Secretly glad for the company, Ashley picked up the quill and resumed her calculations. The flickering firelight cast a golden glow on her features as she concentrated on the precise figures. Like most of the tobacco planters on the Tidewater, Ashley was heavily in debt. But unlike most of them, her problems were compounded because she was a woman.

Since her grandfather's death nearly a year ago, she had discovered that it was almost impossible for her to carry on the day-to-day business affairs of the plantation. Ships' captains who had done business with old Ash for years had suddenly had no room on their vessels for Ashley's tobacco. A neighbor, from whom they had purchased woodland, was demanding immediate payment, even though he had given her grandfather five years to pay.

If she couldn't ship her tobacco, there would be no money to pay the debts, no money to order precious goods from England such as iron tools, needles, or salt for preserving meat.

"Men don't like dealing with a woman," her solicitor, Richard Chadwick, had declared the morning of her grandfather's funeral. "You must hire an overseer, someone to placate the merchants and sea captains, not to mention your London factor. I'm certain he won't renew your contract next year, and then where will you be? Without a factor, you can't sell your damned tobacco if you do get it to England!"

"Morgan's Fancy has never had an overseer," Ashley had declared. "My grandfather didn't believe in them. I'm perfectly capable of conducting my own affairs. Besides," she'd admitted, "I couldn't afford an overseer even if I wanted one." But she knew that once Richard had something in that brain of his, he was like a dog with a bone; he kept gnawing at it. She'd hoped this time would be different.

Ashley slammed the ledger closed and leaned forward to rest her forehead on her clasped hands. Richard or these figures, she didn't know which was worse! Her financial situation was desperate; she had to sell this year's tobacco crop or else.

She'd let Richard convince her that the plantation would be better off with a male overseer, yet secretly she'd hoped he wouldn't be able to find one who would consent to work for a woman. To her delight, Richard's succinct missives had included references to blunt refusals by prospective candidates for the position. As months had passed and the mention of an overseer had disappeared from his reports, Ashley had begun to think the matter was closed.

Richard's latest lengthy letter, received several weeks ago, had proved otherwise. *An overseer has been hired for Morgan's Fancy,* he'd written. *He is a former bondman, but has ten years' experience and comes with a superior recommendation. I'm certain you will be pleased with him. As your solicitor, I've signed a two-year contract with Master Saxon of the Virginia Colony.*

Damn Richard! If she hadn't been able to afford an overseer last spring, she certainly couldn't afford one now. But it would be impossible to break that contract without paying Master Saxon's full salary for the entire two-year period, or without destroying any thread of credibility she had as master of Morgan's Fancy. Like it or not, she would have an overseer as soon as he arrived.

Ashley's thoughts were drowned in a roll of thunder, then forgotten as a bolt of lightning struck so close it lit the bedchamber as bright as day. The resulting thunder shook the house and momentarily deafened her. For two long heartbeats, primitive terror held her transfixed, then her brain snapped into action and she ran to the rain-streaked window. The driving rain made it impossible to see anything, but she was certain the lightning had hit something nearby.

Ashley grabbed a worn cloak from the back of a chair and threw it around her shoulders. "You stay here!" she ordered Jai. Carefully closing the bedroom door behind her, she hurried down the wide stairs and into the entrance hall.

The shadowy form of an old man thrust forth a lantern. "I think it hit close, Miss Ashley," the thin voice quavered. "I was goin' to take a look-see."

"I'll go." She took the lantern from his wrinkled hand.

"You got no business goin' out there. It's a powerful bad storm. You know how you hate thunderstorms. If Master Ash was here . . ."

"Well, he's not here, Thomas." Her voice softened. "I'll be all right. You stay inside where it's dry."

Outside, the rain soaked her cloak in seconds, and she pushed the heavy, sodden mass off her shoulders. Wind tore at her unbound hair and drove needles of icy rain against her skin, threatening to drive her down into the slippery, cold mud. Ashley closed her eyes against the flying sticks and debris, making her way slowly by memory across the familiar farmyard. The wind filled her ears and the rain drenched her linen shirt and breeches, chilling her body.

Another flash of lightning illuminated the barn ahead, startling her so that she slipped to one knee in the mire. A mare's whinny was borne on the wind, high-pitched and full of fear.

Struggling to her feet, Ashley ran the last hundred feet to the barn and yanked open the heavy wooden door. Smoke and the acrid smell of burning hay enveloped her. Flames danced at the far end of the center walkway. Bits of wood flew from the stall on her right as the bay stallion lashed out with powerful hooves against the plank door.

"Whoa! Whoa, boy!" Ashley shot the iron bolt and shielded herself with the door as Baron reared, then plunged through the opening to safety.

She had no need for the lantern. The growing fire provided light enough as Ashley ran from stall to stall, opening doors and trying to drive the terrified horses to safety. The thick smoke choked her and her eyes streamed with tears.

A shrill whinny came from the last stall on the right. Flames had already spread to the walls. Sparks rained down on the chestnut mare, and her colt cowered in the far corner of the box stall. Ashley seized the metal bar, crying aloud as the intense heat raised blisters on her hand. The stall was knee-deep in straw, smoldering now in a half dozen places. Frantically Ashley cast about for something to force back the latch. On the far wall hung a pitchfork; she grabbed it and used the wooden handle to beat against the bar and open the door.

"Where are you?" a man shouted above the din.

Ashley turned toward the voice. "The far side! The stallion! Get him out!" she ordered, then ran to the plunging mare and caught hold of her halter. A hoof grazed her knee as the chestnut reared, driven beyond reason by the fire. Ashley saw stars and gasped to keep from passing out. Pain shot up her leg; it would barely hold her weight. Still she clung to the halter.

"Come on, Scarlet," she pleaded. The mare rolled her eyes until the whites showed and backed farther against the wall, pinning the spotted colt behind her. The colt gave little snorts of fear as he struggled to keep his footing in the smoldering straw.

Ashley felt as though her arm was being pulled from its socket. Her blistered hand was an agony against the leather strap. She let go and grabbed the pitchfork, using the handle to smack the mare's rump. "Get out of here!" she screamed. "Go!" A spark burned through her sleeve below the elbow, and she tore off the voluminous shirt she wore over her cotton shift and wrapped it around the plunging mare's head.

Unable to see, the animal quieted, permitting the woman to lead her, step by trembling step, out of the stall and down the walkway, her colt pressing close on her heels. Strong male hands grasped the halter near the barn entrance, and Ashley would have run back into the inferno but her knee failed, throwing her to the ground. Suddenly someone grabbed her, pulling her to her feet, dragging her toward the open doors.

"No!" she protested. "Let me go! I have to get—" A horse's terrified scream drowned her words as she was swept up into a stranger's arms. "No!" Fiercely she struck out at the bearded face close to hers. "Put me down!" An iron grip closed around her wrist.

"Hit me again, and I'll gi' ye the taste o' my fist!" a gruff voice threatened.

Rain beat against her face, and Ashley coughed, fighting for air. "Put me down!" she repeated.

"Give her to me." The soft lisp of Mari's familiar voice came from the darkness. The Indian woman's arms caught Ashley as the man let her fall. "It's all right," Mari soothed.

"Squire's still in there!" Ashley cried.

"The bearded man went for him," Mari explained. "It's all right. Come away, child. There's nothing more you can do."

Someone threw a cloak over her shoulders. Choking, she wiped at her streaming eyes and stared back at the barn. Flames shot high in the air, piercing the shingled roof in several places. Reason flooded her brain. "Who is he, Mari? Who went after Squire?" Vaguely she made out the forms of Joshua and Edgar in the crowd carrying buckets of water. "Who's in the barn?"

A shout went up as a big man and a horse loomed in the glowing doorway. The stranger was bare-chested, his shirt wrapped around the stallion's head.

"Are you all right?" Ashley called. Her eyes traveled over the valuable workhorse before coming back to rest on the man. A frown creased her face. "Who are you?" she demanded, gazing into the smoke-stained face. His craggy features were obscured by the dirt and ashes, but Ashley would have remembered those blacksmith's arms and broad, muscular chest if she had ever seen him before.

Joshua came forward to catch hold of the stallion's halter. The stranger released the horse and glared at Ashley.

"I asked who you are," she repeated. "Are you hurt?"

"No thanks to you." The burr of the Highlands clung to the deep voice. He rubbed at his cheek, assessing her boldly. "What place is this, where a wench risks her life while men stand back?" His insolent gaze took in the ragged cloak and the clinging breeches. "Your husband should be ashamed."

Ashley stiffened, conscious of the spectacle she must look with her face blackened and her hair hanging in strings. Her lips whitened with anger. "I have no husband," she declared, "nor do I wish any." She met the man's brazen stare with one of her own. "I owe you thanks for saving the stallion; it was a courageous act. A death by fire is not one I'd wish for man or beast."

He nodded. "It seemed none of these"—he glanced about him at the milling men and women—"were willing to go in after ye. Ye showed bravery yourself, or at least more bravery than good sense. Do you make a habit of assaulting your rescuers?"

Ashley bit back a rising oath. "Until you interfered, stranger, I was managing. I could have gotten the stallion out."

"You're a fool if you think so," he snapped back, indicating the bloody gash where she'd been struck by the mare's hoof. "That knee would have been your undoing. You and the stallion would have died."

"You're welcome to your own opinion!"

"A rare bit of feminine logic." Ignoring her discomposure, he arched one dark eyebrow quizzically. "Would it be too much to ask if we could get in out of this damned rain?" He nodded toward the barn. "The rain will put out the fire, and the animals are safe. There seems little to be done here until daylight."

Ashley fought back a rising antagonism as she turned to lead the way back to the house. She paused, her brown eyes narrowing suspiciously. "You didn't give your name. Are you a runaway bond servant that you are ashamed to tell it? A ship's deserter?"

He chuckled deeply. "Do I have the look of a sailor? I've nae the time to bandy words wi' a saucy serving wench, as pleasant as that may be. My business is wi' the master of Morgan's Fancy. I'm Kelt Saxon, his new overseer."

"You? You're Saxon?" Ashley was aware of Mari's twitter of amusement behind her.

"Aye, sweet, I am."

Morgan's Fancy's new overseer, was he? Ashley dropped her gaze to the Scot's muddy boots and affected a meek reply. "I did not know, sir." She turned to the Indian woman. "Mari, will you show Master Saxon to the house?"

"Is your master ill?" Kelt searched the yard for a man in authority. "Is he at home?" Why wasn't the old man here at the barn? Could he be an invalid? "I want to speak with him right now."

"You must have time to change into dry clothes and have Mari look at your burns," Ashley insisted, painfully aware of her own throbbing hand and the knee that would barely hold her. She forced her voice into a servant's humble tone. "I'm certain the master can meet you in the library in . . ." She hesitated, tempted to put off the confrontation until morning. "In perhaps an hour. All your questions will be answered then, I assure you." An hour would give her time to compose herself, to prepare the type of reception this arrogant Virginian deserved. "Please, sir, go along with Mari."

With a final glance at the lass, Kelt followed the Indian woman toward the manor house. He hoped he hadn't made a serious mistake. The sassy wench was well spoken for a servant. Could she be old Ash Morgan's mistress? he wondered. Not likely; a man would take better care of such a shapely wench if she warmed his bed at night. Who was she then? Surely not a decent woman, garbed in men's clothing with her hair unbound like a common slut. Kelt supposed he'd find out soon enough. God, but he'd be glad to get out of these wet clothes! He was nearly frozen to death.

The storm seemed to be slackening as Ashley limped back toward the house. The wind dropped and the rain fell more slowly. The pain in her knee was enough to bring tears to her eyes with every step. Childlike, she held her injured hand palm up to the cooling drops and wondered if she'd be able to manage the stairs without help.

Finally, in her bedchamber, Ashley lowered herself into a high-backed chair by the hearth. Jai came to offer his comforting presence and Ashley stroked his head as Joan, the serving girl, wrapped a homespun blanket about her mistress's shoulders.

"Storm's nigh over, miss," the girl said. She knelt on the bricks and began to feed cedar shavings to the slumbering coals. "Be that the new overseer fer certain?" She rolled her heavy-lidded eyes at her mistress. "Handsome as Satan. Oh!" Joan winced as she saw Ashley's knee. "It's bleedin'. Shall I fetch the medicine box?" Her plain face grimaced with concern. "I kin get Mari."

Ashley's teeth began to chatter as a chill seized her. "No. I want hot water for a bath." She pushed back the blanket and wiggled out of the ruined breeches. "I want soap and some clean linen strips to bind this. Say nothing to Mari; she's tending the Scot." Ashley deliberately ignored Joan's remark about the stranger's appearance. Joan believed any man who walked upright was handsome. To draw attention to the matter would only encourage her fancies.

Ashley rubbed the dog's head as Joan hurried to fetch warm water. "I should have taken you with me, Jai," she murmured. "I'd hate to think you would have stood and stared like the rest of those pudding heads while I was being manhandled by that oaf. You'd have taken a bite out of the seat of his breeches, wouldn't you?"

With a sinking heart, Ashley remembered the loss of the barn. Her grandfather had built it with his own hands. The structure would have to be replaced, and she could ill afford the cost. Still, the animals were all safe. She shuddered when she thought what might have been. Squire, Baron, and Scarlet's new colt could never be replaced; each horse was an individual . . . a friend.

It would be a pleasure to take the new overseer down a peg or two. Mischief lit her brown eyes as Ashley thought of the interview to come. Saxon obviously believed her grandfather was alive and master of Morgan's Fancy. It was undoubtedly Richard's doing that he thought so. Ashley's lips curved into a sly smile. Master Kelt Saxon was in for a surprise.

Anticipation kept her thoughts occupied during the

bath and Joan's clumsy wrapping of the injured knee. She allowed the girl to brush and braid her hair, then waved her away. "Go to bed. I can dress myself." She smiled. "Thank you, Joan, and a good-night to you."

"Night, miss." Joan bobbed a curtsy and left the room.

Biting her lower lip, Ashley forced the swollen leg into a clean pair of gray doeskin breeches. Next she donned a man's full-sleeved linen shirt and leather vest. It was her habit to wear men's attire; she had no time for women's satin and lace. A skirt, even a lady's riding habit, was awkward for attending to the duties of a plantation master. As a child, she'd had her grandfather's permission to dress as a boy. Now that she was a woman grown, there was no one to force her to adhere to custom. Besides, she told herself, if the workers saw her dressed as a man and heard her giving orders day in and day out, in time they might come to forget that she was only a woman.

After tugging on a clean pair of riding boots, Ashley paused to catch a quick glimpse of herself in the tiny mirror. "You've looked better," she admitted to her reflection. Taking a deep breath, she started for the stairs.

In the library, Kelt Saxon waited impatiently for Master Ashley Morgan to join him. The dry clothes and hot tea the Indian woman had offered had done nothing to ease his growing suspicion that something was very wrong here at Morgan's Fancy.

A friend, Captain Philip Fraser of the *Merry Kate*, had brought him as far as Chestertown that afternoon. Good sense would have bade Kelt remain in the port town until morning, but Fraser's tongue-in-cheek gibing about Kelt's new position had struck a chord. Add that to the amused glances he'd received in the

Chestertown Inn when he'd said he'd been hired as the new overseer for Morgan's Fancy, and Kelt was certain something was afoot.

He tried to remember Fraser's exact words when he'd asked if the captain was personally acquainted with Ashley Morgan.

"Me and old Ash shared a few drams of rum from time to time," Fraser had admitted.

"Is he a fair man?"

"When I knew him, Ash Morgan was as honest as they come. Tough as hickory."

From a man like Fraser, that was high praise. Kelt and Fraser had fought side by side against the British during a local uprising in Scotland. No braver man than Philip Fraser ever drew breath, for all that he'd accepted the King's pardon and come to America, leaving Scotland and her heartaches behind. But Fraser had followed that statement with an offer to carry Kelt back to Virginia if he changed his mind about working for Morgan.

"My contract is for two years. I'll need no passage until then," Kelt had replied patiently. What had Fraser been alluding to? He'd been unable to get another word out of him on the subject.

The innkeeper had been equally closemouthed. "It takes a certain kind of man to work for Ashley Morgan," he'd commented. "Course, coming from Virginia, you might be that kind." A ripple of laughter from the men gathered in the public room had followed.

It had been enough to send Kelt back to the stable for his horse and set him on the way to Morgan's Fancy within the hour. The weather and sketchy directions had sent him to the wrong plantation. He could have spent the night there, claiming a traveler's hospitality, but by then he'd already been wet and stubbornly set on making his destination as soon as possible. He'd followed the poor excuse for a trail until he'd seen the light of the fire and heard the shouts of the men.

Nothing Kelt had seen or heard had given him any clue as to what was wrong with the master of Morgan's Fancy, or why he hadn't been in the yard directing rescue efforts.

Restlessly Kelt scanned the rows of books that lined the walls. "Too many for show," he murmured, half to himself. One finger gently touched the spine of a red leather volume. "William Shakespeare." Well read, or more money than he knows what to do with. Kelt had not seen such a library since he'd left his home in Scotland.

Ashley paused in the doorway. The Scot was bigger than she'd remembered at the barn; she couldn't help noticing how his broad shoulders strained the seams of his well-cut gray coat. She swallowed hard. "Kelt Saxon?"

He turned toward her, hat in hand, and their eyes locked. Anger tinted the Scot's high cheekbones. "It's you, again, wench. Did ye tell Master Morgan I'm waiting to see him?" Kelt demanded.

"If you're waiting for my grandfather, you'll have a long wait. He's been dead nearly a year." Ashley crossed the room and gracefully extended her hand. "I'm Mistress Ashley Morgan, and if you work here, you'll be working for me."

Chapter 2

Anger warred with surprise in the Scotsman's rugged face. The silence was so deep that Ashley could hear the ticking of the tall case clock on the landing. A shiver ran down her spine as she stubbornly met the fierce gray eyes. He has the eyes of a hawk, she thought, but he's a man, like any other man, no more and no less.

"If this be some sort of joke, I'm in no mood for it," he said coldly.

"I assure you," Ashley repeated firmly, "I am the master of Morgan's Fancy."

Kelt shook his dark head in disbelief. "No, Mistress Morgan. You've got the wrong of it. I've a contract to work for your grandfather, not you. I dinna work for women. I know not what game ye play, but I'll nae be a part of it. A mon's clothing doesna make a mon." He kept his voice low, controlled. Only a tiny muscle twitched along the line of his granite jaw. Fraser had known! The bastard had known all along! Kelt's face flushed with anger beneath the tan. "I came here in good faith at no little expense." He'd also given up a good job offer in Virginia. Damn! "I expect an explanation for your deceit, Mistress Morgan."

"I had no part in any deceit!" Ashley flared.

"Do you deny that your solicitor, Richard Chadwick, was acting for you when he offered me a contract?"

"No, I don't deny that, but it wasn't my idea to neglect to tell you that I am a woman."

"So ye do admit that much, that ye are a woman." Kelt let his gaze drop to her breeches and riding boots. " 'Tis a wonder."

Ashley fought to control her temper. This Scotsman, whom Richard had praised so lavishly, was as narrow-minded as the captains who refused to carry her tobacco. "What I choose to wear or not wear is none of your concern. You have been hired as an overseer."

Kelt took a threatening step in her direction. Ashley stood her ground, glaring up at him. "I've been deceived, Mistress Morgan—lied to—and ye expect me to stay here and work for you! Are ye daft, woman?"

"I have your written word, witnessed and recorded," she reminded him. "I need you to ship my tobacco. You'll stand by your contract, or you'll never work as overseer in any of His Majesty's colonies again."

"A false contract is worthless!"

"Show me the deception, Saxon! Who told you Ashley Morgan was a man? Where in that contract does it say you are to be employed by a man?"

Kelt's large hands clenched into fists. He had never struck a woman, though more than once he had been sore tempted. But this time . . . He turned away, forcing down the waves of fury that shook him worse than a fever's chill. He would not willingly place himself in a woman's power again. "I am an honest man," he said, "and I expect honesty in others."

"I have as much honor, perhaps more, than most

men,'' Ashley flung back. Her knee was hurting so badly that she wasn't certain how much longer it would hold her. She could feel tears of pain pooling in her eyes, tears she couldn't let the arrogant Virginian see. Time and time again she'd taken insults from merchants, government officials, and fellow planters, simply because she was a woman trying to run a plantation alone—trying, as they claimed, to go against God's natural order. But she'd had enough; she'd not be bullied.

She hadn't wanted an overseer, but now that he was here, she would use him to ship her tobacco. ''Can you blame me if you jumped to conclusions?'' she asked tartly.

Kelt whirled on her. ''It was deception and well ye know it! Your grandfather's name and reputation are well known in Virginia.''

''This verbal sparring will get us nowhere.'' Ashley crossed painfully to an elegant mahogany sideboard and unstoppered a decanter of French brandy. She looked toward the Scotsman questioningly. ''A drink, or are you an abstainer?''

A frown crossed his brow. Tendrils of red-gold hair had loosened to frame her Dresden-china oval face, a face unmarred by pox or the loss of any teeth. Her nose was straight and well formed, the chin a bit too firm for a woman. And her mouth . . . A hint of a smile crossed her lips. The woman was more attractive than he cared to admit. Kelt shook his head. ''Nay, I'm no abstainer.''

Deftly Ashley poured the amber liquid into a snifter and offered it to him. ''I don't like having an overseer on Morgan's Fancy any more than you care for the idea of working for me,'' she admitted. ''I am a good planter, Saxon. My grandfather was one of the best, and he trained me.'' Kelt took the goblet, and she poured a second drink for herself. "But"—her eyes met his—"I have no intention of letting you out of the contract. As much as I hate to admit it, Richard was right. I need you." She took a sip of the brandy. "Since we are forced to work together, I think we should make the best of it." Her smile spread, lighting the almond-shaped eyes with genuine warmth.

Kelt's fingers tightened on the stem of the snifter until the glass neared the breaking point. In the firelight, her eyes were the color of the brandy. The thought was as disquieting as the tightening of his loins. Resentment and confusion clouded his mind. Did this woman have the audacity to believe she could force him to work for her? Who was she to stand there, as bold as any man, drinking brandy and telling him what he would and would not do? He forced a wry laugh. "And what makes ye think that I would be a very good overseer for Morgan's Fancy—if ye forced me to stay?" The burr came thick in his words.

"And risk your own reputation? You're too honest a man for that. You weren't hired at random, you know. My solicitor had you carefully investigated before he offered you the position. He knows I'd have no man on Morgan's Fancy I couldn't trust." Amusement lurked behind the amber eyes. For once I hold the upper hand! Ashley swirled the brandy in her glass and drained it. "Help yourself if you'd like another," she offered.

The crackling of the fire was the only sound in the room, that and the steady pulse of a light rain against the glass panes of the windows.

Kelt's eyes narrowed speculatively. "And if I don't agree to work for you?"

Ashley shrugged. "If you were a fool, you'd never

have gotten where you are today. I've won, and we both know it. The outcome was never in doubt." She forced herself to meet that steely, hawklike gaze without faltering.

A darker flush of anger stained his features. "By God! I'll not work for such a—" The stem snapped and glass shattered. The brandy stained the rug at his feet.

Ashley turned in the doorway. "Leave it. Joan will clean it in the morning. Will your family be joining you soon?"

"I have no family."

"Oh. I had assumed you would." Ashley tried to hide her discomposure. How could Richard have chosen a single man when he knew the overseer would have to live in the manor house? "You will be living here. Morgan's Fancy has never had an overseer before; we have no suitable quarters. I hope the chamber you were given will be sufficient. Normally we start work at daylight. I expect no less from my overseer. I'll instruct you in your duties at breakfast."

"You want me to live here, in the manor house?" he said incredulously. "What of your reputation, Mistress Morgan? Surely an unmarried male cannot—"

Ashley folded her arms across her chest. "You may as well know the worst of it, Saxon. My grandfather had no sons. I am the child of his daughter, Cicely. My name is Morgan because I was born a bastard. According to the accepted standards of our society, I have no reputation to lose." She smiled sweetly. "I bid you good-night, sir."

Speechless with fury, Kelt stared after her retreating back. The woman was mad! He'd gather his belongings and be gone on the next boat. His belongings! "Damn!" He'd forgotten. Everything he owned was still sitting in that whoreson's inn at Chestertown.

There'd been no way to carry his sea chest and his canvases on horseback.

Kelt swore fiercely, jammed his cocked hat back on his head, and stalked from the room. If he was overseer here, he'd be damned if he wouldn't order someone to go and fetch his things.

Good sense overtook Kelt before he could wake the servants. Morning would be time enough to send someone for his personal belongings. He would send a shilling along to pay for the night's safekeeping of his trunk and thus would owe the innkeeper no obligation.

Two full notebooks of sketches were safely wrapped in oilcloth and packed in that sea chest, some of his best work, along with his oil paints and brushes. His clothes could be replaced, but not his paints. The brushes had come from Amsterdam, the oils from Venice. If one brush had been disturbed, he'd have the innkeeper's head on a platter.

Wearily he turned toward the stairs; a single tallow candle burned on the stand. Gratefully Kelt took it. He felt as if he'd been on his feet for days. At the top of the staircase, he silently made his way down the hall to his chambers. A fire had been laid, and the bedcovers had been turned down.

To give the devil his due, or in this case, *her* due, he had to admit his quarters were excellent, consisting of a large bedchamber with windows facing south and east, and a smaller room with a desk and shelves for his books. The south light would be perfect for his painting.

Methodically Kelt undressed and hung his clothes neatly over a chair, then blew out the candle and climbed into bed. His sleep, when it came, was troubled, full of friends and enemies who were long since dead and the bittersweet memories of Highland heather in bloom.

* * *

Ashley woke in the early dawn. For a few minutes, she tossed on the thick goose-down mattress, trying to find a position that would not add to the discomfort of her injured knee and burned hand. Sleepily she rubbed her eyes and sat up, dropping her bare feet to the icy floor.

Ignoring the chill, she went to the window and stared out through the morning mist at the blackened outline of the barn rafters. So much for the foolish hope that the fire wasn't as bad as she'd thought last night.

Awkwardly she donned the clothing she had worn to meet with Saxon. Her knee was painful, but it would bear her weight. The burn would need careful watching to be certain it did not become infected. Ashley would have liked nothing more than to go back to bed and sleep for two days, but there was no time to coddle herself.

Ash Morgan had made her tough, not from a lack of feeling for her, but because he loved her so deeply. His unfailing love had sustained her many times during her life and had helped to make up for her mother's rejection.

For just an instant, the image of Ashley's mother came before her. Even at forty, Cicely Morgan Randall had a delicate beauty that few women could ever hope to match. Blood had been spilt for a dance with her; songs had been written in her honor. Her flaxen hair, her porcelain skin, and her china-blue eyes had broken hearts from Philadelphia to the Carolinas. Ashley chuckled softly. No, Mother would definitely not approve of Ashley's new overseer living in the house. But then Mother rarely approved of anything Ashley did, and the feeling was mutual.

Ashley had been born at her stepfather's plantation, Rosewood, on the James River in Virginia, but Cicely had sent her to her grandfather in Maryland while she was still a baby. After that, there had been only brief visits with her mother. Cicely's husband, Nicholas Randall, had wanted no reminder that his wife had been pregnant with another man's child when they wed.

During those visits, Ashley had thought of Cicely as some beautiful stranger, a fairy-tale figure. The fact that this glorious creature had asked Ashley to call her Mama was irrelevant. How could there be any connection between herself, a knobby-kneed, freckle-faced hoyden with flaming red hair, and this exquisite, sweet-smelling lady who never raised her voice in anger? Who even wept daintily?

Cicely's only mistake in life had been Ashley's birth, and presumably the actions that had foreshadowed that shameful event. The scandal of an illegitimate child had been hushed by a hasty marriage to a wealthy suitor, or at least one who lived as though he were financially secure. Once Cicely had sent the infant Ashley to Maryland, the gossips along the James River had found other quarry.

Cicely had spent the twenty-three years since then as the ideal Virginia Tidewater lady. In all things she deferred to her husband, accepting his actions and decisions without question—even when he gambled away her land and spent her considerable dowry on other women.

Despite his continuing love for his only child, Grandfather had told Ashley that Cicely was weak. He didn't want Ashley to make the same mistakes in life; he would teach her to be strong. He would train her to be the equal of any man in wisdom and education. He would make her an independent woman—so independent that she need never marry if she didn't wish to. He had proved his belief in Ashley's worth by leaving everything he had to her, bypassing Cicely and her two sons by Nicholas Randall.

Randall had been so furious that he'd prevented Cicely from coming to the old man's funeral. Even now, he was attempting to break old Ash Morgan's will in a court of law, claiming that Cicely should inherit Morgan's Fancy.

The matter was still under consideration by the governor, but Richard had assured Ashley that there was little chance of her stepfather winning the case, so long as the decision would be made in Annapolis and not Williamsburg. Both colonies might be under English law, but the fierce competition and antagonism between Virginia and Maryland would be a definite factor in the outcome of the case. Annapolis officials would favor Ashley's claim because she held land in Maryland. Nicholas Randall was an outsider despite his wealth and position, and despite the fact that he was a man contesting a woman's rights.

Ashley quietly let herself out the kitchen door. Jai bounded along behind her, as frisky as any pup. The mist was fast disappearing, and morning light sparkled on the grass. It's beautiful, Ashley thought, as green and new-washed as the earth must have looked on the first day of creation. She breathed deeply, inhaling the tangy salt air, letting it banish the terror and despair of the night before.

Lucifer trotted to the split-rail fence, nickering, his black hide as smooth as satin, his eyes full of mischief. Ashley paused to pat the velvet nose. "No biscuit today," she apologized. The pony had an insatiable appetite for Joan's beaten biscuits, and Ashley gladly contributed all of her daily portion.

Joan cooked as well as she cleaned house. Her biscuits were more suited to ship's ballast than to a keen palate.

Bondmen who had gathered around the blackened barn caught Ashley's attention, and she hurried toward them.

"Morning, mistress," one man called. He snatched off his cap as the others quickly acknowledged her presence.

"It coulda been worse. The roof caved in and the rain put out the fire," Edgar offered shyly.

"Hay's gone," Joshua said, then spat a wad of tobacco into the mud.

Ashley walked around the barn, then made her way inside the skeletal structure. The stalls where the horses had been were ruined caves. Ashley shivered as she recalled the smell of horses' burned bodies on a neighbor's plantation several months ago. Will Johnson's barn had gone up in flames, taking four of his workhorses and his best hunter. Ashley swallowed hard, imagining Scarlet's gleaming chestnut coat charred beyond recognition.

The back section of the barn was worse, covered with blackened timbers and ashes. The door to the tack room was still warm to the touch. Ashley flinched, then dragged it open with her good hand. It smelled awful inside, but the saddles and bridles seemed undamaged. She blinked back gathering tears of relief. She couldn't even begin to put a value on the harness, and it was safe.

Joshua waited a few steps away, faded cap in hand. "Baron's got a gash on his hind leg. Won't let nobody near it. He tried to take Edgar's head off this mornin'." He took a breath and plunged on. "Scarlet's got burns that oughta be looked at, and Geordy swears he pulled his shoulder out trying to hold

Baron. Short John's got the bellyache. His old woman say he can't do no work today."

"Enough!" Ashley protested. "I want every hand on this place, man, woman, and child, here at this barn after breakfast. I want all the burned wood carried off. Anything whole enough to be used again is to go in one pile, the rest goes for firewood. Whatever hay isn't ruined is to be spread on the grass. The children can turn it every day until it's dry. By the time it's ready, we'll have a roof to put over it."

"The plantation sloop sunk; the bow's stove in. The flat-bottom boat's washed up in the sheep meadow." Joshua scratched his close-cropped gray hair. His washed-out blue eyes seemed like those of an old man, yet he was barely forty. "Sheep are scattered God knows where, and the cows didn't give a bucket o' milk between them this mornin'."

Ashley's fingers curled into fists and pain from her burned hand shot up one arm to her shoulder. "The sheep can find their own way home. I want this mess cleared away—now!"

"We're short on nails and it's gonna take a lot of pit-sawed lumber to build a new barn, not to mention cedar shakes for the room," Joshua said. "Some of them beams are still good, but I don't know, might be better to pull the whole thing down and build from scratch."

"Send a boy to Canterbury. Tell Martin Hopkins he can have that team of oxen he was offering for, in exchange for enough hay to get us through the winter. Prime hay—none of his moldy seconds."

"Without them oxen, we'll be slow in gettin' timber out in spring. Unless you want to start them half-trained ones in their place."

"Without the hay, we won't get the rest of the

stock through the winter. And Mari says it's going to be a hard one.'' The faintest trace of satisfaction showed in her voice. ''Oh, tell Master Hopkins he doesn't get the oxen until I've got a place to put the hay.''

''Can't build without lumber and nails. And timber.''

''I'll get it! You pass on my orders. Any free man shirking can pack his blanket and walk. As for the rest . . .'' Ashley's eyes narrowed, and her tone assumed a thread of steel. ''I've not used the cat-o'-nine yet . . .''

Joshua chawed his fresh wad of tobacco and shifted his feet. ''Gonna be slow, Miss Ashley. Bad time of year for this to happen. Carpenter's got his hands full workin' on them hogsheads. Oronoco's got to be packed and—''

''I don't need you to remind me what has to be done with the tobacco, Joshua. You probably all know the new overseer arrived last night during the fire. His name's Kelt Saxon, Master Saxon to you. I expect his orders to be carried out the same as mine. You pass the word to the rest. If there's trouble, you'll answer to me personally.'' Ashley looked around at the others. ''Master Saxon is to be obeyed. But if there's anything you don't understand, or if he tells you to do anything I've forbidden, you're to come to me. Understand?''

Murmurs of assent came from the bondmen. Joshua nodded. ''Yes'm.''

Ashley turned to Edgar. ''Where did you put Scarlet?''

''In with the oxen, mistress. I put her and the colt together.''

Ashley sent a boy to fetch her burn ointment, then crossed the farmyard to the old log barn. She could have ordered one of the grooms to care for Scarlet's injuries, but she preferred to see to it herself. Servants had a way of forgetting annoying chores, and old Ash had taught her that the animals had to come first—even ahead of the workers.

"A man with blisters on his hands will complain," Ashley's grandfather had explained patiently, "but a horse can't. Before you know it, infection can set in and you can lose a valuable animal. If you want something done right, do it yourself."

A stableman mumbled a greeting as Ashley entered the shadowy building. He dropped the front leg of the ox he was tending and rubbed his hands on his coarse breeches. "Sugar's got a stone bruise. Noticed him favorin' his foot yesterday when we were movin' those timbers." He offered a bit of crumpled tobacco leaf to the animal and grinned when the broad tongue licked his palm clean.

Ashley walked down the center of the barn, speaking softly to the horses tied along the wall. A spotted ox turned his broad face toward her and bawled.

The bondman grinned. "It's dry in here and clean, if a mite crowded. Them oxen, they'd as soon get the horses out as we would. They don't like horses much."

Ashley stopped to pat the velvet nose of an unfamiliar horse. "Nice animal." The dappled-gray stood unafraid, allowing himself to be petted.

"Belongs to that new overseer. Particular about him he was, too. The horse's name is Falcon." He dropped an armload of hay in the feedbox. "Tells a lot about a man the way he keeps his horse."

The boy came in with the birchbark box of salve and delivered it to his mistress with a shy grin. Ashley thanked him and moved slowly to the mare and colt. "How are you doing, Scarlet?" The high-strung animal quivered, but allowed Ashley to run her hand along her back. "Feeling better?" Gently she began to apply the ointment.

Maybe having Saxon on the plantation would take some of the burden off her, Ashley thought. She decided to put him in charge of the work detail rebuilding the barn. She had to ride to Chestertown in a day or two. A planter over there was thinking of buying some sheep. If she sold some of her ewes, she wouldn't have to worry about feeding them through the winter.

The mare danced nervously, and Ashley whispered endearments to her. Saxon had been mad as a bee-stung bear when he'd found out he'd be working for a woman. She wondered if it had been wise to deal with him as bluntly as she had. She exhaled sharply. The Scot had disturbed her, made her uneasy, something that rarely happened when she was dealing with men. It was best if he learned who was master on Morgan's Fancy from the first!

She finished the treatment, then took a currycomb and began to brush Scarlet's rump and hindquarters. She had overreacted last night, and she knew it. She had blamed Kelt Saxon for the actions of other men, and she'd deliberately baited him. It wasn't like her to behave so unfairly. The man had come here in good faith, and she would gain nothing by making an enemy of him. Ashley patted the animal's neck; she'd give Scarlet a few weeks' rest before riding her again.

The colt pushed under Ashley's arm, sniffing her pockets for a sweet. Ashley scratched behind his ears. "It's time to put a halter on this colt, Daniel," she said.

"None left that small, mistress. Have to make one up special. Would take all afternoon," he warned. "I'm pretty busy today."

"Do it today, and be gentle when you put it on him."

The door creaked on its leather hinges. Ashley looked up to see the tall Scot stride into the barn. "Good morning," she said.

Kelt threw her a black look. "Mistress Morgan. I came to look after my horse." Catching Kelt's scent, the dappled-gray gelding gave a welcoming nicker.

"Guess I'll see about that halter," Daniel grumbled. With a bob of his head in Ashley's direction, he hurried out of the barn.

"My belongings are still in Chestertown. I sent one of the men to fetch them." Kelt crossed to the gelding and checked his water bucket. "At first he wasn't certain he should go without speaking to ye first. It's easy to see discipline is lax on Morgan's fancy."

Ashley stiffened. "A man's discipline, you mean?"

He shrugged. "Take it as ye will. The mon knew I was the new overseer, but he was still surly."

Ashley felt the heat of her inflamed cheeks. "You form opinions quick enough, Scot." She glared at him. "I've run this plantation well enough since my grandfather died. My men are used to taking orders from me. I hardly need criticism from an outsider who's not been here twenty-four hours." Tension knotted her insides. She was doing it again—overreacting to the man. What was it about him that touched off her temper every time she looked at him?

"An outsider ye admitted ye need," he reminded her. "It's nae a woman's place to run a tobacco plantation, and well ye know it. Ye canna ha' the strength or the authority to rule over men."

"Authority or intelligence?" she flared. "That's it, isn't it? You don't believe a woman possesses the mind to manage a tobacco plantation—or any mind at all, save that needed to pick out ribbons for her bonnet.'' Ashley's hands tightened into fists, and she pushed down an urge to slap his insolent face. ''Let me assure you''—her voice dropped to a husky whisper—''that this woman has the intelligence *and* the authority. *I* run Morgan's Fancy, and don't you ever forget it.''

''I think I can remember that, just as long as you remember not to undermine my authority with your people.'' He stroked his neatly trimmed beard thoughtfully. ''And . . . since we're delivering ultimatums this morning, let me present a few. First, I'm verra good at what I do, and I give more than what ye can expect for what I'm being paid. During my personal time, I expect privacy. That includes Sundays. I paint on Sundays unless there's an emergency. No one is to go into my rooms for any reason. I clean up after myself and change my own linen.'' He lounged against the gelding's back.

''Second, I expect regular meals, hot and well prepared. I won't be shortchanged on my food. It doesna have to be fancy, but I won't eat that swill your girl set before me this morning.'' He grimaced. ''Ye could have used that cornbread as mortar to build a new barn.''

Ashley stared hard at her boots and tried to keep from smiling. The only cornbread in the kitchen this morning had been the pan of it Joan had baked three days ago, without salt, for chicken feed. Joan had her own ways of dealing with those above her station.

''And lastly,'' Saxon continued, ''you and I will sit down together very soon and list my duties and responsibilities. That way we will both know where we stand. I have no intention of arguing with ye every morning over who gives what orders. Is that verra clear, Mistress Morgan?''

"And if I don't agree to your demands?" She could not keep the light of challenge from her eyes.

He grinned wolfishly. "Then ye can release me from the contract, can't you?"

And I'll do just that, as soon as the tobacco is safely on a ship bound for England. If they both agreed to cancel the contract, it could be done without her paying two years' salary, and without Saxon losing his credibility. "Surely you don't expect me to go into the kitchen and prepare your meals myself," Ashley soothed. "Joan's an honest girl, if not too bright. You just have to explain what you want prepared." She spoke slowly and distinctly, as though to a backward child. Richard would just have to find her a replacement next fall, she thought. She wouldn't need an overseer again until it came time to sell her tobacco. Having this arrogant Scot on her plantation for two years would be intolerable. "I believe we understand each—"

"Mistress!" Ashley was cut off by Edgar's entrance. His face was red from running. "They need you at the prize house. There's a fight! Short John and the new bondman! He said Short John's wife was a—"

"Never mind!" Ashley grabbed a saddle and blanket and threw them across the bay stallion's broad back, tightening the cinch and knotting the strap with a horseman's practiced hand. Edgar was ready with the bridle, and she forced it over Baron's tossing head.

"Wait!" Kelt protested. "I'll go." He began to saddle his dappled-gray.

"Come if you like, Saxon," Ashley called, vaulting into the saddle, "but hold your tongue until I ask for it." Ducking her head low over the bay's neck, she urged him out of the barn and across the yard at a gallop.

"How do I find the prize house?" Kelt asked as he mounted the gelding.

Edgar pointed. "Jest follow the lane to the river. That way."

The dappled-gray responded eagerly to Kelt's signal. Ashley's stallion already had a good lead, too good to catch unless she slowed the animal. Kelt slid a hand inside his vest to check his pistol. Why the hell hadn't she waited for me? "Damn you, woman," he muttered. A fight between rough laborers could well end in a killing. It was no place for a woman's tears or hysterics. He pulled his hat down low over his forehead and nudged his horse into a canter. Mud and water splashed the horse's legs, chest, and belly. "What the hell," the Scot murmured, then chuckled. "I can't get any wetter than I was last night."

Ahead, Ashley reined the bay off the lane and through a stand of white pines. She leaned low over Baron's neck as they pushed their way through the low-hanging boughs. Branches caught her hood and pulled it off, letting cold water drip down the back of her neck, soaking her shirt and jacket. "Damn that stupid slut!" she said. Short John's wife had been nothing but trouble since the day the two had arrived on the plantation. She was a lazy good-for-nothing whose swaying hips and come-hither eyes had caused a half dozen fights among the men, and almost constant bickering among the women.

Short John and his wife had three and a half more years to go on their indenture. He was a passable worker when driven to it, but enough was enough. She'd sell their bond at the next possible opportunity. It was better being without the extra workers than putting up with fights and bickering.

Ashley was yanked from her thoughts when her horse's right foreleg slipped on the wet needles. She threw her weight to the left and pulled hard on the reins. "Easy boy," she cautioned. "We're almost out of the trees."

Taking the game trail through the woods would save her minutes over the dirt lane. Morgan's Fancy stretched from the Chesapeake to the Chester River, with two major creeks and several smaller ones deep enough to anchor an oceangoing ship weaving across her property. The prize house was located near the mouth of Maiden's Creek in a sheltered cove. It had its own dock, several cabins, and their dependencies. Two married men and their families lived there year round.

Baron trotted out of the trees and into an open meadow. The prize house lay just ahead, beyond a split-rail fence. Ashley urged the stallion into a canter as she remembered her new overseer. Kelt Saxon could deal with Short John's slatternly wife in the future! Let him unravel the dilemma. Doubtless it would help to keep him occupied and out of her affairs.

Laughing, Ashley rose in the saddle as the bay soared over the fence. A few strides beyond, and she was swinging out of the saddle in front of the prize house, the shouts of angry men loud in her ears.

Chapter 3

A woman with an infant in her arms burst through the doorway of the wooden structure. "They're killin' each other, Mistress," she cried. "You got to stop them!"

Ashley untied her cloak and let it fall, then unfastened the leather whip from her saddle. "I'll tend to it, Cara. This is no place for your baby. Get back to your cabin." She glanced toward the stallion. "Send someone to look after Baron." Taking a firm grip on the bullwhip, Ashley entered the prize house.

The interior of the large building consisted of space from the floor to the massive beams and high, peaked roof. The small windows were shuttered against last night's weather; the only light came from several torches along one wall. At the center of the room stood a huge horizontal press, or prize, used for packing the cured tobacco leaves into casks. Beyond the filled casks and hogshead, in the far corner of the structure, a knot of men and women surrounded the struggling opponents. Thuds of flesh against flesh sounded above the catcalls and cries of the crowd. Her mouth dry, Ashley pushed her way through the circle.

"What's going on here?" she demanded.

A man appeared at her shoulder, doffing a worn cap with exaggerated deference. "Gideon called Short John's wife a dirty whore. You'd best let one kill the other one an' hang the one what's left." He nodded toward a screaming black-haired woman. "She told Short John that Gideon jumped her and tried to—"

Spying Ashley, the woman began to shriek louder. "He tried to have his way with me, Gideon did." The sensual features twisted as she waved clenched fists. The bodice of her gown was torn, exposing large, heaving breasts. "Kill him, Johnny!" she urged. "Kill the Welsh bastard!"

"Stop it, both of you!" Ashley ordered. "Short John! Gideon!" Deliberately, she uncoiled the whip. "Do you hear me? Stop fighting at once!"

The Welshman was a head taller than his opponent, with long, muscular arms and hamlike fists. But the smaller man had the quickness and cunning of a street fighter. With a wild cry, Short John drove his head into Gideon's belly, knocking the big man to the floor and flinging himself on top, fists flying.

The jeering mob surged around them as they rolled over and over on the hard-packed floor, locked in mortal combat. Short John caught the Welshman square in the nose with a well-placed blow, and the sickening crunch of bone came clearly to the spectators. Blood flew, and a knee in the little man's groin doubled him up with pain. The Welshman swore and came to his feet, pulling a wicked-looking knife from his boot. The onlookers screamed in outrage. A man stepped forward, then stopped as the big man cut an arc through the air with the gleaming blade.

"Stand back! I'll kill any man who comes near me!" he threatened. With an animal cry, he advanced on Short John. "When I finish with you," he promised, "you'll need no woman, slut or nun!"

* * *

As Kelt galloped up the road toward the prize house, he saw Ashley's bay stallion being led away by a young black boy. He pulled the dappled-gray up sharp and threw himself out of the saddle. "Where's your mistress?" he shouted.

"In there, sir." The boy pointed. "In the prize house. There's a fight between—"

"I know that!" Kelt dropped the reins and ran through the open doorway. He had crossed half the distance between the entrance and the inflamed throng when the crack of a bullwhip cut the air. The crowd scattered, stunned to silence, and he saw Ashley advancing slowly on the struggling figures. For an instant Kelt froze. Didn't she have sense enough to realize how much danger she was in?

With a sound as sharp as a musket shot, the whip snapped again. A man screamed in agony and something flashed through the air, struck the floor, and rolled almost to Kelt's feet. He stooped and picked up a razor-sharp knife.

The two men parted; the smaller man, covered in blood, threw up his hands in surrender. The other lunged toward Ashley, his eyes distorted with rage. Time seemed to slow as Kelt shouted a warning and pulled his pistol from the shoulder holster. "Halt or you're a dead man!" He leveled the weapon at Ashley's assailant, his finger tightening on the trigger.

Ashley held her ground, and the whip snaked around the bondman's legs. He fell heavily, and before he could gather his wits, Kelt had one knee on the man's chest. His left hand was at the Welshman's throat, the right held the pistol inches from his skull. "Don't even breathe," Kelt cautioned. The gray eyes held no mercy. " 'Tis easier to make an end of ye here and now, than to turn ye o'er to the high sheriff for trial."

Ashley moved to stand beside Kelt. "Will you go quietly, Gideon?" she asked.

Beads of sweat broke out on the man's head as he grunted his assent. Ashley rose and turned toward the onlookers. "This is the new overseer, Master Kelt Saxon. You'll obey his word as you do mine." She coiled the whip and turned her attention to Short John. "Go to your cabin. You and your wife have been warned about these fights before. Master Saxon will deal with you tomorrow."

"You and you"—Kelt pointed to two men—"bind him securely." One muscular arm yanked the bondman to his feet and shoved him into their grasp. "If he escapes, ye take his punishment." The angry hawk eyes scanned the room. "The rest of ye—ha' ye no chores to attend to?"

Quickly the men and women dispersed. Kelt watched Ashley out of the corner of his eye, still shaken by what he had seen. Her composure surprised him. No, he admitted to himself, it rankled. His irritation was all the more pronounced because of its irrationality.

"What manner o' woman are ye?" he demanded through clenched teeth.

"A self-sufficient one." She stared back at him arrogantly, with no hint of feminine timidity. "But a sensible one, I hope. That was quick thinking and quicker action. Thank you."

"Ye handle that whip like a drover," he said, ignoring her thanks.

Mischief lit Ashley's brown eyes. "Thank you again. Old Ash would be pleased at the compliment. He taught me how to use a whip and had this lighter one made especially for me."

"An odd choice of gift for a lady." Unbidden, a

hint of sarcasm crept into Kelt's burr. He knew he'd been badly frightened for her, and now that fear was fast becoming irritation.

Ashley laughed. "I'd say that depends on the lady." She nodded at the departing workers. "My grandfather was a small man, and in his later years too weak to enforce his authority with his fists. He knew I would have the same problem, so he made certain I could take care of myself." She arched one auburn eyebrow in amusement. "I can shoot, too. I trust that doesn't offend you, Scot."

Kelt frowned. "Damn it, this is no matter for jest. Ye should have left this trouble to me. The mon could have taken that whip from you and killed you! A fight between men is no place for a woman."

Ashley shrugged. "It was a woman who started it. It's only fair that it be settled by a woman." No need to tell him that her men would have come to her rescue if they'd thought she was in danger.

"If one mon had killed the other, ye would have shared in the responsibility." Kelt's expression softened. "Ye show more courage than common sense, lass."

Ashley fought to control an inner trembling. Did he want her to admit she was frightened? Of course she was. Old Ash had taught her never to show fear, never to admit doubt. She had become a skillful actress, but the fears were still there, some real, some childish, like her overwhelming fear of thunderstorms. "On the day I can't control a fight between my workers, that's the day I lose my authority as master of Morgan's Fancy," she said.

"A woman is a woman, and a mon a mon. There are things ye canna do, and the sooner ye learn it, the better." Kelt fumbled with the clasp of his cape. "You're shivering. Let me give ye—"

"No!" She waved him away. "I have a cloak. It's outside." She'd not invite the familiarity of accepting his clothing. "Since you're so eager to take charge, I'll leave the settling of this matter in your hands. Both men are indentured servants. The one with the knife has been here only a short while; he's lazy and a troublemaker. Short John's wife . . . Well, you must talk to her and form your own opinion. Short John's a good hand with the oxen, and he can even read and write a little. We can ill afford to lose them. We don't have enough workers as it is."

"Ye want me to get rid of them all?"

"That's for you to decide, Master Saxon. The Welshman must be dealt with severely. It is forbidden for him to carry that kind of knife, let alone to threaten me with it." Ashley pushed a strand of hair away from her face. "I'm not such a fool as you think. On the Tidewater, only a madman would kill a woman in full view of witnesses. I was in less danger than you would have been. If he had harmed me, the others would have torn him to pieces."

Kelt nodded reluctantly. "Aye. It's the same in Virginia." There was an odd thickness in his voice. When he had seen that man advancing on her with the knife . . . What was there about this woman that had affected him so? It had been more than a man's natural protective instinct toward a woman in danger; the fear had touched a deeper chord. He shrugged, pushing away the unsettling thoughts. "Tomorrow is time enough to deal out punishment. Give them a night to worry on it." He grimaced. "Is there a chance of a decent meal in this godforsaken place? I've not been so empty since I came to the Colonies!"

Ashley laughed. "We've shown you poor hospitality, haven't we? Come with me. We'll warm ourselves at Cara's hearth and sample some of her cooking. She always has something in the kettle, and her cornbread is the best I've ever eaten.'' She moved briskly toward the door, then paused and looked over her shoulder. ''Well, Scot, are you hungry or not?''

''My name's Kelt, and I am.''

She nodded. ''Kelt, then, and you may call me Ashley when we're alone or off the plantation. I hear naught but 'mistress, mistress' from dawn until dusk until I'm sick of the word.'' She motioned toward the door. ''Come on. You might as well meet some of our people.''

With a sigh Kelt followed her. Leftovers snatched in a servant's kitchen wasn't what he'd had in mind when he suggested a meal, but it seemed all he was likely to get.

In the afternoon Ashley gave Kelt a tour of the plantation, beginning with the prize house and continuing through the fertile fields and meadows. The corn stood in shocks, evenly spaced, running down to the banks of the Chester River. Rabbits and game birds leaped up before the horses, and the sky overhead was filled with flocks of ducks and geese. The cloud-strewn sky echoed with their mournful cries.

Kelt stood in the stirrups and looked around him. He'd never seen a land so hauntingly beautiful since he'd left the misty glens of Scotland. '' 'Tis bonny, this Tidewater country,'' he conceded. The autumn colors blended one into another until he ached with an artist's bittersweet longing to capture the blue-green waters of the creek framed in marsh browns and cedar green.

''My grandfather carved every foot of it from wilderness. He traded with the Indians for this ground, even though Lord Baltimore claimed it. He gave three wives to this soil; one by drowning, another by fever, and my grandmother by childbirth. He was already old, some said, when my mother was born. His other children all died in infancy."

Kelt sighed. "I ken your love for the land. 'Twas so in my native Scotland. The house I was born in had been in my family for centuries."

"Your family, are they still there?"

"Nay." He looked away, blinking at the moisture gathering behind his eyelids. "They are all dead; the land belongs to a fat English lord who has probably never traveled the distance from London to even look at it." Unconsciously his fingers tightened on the leather reins. "The memories are bad ones; I'd rather nae speak o' it."

"As you please." Ashley had known enough pain to recognize it in another. Quickly she searched for a safer subject. "Being from Virginia, you may have met my mother. She is married to Nicholas Randall of Rosewood on the James."

"I've heard of Randall, but I've never seen his wife."

"A pity. She's quite a beauty." Ashley dug her heels into the horse's side. "We'd best get back. The woodland and the northern fields you can see another day."

"How many fields have ye got in tobacco?"

"Four. The crop was good this year. Now we've got to worry about getting it to England." Briefly Kelt glimpsed the concern in her eyes.

He didn't need to ask if she was in debt. Every planter he knew was. A plantation needed hundreds of items to function; hoes and axes, shovels, harness buckles, leather, iron for cart wheels, fish hooks, barrels, shoes and boots, cloth and china, even glass for windowpanes. All these things came from Mother England and cost dearly. Each piece was taxed, and surcharges were added over and over until the cost of even a pair of boots was beyond belief.

Tobacco was the cash crop of the Chesapeake, the crop that supported the planters' way of life. The price of tobacco fluctuated. Maryland farmers sold according to the word of their factors in England, often going in debt for the year until the proceeds were in.

Matters were made worse by the law that said colonists must buy and sell only with England. Dutch traders might offer far more profit on a cask of tobacco, even three times as much as the legal market. But a planter who sold to such a trader was branded a criminal, a smuggler, and might lose everything, including his life, if he were caught.

"Between the pirates and the weather, tobacco's a gambler's game," Kelt admitted. "Have your shipments been hurt?"

"None of ours so far, and that's a near miracle. They used to say my grandfather had the devil's own luck." Ashley reined in her stallion to ride beside him.

Kelt couldn't help but admire the ease with which she rode astride. Her back was ramrod straight, her hands light on the reins, yet ready to show firm control if the animal shied. "Since His Majesty's warships have been pulled back for that cursed war in Europe, they say you can follow the Carolina coastline walking on water. Pirate ships are so thick, ye can leap from ship to ship without ever getting your feet wet."

She laughed, sounding younger than he remembered, then her brow furrowed in concern and she grew serious. "I can no longer afford shipping insurance on my tobacco. It's jumped ten times over the last three years. Richard, my solicitor, says that by next year no one will be able to insure his cargoes."

"Ye have no insurance?" Kelt frowned. "That's poor business. If the decision were mine, you'd have insurance, regardless of the cost. I know of five ships that were taken this summer, four sent to the bottom."

"Well, it's not your decision." She clicked to the bay, urging him into a canter. Why had he spoiled the first pleasant conversation they'd had together? She had sense enough to know a tobacco shipment needed insurance; she also knew that there was simply no money left to pay for it.

Kelt cursed under his breath and gave the dappled-gray his head. Was he expected to spend the next two years eating her dust?

When they reached the farmyard, Ashley was pleased with the progress the workers had made on the barn site. Ashley introduced Kelt to the people he hadn't met yet and explained to him what orders she had already given.

"There are plans of the barn somewhere in the office. My grandfather recorded everything he did," she said proudly. "I want the barn replaced exactly as it was. We can give all our attention to it as soon as we load the tobacco crop."

Kelt walked around the ruined structure, pausing now and then to kick a beam or tap an upright. Ashley waited patiently, something he was certain didn't come easy to her. "Do ye want an honest opinion?" he said finally.

She nodded. "I may not agree, but I always welcome a man's thoughts."

"Tear the whole thing down. Put in a new brick foundation over there." He pointed. "Maybe a hundred feet from this one. And build from the bottom up; too many of your main supports are weakened. If ye patch this one, it will always be just that, a patched job.''

A tenseness crossed her face. ''You're right, but a new barn won't come cheap.''

''We can log and pit-saw all we need here on the plantation. I know how to set up a brick kiln if you don't have one. It will take a lot o' hours, but winter's a slow time anyway. I think it will be worth the extra effort and expense.''

Sentiment warred with good sense behind Ashley's cool facade. Slowly she nodded again. ''We don't start planting tobacco seed until late January or February. We'll do it your way, Master Saxon.'' Already he was changing things, and she resented it. Ash Morgan's barn would be gone forever.

''Do it then,'' she said softly. ''Spend not a shilling more than you have to, but build something that will last two hundred years and more.'' It was what her grandfather would have ordered if he'd been alive to say so. ''You can begin as soon as the tobacco goes out. I'll hold you responsible.'' Ashley tossed her horse's reins to a boy and strode toward the house. ''I've some figures on the tobacco,'' she called over her shoulder. ''I'll send them out to you. It's prime oronoco, and I want it loaded carefully. I'll have none of the casks spoiled by water on the voyage.''

Kelt was so engrossed in his planning for the new structure that it was sundown before he realized it. When the light began to fade, he went inside to clean up for the evening meal, entering through the kitchen. The girl, Joan, murmured something to him and pulled a smoking skillet off the hearth.

Except for a hound lying on the bottom step of the grand staircase, the house seemed empty. Kelt stopped at the foot of the steps and glanced around him, frowning. A candlestand stood beneath a gilded mirror, the mahogany soiled with melted wax. Dust lay thick in the corners of the hall and cobwebs hung from the ceiling. "Lazy wenches," he muttered. He knew what his mother would say about such careless housekeeping. Womanly and every inch a gentlewoman, she would have no slacking in her household. The manor house at Morgan's Fancy would have fitted neatly into one wing of his father's house in Scotland, but every surface, windowsill, and tapestry had been spotless and sweet-smelling. Mistress Morgan could take a few lessons in managing a household from a woman such as his mother.

He took the steps two at a time, nearly knocking down old Thomas as he came out of Kelt's bedchamber.

"Evenin', sir," Thomas said. "Your things have all arrived safely from Chestertown. I was just lightin' a fire to take the chill off yer room."

"Thank you, but next time I'll tend to it. I prefer to care for my own needs." Kelt frowned, wondering how long it would be before the household staff took his request for privacy seriously. He'd never been lodged in the main house since he'd become an overseer, and certainly never when he'd been an indentured servant. At his last position, he'd had his own cottage; he needed solitude to paint.

He stopped short just inside the door. Curled in the center of his bed was a black and white cat and her assortment of kittens. A curse slipped between his clenched teeth. "Out!" he yelled loudly. "All of ye!" Kelt clapped his hands and cats flew in all directions. Two kittens dived out the door and the mother cat disappeared under the poster bed.

Ashley came running. "What's wrong?"

Kelt noticed that she'd changed into a blue man's shirt made of something silky, but she still wore men's breeches and riding boots. "There's a cat in my room. To bc cxact, there are several. I want them *oot*. Now!"

Ashley's eyes widened. There was no hint of a smile on her lips, but her eyes revealed her amusement. "You're afraid of cats?"

"Of course I'm nae afraid of them. I just don't want them in my room." His voice sounded petulant to his own ears. "I dinna like cats," he repeated lamely. "I've never liked them."

"My grandfather liked them," Ashley said, as she dropped to her knees and began to coax the mother cat out from under the bed. "They're independent animals and very intelligent. Here, kitty, kitty," she called.

"I dinna want anyone in my room."

"So you've said. I'll speak to Thomas, but he's been here more than thirty years. He and my grandfather were friends. I'd have to be careful not to hurt his feelings. Thomas will think you're afraid he'll steal something." Ashley got up with three kittens in her arms. "He won't, you know. Your things are perfectly safe here."

"I'm accusing no one in your household o' being a thief, but I am a private person."

A man who has shared a tiny prison cell values his own space, his own possessions, Kelt thought. And any man who survived the voyage to America in the hold of a convict ship must forever live with the memory of filthy, diseased bodies pressed close around him. He became aware that he was blocking the doorway and stepped aside quickly. "Ye didna catch the big cat."

"Gypsy? She'll follow her kittens. Just leave the door open and don't frighten her."

"What time is supper?" Kelt tried to ignore the mother cat curling around his ankle, purring.

Ashley shrugged. "Whenever Joan gets it on the table. She'll yell."

"I've nae wish to interfere with your staff, but your slave Thomas—"

"Thomas isn't a slave!" Ashley snapped. "There are no slaves on my plantation! Thomas Weaver was born as free as you were."

Kelt threw up a hand. "Peace, Mistress Morgan. I'd no intention of insulting the old man, free or slave. Do ye think me an ogre to mistreat your servants?"

"Thomas isn't a servant . . . not exactly. This is his home as much as mine."

Kelt ran his fingers through his hair. What kind of place was this, where a woman ruled and servants were not servants? He struggled with his temper. "I just want my rooms undisturbed, by people or animals."

She lowered the kittens safely to the floor and shooed them toward the stairs, then turned to face him. "If you dislike animals, Scot, you'll find it quite uncomfortable on Morgan's Fancy."

"I dinna say I didna like your damned animals!" The burr grew thicker as his temper heated. "I am fond o' God's creatures—most of them—but they have a place, and it isna in my bed."

"Would you rather have mice running up and down the stairs? Burrowing though your precious possessions?"

With a snort of disgust, Kelt retreated into his room. "If ye dinna mind, I will dress for supper," he said sarcastically.

Swiftly he stripped to the waist, filled the washbowl from the water in the pitcher, and began to lather his face and neck with the soft, scented soap on the washstand. Kelt was especially fond of bathing, a trait he'd acquired from his mother.

At home, in Scotland, there had been a special bathing room that his father had ordered built for his mother. It contained a huge soapstone tub, heated by its own brick hearth and equipped with piped-in water from a spring outside the castle walls. Many a day in Virginia, after a hard day's work in the fields, he had missed the sheer luxury of that bath.

Kelt stared down at his hands, scarred and callused—not from wielding a burnished claymore, but from a farmer's hoe and ax. Strange were the ways of God, that a hotheaded young rebel from the Highlands could ever find peace in the rich, red soil of Virginia, especially on land that belonged to another.

Kelt sighed deeply as he rinsed away the suds and grime with fresh water, then dried himself with a clean towel. The soil here in Maryland ran to sandy brown and even black. Would he come to love the smell of it as well?

He sat on the edge of the bed and removed his boots and stockings and the tan breeches that smelled of horse and sweat. I'll nae be here long enough to learn the land. Not if she keeps up her kelpie ways! Damn, but the lass got under his skin! Like a fistful of burrs, whichever way he turned and twisted, she dug in deeper.

The arrogance of the woman with her mannish ways! "Nay." He spoke aloud in the empty room. "Not mannish." There was no mistaking the soft curves of a lass in her boy's attire. The skin-tight breeches showed her rounded bottom all too well.

"By God, she is a kelpie!" he swore under his

breath as his finger touched a hot spot on the iron caldron he was lifting off the fire. He sucked at the reddened skin, then used his discarded shirt to grasp the handle. He'd been too long without a woman—that was his problem. He should have stayed the night in Chestertown and demanded the innkeeper search out a likely wench to warm his bed. If he could not keep his thoughts off the thorny mistress of Morgan's Fancy, it was not her charms but the lack of feminine attention that was the cause.

Ashley Morgan was definitely not his type. Kelt liked his women small and soft, gentle-mannered and laughing. Ashley had a seductive smile when she used it, but he had never met a female with such a foul temper. She was as touchy as a Lowland Scot at his daughter's wedding.

Kelt began to whistle a saucy tune as he rummaged in his trunk for clean clothes. His eyes caught a flash of silver and he reached for the source, a flask of excellent Scotch whisky. Slowly he removed the cap and took a long sip. The warmth seeped through him, calming and relaxing. Now that he knew Ashley had no attraction for him, he could go below and enjoy a well-earned meal.

His optimism was short-lived, however; the supper was a disaster. Although the table and dishes were clean, Joan's mutton stew was only one step up from prison fare, and her beaten biscuits were fit only to slip under the table for Jai.

Kelt ate alone, trying patiently to chew the stringy chunks of meat. When he asked where the mistress was, Joan only shrugged. " 'Spect she's workin' on them ledgers again, Master Saxon. Lots o' times she don't come down to eat at night."

I can guess why, Kelt thought. He tried to ignore Joan hovering around his chair. The wench left little doubt as to her intentions; she brushed against him suggestively every time she filled a plate or removed a dirty one.

Despite a missing front tooth, the girl was not without charm. But he had never played with the females that worked for him. It was a rule that had proved to be a sensible one over the years and one he wasn't about to break now.

Kelt finished his portion of stew, took one look at the ancient bread pudding, seized an apple off the sideboard, and went back upstairs to his rooms.

Ashley heard his tread on the hall floorboards and tried to concentrate on her records. She had deliberately decided not to go down to supper. This dark Scotsman stirred emotions within her that were too disturbing. Doubtless it would please him no end to know she could not banish his rugged face from her mind, could not forget how his dark hair lay on his neck.

With an oath she slammed the ledger shut and went to retrieve a book from the mantel. If she couldn't make sense of her figures, she would read. She'd be damned if she'd sit there dreaming over a man's lean backside like some tavern slut.

An image of Kelt's hand holding the pistol to the Welshman's head came to mind. Although his hands were large, the fingers were long and well formed, the nails clean and cut straight across. A faint scattering of black hair covered the backs of his hands. A tantalizing possibility tormented her brain. What would it be like to be touched by those hands? "Not worth the cost," she whispered into the empty room. She might admire Kelt Saxon's physique, but she didn't need him complicating her life. In a few weeks, at most, he would be gone. And since she saw where her weakness lay, she would make sure the next overseer was gray-haired, overweight, and happily married. Chuckling, she opened her book as a picture of Kelt Saxon, twenty years older and surrounded by a nagging wife and throngs of children, skittered across her mind.

Across the hall, behind a locked door, Kelt settled into a comfortable chair before the fire and balanced his sketchboard on his lap. Swiftly his fingers flew over the paper, creating ghostly outlines of Morgan's Fancy—the two-story brick manor house, the barns and dependencies, horses. And almost of their own volition, the charcoal lines and smudges began to form the face of a woman . . . the hauntingly beautiful face of Ashley Morgan.

Chapter 4

Ashley gazed thoughtfully at the merchant vessel as wind filled the square sails and carried the tall ship swiftly across the sparkling waters of the Chesapeake. The bite of the autumn wind brought spots of bright color to her cheeks and filled her cinnamon-brown eyes with tears, but she didn't notice. Her thoughts were with the ship and the precious cargo in her hold. If anything happened to this year's tobacco crop . . . Ashley shivered and pushed away the lurking fear.

The tobacco would be safe. It had to be! Wasn't old Ash Morgan's luck a legend in the colony? "If you've got any pull with the Lord, now's the time to use it," she whispered. If her grandfather's spirit was anywhere, it would be here on Morgan's Fancy at tobacco shipping time. Somehow she didn't think even death could stop the tough old man from watching over what he had loved most in life.

Ashley sighed and walked back toward her horse. The Morgan luck had seen them though some tough times; the plantation had survived political upheaval, drought, and Indian attack. Once a forest fire had swept down toward the house and barns, only to be drowned in a rainstorm at the last moment. Old Ash had even argued publicly with a royal governor once and got away with it. So far, Morgan's Fancy had never lost a tobacco crop to pirates on the high seas or to insects in the fields. There was no reason their luck should change now.

Ashley nodded to the serving boy and took Baron's reins in her hands. Why do I feel so uneasy? she wondered. Kelt Saxon was a better overseer than she'd expected. He was intelligent, and he was fair with the plantation workers. Although she didn't care for his arrogant manner, the Scot had solved her most pressing problem by finding a captain to carry her tobacco to England. She had to admit Kelt was a good man, and if Ash were alive, he and Kelt would probably be friends.

Sadness came over her as she realized how acutely she still missed her grandfather. They had always celebrated on the day the tobacco sailed. They would ride into Chestertown and have dinner, and he'd buy her some special gift. "I miss you, Ash," she murmured as she swung up into the saddle. The bay stallion tossed his head and snorted, pawing at the fallen leaves with his powerful hooves.

"It's chancy, sailing with such a small fleet."

Startled, Ashley whirled in the saddle to stare into her overseer's face. She'd been so intent on watching the ship sail she hadn't heard the Scot ride up behind her. "It wouldn't be if we had the protection the King owes us," she answered sharply. "A man-of-war would go a long way toward making the *Isobel*'s voyage a safe one. She only carries eight cannons, not much defense against a Spanish or French privateer. It's open season on tobacco ships."

Kelt's gray eyes burned into her own; the soft burr of his voice made the skin on her arms and the back of her neck tingle. Damn him! How could he affect her so strongly just by being near? She forced herself to listen to what he was saying.

"Word is, Morgan's Fancy's never lost a tobacco shipment. I told Captain Dayton he should charge the other planters extra to ship with him just because your tobacco was aboard."

"And he agreed, I suppose?"

"Nay. He said, 'Morgan luck or not, you're lucky I'm carrying your mistress's crop at all.' "

Ashley couldn't help but notice the dark circles under Kelt's eyes. She wasn't the only one who'd been putting in long hours. He'd worked harder than the men the last few days. "We usually take the day off . . . shipping day," she explained. Her mouth felt dry. Was she coming down with something? She tried to sound normal. "The people expect it. Feel free to do the same if you want to ride into Chestertown or just catch up on some sleep."

She'd heard of no involvement with the serving wenches; surely a virile man such as Saxon must have physical needs, needs that only a woman could satisfy. Likely he'd welcome time off to seek out a willing bed partner. God knows, there were plenty who would welcome his advances, even without payment.

Kelt nodded. "The men deserve a day off. They've earned it." He stared at her intensely. "It's a good crop, and if it gets through to London, you should get a prime price for it."

"Not if, *when*." Ashley's gaze met his squarely. "You'd better hope it gets through if you expect to be paid." Her features softened. "You're right about the price, though. With fewer ships getting through, the tobacco that does arrive in England can command top money."

She guided her horse back along the dirt road and Kelt fell in beside her. The man had said nothing about whether he intended to take the day off. Double damn him! Even when he said nothing, he annoyed her.

The dappled-gray moved with a smooth gait, ignoring the tossing head and laid-back ears of Ashley's stallion. "You did a good job," Ashley admitted, breaking the silence. "Dayton refused to carry my tobacco before."

"He told me so. Said he didna do business with ladies."

"Captain Dayton called me a lady?" Ashley's eyes sparkled with mischief. "That's a first."

"Well," the Scot conceded solemnly, "perhaps that wasna his exact word." He grinned.

"I didn't think so."

Dry leaves, their brilliant colors faded to dusty brown, skittered before the wind, tumbling and rolling across the dirt road in front of the horses. Ashley kept a tight rein on Baron, tensing her leg muscles as he danced sideways. "Whoa," she soothed. "None of that now."

As if to test her, the animal snorted and reared, pawing the air with his powerful front legs. Ashley threw her weight forward in the saddle and smacked him sharply with her riding quirt. The stallion leaped ahead, plunging down the road at a full gallop. Ashley let the big horse have his head for almost a quarter of a mile, then gradually slowed him to a canter and finally a trot.

Kelt frowned as he brought his dappled-gray up beside the stallion, both animals streaked with sweat. "Ye ride well for a lass," he admitted, "but that's too much horse for a woman. Ye lost control of him on the bend. 'Twould make more sense for ye to ride a mare. You'll break your neck on him one o' these days."

Heat rose in Ashley's cheeks under the Scot's fierce glare. "I did not lose control. I gave him his head on purpose." She forced herself to swallow the oath that rose to her lips. "I ride well for a lass?" She looked up at him through thick, dark lashes and smiled sweetly. "Thank you, sir," she replied smoothly. "You ride well enough yourself, for a man."

"Ouch!" He nodded, the anger draining from his expression. "I suppose I deserved that." His deep voice softened. "But the advice was given sincerely, not to insult ye. I'm nae used to seeing ladies riding astride in such"—he raised one eyebrow quizzically—"gentleman's attire." Kelt reached up to touch the brim of his cocked hat in salute. "Can we call a truce for the day? You did promise me a day of rest, and I've no wish to begin it with a quarrel."

"And do you make a habit of instructing your employers in horsemanship?" Ashley demanded. "Your *male* employers?"

"I have apologized, and you'll get no more from me on the subject, mistress." The gray eyes warned her not to push too far. "Other than the fact that the stallion is high-spirited, too much so to make a dependable riding animal. Ye'll come to grief wi' him, mark my words."

Ashley noticed that Kelt's Scots' burr increased with the intensity of his emotion. "I accept the apology, but not the advice. We suit each other well enough, Baron and I. My grandfather taught me nothing if not how to stick on a horse. I want no plodding draft horse. If I did, I could ride Squire."

"Falcon is a gelding, and he's served me well. He's fast and levelheaded. A mon can ask no more of a horse." He leaned forward to pat the dappled neck. "A stallion wastes too much time thinking of other matters to be a steady mount."

"I like the fire and the stamina," she explained softly. "I've been in the saddle from dawn to dusk many a day. Can your gelding match that endurance?"

"If I ask it of him." Kelt gazed at the dirt lane ahead. Did this damnable wench always have to have the last word? She was a stubborn shrew. A man would have to have his head examined to work under her. "I have made arrangements to sell the Welshman's bond to Martin Hopkins of Canterbury. Do I have your approval?" he asked, changing the subject. "I thought to keep the man and wife on and give them a second chance. As ye said, you're short of hands already, and he does have skill with the oxen."

"As you see fit. Did you talk with the woman?" Ashley could imagine that Short John's wife would put her best foot forward for such a lusty specimen as the new overseer. "She has caused trouble before."

"I've warned them both there'll be no more. I'm not soft, but I'm fair. I was a bondman myself when I first came to this country. I know where they stand." Kelt shot Ashley a hard look, then continued when he saw no scorn on her face. "If ye can scrape up the coin, I'll buy more slaves when tobacco planting time comes."

"No slaves."

"What did you say?"

" 'Twas plain enough, Scot. I've told you before we have no slaves on Morgan's Fancy. My grandfather used only free men and bond servants. I see no reason to change."

"Ye brought me up from Virginia to oversee your plantation. Buying and selling slaves has always been one of my duties. You're shorthanded, ye admit as much. With slaves there's less trouble of the kind you broke up in the prize house. They're good tobacco workers, strong, and easily trained in the tedious day-to-day labor."

"Like dumb animals, you mean?" Ashley reined in Baron and regarded him through narrowed eyes.

"I didna say that. A mon is a mon in my experience, some quick and some stupid. Skin color tells you nothing."

"A man is a man? And yet you think it morally right to hold another human in bondage without hope of freedom?" The cinnamon eyes darkened to ebony. "Slavery is a curse, and I'll not sully Morgan's Fancy with it!"

"Ye treat your workers fair, do ye not? You give them all decent food and tight shelter. What difference does it make if ye refuse to buy slaves? Does it free a single man? Does it send one back to Africa?" Kelt scoffed. "I wasna suggesting we finance a raid on the African Coast. If ye purchase men who are already slaves, you might give them a better life than they have already."

"If I had the coin, I would buy them and set them free," she declared vehemently. "A free man does twice the work of a slave. And why shouldn't he? He has hopes, dreams, something to work for."

"Slaves show a better profit than bondmen. By the time you've trained a bond servant to his trade, it's time to free him. Most are the scum of London and Bristol—pickpockets, highwaymen, and—"

"And rebels?" Ashley dared. "Traitors to the King?"

Kelt pursed his lips. "So we come to that, do we?

Aye, I'm one of those rebels ye speak of . . . or I was. But I've paid my price, and the why and how of my arrest is my own business, Mistress Morgan. Ye knew I was a bondman before you hired me. If it's a problem now, you've only to say the word and I'll pack my belongings."

"You're as touchy as a blueclaw. I meant no insult to your precious Scot's pride, man. I was merely pointing out that a man such as yourself, who has been a bond servant, is in a poor place to condemn them."

Kelt shrugged. "'Or in a better place to judge than a gentlewoman. I've worked beside slaves and bondmen, eaten what they've eaten and slept on the same straw. Morgan's Fancy is in trouble financially. I'd be doing less than my duty if I didna advise ye to bring in slaves."

"And I'd be doing less than my duty if I let you." She dug her heels into Baron's sides and reined the animal around Kelt's mount. "No slaves and that's final. We'll not discuss it any more."

They rode back toward the house in single file with Kelt keeping his dappled-gray a good two lengths behind the stallion's hindquarters. Ashley's temper was evident in the rigid line of her spine, but she rode as though she were part of the animal.

"She's got more spunk than sense," Kelt murmured to the gelding.

Ashley's auburn hair was gathered at the back of her neck with a bit of black ribbon. It spilled over her shoulders in a curling mass, perversely enticing beneath the felt cocked hat. "She dresses like a lad," Kelt fumed. "There's no woman in her." But the slender neck and nipped-in waist belied his speech and he knew it. God, but he couldn't keep his eyes off her! Would that red-gold hair smell like honeysuckle?

Kelt removed his hat and wiped his brow, grinning at his own foolishness. If there was sweat on his forehead, he had worked himself into it, thinking about Ashley. The wind off the bay was sharp. A yearning coursed through his veins as strong as the one that had driven him to his first woman.

He chuckled at the memory. Jeannie MacDuff . . . as plump a pigeon as ever claimed a boy's innocence. He'd been mad for her—haunting the tavern where she worked, sketching pictures of her face, and even writing poetry extolling her virtues. Jeannie was a sweet piece, but virtue was not one of her strong points.

Jeannie had been the first, but there'd been too many since to name. There had been one special lass, a long time ago, whom he'd asked to be his bride, but smallpox had claimed her before they'd done more than exchange a few chaste kisses. Dark and tiny she was, no bigger than a child, with a soft voice and a gentle manner. Kelt tried to remember her face, but there was nothing . . . only the sound of bagpipes at her funeral. "Ah, Mary, you were too good for me by far."

Better she died of the pox than was raped and murdered like her sisters. A chill ran through Kelt and he pushed away the bitter memories. "Like my sisters." He bit the soft inner side of his cheek until he tasted the sweet-salt of blood.

"Those times are gone," he said softly. "Best forgotten." A man was wiser to fill his life with something new than to mourn what was finished. A Scot he was born and a Scot he would die, but he'd kill no more for lost causes. His hands had known enough blood. "I'm a planter now, by God!"

He'd ride to Chestertown and find a good-hearted wench with breasts like ripe melons. A man had to be hurting when he developed a yen for a woman as hard and shrewish as Ashley Morgan. "She'd be naught but ice in bed," he assured the dappled-gray. "A sour apple, left too long on the tree."

The gelding snorted and flicked his ears, and Kelt laughed deep in his throat. "Nae much of a liar am I, boy, when I can't even convince you of my prevarications."

A boy on a workhorse galloped down the road toward them, bringing Kelt out of his reverie.

"Mistress! Mistress! There's a message come from Annapolis fer ye!" The towheaded child waved excitedly. "A letter, Miss Ashley! Wi' seals an' such on it! Thomas said to fetch ye right away! He's holdin' it at the house."

Kelt urged his gelding up beside Ashley's mount, glancing from her pale face to the lad's red-cheeked one. "Were ye expecting bad news?" he asked.

"Thomas told me to take a horse, mistress," the boy insisted. "I've rid ole Dan before." The clear blue eyes grew anxious. "Did I do wrong?"

"Ye did exactly right," Kelt said heartily. He dug in his vest pocket for a ha'penny and tossed it to the boy. "You're a smart laddie." Kelt looked the boy over; he couldn't be more than eight, but he rode well enough and he seemed to have his wits about him. "What job do ye hold?"

"I'm kitchen boy, Master Saxon. I turn the spit and fetch and carry. Whatever Joan bids me."

"No more. I'm in need of a sharp lad to carry messages for me. I don't suppose ye can read and write, but no matter. I—"

"Dickon can do both," Ashley assured him. "He'll never make a scholar, but he is fair enough at sums."

Her eyes twinkled at Kelt's disbelieving expression. "We have a school of sorts, two afternoons a week. Thomas is the schoolmaster. All my children learn to read."

"I was not aware, mistress, that ye had any offspring," Kelt said solemnly.

Dickon barely stifled a giggle.

"I meant the children of Morgan's Fancy," Ashley snapped.

"An honest mistake," Kelt soothed, fingering his beard. "Do ye have any objections to my using Dickon as a runner, or had ye planned to make a cook of him?"

"Dickon?" Ashley glanced toward the boy. "Would you like that?"

"Oh, yes, Miss Ashley." He leaned forward on the bay's neck, twisting his thin fingers in the horse's mane. "I'd like that fine. I'm a good rider, Master Saxon. I'll do good fer ye, I promise."

"I intended to offer the boy a better opportunity than Joan's kitchen," Ashley said. "He'll learn more with you than he would scrubbing pots. Just be certain your duties do not keep him from his lessons." She gathered the leather reins in her hands. "Now I must see to my letter." She clicked to the stallion and urged him forward in a canter.

Kelt stared after her for a long moment. He'd read uncertainty in her eyes. She was expecting bad news. What could be coming that would cause such a reaction in a lass who had faced down an angry bondman with a knife? There were mysteries at Morgan's Fancy he did not yet understand.

"Sir." The boy spoke timidly. "Will ye need me to do anything now, sir?"

"Not now. Yes, on second thought you can. Ye

can ride to the prize house and then down to the lumber camp and tell everyone that they have the day free.'' He raised a hand. ''Wait. First go back to the barn and take a riding horse and put a saddle on it. The little gray mare will do. Be certain ye touch none of the blooded horses or any your mistress uses.''

A smile spread across the child's face. ''Aye, sir.'' He nodded. ''I know the horse well. I'll tell the groom you gave me leave to take her.''

''She's old but steady. We'll see about a decent mount for ye in time. If you're to carry my messages, you must have good horseflesh under ye. Wait by the well for me after breakfast tomorrow morning. I'll have a task for ye then.''

''Yes, sir.''

A groom was leading Baron toward the barn when Kelt reached the farmyard. Ashley was nowhere to be seen. Kelt handed his horse to a waiting servant and went into the house. He meant to find out what the message concerned, if it was plantation business.

Thomas was coming down the front steps with an armload of books. ''Sir,'' he called out softly in greeting.

''Your mistress—where is she?''

''In the library, Master Saxon. She had a letter come from Annapolis by boat.''

Kelt nodded and made his way down the hall. The library door was closed; he hesitated, then rapped sharply. ''Mistress Morgan? May I come in?''

''Yes.''

Ashley was alone in the room, standing in front of the fireplace with her back to him.

''Bad news?'' Kelt asked. If it was, he hoped she wouldn't start crying. Weeping women distressed him; he never knew what to do or say.

Ashley turned to face him, her russet eyes sparkling with unshed tears. ''Good news!'' she said, holding out the creased parchment. ''I've won.'' A glow of triumph lit her face. ''My stepfather thought to contest my grandfather's will. He took me to court, claiming Morgan's Fancy by my mother's right as daughter, but his claim was thrown out.'' She took a step toward him. ''Don't you see, Kelt? The will stands as written. Morgan's Fancy is mine!''

Chapter 5

Kelt stared into Ashley's shining eyes for a long moment, fully aware of the flood of emotion her excitement caused within his own soul. She stood so near he could have taken her in his arms; the impulse to do so was almost overpowering. His gaze fastened on her parted lips. They were full and sweetly curving, trembling ever so slightly as they both became acutely aware of the silence in the room.

Ashley broke the spell. "My solicitor wouldn't let me go to the proceedings," she said. "He was afraid I might say or do something that would prejudice my case."

"I canna imagine why he would think that," Kelt murmured wryly. "Ye are the image of a Tidewater lady." He dropped his eyes to the muddy riding boots and then solemnly regarded her breeches. Even they had seen better days, he decided. A tiny three-cornered tear had begun to fray just above the knee and the material was wearing thin. What could old Ash Morgan have been thinking to raise a lass as wild as a woods colt? She was in need of a firm hand, male or female, to keep her in line. But as she was, what man would even think of taking on such a handful?

Ashley ignored his gibe. "The royal governor himself bade my stepfather's solicitors hie themselves back to Virginia. Nicholas will be furious, of course. I'd love to see his face when they tell him."

"And your lady mother?"

"Cicely will be secretly glad, I think. Nicholas has run through the majority of her dowry, both land and gold. I can't believe she'd want him to have Grandfather's estate, too." Ashley pulled off her cocked hat and sailed it across the room. "There is no love lost between Nicholas and me," she explained. "My stepfather despised me from the moment I was born." She chuckled. "Cicely told me he called me a worthless redheaded bastard and threatened to drown me in the James if she didn't keep me out of his sight."

Kelt frowned. " 'Tis a cruel thing to tell you, even if it's true."

"It's true, all right. Nicholas never referred to me by my name when I was visiting Rosewood; it was always 'little bastard,' or if he had company, the more polite 'you.' "

"Didna your mother try to protect you from him?"

Ashley looked away. "I was proof of her shame. It's why she sent me here to be raised by my grandfather. She said that if I'd been a boy, she might have tried to keep me, but since I wasn't, I was better off in another household."

"Why did ye nae tell me o' the court case? Ye ha' said nothing."

Ashley smiled. "And give you more reason to mistrust me? Would you have stayed if you thought my claim to the plantation was in doubt?" She fixed him with an intense gaze. "You're not certain, are you?" Her expression became serious. "Cicely said that Nicholas wanted Morgan's Fancy for my half brothers, but that's a bald-faced lie. Robert's not sober long enough to make the journey to Maryland, and Henry . . ." She shrugged. "Henry's not but a whining fop."

"Ye dinna seem overly fond of your brothers," Kelt observed.

"They've shown no great fondness for me. Do you have brothers? Parents living?"

Kelt turned away and walked to a window. "No." He stared out at the gently bobbing sloop moored to the dock. Seagulls swooped down toward the gray surface of the water; their raucous cries came faintly through the glass. "All dead," he said. A sharp pain knifed through his gut. Why did it still hurt so much? Time healed all wounds, didn't it? Why not this one?

"I'm sorry." She crossed the room toward him and her shocked tone penetrated his sorrow.

"It was a long time ago," Kelt said.

"Noon meal!" Joan cried, sticking her head into the room. "You'd best eat while it's hot."

"Coming," Ashley replied. She half turned to Kelt. "I have not told you," she said softly, "how much help you've been to me. I know I've been difficult. I'm not"— She took a ragged breath and plunged on—"like other women, but . . . Oh, damn it, Saxon, you know what I mean. Thank you."

He nodded. "Aye, you've the right o' that, you're nae like other lasses. But it comes to me that ye may ha' a few good qualities just the same." He placed a hand lightly on her arm. "I dinna—"

Ashley jerked away as though she'd been burned, then tried to cover her chagrin with a hasty jest. "You'd best hurry and wash. I'd not want to keep you from your meal. I know how you enjoy the delicate flavor of Joan's cooking."

* * *

Kelt was already seated at the dining table when Ashley joined him a few minutes later. She noticed that he had changed into a fresh white linen shirt and stock. His hair was neatly brushed and tied back with a clean leather thong, and his russet leather vest was spotless.

He stood politely as she neared the table. Despite his size, he moved as smoothly as a dancer—or an Indian, she thought. He'd not learned his fine manners in the tobacco fields. Kelt Saxon was born a gentleman—she'd bet a hundred cleared acres on it. She allowed him to pull out a chair for her, secretly glad she'd taken the time to change her own clothing. Even her grandfather had chided her as a child for coming to the table smelling of horses. She'd give the Scot no such opportunity.

She'd been unprepared for his touch in the library. If she hadn't pulled away, what would have happened? Would he have tried to kiss her? Was it possible he thought she was a desirable woman? Or did he think she shared Cicely's moral code?

No, she admitted honestly, it wasn't Kelt's action that had shocked her; it was her own reaction. She wasn't a child; she'd been held and kissed by other men. But none of those kisses had affected her like the mere touch of Kelt's hand. What was there about him that made her tell him things she'd never told anyone, that caused her insides to feel as if she'd swallowed a butterfly? Whatever Kelt's attraction is, I'll have to get over it. There's no room in my life for a man—not even him.

She glanced sideways under her lashes to the end of the table. Kelt's size never ceased to amaze her. Even seated, he was immense, the rippling muscles barely concealed by the thin folds of the shirt. She pretended to unfold her napkin as she watched him. His attention was fixed on the covered tureen Joan was placing in the center of the table.

There'd be hell to pay, Ashley thought with carefully concealed amusement, if Joan had reheated the fish soup from yesterday. Even then, the extra dose of pepper had failed to cover the burned taste. Kelt had grumbled, but he'd eaten it. Ashley didn't believe Joan's ruse would work a second time. The cornbread was fresh, but cornbread was never Joan's strong point. In fact, the only thing one could say with honesty about Joan's cooking was that the wench was clean. The food might taste awful, but there'd be no rodent droppings floating in the stew, as she'd pointed out once to her mother at Rosewood.

Joan lifted the lid and began to ladle out generous helpings of the soup. Ashley tried not to giggle as Kelt took a suspicious taste.

"What in God's name is this?" he roared. "By the King's pink backside! Is this hog swill the same ye served last night?"

Joan dropped the pewter ladle to the floor, oblivious to the spilled soup on her skirt. Her eyes grew large in her face as she covered her mouth with her hands and began to wail. "I tries me—me best," she sobbed. "I ain't no cook. I never was train—ain—ained." Throwing her apron over her face, she ran from the room followed by the half-grown girl who helped her.

Ashley dissolved into laughter. "You've frightened the girl half to death. For shame! She'll serve us even worse now until she gets her nerve back."

Glowering, Kelt stood and poured his bowl of soup back into the tureen. "Better starved than fed that muck," he spat. "Enough is enough! 'Tis worse than prison fare. Dickon! Dickon, I know you're out there! Get in here!''

The boy peeked around the door. ''Sir?''

Kelt picked up the plate of cornbread and dumped it unceremoniously into the soup. ''Take this where it belongs—to the hogs. Now!''

''Yes, sir.''

The hawklike eyes fastened on Ashley. ''I suppose you're useless in the kitchen?''

She nodded, certain that if she tried to speak, she'd burst into fresh laughter.

''Sit here. Dinna move. Just sit here until I fetch us something fit for humans to eat.'' The broad shoulders disappeared through the doorway.

Ashley heard rustling and frightened squeaks in the hall, then the sound of hurried footsteps. Still chuckling, she pushed aside her bowl and dug a small book of poetry from her vest pocket. She had no intention of going anywhere until she tasted the fruits of her overseer's efforts. Even an apple and some cheese would be better than the burned soup.

She'd not bothered to tell the Scot that Mari often cooked when she was at the house. Her friend had been away since the fire, visiting relatives near Assateague. The Indian woman was an excellent cook if you had a taste for Indian food. Her stews and seafood were delicious, not to mention the honey cakes she'd made for Ashley since she was a child.

Mari had offered to teach Ashley time and time again, but Ashley had no desire or time to learn. There was always too much to be done outside—a lame horse or a leaking sloop to be seen to. She wasn't much of a housekeeper, either, she had to admit. The house had been neglected since her grandfather's death. But their livelihood depended on the land, and the land took every minute of her time.

With a sigh, Ashley opened the tiny leather-bound book. Kelt would be better pleased when Mari returned. And she would have to find someone to replace Joan. The trouble was, she liked Joan. The wench was honest and had a good heart. To put her to work outside would cause even more problems, not to mention the shame Joan would feel at being demoted.

As minutes passed without the Scot returning, Ashley's curiosity got the better of her. She put the book back into her pocket and made her way silently down the hall to the kitchen. She could hear Kelt giving orders before she reached the doorway.

"Slice those apples thin. I want no seeds or peel in the fritters."

Joan's reply was muffled.

Cautiously Ashley pushed open the heavy door. To her surprise, Kelt stood by the kitchen table, sleeves rolled up, patting dough into neat little biscuits. He glanced up at her.

"It's taking a little longer than I thought. Sit and watch if ye like. Are those oysters shucked yet, Thomas?"

"Yes, sir." The old man winked in Ashley's direction. "They're fresh, just like you said, tonged just this morning."

"Leave a few in the shells to eat raw and cut up the others for stew." Kelt wrapped a piece of leather around his hand and pulled a three-legged spider from the hearth. Deftly he greased the bottom of the pan with lard and placed the flat little biscuits inside, then covered it with a heavy lid. Placing the frying pan back in the fireplace, he used an iron hook to pull hot coals over the lid.

In less than an hour's time, Kelt and Ashley were

seated at the elegant table once more and a red-eyed Joan was dipping out bowls of steaming oyster stew. There was broiled filet of rockfish, applesauce with a sprinkling of precious cinnamon, and the tiny biscuits done to a golden brown. Boiled potatoes mashed with turnips completed the main course. For dessert, Thomas carried in a silver platter of apple fritters.

"Given time and the proper ingredients, I could have done better," Kelt boasted. "This is simple fare, but fit for a gentleman or a lady. Do ye agree, mistress?"

Ashley swallowed the last of her biscuit and nodded. "If you ever decide to seek another trade, you can work for me as cook. But a few weeks of sitting at your table and I'd weigh more than a cask of tobacco." She smiled at him. "There's more to you than meets the eye, Kelt Saxon."

Kelt raised his napkin to wipe at his lower lip. "Ye should smile more often; it becomes ye."

"And you." Ashley raised her wineglass in salute. "To a fine dinner and to the man who prepared it. My stomach thanks you, sir."

"For Christmas, I'll prepare a haggis. No Yuletide celebration is complete without it. Ye'll have to part with a sheep or two." His gray eyes narrowed. "Ye do celebrate Christmas here in Maryland, don't ye? There are no religious rules against it?"

"There is a great deal of merrymaking and a mighty lifting of cups," she assured him. "In fact, we have received an invitation to a Christmas dance at Canterbury. Martin Hopkins mentioned you by name. I'll not be going, but you are welcome to."

Kelt waved away Joan's offer to refill his wineglass with a slight motion of his long, well-formed fingers. They were exceedingly clean for a man of the soil, Ashley decided. Both of her hands would have fit neatly into one of his, but Kelt's hands were far from clumsy. She had never known an artist before, but she wondered if— Her reverie was cut short by Kelt's insistent question, repeated, she was certain by the amused expression on his face, more than once.

"I hope it is my cooking you're engrossed in," he said. "I wouldna want to bore ye at your own table, mistress."

The gray eyes twinkled at she struggled to remember what he had asked her. "I'm sorry," she hedged. "I was thinking of the tobacco shipment." She pushed back from the table and stood up. "I have enjoyed your meal and your company, but I will impose on you no more on your day off. Lord knows you have few of them. You are free to ride to Chestertown if it pleases you. I have accounts to do. If you'll excuse me."

"Aye, I'm certain you do. But you'll give me the favor of a reply to my last question, or tell me it's none of my business. I asked why ye would not be going to the Christmas gathering at Canterbury. Is there bad blood between ye and your neighbors?"

"Are you always so direct?" she asked. Her cheeks felt flushed, and she knew the heat had not come from the wine. His gaze was unnerving. "I get on well with my neighbors, if you must know. As to why I don't go to their parties, it is my own affair." Her voice softened. "They would welcome you. An eligible bachelor is a much sought after commodity."

"Even an overseer?"

"Martin Hopkins was once an indentured servant. He was transported to Annapolis as a horse thief thirty years ago. I doubt he would look down his nose at you or any other. You have a respectable occupation, and Martin has two unmarried daughters." She chuckled. "Believe me, you would be well received."

"Fair flowers, are these Hopkins lassies?" His voice was strangely choked. "As lovely as the acres their fond father will add to their marriage portion?"

"As to that, sir, you must make your own decision. But this much I will tell you. A poxed face often conceals a sweet and gentle nature, while beauty can cover much that is undesirable."

"Now I know ye speak truth, Mistress Morgan. 'Tis common knowledge that a sensuous mouth and come-hither eyes often hide an evil temper. Methinks I must see these lassies for myself. What better time and place than a Yuletide fete?" He stroked his neat beard. "But I would feel more comfortable if you would accompany me. You could point out the unattached ladies and tell me all their faults before I waste time in idle conversation with the wrong woman. As ye so wisely pointed out, my free time is limited." He grinned wickedly. "Remember, I am a stranger here. Would ye leave me to the mercy of scheming mothers?"

"You'd be naught but a lamb among wolves, I'm certain," Ashley replied more sharply than she intended. She knew her hired overseer was making fun of her and she wasn't sure she liked it. "Thank you again for the meal. If I don't see you at eventide, we'll meet over breakfast to discuss tomorrow's chores."

Kelt gave a courtly bow and stepped back to let Ashley pass. "You're sure you willna reconsider about the dance?" His shoulders quivered slightly with barely suppressed mirth. "For the sake of the season and good relations with your neighbors?'' He paused. ''Or, if you willna go, at least give me the name of the most eligible young maid.''

Ashley stopped short in the doorway and turned to glare back at him. ''That will be no problem. You would want to court Mistress Honor Horsey. She is the only heir of doting parents. She has all her teeth, and is sound of body and wind.''

Kelt chuckled. ''Why do I suspect the lass has a face like a toad?''

''If you believe that, sir, you are greatly mistaken,'' Ashley protested. ''There may be few eligible maids in Chestertown, but I assure you she would be considered a beauty even in Virginia.''

''A shrew, then?''

Ashley shook her head. ''Of gentle voice and manner . . . if a bit shy.''

''Beautiful and good, a paradox.'' Kelt folded his arms across his chest and pursed his lips in feigned puzzlement. ''Hmmm,'' he mused. ''Can the lass be simple?''

''Bright as a new penny,'' Ashley countered.

''Overly plump?''

''Nay.'' Ashley's eyes sparkled with mischief. ''And neither is she an old maid.''

''When did you say this dance is to be held? Will there be time to cry the banns before Christmas? If Mistress Horsey is as you say, you may well dance at our wedding.''

''Gladly, Saxon. For then you would have so much of your father-in-law's land to tend to, you would have no time for mine. We could part friends.''

''We can part whenever you like, if you'll but pay me for the full contract,'' he shot back.

''A cold day in hell,'' she answered sweetly. ''Until morning, sir.''

* * *

Kelt knew his head had barely hit the pillow when he heard someone call his name. He moaned and opened his eyes; it was pitch black. He yawned and fumbled for the pistol on the candlestand beside his bed. "What is it?" he answered sleepily. "Is something wrong?" Even in his semiconscious state, he knew that if he was being called from his bed, something must be amiss.

The doorknob turned with a soft click. "Scot? Are you awake?"

"I'm awake," he said thickly. "Ashley?" Kelt scrambled from the bed and grabbed for his breeches. The damp air was cold against his bare skin and he shivered. "What the—" He clamped his teeth over the final word. "Is something wrong?" he repeated. "Just a minute, I'll light a candle." He padded barefoot across the icy floor to stir the coals of the dying fire, then knelt to hold the candlewick to a flickering ember.

A pale circle of light illuminated the room. Ashley stood beside the door, fully dressed. "You sleep like the dead."

"Why in the name of Mary's son have ye roused me from my bed? It can't be long past the witching hour." He ran a hand through his thick, tousled hair. "Have the bondservants all run away? Is there another fire?" he demanded dubiously. The house was silent. Whatever had brought his mistress to his bedchamber at this hour, it didn't seem to involve the rest of the household. Kelt regarded her suspiciously. If she'd come to seduce him, she'd wasted time in dressing.

"Actually, it's closer to four." She took a few steps toward his easel. The partially completed canvas was hidden in shadows. "You were awake until nearly midnight. Were you painting? Can I see?"

"No." Kelt moved to cover Ashley's portrait with a linen sheet. "Are you tight with candles that you care how late I work?" he grumbled, turning his back to put on his shirt. "This is not decent. If ye wanted me, ye should have sent Thomas."

Ashley laughed. "I'm not one of your frail English ladies that a man's bare chest will send me into vapors, or ecstasy for that matter. It's foggy out."

Kelt inhaled sharply. If she had awakened him from a sound sleep to tell him it was foggy . . . His fingers itched to tighten around her throat. No jury would convict him of murder with such provocation, not even a Maryland jury. "Woman . . ." he threatened.

"It's foggy out, so it's a perfect morning for goose hunting. We can use a goose for the house and as many as we can shoot for the workers. I thought perhaps you'd like to come. We've shown you little but hard labor since you've come to Morgan's Fancy." She reached out nonchalantly to lift the corner of the cover over the painting.

"Don't touch it," he ordered. The near whisper did not soften the authority in the Scot's burr. He nodded, motioning to the open door. "I'll come wi' ye and gladly, if you'll but give me a few minutes to pull on my boots and wash the sleep from my eyes. I favor a good hunt as long as the game's not wasted. God knows enough geese have passed over this house in the last few weeks."

"We'll grab a cup of tea and some of your biscuits in the kitchen, but there'll be no time for a proper breakfast," Ashley warned. "And if you're not sharp, I'll leave without you." She hurried out of the room and down the dark stairway. There was no need for a light; she knew every inch of Morgan's Fancy.

Jai pushed his cold nose into her hand and she patted the dog's shaggy head. "Yes, you're coming," she promised. "Did you think I was going to swim after the dead geese myself?"

The kitchen was still and dark. Only a faint glow from the coals in the corner of the wide fireplace gave off any light. Ashley knelt and began to make up the fire, adding cedar chips and blowing gently to ignite them. There was no sound in the room but the crackling of the new fire and the dog's breathing. Deftly Ashley hung the iron kettle over the flames and stood up, brushing the ashes from the knees of her leather breeches.

Sooner or later, she'd see what it was that the Scot was painting. She wondered if he was any good. Most itinerant artists she'd heard about were nothing at all like Kelt Saxon. There was more of soldier than limner about him. He was an educated, sensitive man, someone she would have liked to have as a friend. Why then did he constantly infuriate her? He didn't even have to say anything—a look was enough to send her temper soaring! It would be better for her and for Morgan's Fancy if he were gone.

"Do ye make it a habit to rise on the worst of nights and hunt for your people?" Kelt's question came from the shadows by the door. He lifted a candlestick from the trestle table and brought it to the fire. "Ye constantly surprise me, Mistress Morgan." He rubbed at his arms briskly and yawned as Jai twisted about his ankles, pushing his massive head against the man to be petted.

"Jai," Ashley scolded. "Come here."

"Leave him." Kelt patted the shaggy, multicolored coat. "Good dog, good Jai." The animal's heavy tail thumped vigorously against the floorboards.

Traitor, Ashley thought. Even my own dog likes the rogue! "You must remember," she said, "my upbringing was unusual. For all intents and purposes, I was raised as a boy. Didn't your grandsire take you hunting?"

"As a matter of fact, he did. I shot my first stag when I was nine and he carried it back across his saddle bow. Ye would have loved him. He had a beard halfway to his waist. It was as red as your own locks in his prime, but when I knew him, it was snow white. He wore a belted plaid, wi' his old legs bare summer and winter, and a great pagan brooch of beaten silver. There was a man! 'Til the day he died, few could best him in arm wrestling. He carried his bride off by force, riding fifty miles through English territory with her in his arms."

"A kidnapper? And you boast of him? She should have cut his throat with his own broadsword."

"And make my own father an orphan? Nay, my grandmother was not unwilling. She was already five months gone with his child. They were sweethearts, if enemies by birth." Kelt took two mugs from the Welsh dresser and carried them to the table. "It was a love match, one that lasted for half a century."

Ashley looked unconvinced. "I think you spin your tales as easily as you swallow food, Scot." She sprinkled a handful of loose tea into the china pot. "I'm never quite certain what is truth and what is feigned charm." It was happening again! Damn it! She was turning a pleasant morning's hunt into a sparring match. She forced a smile. "I hope you're a good shot. I'd like to bring back some birds this morning. With the fog, it should make for good hunting."

"Aye, I've found it to be so." He unwrapped the biscuits and popped one in his mouth. "Ye should have roused me a little earlier, so I would have had time to make us a decent meal. It will be raw out this morning, mark my words."

"At least it's not raining. My grandfather always took me duck hunting in the rain," Ashley said with a shudder. "And you'll appreciate the effort when you're sitting over a platter of roast goose with berry dressing."

"If Joan touches so much as a feather of one of my geese, I'll sell her indenture north to the Puritans."

Chapter 6

The sound of the horses' hooves hitting the trail was muffled by thick fog. Even the creak of saddle leather and the heavy breathing of the animals seemed distorted and far away. Mist swirled about the riders, making it impossible to see more than two arms' lengths ahead. The ghostly shape of a great horned owl fluttered before them, and Ashley's horse snorted in alarm and shied sideways, bumping into Kelt's mount.

"Whoa, whoa," Ashley soothed. She tightened the reins, pulling the nervous mare's head down, and patted the animal's neck. "Easy, girl. You're not afraid of a bird, are you?"

"It's a good thing ye listened to me and left that devil you usually ride in the barn. He'd have dumped you in the dirt," Kelt said.

Ashley chuckled. "For once you're probably right." She glanced sideways at him. His features were lost in the fog and darkness, but the soft burr of his deep voice was reassuring. No need to tell him that the owl had startled her or that she was afraid of the dark.

If Mari was home, Ashley would have taken the Indian woman hunting with her. She wouldn't have come alone. In the daylight, she wasn't afraid to go anywhere or face anything. But with the coming of night, a child's fears of the unknown assailed her.

Her grandfather had despised cowardice; nothing dead or alive had frightened him. There was no way Ashley could admit to being scared of the dark. He had raised her as he would a son, and expected the same courage of her as he would of a man.

"Are ye sure ye know where you're going?" Kelt's query brought her back to the fog-shrouded lane. "I'd hate to get up at this time of the night and not get a shot at some geese."

"There's a blind along the river. We'll tie the horses a little way off the road and walk down to it. As soon as the sun comes up, you'll get your fill of shooting."

Ashley liked the excitement of the hunt, but not the killing. She hunted deer and small game, shot wolves and other creatures that preyed on the poultry yard and livestock. She killed for food and to protect what was hers, but she never got over the sense of loss . . . the pain of putting an end to something wild and free.

"I suppose ye be a fair shot, for a lass," Kelt said.

"You'll have to be the judge of that." She hoped she could shoot straighter than he could; he'd never let her hear the end of it if she couldn't. "No fair shooting on the water."

"I wouldna think of it."

"We'll take no more than we can carry home. Be sure you kill what you aim at. Mari says a crippled bird is an insult to the South Wind." Ashley glanced over at Kelt, waiting to hear his amused reaction.

"I knew it was an insult to someone to waste one of God's beasties, but I never knew which wind it was," he said solemnly.

"Indians claim the wind is alive. They say they can see it."

"Aye, I've heard that tale myself. But if they can see it, it must have a color. Did she say what color the wind was?"

"Red."

"I see."

"You don't believe me."

"I know little of redmen, or redwomen for that matter. Mari sounds a strange sort."

"Only if you don't know her. She isn't strange to me. She's been half mother, half friend to me all my life." Ashley unconsciously reined the mare closer to Kelt's horse. "She has her own ways, Mari has. That I'll admit. All the years she's lived on Morgan's Fancy haven't changed her Indian beliefs one iota."

"You said she wasna a servant. What exactly is she?"

"She was my grandfather's woman."

"Nae his legal wife?" Kelt couldn't quite keep the shock from his voice. "I wouldna think such a woman a fit companion for an innocent young girl."

"A better companion than my lady mother." Ashley slapped the reins against the mare's neck, urging her into a trot. "He would have made her his wife any time, right up until the day he died, but she wouldn't have it. She said the white men made slaves of their wives. Ash was good to her, but if she'd married him, maybe he'd have changed like all the rest. She preferred to keep her freedom and her own home. He built her a cabin and deeded a hundred acres of land to her. It still stands, right in the center of the plantation."

"And ye dinna begrudge her any of your precious land?"

"You don't understand, Kelt." Ashley's voice

cracked. "I'd give Mari a thousand acres if she wanted it. She's the closest person to a real mother I ever had." A cedar leaning over the trail brushed against her leg. "Pull up," she said. "We leave the animals here."

They tied the horses to a branch and Ashley led the way down a faint path, feeling her way step by step. "No more talking," she warned. "And be careful with your musket. I don't care to be shot in the back or to have you shoot my dog."

"Do ye think me such a fool?" he snapped back. "Mind your own weapon and I'll mind mine."

"Quiet, you'll scare the geese," she whispered. "You talk more than any man I've ever known."

They walked in silence for several hundred yards until Ashley felt the ground begin to soften. She felt for a fallen log, warning Kelt when her right foot touched it. "Watch your step."

The blind wasn't far now. She didn't need light to find it; she'd been here too many times. She moved the heavy musket to rest in the crook of her left arm and reached back to catch Kelt's hand. It closed on hers with a confident grip that made her pulse quicken.

She swallowed hard and prayed her voice would betray none of the strangeness she felt. "Careful. There's a log bridge to cross. It's narrow and the river too cold to swim in this time of year." She forced a laugh. "I know because I tumbled in one morning and ruined my grandfather's duck hunting. They had to fetch me home to thaw me out."

"As much trouble as ye must have been to him, it's a wonder he didna let you drown."

"Here's the beginning." Ashley freed her hand, warm and tingling from his touch.

The first promise of dawn was beginning to illuminate the eastern horizon. The duck blind was a faint outline against the darker shadow of the water ahead of her. The structure had been built on cedar posts set deep in the riverbed, accessible by a log walkway over the water. Nervously Ashley stepped onto the log, placing each foot with care. Normally she could have run across the makeshift bridge with her eyes blindfolded, but Kelt's presence behind her made her oddly unsteady on her feet.

"Jai," she whispered. "Come on, boy." She could hear the soft padding of the dog's feet and the rhythm of Kelt's steady breathing behind her.

Gratefully Ashley took hold of the sturdy support on the corner of the blind and stepped inside. The cedar post and reed structure was a good eight feet square with a woven reed roof over the back two thirds. The front wall of the blind, facing the river, was only waist high to give the occupants room to shoot. It had been freshly repaired just that fall, and the floor was ankle-deep in fresh hay. Ashley leaned her musket against the far wall and sat down on the bench. Jai curled up at her feet. Absently she patted his head. "He'll fetch the geese in for us," she said.

Kelt put his gun down and crouched on the other side of the blind. "Nice," he offered.

"The hay's to keep your feet from freezing. Goose hunting's cold sport."

"Aye." He pulled a piece of hay from the floor and sucked on it. "I allow a lass would think that."

Ashley bit back a stinging retort and turned to look out at the mist-covered river. Even in winter, the river teemed with bird and animal life. She willed herself to push the Scot from her thoughts and let the peace of this quiet place seep through her. The rippling of the tide beneath the blind was curiously soothing. Even the echoing splash of a muskrat blended with the mournful cry of the geese winging overhead to play out a wilderness symphony.

Now Ashley remembered why she liked to rise in the blackness of the night and come here. There was something almost mystical about the river in winter, something indefinable. A quick glance might give a stranger reason to believe that the scene was cold and barren. But she didn't see it that way. To her, there was a sense of waiting, a promise of the full bursting of life that would come again in the spring.

Sitting here in the dark, waiting for the sun to come up over the trees, was like waiting for the creation. Ashley knew the light would come, but still she watched with bated breath for each ray of shimmering light. The magic had never failed to work. The sun always rose.

This morning was no exception. Iridescent coral and gold spilled across the cloud-strewn sky, so beautiful that Ashley caught her breath in wonder. By almost imperceptible degrees the blind and the river became more visible. The far bank was still shrouded in mist, but she could make out the puffy black and white heads of a pair of buffleheads swimming a few yards from the blind and a larger group of black ducks feeding just beyond them.

"Ashley."

It took a second to remember she was not alone in the blind. She exhaled sharply. Kelt was standing barely an arm's length away, his eyes fixed on her face. A strange note in his voice sent a wave of excitement surging through her.

"You're a bonny sight fer a mon, with the light playin' across all that hair."

Ashley's breath caught in her throat as she stared up at him. The light was dim at the back of the blind, and Kelt's face was shadowed. He's going to kiss me, she thought. And I'm going to let him. With the patience of Eve, she waited . . . knowing, anticipating the feel of that masculine mouth pressed warm and firm against her lips.

"I want to kiss ye," he murmured. "Only kiss ye . . . nothing more."

Trembling, she rose and took a step in Kelt's direction. An unfamiliar weakness flowed through her limbs as she stared up at the big man. *Run!* her inner voice cried. *Stop before it's too late*. His arms encircled her as he lowered his head to gently brush her lips with his.

Ashley slipped her arms around Kelt's neck, savoring the warm pressure of his mouth against hers, reveling in the strong, male scent of his hard-muscled body and the exquisite sensation of his broad hand pressed against the small of her back. A bittersweet ache grew in her breasts as they pressed against his chest, and her lips parted of their own volition, allowing his tender, exploring kiss to deepen.

Time stood still as she strained against him, nearly overcome by the hot, tingling desire that raced through her veins. Her fingers tightened in his hair, pulling him still closer until suddenly, with a shuddering breath, Kelt released her and stepped back.

"Ashley," he murmured hoarsely. He laughed deep in his throat. "By all that's holy, lassie, 'twas stop now or not at all."

Shaken, Ashley touched her passion-swollen lips as the unfamiliar sensations slowly receded, leaving her breathless and weak-kneed. Slowly she lowered herself to the bench and smiled. "Thank you," she whispered.

"For stopping or for the kiss?" He ran a hand through his hair. "I'd nae harm ye. I didna mean for . . ."

"For the kiss. She moistened her lips with the tip of her tongue. "Every woman should be kissed like that at least once in her life."

"And you haven't?"

Ashley shook her head. "Never." She sighed deeply and smiled shyly. "For a wild Highlander, you have a gentle touch."

Kelt reached out to touch a curling tendril of auburn hair that fell across her forehead. "I'm no thief. I'll nae take what's not offered freely or mine by right."

She nodded solemnly. "You are a dangerous man, Kelt Saxon." What power did he have over her that he could cause these new and disturbing emotions with a kiss? Was it Kelt or her own weakness? No matter which, she needed time to think and she couldn't think clearly with him so close.

Ashley forced her voice to a semblance of normality. "Come, Jai." She motioned to the dog. "The geese have had a reprieve," she said huskily. "I find I'm in no mood for killing this morning."

"Nor I," Kelt agreed readily. He handed Ashley's musket to her. "The bondmen can get by on pork and cornbread for a few more days."

Ashley nodded. "As long as it's not Joan's."

He laid a big hand on her shoulder. "I canna promise that what happened here won't happen again."

She pulled away and led the way from the blind. If it does, I must find a way to deal with it, she thought.

They made their way back to the tied horses and returned to the manor house in mutual silence.

Ashley walked around the frame of the new barn with pride. With the tobacco shipped, Kelt had been free to use field hands as well as the plantation craftsmen to work on the construction these past weeks. Precious time had been saved when they were able to trade the sheep and some cows to a neighbor for seasoned lumber. Kelt had borrowed ten men from Martin Hopkins at Canterbury to help raise the walls and cross beams. Kelt had assured her he knew a little about construction, and she was well pleased with the results. When the last of the shingles were nailed down, they could start moving the horses into the spacious stalls.

It would be a long time before she'd stop looking from her bedchamber window for the old barn—old Ash Morgan's barn. Would she always think of this new one as Kelt Saxon's? The men called it that. "The Scot's barn," they said. In fairness, she had to admit it was larger and safer than the one they had lost by fire; each box stall now had an outside door as well as a gate to the center hall. The plan had required extra hinges at a time when iron was precious, but the Scot had convinced the master carpenter that it was worth the expense.

"One blood horse lost would be more than the cost of the hardware," he'd insisted.

Reluctantly Ashley had dug into the small box of coins she kept in the library beneath the loose brick in the hearth. Kelt was right. The livestock was the life's blood of Morgan's Fancy. They couldn't afford to lose a single animal.

"Are ye satisfied?" Kelt handed the armful of cedar shingles to a workman and dusted off his hands. "I thought to stable the beasts here tonight."

"With only half the roof done?" Ashley met his intense gray eyes without flinching. She hadn't actually avoided him since that morning in the duck blind, but she had wanted to keep her distance; it would have been far easier. But she couldn't give him the satisfaction of letting him know how deeply she had been shaken by a single kiss.

"They'll finish or I'll know the reason why. Look at that sky." He motioned toward the west. "We'll have snow before morning or I'll miss my guess. It's gotten colder in the last hour."

"It would suit me if it snowed two feet and the bay froze over. We'd have less to fear from raiders if there was ice to hold back the ships."

"Aye. There's much we should talk about, Ashley." His brow creased in genuine concern. "Word from Chestertown is that murder's been done on the Eastern Shore. A house was burned and stock slaughtered."

"How many dead?"

"Two men and a child. Four slaves and a woman are missing," he said. "Pirates, 'tis believed. They came by water and left that way."

"They're certain it wasn't a slave uprising?" Mentally, Ashley began to count the flintlocks, wheel locks and other weapons belonging to Morgan's Fancy. She'd break the law and arm her bondmen if necessary.

"Nay." The Scot shook his head. "The evidence was plain enough. They came to steal slaves and whatever else they could carry off." No need to mention that the missing woman was only nineteen and big with child, or that her husband's head had been nearly hacked off with a cutlass.

Ashley's face paled and her lips tightened. "Brave men to murder a child." She pushed back the icicle of fear that formed within her. "Human vermin," she murmured. "How did the child die?"

Kelt exhaled and turned away. "Leave it, lass. Dead is dead. No need to fash yerself."

"Do you think I'm a child that you must keep things from me? I've seen death before. It's ugly and senseless, but it will be none the less for my knowing the truth." Ashley's eyes darkened with rising anger. "Who was it? What plantation?" Kelt shook his head stubbornly. Ashley whirled on the man standing just beyond Saxon. "Joshua? Who was murdered?"

Joshua scratched his chin and mumbled under his breath.

"Who? I can't hear you."

"Martin Briggs and his brother John from Swan Point." He looked sheepishly at Kelt. "I can't rightly go agin' the mistress, sir."

"The child?" Ashley asked softly.

"Martin Briggs's young'n. Don't rightly know his name, but 'twas a boy."

"They came to buy a milk cow of me last spring." Ashley clenched her trembling hands into fists, locking them against her sides. "He was a babe in arms."

"He was in his cradle when they set the house afire," Joshua said. "Poor little tyke never had a chance."

"Damn you, man!" Kelt swore. "Have you no more sense than a—"

"I asked him, Saxon," Ashley snapped. "Do you think I'm too frail to hear the truth?" Her stomach lurched as she remembered the blond-haired babe she'd held in her arms. Whoever the raiders were, it couldn't be any of Gentleman Jim's men. A pirate he might be, but he had an honorable name with women. He'd never been known to harm one. "Damn." The missing woman had to be Martin's wife, Jane. Ashley turned and walked quickly to where a stableboy waited with her horse. She needed to be alone, to have time to think. An image of the baby's chubby face hovered just behind her eyes. She stopped and glared back at Kelt. "When was the attack?"

"Two days ago." He took a step toward her. "We should make plans for setting a guard around the plantation. And . . ." Kelt's jaw was set as though carved in granite. "I think you should stay close to the house for a few days."

"I'm certain you would, Master Saxon." Ashley put her foot in the stirrup and swung up onto the bay stallion. "This is my land and my people," she said hotly. "I'll not skulk about like a craven because of a few human scavengers. Let them set foot on Morgan's Fancy, and they may get more than they bargained for." With a firm hand on the reins, she pulled the horse's head around and set her heels into his flanks. "Ha!" she urged. Horse and rider crossed the farmyard and headed toward the prize house.

Cursing women, horses, and Marylanders in general, Kelt mounted his dappled-gray and galloped after her, leaving the workers mumbling among themselves behind him.

Joshua glanced in Short John's direction and spat onto the hard-packed dirt floor. "Them two . . ." he ventured. "Them two is somethin' else."

Short John made an obscene gesture and dropped the hammer. From a pocket beneath his leather apron he pulled a tin flask and took a long swig. Smacking his lips, he wiped his mouth with the back of his sleeve and offered the flask to Joshua.

The older man scratched the salt and pepper stubble on his head and frowned. "Scot's gonna smell it on yer breath, way you been suckin' it in. Take the hide offen yer back, he will!" He shook his head. "Not me. Roof's too high. I'm layin' shakes, I don't drink none. Not me. Knew a fella once, fell offen a roof." Joshua paused for effect and blew his nose between his fingers. "Broke ever bone in his body. Just like a jellyfish, he was. Lived fifteen year like that. Had to be carried ever'where in a sack like a papoose. S'God's truth. Seed him wi' my own eyes."

"Bull."

Edgar laughed as he came down the ladder. "Thought you said that fella buried his legs so far in the ground they had to cut 'em out." He reached for Short John's flask and took a nip. "Got to keep your stories straight, Joshua. What about the little cart you said his woman pulled him around in?"

"That was another fella, in London, close by the bridge. This fella was a Welshman, fell off a church. Broke ever' bone in his body. Swear to God!"

Edgar leaned against the ladder and peered up at the sun. "Close on to noonin', wouldn't you think? My belly's bangin' against my backbone."

"Yer belly's alway's clammerin'," Joshua protested. "It ain't time for quittin' yet. He'll be back here wantin' to know why it ain't done, and I'll ketch hell. You got another hour to go before dinner, Edgar, and well you know it."

"Well, I don't know about the rest of you, but my woman's waitin' fer me. I've a mind to get some of what thet overseer's gettin' afore my dinner." Short John leered suggestively.

"Hold yer tongue," Joshua threatened. "There's no cause to talk dirty about the mistress." He reached for his hammer and tossed it meaningfully from one hand to another. "She's different, I'll grant ye that, but she ain't no whore. Mistress Ashley's a lady. Don't ye be fergettin' it."

Short John scoffed. "A lady? A apple don't fall far from the tree to my way o' thinkin'." He winked at Edgar. "A lady ain't what you'd call her mother, is it?" He sipped at the rum again. "Put a sow in silk, she's still what she is."

Joshua took a step in Short John's direction and his

eyes narrowed in warning. "Enough. Git back to work, all of ye."

"Iffen she's sech a lady, how come she's got the same name as her mother's people? And how come the new overseer sleeps under her roof?" Short John laughed and shrugged. "You bang cedar shakes if ye want to. I'm off to take some sweet between my woman's thighs."

Kelt swore under his breath as he watched Ashley rein the big bay horse off the road. She was taking that damned short cut again, but he was certain she was riding to the prize house. He'd intended to warn the families there of the danger of pirates. A prize house was too tempting for raiders. Tobacco was as good as gold in any port, and the pirates would have no way of knowing that Ashley had shipped all of hers to England. "May their souls burn for all eternity." He'd have to pull men from other work and set a watch at the prize house as well as on the rivers and the main dock near the manor house.

Kelt grunted. God knew he was probably better suited to be a military man than a farmer. Few of his family had ever died in their beds; he'd sprung from a bloodthirsty lot of warriors.

He'd need a complete list of weapons and ammunition, as well as information on who was trustworthy and could shoot. Boys could serve as riders, or better yet, watch for smoke signals. Ashley could have saved them time and effort if she hadn't gone riding off in a huff. She'd have the information he needed, probably without even going to her account books. "Hell, she probably knows how many rocks each boy has in his slingshot bag," he muttered to the horse. "Damnable woman!"

He'd gotten precious little sleep since that morning

in the duck blind several weeks ago. Ashley had come into his arms willingly enough, as passionate as any wench he'd ever tumbled, more so for the innocence that had been behind it. He wanted her in his bed, hell yes, but what worried him even more was that he knew making love to her wouldn't be enough. With Ashley, it wouldn't be just the joy of her body—and hers was meant to give a man joy if any woman's was. It would be something he had never felt before. Something he had stopped searching for . . .

His loins tightened with desire as he remembered the feel of her satin-soft skin against his . . . the faint lavender scent of her hair and clothes . . . and clean, sweet taste of her ripe lips. Every instinct had urged him to push her down in the hay and take his pleasure. She wouldn't have fought him. But in winning, he would have lost. He might have had use of that lovely body, but Ashley Morgan would have slipped through his fingers like river mist. She was like some wild forest creature. She'd have to be tamed before he put his mark on her. And the fear was that if he did, he might become the captured quarry.

Why didn't I have sense enough to seek a whore in Chestertown, or accept Joan's open invitation? Instead, I spend my nights with a brush and canvas. Poor comfort for a man.

The portrait was another thorn in his side. The image he carried of Ashley in his mind and the one he sweated over in oil were not the same. He had the eye and hair color, the lines of her chin, the stubborn mouth, but the essence that was Ashley Morgan eluded him.

Kelt was jerked from his reverie by the sight of Ashley crossing the meadow at a full gallop. A high split-rail fence stretched between the horse and the prize house compound. He unconsciously caught his breath as he watched her tense for the jump, leaning forward on the stallion's neck, blending with the magnificent animal.

The bay soared upward. For a heartbeat, horse and rider seemed almost one and Kelt's artist's soul longed to capture the moment on canvas. Then, suddenly, Ashley fell to the right, grabbed frantically at the stallion's mane, lost her grip, and tumbled to the ground.

By the time Kelt reached the fence and threw himself out of the saddle, the bay had limped back to where Ashley lay and was sniffing her still form. Kelt dropped to his knees beside her. Her face was as white as tallow, her eyes shut. Over her left eye a purpling bruise seeped dark blood. "Ashley! Ashley!" he called. He brought his cheek to her lips; her breathing was so shallow as to be almost nonexistent.

"Ashley. Ashley. You're bleeding, damn it." Kelt's voice dropped to a harsh whisper. "If you're bleeding, you've got to be alive. Dinna ye ken, lass? You've got to be alive!"

Chapter 7

Kelt gathered her in his arms, cradling her limp form against his chest. The thick lashes lay unmoving against her ashen cheeks with no hint of consciousness. She was heavier than he would have believed; the muscle and sinew of an athlete lay hidden beneath her womanly curves. Still he lifted her easily and carried her with sure strides toward the nearest cabin.

The wound on her forehead continued to bleed. The trickle of blood ran into her hair, matting the red-gold tresses with an uglier shade of crimson. "Hold on," he said between clenched teeth. "Just keep breathing, lass."

He could feel no broken bones, but her head must have struck a fence rail as she fell, or else that bastard stallion had caught her with a hoof. Kelt bit back an oath. He'd known the animal was too much for a woman . . . known she would come to grief. But he hadn't known how much he would care.

A thick ache rose in his throat. He felt no fear, only an emptiness in the pit of his stomach. He'd seen men die from less of a blow than this. If Ashley died . . . He pushed back the thought. She was alive now and he would keep her that way. Where in

God's name was the nearest physician? And if they found him, would he know anything about head wounds? Kelt would stand for no senseless bloodletting. What she needed was quiet and warmth to give her body the chance to mend itself.

Ashley's saddle lay on the grass not far from where she had fallen. When Kelt found out who had saddled the stallion, that man would rue the day he'd left his mother's apron strings. He'd known from the first that it was the saddle that had failed, not the horse or rider. The bay's form had been perfect as he started the jump. When the cinch came loose, Ashley had lost her balance and gone over with it.

"Ashley?" He might have been carrying a rag doll in his arms. Her lips were parted slightly; the bottom one was fast swelling. Her breathing was still faint, but it was the color of her face that frightened him. Except for the injured lip and the bruise on her forehead, she might have been carved from marble.

"Cara!" he shouted as he neared the cabin door. "Your mistress is hurt! Make ready a bed!"

The bondwoman threw open the door; behind her stood Mari. They moved away as Kelt carried Ashley into the cabin. The Indian woman pulled back the quilt on the bed and watched as the Scot laid her on the clean linen sheets.

"She fell from her horse," Kelt said gruffly. His eyes met Mari's and he was stunned by the compassion and peace she radiated. "I canna wake her." His voice trailed off and he moved back to let Mari examine Ashley's head wound. Behind him, a child whimpered and Cara hushed it with a sharp whisper. "I think she hit her head on the fence," Kelt explained.

Swiftly the copper-skinned woman brushed fingertips across Ashley's lips and then down to rest on the curve of her throat. "Bring water," she ordered in a soft lisp. She turned fierce obsidian eyes on a small boy. "Cold—from the well. Quickly." She motioned Kelt to a three-legged stool. "Sit there, or go if you will. I will tend her."

To his surprise, Kelt obeyed. There was no sting to the crisp order. The woman's hands were knowledgeable; Ashley would come to no harm through her ministration, of that he was confident.

He removed his hat and fumbled with the tie of his cloak. The room was low ceilinged and overly warm but spotless. The neatness of the cabin had struck him when he'd eaten here with Ashley once before. In his experience, most bondmen's quarters were barely inhabitable. A small girl-child tugged shyly on his sleeve.

"Yer cloak, sir." She bobbed her head and reached for it. "Ahh . . ." Her face blushed crimson and she stared down at her scuffed leather moccasins. "Do ye . . ."

Cara cleared her throat loudly, coming to the child's rescue. "Will ye take 'freshment, Master Saxon? Somethin' to drink?"

He shook his head. "No."

Mari moistened Ashley's lips with a wet cloth, then gently wiped the blood from her forehead. The bleeding had nearly stopped, but the bruise was now an uglier purple.

Kelt's eyes followed Mari as she continued to care for her patient. Her hands were scrupulously clean, her hair neatly braided in waist-long plaits. The decent gown was augmented by a brightly beaded vest and headband. Azure glass beads dangled from her ears. He wondered how old she was. There was no hint of gray in the crow-black hair; no wrinkles lined her face. And when she spoke, he caught a glimpse of white, even teeth. She could have passed as a woman of twenty, but he knew that must be impossible if she had acted as mother to Ashley when she was growing up.

"Why doesn't she wake?" he demanded. The warmth of the room seemed to close in on him. "Do you know if there is a physician in Chestertown?"

Mari shook her head gently and laid a finger on her lips for silence. "Her soul has left her body." She sighed and the dark lashes drooped like birds' wings across the high cheekbones. "We must not move her. Only wait awhile. It will return. Her life force is strong." A faint smile lit the ebony eyes. "You care more for her than you know, Kelt Saxon. It is good."

For one hour, two—Kelt couldn't be sure—he waited. Others pressed into the cabin, asked questions, and were shooed away by the women. The strong smell of cooking soup filled the room. Children fussed and were fed. A baby cooed. Someone put a mug of ale into Kelt's hand; he raised it to his lips but couldn't swallow. I think I love her, he thought with sudden clarity. God, help me, I think I love her, and I'll never have the chance to tell her so.

Suddenly he was startled by the Indian woman calling his name.

"Now, Kelt Saxon. Call her back from across the river. Call her. Now!" With surprising strength, Mari caught his arm and pulled him to the bedside.

His breath came in ragged gulps. Ashley looked no different than she had since the fall. Her breathing might be a little stronger, but he couldn't be certain. He had gazed so long and hard at her pale face without seeing any hint of conscious. Still, it did not occur to him to doubt the urgent command. "Ashley," he whispered.

"No!" Mari's bronzed fingers bit into his forearm.

"Call her! Bring her back now or you will lose her forever!"

"Ashley!" He bent over the still form and took hold of her shoulders. "Ashley!" he ordered. "Come back!"

A flicker of color stained her cheeks and she drew in a long breath. The fingers on her right hand moved.

"Ashley." Kelt's bones felt as though they had turned to milk. He cupped her face between his callused hands. "Ashley, lass," he pleaded. "Wake up. Ye've slept long enough."

Her eyelashes fluttered, then opened. For a fraction of a second Kelt gazed into the familiar spark. Then, as quickly as it had come, the light faded; the eyes staring back at him were empty. Her lids closed and the faint breath ceased.

"*Dah-hai-tha!*" Mari cried. With a wail that chilled his blood, the Indian woman fell to her knees and began to weep.

"Ashley!" Kelt shook her roughly. "Damn you, Ashley, you canna die on me!" Instinctively he leaned down and pressed his lips to hers in a bittersweet kiss of unsuppressed longing. Tears clouded his eyes as he cradled her against him, gently kissing the curve of her brow, the swollen bruise, and the corners of her mouth. "Nay, lassie," he entreated. "The grave shall not have ye. Now now . . . not yet."

Ashley gave a little moan deep in her throat and stirred in his arms. The awful pallor of her skin darkened to rose and she sighed, opening her eyes. "Kelt?" Her lips moved in a silent question.

Kelt's sigh of relief was heard above the whispers. Trembling, he laid her back against the pillow, answering her weak smile with a crooked grin.

Ashley took another deep breath and raised a hand

to her forehead. "What happened?" she whispered huskily.

"You fell off your horse," Mari scolded. "What would your grandfather think?" She brought a cup of water and offered it to Ashley even as her eyes signaled Kelt that all was well. "Must I strap you to a cradleboard like a papoose? You frightened us half to death."

"Aye," Kelt agreed. He cleared his throat and ran a hand through his tousled hair. "I told you that stallion was too much for a lass."

Ashley chuckled, then winced at the pain. "Go away and leave me in peace. I've no wish to have you laughing at me, and me as weak as a kitten."

Kelt mumbled a reply and walked stiffly from the cabin. A throng of men immediately surrounded him.

"Is she dead?" Joshua demanded. "Is the mistress kilt?"

"Cara said—"

"It was a bump on the head, nothing more," Kelt said. "She is awake and giving orders." The cold air felt good on his skin, but he wanted to be alone. *What in the name of all that was holy had happened in there?* He had believed her dead . . . or had he? "Back to your work, all of you!" He turned to Joshua. "Find me the man who saddled Baron this morning." Anger was slowly replacing the confusion Kelt felt, and he was glad. He could deal with anger.

Joshua tugged at his forelock, not deceived for a second by the overseer's soft burr. "Yes, sir. I will, Master Saxon. Right away."

A servant held Kelt's dappled-gray gelding for him to mount. The Scot set a booted foot into the stirrup. "Was the stallion hurt?" he demanded.

"No, sir. He's over there."

Kelt waved them away and rode over to where the

bay was tied. Dismounting, he ran his hands over the stallion's legs, searching for swollen tendons or cuts. "The devil looks after his own, I see," Kelt murmured to the horse. "You seem to be all of a piece."

The stallion nickered and turned his head to gaze past the man. Kelt looked up to see Mari standing there, wrapped in a red wool blanket. "What happened in there?" he asked.

The Indian woman shrugged and glanced up at the gray Tidewater sky, making a slight motion with her right hand. *"Mesawmi,"* she said. The Algonquin lilt to her words made it almost a prayer. Stepping forward, she touched his arm "Wishemenetoo has blessed you. Do not question the power."

"She was dead."

Mari favored him with an elusive smile. "What is death, Kelt Saxon?" She took her hand away and the tension drained from his muscles. *"Lenawawe* . . . she lives. Accept it, and accept this." The narrowed eyes of the squaw gleamed with ardent fervor. "From this time on, your lives are joined. You will find no happiness without her . . . or she without you."

Kelt shook his head. "I dinna ken your ways and they are hard for me to reconcile with logic." He let out a long breath and his brow furrowed. "Ye ask me to believe what I know is impossible, woman. I must think on this. But . . ." Gray eyes met black. "If anyone saved her life, it was you." He colored. "I've not had the best opinion of ye, but I was wrong. I can see why a mon would choose a woman like you. And I'd like to count ye as my friend, if it's still possible."

"A man or a woman cannot have too many friends, overseer. Ashley has been the child of my heart. I would love you for her sake, no matter what you thought of me."

"No," Kelt protested. "Now 'tis ye who doesna understand. There can be nothing between Ashley and me. I'm naught but her hired man."

Mari's laughter was quick and tinkling. "Nothing between you and *Ashley?* Not *Mistress Morgan?*" She chuckled again, covering her mouth like a child. "Because I do not use the silly titles you English give each other, don't think I don't know them." She pulled the scarlet blanket up over her hair. "Protest all you like, Kelt Saxon. What will be will be."

"Aye, there's sense enough to that, I suppose," he granted. "You're certain she'll be all right?"

She nodded. "She is strong. All she needs now is sleep and time for her head to heal."

Kelt looked unconvinced. "The cut looked deep enough to need stitching. Perhaps we should fetch a physician."

"To sew the wound would cause a scar. I will pull it together and bind it with herbs." Mari flashed another smile. "When the corn is green again, you will see it only when she is angry." She nodded to him in regal dismissal and turned back toward the cabin.

"I'll take your word for it . . . and"—he grinned at her—"I'm nae English. Would you have me call ye Iroquois?"

Mari's laughter echoed across the deserted yard.

Tears rolled down Dickon's face as the boy struggled to keep from crying. "I saddled Baron, Master Saxon. But I done it right! I swear it!" He rubbed his face with a dirty sleeve. "The cinch was tight. I checked it afore I led him out!"

Kelt closed the account book on the desk in front of him and considered the protesting child. The blue eyes were full of desperation, but there was no guilt.

Dickon was innocent; Kelt was certain of it. "All right, then. We'll say no more about it. It was an accident, and your mistress is on the mend."

"Is she fer certain, sir?" Dickon sniffed and wiped his nose. "She ain't dyin'?"

"Mistress Morgan will be about her business in a few days." It was true. Even now, Ashley was installed in her bedchamber upstairs. He'd heard her arguing with Joan only a few minutes ago. By the week's end, she'd be on that bay devil again, jumping fences, or he'd miss his guess.

"Sir." The boy shifted nervously from foot to foot. "Am I to be beat?" The small chin stiffened. "I don't mind it, Master Saxon. But if I am, could you do it here?" The boy reddened even more. "I don't want to cry in front of them." He made a motion with his head toward the farmyard. "I ain't a coward, but I ain't sure I won't yell if you use a strap."

Kelt got to his feet. "No, you're nae to be whipped. I'll take your word on it. I only wanted to be sure you had tightened the cinch properly."

"Oh, thank you, sir." The tears flowed harder. "Thank you."

"Off with you now. And I'll be wanting a horse after the evening meal. I want to check the guard posts myself. You can come wi' me if you like."

"Yes, sir. I'll have Falcon ready at the gate for you. Right after supper." Dickon yanked at the hair that fell down over his forehead and backed from the room.

Kelt closed the library door and walked to the fireplace. Kneeling before it, he added a cedar log to the fire. Ashley's fall had been no accident. He'd examined the saddle himself. The cinch strap had been cut nearly through; only a small fraction had been torn from Ashley's weight at the jump. The culprit was clever. He had covered the slice with molasses, rubbing it into the leather so that the person saddling the horse wouldn't notice the severed spot underneath. The problem was, Who was trying to kill Ashley and why?

He'd told no one of his suspicion so far, not even Ashley. He'd taken the cut strap and hidden it in his room until he could decide what to do about it. As long as the culprit was unaware that they were on to him, it would be easier to catch him. A renewed fury surged through Kelt as he remembered the seconds he had believed Ashley to be dead. He'd find whoever was responsible and they would pay dearly. It was a promise!

He'd not been idle in the two days since the accident. With Joshua's help, he'd set armed guards patrolling the shoreline of Morgan's Fancy. Ashley had given him the key to her armory and he'd passed out weapons to all the grown men and boys over twelve. Not all had received guns; there was a crossbow, and even two old wheel locks as well as Indian trade hatchets and a few flintlock pistols. Those went to the women who'd proved they could shoot straight. If raiders landed on Ashley's land, he meant to give them a warm welcome.

Upstairs in the hallway Mari paused by the open doorway to leave final instructions with her patient. "You are not to leave the house for this many days," she ordered, holding up two fingers. "I will come every morning to change the bandage on your head. No horseback riding until I say so, and if you have pain, you are to send a boy for me. Do you understand?"

Ashley drew her knees up under the blanket and wrapped her arms around them. "You're a tyrant,

Mari. There's nothing wrong with me. I feel fine except for this." She touched the linen bandage. "I'll die of boredom cooped up here. The least you can do is stay with me and tell me all the gossip from your family. Did Kitate Ki-be-tar-leh have her baby yet? Does it look white or Indian?"

"The news will taste better if I give you a little at a time on long winter evenings." Mari's dark eyes twinkled. "Yes, my cousin was safely delivered of a healthy girl child. Her hair is the proper color for humans, but . . ." Mari sighed. "I fear her eyes will remain Dutchman blue."

"But has Hans's mother accepted them?"

"For that part of the story you must wait." Mari wrapped her red blanket around her shoulders. "My cabin will be full of mice and squirrels. I am going home."

"Don't go. Just stay another two days. We'll starve!" Ashley said. "Think how grateful Kelt was for your crab soup and the baked pumpkin. Would you leave an invalid to Joan's cornbread and mutton stew?"

"I have told you what to do with Joan. Send her and her cornbread to your stepfather in Virginia. Then he will die of her cooking and your mother will be free of him."

"Mari . . ." Realizing she was gone, Ashley lay back against the pillow and stared at the ceiling.

The ache in her head had subsided to a dull throbbing. The worst thing about the accident was having Kelt see her fall off her horse. She'd felt the saddle slipping; ten to one the cinch had broken. It had felt snug enough when she was riding. She'd taken falls before; every rider did. If she hadn't hit her head, she would have walked away from this fall, too.

"Miss Ashley." Thomas's soft voice penetrated

her self-pity. "Can I come in?" In his hands he carried a leather strap. "There's somethin' I think you oughta know."

Ashley sat up straight and motioned him into the room. "What is it?"

The old man closed the door behind him and put a finger to his lips. "I was checkin' Master Saxon's closestool to see if Joan was keepin' his rooms decent an' I found this inside the chamber pot." He held up the broken cinch. "This is off yer saddle. And it was cut in two before it broke!" He handed over the evidence.

Ashley paled. "You're right, Thomas. It was cut." For a long minute she stared in silence at the altered saddle leather. There was no doubt that it had been cut, but why would anyone want her to fall off Baron? And the thought that Kelt had done it, or had ordered it done, was beyond belief.

"What you want me to do about this?" The lined face was stern. "I'll kill him for you, if you say."

"No!" Ashley shook her head. "No. I don't know what's going on here, but I'd bet next year's tobacco crop that he wouldn't do it. He couldn't . . ." She exhaled sharply. "If I'm that bad a judge of men, I deserve to be done in. Send him up to me. And, Thomas, leave us alone."

"That bump on the head rattled yer brain for certain. You think I'm goin' to leave you alone with a man that maybe tried to kill you?" Thomas glared at her. "If you don't have sense enough to watch out for yourself, we'll have to look out for you."

She shook her head again, wincing from the pain when she moved too quickly. "If he wanted to kill me, he's had lots of chances. I'd be more likely to break an arm or leg falling off a horse than my neck. A lot of people could have put that strap in his chamber. I want to talk to him about it. Don't say anything to anybody."

Thomas wiped his gnarled hands on his breeches. "I'll do as you say, Miss Ashley. But I don't like it. And if anything bad happens to you—he's a dead man. I may be old, but I'm still a crack shot."

"I'll be fine, really. Send him up. And no lurking about the hall listening. Wait downstairs. If he tries to smother me with my own feather tick, I promise I'll scream. Then you can come up and shoot him."

"Hmmmp." Frowning, he left the room.

Ashley ran a hasty brush through her unbound hair, pulled the cover up to her neck, and waited.

Kelt barged in without knocking. "Damn it, woman. Didn't I tell you I didn't want anyone in my room!" He stormed across the chamber and stood threateningly over her bed. "What the hell were Joan and Thomas doing in there?"

Ashley's eyes widened. "What did Thomas say to you?"

"My privacy has been violated! Joan's wailing something about a chamber pot and Thomas stopped me on the stairs threatening to shoot me. Is this a tobacco plantation or an asylum?"

Ashley tried to keep a straight face. "Pull up a chair," she said. "No, first shut the damned door. Joan and Thomas will be falling all over each other trying to hear what we're saying."

Kelt slammed the door with a resounding bang, shot the bolt, and came back to the bed. "I'll stand. Ha' I or ha' I not made it plain that no one shall enter my quarters?"

"If you could but see yourself, Scot. You've been called up here to answer serious charges. Instead of showing proper respect or concern, you prattle on about maids and chamber pots. Perhaps this is an asylum and we're all inmates.'' She sat up, tucking the quilt around her waist. The ample linen nightshirt covered her from ankle to chin. Even Thomas would think her decent before her overseer. ''This is what all the fuss is about.'' She whipped the leather straps from under the cover. ''My cinch was cut.''

''Aye.'' Kelt set his lips in a hard line and glowered at her. ''I knew as much.''

''Obviously you knew. It was found in your room.''

''In my closestool, for God's sake!'' Bright spots of color flamed on his cheekbones. ''What was Joan doing in my room? I haven't used a chamber pot since I was three years old!''

Ashley bit back the laughter that was adding to his anger. ''I'm surprised you admit to using one at all,'' she ventured. She wiped at her eyes. ''Well, it's my own fault. I was complaining about it being too dull in here. Can we sort this out, Kelt?'' Her voice became serious. ''If you knew my fall wasn't an accident, why didn't you tell me? And why did you hide the cinch?''

Kelt let out an oath that rattled the windowpanes. ''Am I being accused of trying to murder you, now? By Mary's sweet blood, I would have told you! I didna want to make it public knowledge, lest we frighten the weasel away.'' He brought his face dangerously close to hers, so close she could see where he'd nicked himself trimming his beard. ''Do you believe it of me?''

''No.'' She caught his hand. ''Stop yelling at me. My head feels like I've been drinking nonstop for a week. Sit down. On the bed, for God's sake. I'll wager my virtue's safe enough.''

''Aye, as safe as though ye were a nun!'' He lowered himself stiffly to the edge of the bed. ''And you haven't answered my question. What was Joan doing in my room?"

Ashley sighed. "We're going in circles. Joan went in to see to your chamber pot. Thomas only went in to be certain she'd done it."

"I've told you I dinna use one, and if I did, I'd not ask another to carry it for me." He folded his arms across his chest and his gray eyes narrowed. "I'll not move from this point. My chamber is my own. I want no one messing with my paints."

"Joan told me she thinks you paint naked women," Ashley teased. "I think she's hoping you'll offer to sketch her."

"I'll paint naked clerics if it please me, but keep your servants out of my chamber!"

"I'll tell them again, I will," she soothed. "Don't scowl at me so. I'd be a fool if I believed you a murderer and then called you to my bed to ask if you were. A murderer wouldn't stoop to lying, now would he?"

"Aye, so how can ye be sure I'm tellin' the truth? With your own lips you've said the murderer wouldn't admit to the truth." The stern jawline softened. "You could be in great danger, even now."

Ashley moistened her upper lip with the tip of her tongue. "You don't kiss like a murderer," she murmured. Kelt's nearness was vaguely disquieting. Invisible bands seemed to tighten around her chest as her gaze fastened on the curling dark hair that showed above his spotless linen shirt. She smelled the sweet, rich scent of tobacco and knew he'd been smoking his pipe. "Joan's claiming you brought me back from the dead with a kiss," Ashley said boldly.

"She also says I paint naked women in my room at night."

Ashley's fingers lay lightly on Kelt's wrist. "I

remember nothing from when I started to fall until I woke up in Cara's cabin in your arms.''

Kelt stood up suddenly. ''You were hurt. I was concerned.''

''But you did kiss me?'' Ashley leaned forward, suddenly very vulnerable. ''I wasn't sure if it was a dream or . . .''

''Aye. I did.''

''Joan says—''

''To hell with what Joan says, or anyone else!'' Kelt knotted his hands into fists at his side. ''Do you think I'm made of stone, woman? I'll nae be a plaything. Not yours . . . not any woman's.'' He moved toward the door, then stopped and looked back at her. ''We'll talk more of the accident when you're well. Until then, say nothing to anyone.''

Ashley stared after him as the tightness in her chest increased. Furiously she blinked back the moisture that threatened to cloud her vision and turned her face to the wall. ''I'm not made of stone, either,'' she whispered into her pillow. A single crystal tear slipped from under her lashes and rolled down her cheek.

Chapter 8

December 17, 1743

Ashley and Kelt walked across the orchard toward the dock. A light blanket of snow covered the ground, laced the winter-barren apple trees with garlands of glittering fairy dust, and muffled the shrill cries of swans winging overhead. The midmorning sun was bright, despite the dropping temperature, and a light wind off the Chesapeake brought the strong, sharp smell of salt.

Kelt glanced sideways at the woman striding briskly beside him. Ashley's mood was light and her cheeks glowed like roses. She had removed the bandages and, except for the bruise across her forehead and the smudge of purple beneath her eye, she looked the picture of health. The auburn-haired lass had recovered even more quickly from the fall than he could have imagined. Still . . . something was different about her since the accident.

She smiled up at him questioningly. "Soot on my nose, Scot?"

"I was wondering what you would say when I told you what I did this morning," he lied. He quickened his step, averting his eyes to keep her from reading his thoughts. I'd like to paint you as you are now . . . with the green wool hood of your cape framing your face and the snow behind you.

Ashley stopped short, folded her arms across her chest, and waited. "Well?" she demanded when he didn't explain. "What exactly did you do?"

"I accepted Martin Hopkins's invitation to the Christmas fete . . . for us both."

"You did *what?*"

Kelt shrugged and grinned. "Hopkins rode over and asked me himself. What else could I do?"

"You could have accepted for yourself." Ashley pursed her lips in a frown. "They tolerate me, for all my idiosyncrasies, but I don't really fit in." Doubt flickered behind the cinnamon-colored eyes. "Now there's no way I can get out of going without offering insult."

"It's Christmas. Surely you can allow yourself a little pleasure. Life's not all work, Ashley."

She stepped past him and hurried toward the dock, her knee-high Indian moccasins almost soundless on the crust of the sparkling snow.

"Wait, lass," he called, catching up to her with a few easy strides. "I thought ye'd be pleased. I never knew a woman who didn't like a party." He lay a gloved hand on her sleeve. "Is it that ye have nothing appropriate to wear?"

"No." She brushed away his hand and kept walking.

"Then what is it?" he demanded. "Are ye too proud to go to such an affair with your hired man? Do ye think 'twould cause talk among the gentlefolk of Chestertown?" The sarcasm in his burr was barely concealed.

" 'Tis neither, you great Scottish ox!" Ashley

retorted. Her voice dropped and she walked faster. "I can't dance."

A chuckle erupted from deep in Kelt's throat as he caught her around the waist and swung her in a half circle. "What did you say?" he demanded. "The mistress o' Morgan's Fancy canna dance? I dinna believe it."

Ashley's eyes narrowed dangerously and she stiffened in his hands. "Put me down," she ordered. When he complied, she stepped back, the tint of her cheeks revealing the depth of her anger. "Do you think a single kiss gives you leave to take liberties?"

"Two kisses," he reminded her. And I've half a mind to make it three.

"I don't deny that you're an attractive man, Saxon, or that I haven't thought about . . ." Ashley paused, searching for the right words. She shrugged. "Perhaps my grandfather taught me too well. My directness of thought and speech would be better suited to a man." Her lower lip trembled as she fixed him with a steady gaze. "I am no lightskirt, and I tell you straight out that I do not mean to wed—not ever! So, you'd be best advised to turn your charm on one of Martin's offspring."

"Marriage, is it? Marriage? Don't flatter yourself, *cailleach!*" Kelt threw his head back and glared at her arrogantly, his fists resting lightly on his slim hips. "When and if I take a wife, it won't be for her land and fortune! God knows there'd be no other reason a man would want such an ill-tempered harpy as ye." His gray eyes clouded with anger. "Do ye think the English have stripped me of my pride, woman?"

The question hung in the crisp air between them. For an instant, veins stood out on Kelt's forehead and Ashley was keenly aware of the straining sinews that threatened to rip the seams of the heavy leather vest. Frightened by the intensity of his barely controlled fury, it was all she could do to hold her ground and not back away.

"It is a man's place to support his wife and bairns, not the other way around." Kelt slowly relaxed his tense muscles. "King George's soldiers took much . . . but they didna take my pride." He pulled off his cocked hat and ran a hand through the dark hair. "I meant you no insult by my kisses—nor by my touch. But I didna speak a word of marriage. And when I choose, 'tis *I* will do the askin'."

"Good," Ashley replied. "Then we both know where we stand. I meant no insult to your damned Scot's pride, either. You wouldn't be the first man to look at broad fields and deep water docking. Even in the Highlands, property must be a consideration in deciding who to wed."

"Aye, I'll grant ye that. But 'tis different. In Scotland I have . . ." He shook his massive head and laughed wryly. "Nothing." The word was barely a whisper. "Nay, lass. I've unleashed my foul temper on you without cause." He replaced the hat and pulled it low over his forehead. "I am doubly sorry. A shrew ye be, but no cailleach. 'Tis my own bile that poisons me." The gray eyes softened. "I've seen too many make their fortune in this new world through a marriage bed and then betray the lass that brought it. I be no such mon, and I fear I have strong opinions on the matter."

"Agreed." Ashley gave him a faint smile. "My mother received much the same treatment from my stepfather, Nicholas Randall—and he was supposed to be a Virginia gentleman of breeding." She tilted her head slightly to gaze into his eyes. "What happened in Scotland, Kelt? Why were you transported to the Colonies?"

For several seconds he did not answer, then he sighed and shook his head. " 'Tis over and done with. Better not to speak o' it."

Ashley caught his work-roughened hand and gripped it. "I know you, Kelt. You are no criminal."

"So my mother always said."

They reached the edge of the dock and sat down on an overturned rowboat. The gentle swish of the water lapping against the shore was oddly comforting to Kelt. "I think my mother would ha' liked you," he murmured finally.

Ashley laughed. "If she did, it would be the first time anyone's mother liked me."

"She admired spirit in others, and she was firm in her conviction that none of my sisters be married off to men they didna like."

Mischief twinkled in Ashley's eyes as she released his hand and crossed her legs under her. "And here I thought you were going to tell me she was a gentle, sweet creature with no thought but your father's wishes."

Kelt smiled wryly. "She was, and she would be shocked at your standards of housekeeping, but my mother had a wonderful sense of humor." He leaned forward, resting his hands on his knees, and stared at the water. "Even though my father had no title, we were wealthy, owning estates in England and Ireland as well as Scotland. My father's two younger brothers were declared Jacobites. They were both killed in 1719 at the Battle of Glenshiel."

"You must have been a child then," Ashley said.

"Aye, but the rebellion was our downfall just the same. My father was the oldest son, the heir; even though he took no direct part in the rebellion, his enemies tried to have him arrested as a Jacobite traitor. My father had no love for King George, but he was no rebel. He cared more for his land and his family than politics."

"And you?"

Kelt grinned wolfishly. "Young men are ever ready to do battle for some great cause. It was easy to hate the British soldiers; they burned farms, murdered whole families, carried off young girls to serve as whores in their camps. We saw little English justice in Scotland."

Ashley nodded. "I've heard the same thing from others."

"An English officer, the younger son of an earl, saw my sister Ceit at a ball in Edinburgh and he wanted her for his bride. Ceit was promised to my cousin Parlan. The earl's son, Richard Humphry, came to Ceit's wedding uninvited. He drank too much and insulted Ceit. He and Parlan fought, and Parlan killed him in self-defense. When Parlan was arrested for Humphry's murder, I testified on his behalf, but he was found guilty just the same. I stayed in Edinburgh to try and arrange a new trial while my brothers took Ceit home." Kelt's eyes glazed. "English soldiers went to my father's castle a week later. He'd been an invalid for months, but they accused him of attacking them and of perpetrating high treason against the King. My parents, my sisters and brothers, and their children, were all slaughtered, along with our family retainers. I escaped arrest and was declared an outlaw."

"And your cousin?"

"Hanged. I went to Humphry's quarters that night and killed him. It took the British nearly two years to catch me. I was convicted of murder and treason, and sentenced to die in a particularly unpleasant manner."

"But you were spared?"

"Aye. After I spent a long time in prison, someone in power, a real Jacobite, I suspect, arranged to have me pardoned on the treason charge. As a common murderer, I was worth more alive than dead, so I was shipped off to Annapolis to be sold as an indentured servant."

"Maryland? But I thought—"

"My indenture was purchased in Maryland, but my first master had a plantation near St. Mary's. I was only there a few weeks when he moved south to Virginia. I served nine years as a bond slave before I got my freedom."

Ashley blinked back the tears that threatened to spill down her cheeks. "I'm sorry about your mother . . . your family. You have reason to hate."

"Nay, no more," he said softly. "Hate eats at a mon until it destroys him. Hate willna bring them back."

"But you don't forget."

"Nay, you don't forget."

They sat in silence for a while, then Kelt turned to her quizzically. "I've satisfied your curiosity, now ye can do the same for me. How is it that a lady such as yourself canna dance? You must admit it is somewhat difficult to ken." He grinned at her discomfort. "Never mind, lass, it just so happens that I'm a wonderful dancer. We've a week before the party. I'll teach ye to dance."

"I can't wait." Ashley grimaced. "But I warn you, I sent my last dancing teacher away raving like a madman."

"What did ye do to the poor woman?"

"He was a man, and I poured honey in his wig and ants in his bed." Ashley got to her feet. "Unless you've forgotten, we came to check the repairs on the sloop.'' Her dancing ability, or lack of it, was not something she wanted to discuss with him. That she couldn't dance was her own fault. God knew her grandfather had gone to enough effort to give her lessons in the finer arts.

She walked cautiously across the dock toward the moored sloop. The wooden boards were icy beneath her moccasins and she had no wish to fall flat on her bottom and give Kelt even more reason to laugh at her. The storm that had caused the loss of the barn had done considerable damage to the plantation sloop. Repairs had been made in Chestertown by John Saloway, master boat builder; even now, his considerable bill lay on her desk. He must be paid at once, but she'd be a fool to pay without examining the work first.

Ashley knelt beside the sloop and ran her fingers along the seams of the new wood. The old and new boards were joined so tightly that it was almost impossible to tell where the hole in the hull had been. The boat builder had earned his fee—if only she could figure how to come up with the silver to pay for the repairs.

Kelt's teasing brought back memories she hadn't thought about in years. She'd been hiding from her dance master the first time she met Gentleman Jim. She couldn't abide Roger de Ives, with his powdered wig and affected manners. She'd accidentally stepped on his satin slipper and the other children had laughed at her. She'd been so angry, she'd taken her pony from the barn and ridden to the far end of the plantation.

She'd heard voices from the woods, tied her pony, and crawled on hands and knees to peer through the bushes at an unfamiliar ship anchored in the creek. Even a child knew a hundred-ton schooner with eight cannon and swivel guns was no honest merchant vessel. They were pirates. They had to be. Pirates on Morgan's Fancy! So intent was she on her spying that the first indication that she'd been seen was when a powerful hand seized her ankle and lifted her upside down into the air like a captured rabbit . . .

"Ashley!"

She blinked and looked at Kelt standing beside her. "What?"

"I said I was riding to Chestertown for lead and powder. Do ye wish me to settle with the boat builder? His apprentice was insistent on being paid immediately. They didn't even want to let Joshua sail it out of the boatyard." Kelt ran his hand along the hull approvingly. "They did a good job on this." His brow furrowed. "I'll be needing more axheads for the lumbering. The harnesses can be made here on the plantation, but I must have iron for billhooks and brass—"

"I know," she interrupted. "I'm not questioning your need." She pushed back the vivid memories of childhood and fixed her attention on the problems Kelt's requests would cause. "Frankly, I'm short on coin." She sighed. "Until word comes from London with the total of our crop, we'll get no credit from the merchants." She swore under her breath. "As if the colony did not live and breathe on borrowed monies! Martin has half the land I do and the merchants will carry his accounts for years. It's because I'm a woman. They fear I'll not pay."

"Well, they could hardly have you thrown into the stocks if you didn't. How would it look?"

"You're no better than the rest of them. 'Tis custom that debts cannot be collected before the tobacco sales are completed—yet I am not even given benefit of that consideration." Ashley began to walk quickly back down the dock.

"I take no sides, woman. I only state the facts." Kelt lengthened his stride to catch up with her. "And have you forgotten? Seven men finish their indentures next month. We must give their release money and find other men to replace them. We are short-handed to begin with—we cannot operate without skilled labor. I think you should buy slaves."

She whirled on him. "I have told you over and over, no slaves! Bondmen if we must, but no slaves."

"They are not practical. Most are but lads or men past their prime. Lumbering is men's work. It takes a strong back and a constitution of iron. There is a stand of white oak near the river I mean to level before plowing time. We can float the logs to Chestertown for sale as masts. The navy has raised its price again for prime wood. That will solve some of your money problems, but I canna cut trees without muscle."

"Then you will have to choose the new bondmen carefully. I would sooner lose Morgan's Fancy than grow her crops with the sweat of slaves." She slipped in the snow and Kelt caught her arm. "I'm all right," she said, pushing his hand away. "I can walk without help."

"So it seems," he murmured. "But that doesna solve the problem. Where is the silver to come from?"

"I'll sell some of grandfather's books." Ashley swallowed hard as a tight knot rose in her throat. "There is a copy of Pindar that Lord Miles has been after me to sell him and . . ." She sighed. "He can have the engraved Virgil as well. They should pay for the repairs and all the rest, including some new bondmen."

"The books are precious," Kelt said. "Is there no

other way?" He knew Ashley valued her grandfather's extensive library beyond price.

"None that I can think of." She shrugged. "I'll change and ride with you to Chestertown. I can see Lord Miles on the way and then help with the other dealing. If there are decent men to be had, he'll know." Ashley kicked at an unbroken drift of snow. "If I am to charm Lord Miles out of his hoarded silver, I must dress as befitting a gentle maid. Doubtless it will please you no end to see me in women's garb."

"Aye. To see such a sight is worth a long ride in winter," he agreed. "But I must see it to believe."

The following evening, Ashley paused on the wide staircase to pick up a stray kitten, then descended to the hall. The mother cat rubbed against her boot, purring loudly. "You should keep a closer watch on your kittens," Ashley chided the cat. "That cursed Scot's been seeking out all ingredients of things to mix into a haggis."

"I've not come yet to eating cat," Kelt said from the open doorway. "And if I did, I'd not ruin a good haggis with that one."

She laughed and led the way into the great hall. Several candelabras cast pools of light across the polished floor of the elegantly furnished room. Shivering, Ashley glanced toward the cold hearth. "It's freezing," she said. "You could have lit a fire in here."

"I didna think fire building was part of my responsibilities," he answered, dropping smoothly to one knee to light the kindling with a flickering candle. "Besides, little will come of the lesson anyway. I've never taught a lass in breeches to dance before. You should have put on a gown,'' Kelt accused, eyeing the snug fit of Ashley's doeskin breeches.

''If I must pretend music, then you must imagine the dress,'' she parried.

''Aye. There's truth in that. I can tell ye that 'tis easier for a mon to imagine skirts off a lass than on.'' Gallantly he took her hand and led her to the middle of the room. ''Dancing is simple. Just think of dance as an exercise in mathematics—so many steps one way, bow and curtsy, toe point. Once you memorize the pattern, it's the same thing over and over. We'll start with the minuet; it's in three-quarter.''

''I feel silly.'' Ashley's fingers tingled where Kelt grasped them firmly in his large ones and her heart was beating much faster than normal. Why do I feel like some fourteen-year-old chit? She forced herself to follow his softly spoken directions.

''Relax,'' he instructed. ''Pretend you're on horseback. You've no trouble there.'' Kelt put his hand on her waist and positioned her body. ''Stand this way, chin up, and smile—this isn't a hanging.''

Could he feel her trembling? She was suddenly warm in the icy room as waves of emotion coursed through her. I'm no better than a mare in heat, Ashley castigated herself. Her feet stopped moving and she pulled free. ''Must you hold me so tightly? I've not seen partners in a minuet so near.''

''St. Stephen give me patience,'' Kelt muttered. ''During the actual dance, my hand would not be on your waist. I must lead to teach ye the steps. How can I lead if you dinna follow?'' He seized her hand. ''Step. Step. Now, balance, curtsy . . . point your toe. Your toe, not the—'' Kelt bit back a curse. ''Riding boots are nae for dancing. You must have slippers. Change, or forget the whole thing.''

With a feigned pout, Ashley left the room and ran

upstairs to rummage in her great-grandmother's cherry chest for a pair of dancing slippers. The first one she dug out was red satin and belonged to Cicely. She threw it over her shoulder; she'd not been able to fit into her mother's shoes since she was eleven. Cicely's feet were so tiny that even her riding boots were probably suitable for dancing.

"What you lookin' fer?" Joan called from the hall. "He said—"

"My old slippers, the black kidskin ones."

"You throwed them out last year," Joan obliged. "Yer good ones is all—"

"I don't want my good ones. I just need something to— Here! This should do." Ashley perched on the edge of the bed and tugged off the leather boots, then replaced them with a pair of scuffed olive-green slippers.

"Them's the pair we shoulda throwed out, miss," Joan said. She leaned against the doorjamb and scratched her head. "I done somethin'," she admitted. " 'Tweren't me fault. Jest happened."

Ashley shoved the boots under the high poster bed. "What wasn't your fault?"

"Thet spider thing sorta fell over."

"What spider thing?"

"In his room. That spider kinda thing his pitchers sit on." Joan threw up one hand. "I didn't go near it—swear to God, Miss Ashley. I was just chasin' the cat and the damned spider thing started shakin' and fell over. You s'pose that room is haunted?"

"Master Saxon's door is kept shut. How did the cat get in there for you to chase?"

"I heard a noise. The funniest little noise. Thomas said there was ghosts in that room, thet it used to be yer grandmother's room and thet she died there."

"Go on, Joan," Ashley insisted, trying to keep a straight face. "You heard a noise?"

"Yes'm, I did. I heard this rustle-rustle like somethin' creepin' around—and I knew he was down in the great hall wi' you doin' somethin'."

"Dancing."

"Dancin wi' his arm around you and no fiddler."

Ashley fixed Joan with a threatening look and took a step in her direction.

"I knew he warn't there, so I opened the door jest a crack and that ole mama cat flew in there like she were possessed! Why do you suppose she went in there, unless she heard it too?"

"I wouldn't have any idea, Joan."

"So I figured I better catch her on account of how he hates cats in his room. So . . ." She paused for breath. "I jest dived fer her and bang, down went thet spider thing. I didn't move thet sheet. I just snatched up that cat and run to tell you." Joan stared at the pool of candlelight on the floor and drew a small circle with her toe. "He's gonna be mad."

"If you didn't touch it, if you didn't go near it, it must have been the ghost." Ashley shrugged. "Don't tell Master Saxon. He can pick it up himself. But . . ." Her voice dropped to a near whisper. "I wouldn't go in there anymore if I were you. I wouldn't even open the door. Ghosts can't leave a room they died in. If you don't go in, it can't haunt you."

"It can't?"

Ashley shook her head slowly. "You took a big chance when you opened that door. You were brave . . . but a person can be too brave. I heard of a girl once . . ."

"What?" Joan's eyes grew large in her pale face.

"Never mind. You don't want to know." Ashley

feigned a shiver. ''But they had to bury her in a closed box.''

''Mistress Morgan!''

Kelt's shout from the bottom of the staircase reminded Ashley of the dancing lessons. ''Go on.'' She motioned impatiently. ''You're finished for the evening. I'll say nothing to Master Saxon of your trespassing. But unless you want something unearthly creeping down your throat at night, I'd stay clear of that haunted room.''

''Are we to do this or not?'' Kelt demanded.

''Coming.''

Chapter 9

December 24, 1743

Kelt stood by the window in the great hall of Canterbury, staring out at the gently falling snow. In the distance, beyond the great oaks that surrounded the manor house, he could see the glow of lights from the workers' cabins. It's only a short distance, he thought, between Hopkins's mansion and the bond servants' quarters, yet they're oceans apart.

Ashley had told him that their host, Martin Hopkins, had come to the Colonies as a convicted horse thief. In Scotland, such a man lucky enough to escape hanging would carry the stigma of prison for the rest of his life. What was there here in this new land that made a man's past irrelevant? How could a convict rise in society to be the master of such a vast estate and earn the respect of important men in the colony?

"Master Saxon!" Martin Hopkins threaded his way through the crowded room toward Kelt. "You're not joining in the dancing, sir?" He motioned to a maidservant. "Annie, a drink for our new neighbor."

Kelt accepted the brimming cup of punch, offered

the red-cheeked girl a nod of thanks, and leaned close to Hopkins to hear him above the music.

"Unseasonable weather, wouldn't you say? You don't see much snow in Virginia, do you?" Hopkins was a tall, stout man with pale eyes and a pocked face. "February and March, that's when we get our snow. Sleighs in December—it's not natural. Course the young ones like it."

"Aye, I found it pleasant enough myself," Kelt said. He'd ridden with Ashley and her driver to Canterbury in a two-horse sleigh. It had snowed two days ago, and that snowfall had provided a hard-packed crust for today's snow, making a perfect surface for the sled runners. "I wondered if the weather would cause problems for your gathering."

Hopkins laughed. "Not likely. I've seen Eastern Shore folks go to a wedding in a hurricane. They'd not miss the dancing and good food unless the Frenchies were marching on Chestertown—and maybe not then!" He slapped Kelt on the back. "Don't know how you got Ashley here, but I'm glad you did. Girl's a little odd, but she comes of good stock. No better neighbor anywhere than old Ash Morgan."

Kelt kept an eye out for Ashley as he listened halfheartedly to Hopkins's chatter. She'd been strangely silent on the ride, had introduced him to their host and a few other men and women, and then had made herself scarce. He'd watched in vain for her among the dancers. There were women here of all ages, from white-haired grandmothers down to little girls. None seemed to lack for dancing partners.

Hopkins nudged him.

"Aye, sir," Kelt agreed and hoped he hadn't consented to marry the man's homely daughter. Where the hell was Ashley?

Hopkins bobbed his head up and down and finished off another drink. "You've the right of it, Scot. If we could trade freely with the Dutch, the price would soon go up in London—you can bet your soul on it." He waved to a balding gentleman. "Nathaniel! Come and meet Mistress Morgan's new overseer. Saxon, Nathaniel Godwin. Nathaniel hails from the Lower Counties on the Delaware."

The man offered his hand and Kelt shook it. Nathaniel Godwin identified himself as a planter and a boat builder. Within minutes, Godwin and Hopkins were involved in a friendly argument concerning the merits of wheat growing versus tobacco growing. Kelt was beginning to wonder what excuse he could give to go in search of Ashley when she came up behind him and tugged at his sleeve.

"Gentlemen." She smiled at their host. "If I might have Master Saxon for a moment, there's someone I'd like him to meet."

Kelt turned to Ashley with relief. "Mistress."

Her dark eyes met his and a tremor of desire washed through him. He had drunk several cups of the strong punch and a glass of wine, but the growing warmth beneath his skin came not from the drink.

Ashley took his hand and led him across the room to the entrance hall. She paused in a circle of candlelight and looked up at it. For an instant, he caught a glimmer of mischief in her gaze.

"Master Saxon," she said formally, "this is the young lady I told you so much about—Mistress Honor Horsey."

Kelt murmured something and offered a slight bow to the blushing child who stepped from the shadows, but his attention remained clearly fastened on the curve of Ashley's creamy throat above the square-cut neckline of her magnificent forest-green velvet gown.

"This is Mistress Horsey's first dance," Ashley murmured.

The heavy-limbed ache spread as Kelt allowed his eyes to rove boldly over Ashley's lush bosom and neat waist above the skirt with its green silk hooped petticoat. I asked her if she had anything suitable to wear, he thought. Ashley's green gown would do for the court of King George himself . . . the gown and the woman wearing it. Where in the name of all that was holy had she gotten it? It was no borrowed gown, that he'd wager. It had been made for her, made to fit every line and curve. His mouth felt suddenly dry and his head felt as if he'd been drinking barley beer instead of punch.

"Would ye do me the honor of this dance, Mistress Morgan?" he asked gruffly. "If you will excuse us, Mistress Horsey." Without waiting for her answer, he caught Ashley's hand and pulled her onto the floor where couples were lining up for a Sire Roger de Coverley reel.

"That infant is the one you would have me court?" he demanded huskily. "She canna be above twelve years."

"Shhh." Ashley smiled at Martin Hopkins and his wife. "Mistress Horsey is all I told you," she whispered. "She is fourteen, an heiress, and free to contract an alliance."

"With mother's milk still on her lips?" Kelt whispered.

The dance parted them, then brought them together again as Kelt swung her around. "I thought you couldna dance," he accused. "We didna practice this one."

Ashley laughed and the color rose in her cheeks. "This is different. It's a country dance." Kelt's hands were strong and warm on her back, so warm they seemed to burn through her gown when he touched her. Suddenly she realized she was having a wonderful time. Was it her imagination, or were the other couples smiling at her with genuine affection?

"You dinna lie, but you gi' the truth your own slant," Kelt whispered as he guided her through the steps. God, but she's a rare beauty, he thought. The loud music, the laughter of the gathered crowd, faded as Kelt struggled with growing desire. Was the lass mocking him with her provocative glances . . . with her ripe, laughing mouth? You are her overseer, nothing more, his voice of reason cried. Has she not made that plain? She'd not be the first mistress to dally with a hired man, if dally it was. Common sense told him to forget her and seek out a more suitable target for his burgeoning need, but it was Ashley he wanted—Ashley he must have.

The reel ended with laughter and thunderous applause. Mistress Hopkins stepped to the center of the room and clapped her hands. "Come now, all of you, and eat," she called out. "Share our Christmas bounty and welcome."

Servants opened the double doors to a dining room festively decked in fragrant cedar boughs, holly, pine, and mistletoe. Kelt was astounded at the bounty that lay before them: roast beef and ham, wild duck and roast goose, venison, suckling pig, and all manner of seafood. Gleaming silver punch bowls held eggnog and steaming wassail. Servants carried trays of hot biscuits to add to the profuse variety of vegetables and pies, cakes, jellies, and custards. The overflowing tables had been pushed back against the walls, and the room glowed with the light of dozens of sweet-smelling bayberry candles.

"There should be enough food here to fill you,"

Ashley whispered. ''And I promise that Joan hasn't cooked a single dish.''

''Come! Help yourself, help yourself,'' Mistress Hopkins insisted. ''Please, take a dish.'' Eagerly the guests began to form lines to sample the delicious-smelling food.

A pretty blond woman tapped Kelt's arm with her folded fan. ''Good evening, thur,'' she lisped, ''you musth be Ma'ther Thaxon. I'm Thible Hopkins.'' She turned to Ashley. ''For thame, Ashley, not to introduth us.'' She rapped Kelt again with the fan. ''This ist tho nice to have you here with us. You muthn't be a thranger. Mama loves guests and it must be tho dull for you at Morgan's Fancy.''

Ashley rolled her eyes as Sibyl continued to babble. Usually Sibyl Hopkins avoided her as though she had the plague. Doubtless the silly pea hen intended to add Kelt to her list of devoted admirers. Ashley was about to pull Kelt forcibly away when Sibyl's father came to their rescue.

''Saxon, there you are! You've met my little Sibyl, have you?'' Hopkins's cheeks had taken on a puce color and his eyes twinkled with good humor. ''I've something in the music room to take the chill off, if you've a mind, Saxon.''

''I'd not refuse a drop, sir,'' Kelt replied gratefully. He wasn't certain what he'd do to the Hopkins wench if she hit him one more time with that damned fan.

''Christmas Eve and all,'' Hopkins said. ''You'd not begrudge your overseer a cup of good Scotch for Christmas, would ye, Ashley?''

''I would,'' she answered tartly. ''Unless you were planning on offering me a glass, too?'' She winked at Martin. ''For the day's sake.''

Sibyl gasped.

"Atchh, Ashley, you're a case, you are!" Hopkins began to chuckle and took her arm with a grand gesture. "Your grandfather ruined you, he did. You'll never find a husband and that's certain." He shook his head. "What would the missus say if I offered Scotch to a lady under her roof?"

"Nothing, if you don't tell her," Ashley replied. She winked at Sibyl. "You wouldn't want to get your father in trouble, would you, Sibyl?"

The girl sniffed. "Well, I—"

"If you do, I'll tell her about you and the minister's son in Chestertown."

"What's this?" Hopkins demanded.

"Ashley Morgan, thas a lie! I never—"

Ashley laughed. "Of course you didn't, but would your mother believe it?"

"Oh, oh!" Sibyl's mouth puckered and her eyes began to water. "You're horrid, just horrid." Throwing up her hands, she turned and fled as fast as her wide skirts would permit.

"What's this about the minister's son?" Hopkins repeated.

"You know Sibyl better than that, Martin," Ashley assured him. "I was only teasing her."

"Hmmmp," Hopkins grunted. Slowly he began to grin. "But she won't tell about the drink, now, will she?"

"No, she won't," Ashley agreed.

Laughing, the three left the crowded room and went down a hall to a small room. Two gentlemen were seated there, and they rose to greet Ashley, their host, and Ashley's new overseer. Jovially Hopkins poured generous helpings of Scotch from a cut-glass decanter on a sideboard.

To Kelt's surprise, the men showed no distaste when Ashley joined their imbibing and conversation.

They included him matter-of-factly and asked questions about planting methods in the Virginia Colony. After several drinks around, Ashley suggested that they return to partake of supper.

"Master Saxon is very fond of eating," she teased. "I've given him a poor impression of Tidewater cooking, and I'd like him to see what Mistress Hopkins can offer."

The gentlemen laughed, and one said, "The last time I ate at Morgan's Fancy, I went straight home and kissed my wife and my cook—and he's fifty years old if he's a day!"

Ashley and Kelt stepped out into the hall, and Ashley caught his arm. "Before we go back," she said softly, "there's something I've been wanting to do." Trembling, she tugged at his hand until they reached a spot beneath a ball of mistletoe. She glanced up and down the shadowy hall to be certain they were alone. Then she slipped her arms around his neck and pulled his head down to brush his lips with hers. "Merry Christmas, Kelt," she whispered breathlessly.

For an instant he hesitated, then returned the kiss, enfolding her in his arms and lifting her up until only her toes touched the floor. His lips were hard against hers, and she felt her pulse quicken as sweet desire spilled through her veins. When he released her, she stepped back, unable to speak, her mind clouded by the strong Scotch and the even stronger stimulus of this man.

"Ye bold baggage," he declared and then laughed. "A Christmas kiss?" he asked. "In Scotland, that wouldna be considered a decent buss." He put out his hand. "Come and I will—"

They jumped apart as the door to the music room opened and Martin Hopkins stepped out into the hall.

"Why are you two lingering there?" he demanded. "You've not had a bite to eat yet. Come along, quick, before the dancing starts again."

"Aye," Kelt replied. "I've a hollow within me that needs filling." He took Ashley's arm. "Later, lass," he murmured, "I'll ha' that Christmas buss."

As Hopkins had promised, the musicians began to play. As soon as they had eaten, Kelt led Ashley into a country dance, then a minuet. Martin Hopkins asked her to dance, and then she danced with Kelt again. There were games, and singing, and still more games. And every time Kelt touched her hand, Ashley was seized with the same breathless joy.

It was long past midnight when the guests began to call for horses and sleighs. The snow was still coming down, and the air was cold and crisp. Men and women exchanged well wishes and hugs and handshakes as servants hurried to find cloaks and mittens and to bring blankets from the kitchen where they'd been warming before the fireplace.

Kelt sent a boy to the stables for Ashley's sleigh, and when it didn't come, he put on his heavy cloak and walked through the falling snow to the barn himself. The matched grays, tied to a post, were eating hay; the sleigh was properly covered to keep it from filling up with snow, but the driver was nowhere to be found. After a few minutes of fruitless search, Kelt and the groom harnessed the horses and hitched them to the sled.

"He's drunk somewhere, I'll wager." Kelt swore. "When you see him, tell him I have business with him at home." Kelt climbed up onto the padded seat and took the leather reins in his hands, clicking to the animals. Will it jeopardize Ashley's reputation to be driven home late at night by her overseer? he wondered. If it would, he knew of no alternative, save to borrow a driver or a maid from Master Hopkins. And it would be a foul piece of luck for the drafted servant to be pulled from home for a cold ride on Christmas Eve.

Ashley laughed away the suggestion as she pulled her fur-trimmed hood about her head. "As Mistress Hopkins can attest," she said, "I have no reputation among the Chestertown ladies, so obviously I have none to lose."

"Such talk," Mistress Hopkins scolded. "What a thing to say. I can send Grace with you for company. The girl can spend the night and come back in the morning."

The black woman cast her eyes floorward, a gesture that was not missed by Ashley. "We'll be safe enough. I thank you for your concern and a Merry Christmas to you all," she said sincerely. "At least we'll have no fear of pirates tonight."

"I'd say you have no fear of them tonight or any other night," an elegantly dressed woman said. "My John says the Morgan luck smacks of witchery."

Ashley smiled sweetly at the rail-thin woman. "I am heartily glad, Mistress Anne, for it means that John is permitted an opinion at home. I feared otherwise, since you so closely guard his speech in public."

"Now, Anne, Ashley." Mistress Hopkins stepped between them and pushed Ashley toward the door. "We are all weary with the celebration. Let us not say things we do not mean."

"Why is it that her grandfather's ships were never bothered by pirates? Or his prize house and livestock? He was in league with them, I say. And she might be, too, trading her favors for—" Mistress Anne's tirade was cut short by a shove from Mistress Hopkins.

"Good night and merry Christmas. Safe journey," their hostess called.

Kelt's hand tightened on Ashley's arm and his left arm went around her waist. "Watch the entrance-way, Mistress Morgan," he said. " 'Tis slippery."

"Thank you," Ashley said as he guided her down the steps and swung her easily up into the sleigh.

A maid tucked a bearskin around her lap and handed her another blanket of thick wool. "They's heated bricks under yer feet, mistress, an' a bottle of hot apple cider." She bent close to whisper. "Thank ye fer not needin' me tonight. Now I kin be wi' my children."

"Merry Christmas," Ashley bid her. She waved to Martin Hopkins and his daughter on the step. "Merry Christmas to you all."

Kelt slapped the reins over the grays' backs and drove away from the lights of the manor house into the cold night. "Can ye never mind your manners, lass?" he demanded, when they were out of earshot of their host. "Another minute and you two would ha' been screaming at each other like harpies. 'Tis no way for a lady to act, no matter the provocation."

"Another minute and Mistress Anne would have been sporting a black eye."

"Cease your shrewish caterwauling, woman. 'Tis Christmas and I've a mind to drive home in peace and quiet. Curl up in your robes and go to sleep. 'Tis no day to be harboring ill will."

A choice response rose to Ashley's lips, but she bit it back. She took a deep breath of the cold, clean air and pulled the thick bearskin around her. Kelt was right. She'd had a wonderful time, and it was too beautiful a night to let Anne Moore ruin it for her. She put out a gloved hand to let the whirling crystal snowflakes settle on it. A bubble of happiness glowed deep within her. She had danced and danced, she'd been kissed, and she'd felt a part of the celebration as she never had before. She lifted her right hand to lick a snowflake and wiggled her slippers until they rested on the warm bricks.

"That's better," Kelt said. "You're a bonny lass when your lips are sealed. Bonny as a field of heather in springtime."

To Ashley's amazement, he began to sing the words of a French Christmas carol in a rich, deep voice. Lulled by the warmth, the singing, and the jingling of the harness bells, Ashley drifted into a dream-filled sleep.

Chapter 10

A sudden jolt wrenched Ashley from her slumber. She was vaguely aware of Kelt's shout of warning and the frantic whinny of a horse, then she was tumbling out of her warm nest of furs and was thrown rudely into the snow. For long seconds she lay there stunned, the breath knocked out of her. Cautiously she moved her arms and legs. Nothing seemed to be broken, but she was pinned to the ground by a heavy weight pressing against her back.

"Ashley!" Kelt called from the darkness. "Are you hurt?"

"I . . . I think I'm all right," she managed. "What happened?"

"We struck something in the snow and the sleigh turned over." Kelt's anxious voice came from only a few feet away. "I think I can turn it back, but not until I get the horses unhitched. Dinna move. I'll just be a minute or two."

"Wait!" she called. The cold snow against her face and neck had cleared her brain of its shock. "I think maybe I can . . ." A firm hand groped in the darkness and touched her head. She wiggled an arm free to grasp the strong fingers. "If you can raise it a little, I think—"

"No." The warmth of his hand was reassuring. "The horses might spook and drag the sleigh over ye. Trust me, lass. I'll not fail ye."

Stifling the coil of icy fear in the pit of her stomach, Ashley released Kelt's hand. "Just don't take all night," she said with feigned bravado. "I've slept in warmer beds."

"Aye, I'll venture ye have." His deep voice was farther away now. Ashley could hear Kelt's soothing words to the snorting animals, lapsing now and then into his native Gaelic as he unhitched them. "Whoa, boy. Good *eich*, good *glasa*. Easy . . . that's it. Nice and easy."

There was a jingle of harness and bells as Kelt led the horses away one at a time. Ashley turned her head to one side and dug away the snow with her free hand. Her teeth were beginning to chatter; not even the thick cloak could still the shivering of her chilled body. Hurry, she urged silently. The worse thing was being trapped. The cold she could endure. If she had been alone with the sleigh turned over . . . If the sleigh had broken her back . . . She pushed the frightening thoughts from her head. If . . . if . . . Such imagining was for children. If she'd been alone, she'd have done her damnedest to get herself out. Now she must rely on Kelt.

Soft footfalls in the snow told her he was back. "I'll have ye free in a heartbeat, lass," he promised. He stood only a few feet from her head. "Now I'll raise the thing and ye scurry out. Can ye do that?"

"Stop talking and get this thing off me," Ashley demanded.

The weight above her shuddered and then eased. Kelt's grunt of exertion signaled the patch of light now visible under the edge of the sleigh. Ashley scrambled out from under and rolled free as Kelt lowered the overturned sleigh to the ground.

Strong arms helped her to her feet and began to brush the snow from her face and neck. "Are ye certain you're nae hurt, lass?"

Tears of cold spilled down her cheeks. "I'm fine," she insisted, half laughing and half crying with relief. "Just freezing to death."

"Are ye well enough to help me right the sleigh? If we can get ye back in it and under the bearskin, ye'll warm up quick enough. I'm afraid the left runner snapped when we overturned."

"We should have brought the maid." Ashley's teeth were chattering with cold.

Kelt frowned. " 'Tis a strange time to be worrying about your reputation. Ye could have been killed."

She shook her head, wrapping her arms around herself and stamping her feet. "I wasn't thinking about that. I was wishing for an extra pair of arms to help us turn the sled."

"We'll give it a try." He lay a mittened hand on her shoulder. "Dinna fash yerself. If it's too heavy, I can use the team to right it. 'Twould just be faster if we could manage it ourselves."

The sleigh turned back on its runners on the second try. Kelt scooped the loose snow out and shook the bearskin. "In ye go," he said, helping Ashley onto the wide cushioned seat and wrapping her in the fur side of the robe. Tenderly he pulled the hood up over her hair and covered her with the wool blanket. "Those slippers were never meant for snow." He sat on the facing seat and pulled off his gloves, then reached under the robe to take one of her icy feet in his hands and began to rub it briskly.

"I suppose I should have worn my riding boots," she teased. "They wouldn't even have showed under the gown." The numbness in her foot was turning to shooting pains. "You do that as if you've had experience."

"Aye, the Highlands have their snap in winter."

"And you have doubtless rescued dozens of maidens in distress." The shock of the accident had left Ashley with a heightened sensitivity as the fear she'd felt earlier was transformed into excitement. Sounds and smells seemed magnified, and Kelt's nearness, his touch, thrilled her. The steady stroking was at once soothing and disquieting. Unconsciously her eyes widened as she gazed at him in the twilight; the softly falling snow dusted his dark hair and beard with a frosting of white and outlined his rugged form in a faintly luminescent light.

"Dozens," he agreed. "But none so ungrateful." He chuckled deeply and reached for her other foot. "I save ye from an icy grave and my reward is naught but a sassy tongue."

"Would you prefer the honeyed dribble that Sibyl Hopkins affects?" Ashley tilted her head and fluttered her eyelashes in exaggerated mockery. "Dear Mather Thaxon," she cooed. "How wonderful it isth to have a gentleman suth as yourself to be our neighbor. We'll all feel tho muth safer, knowing Morgan's Fancy isth in the capable hands of a throng man again."

"I hadna noticed that Mistress Hopkins's lisp was quite that pronounced."

"You did notice her flawless features? The golden hair? The eyes as blue as robins' eggs?"

"If I didna know better, I'd say ye have the sound o' a jealous woman."

"Jealous? And of what, pray tell? Her ability to make blackberry preserves or beat up a whitepot?" Ashley scoffed. "She cannot ride, or shoot, or count past eleven. The only book she can read is the Bible—and that's because she's memorized the Psalms."

"Jealous as a cat," Kelt murmured. "Lass, ye

never cease to amaze me." He chuckled. "Actually, had I been aware that Mistress Sibyl was known for her whitepot, I would have asked her for the recipe. I make quite a good one myself. You mix cream, sugar, and rice with currants and cinnamon—"

"Damn your whitepot!" Ashley pulled her foot out of his hand. "Must you be forever rattling on about your recipes? 'Tis not manly."

"Not manly to relish a good meal?" He stared at her as though she were slow-witted. "I never thought whitepot to be a frivolous matter—'tis most serious. Some think it can be made with barley, but that is heresy. Decent whitepot must be—"

"Enough!" Ashley cried. "What are you going to do about getting us home? Are we to sit here in this sleigh until we freeze solid?" She exhaled loudly. "If I were not dressed in this"—she motioned toward the velvet gown beneath the fur robe—"we could simply ride the team home."

"Aye." Kelt sobered. "What ye say is true." He thought for a moment, then rose to his feet. "I'll build you a fire to keep off wolves and leave you my pistol. If I take both horses with me, you should be safe enough until I get back with proper clothing for you. Unless, of course, you'd prefer I carry you in front of me on the horse?"

"No. It's too cold for that," she protested. "In this dress, I'd freeze before we went two miles. Are you certain you can find your way in the dark? The trail is covered over with snow and you can't see where the trees are marked." I'm making excuses, she thought. I don't want him to go. I want him to stay here with me.

"Aye, I'll find Morgan's Fancy. I have an unwavering sense of direction. It never fails me." He grinned and fumbled inside his cape. "Besides." He produced a metal case. "I never go anywhere in this forsaken wilderness without my compass."

Ashley nibbled at her lower lip. He would go for help and she would be left alone here in the darkness. A thread of cold fear wound through her. "You won't be able to build a fire," she said. "The snow is wet. You'll find nothing but damp wood. It's better if you wait until dawn and then ride for the plantation. It can't be that many hours until daylight."

Kelt hesitated. He'd wanted to be alone with her all night. If they rode on to the manor house, the servants would be there, and the magic they'd known earlier would fade. He rubbed his chin. "There's sense in that." Before she realized what he was doing, he moved to her side of the sleigh, pulled off the bearskin and the blanket, and slid in next to her."

"What do you think . . . ?" Her protests were cut off by the shock of his arm coming around her shoulder. "You can't . . ." Kelt's touch brought the uneasy sensations roaring back. "I don't think . . ." she added lamely.

"Do ye think I'm a complete fool, lass?" he demanded. "To sit over there and freeze when you are toasty warm beneath the blankets?" He brought his lips close to her ear. "Remember, 'twas your idea that I stay. You canna expect me to give my life without cause."

The length of his body pressed against her warmed Ashley as the furs could never do. The heat settled in her breasts and loins, causing intense trembling and growing need within her. Her breathing quickened and her heart began to beat so hard she was certain the man beside her must hear it.

"Atchh, lassie, ye're shivering," Kelt murmured. His hand moved beneath her cloak to feel the hem of her skirt. "No wonder. Your gown is soaked. Why didna ye say so?'' His searching fingers touched her knee and Ashley jumped as liquid fire seemed to shoot up her leg and thigh to meld with the burning ache in the center of her being.

She turned her face up until she could feel the warmth of his breath against her lips. ''Kelt,'' she whispered.

''Aye, lass.''

She did not miss the breathlessness in the deep burr. Ashley blinked back the moisture that clouded her eyes as she slipped an arm behind his neck. ''I want you to kiss me.''

''Are ye certain?'' he asked hoarsely.

She strained toward him and their lips met in a gentle caress that quickly deepened into one of scaring passion. Ashley clung to him as the smoldering embers she had banked for so long flared out of control.

Kelt groaned deep in his throat and gave a long, shuddering breath. ''Ah, lassie . . . I've wanted to kiss you like this . . . to touch you . . .'' Tenderly he cupped her face between his palms and kissed the corners of her mouth and the trembling lower lip. ''You're so sweet,'' he breathed. ''So sweet . . . darlin'.'' The tip of his tongue parted her lips, sending waves of fluttering sensations through her veins.

Instinctively Ashley molded her body to his, opening her mouth to receive the honeyed velvet of his thrusting tongue. She wrapped her fingers in his hair, wanting only to be closer, wanting the taste and smell of him to cool this burning in her veins.

''Lass . . . lass,'' he murmured. ''Do ye know what we're about?'' He pulled back to stare into her eyes. ''There'll be no stopping if we—''

Ashley halted his protests with a kiss, letting her fingers slide down the back of his head to pull him even closer. ''Hush,'' she said. ''Hush.''

With a cry he pushed her gently back against the seat, parting the woolen cloak to caress her neck and shoulders and then to brush the top of an aching breast. Ashley moaned with delight as he trailed a path of fiery kisses down her neck to tease the cleft between her breasts. She half rose, helping him push back the cloak. The bearskin fell away, but she did not feel the cold.

"*Ulaidh,*" Kelt whispered as he fumbled with the ties of her gown. Trembling, he freed a breast and kissed the love-swollen nipple, then took it between his lips and gently sucked. Ashley shuddered beneath him, urging him on with little cries of joy. "Darlin'. . . darlin'."

Her breath came in ragged gasps. She wanted his touch . . . needed it . . . needed to touch him. "Kelt," she whispered. "Love me, Kelt. Please . . . love me." She was vaguely aware when he slipped off her gown and then her shift. Quickly he shed his own clothes, pulled her into his lap, and enfolded them both in the warm darkness beneath the bearskin.

She buried her face in his chest and Kelt tilted her chin and kissed her full on the lips, then nuzzled against a full breast. "You were made for love, lass," he murmured softly.

The gentle tugging at her nipple brought an exquisite wetness between her thighs, and her hand slid down to trace the hard muscles of Kelt's stomach and hip. His hand captured hers and moved it lower. Ashley gasped as she delicately explored the proof of his full male arousal until Kelt groaned and arched toward her. With shaking hands he cradled her body and laid her back against the seat. "I can wait no longer, sweet," he whispered. His mouth covered hers and the length of his hot, naked body seared her inflamed flesh.

For long heartbeats, they savored the deep kiss as his hands moved over her burning skin, touching, stroking, bringing hoarse cries of all-consuming passion to her lips as he caressed the secret places of her body. His weight moved above her, pressing her down. Without hesitation, she opened to him, welcoming the powerful male thrust, welcoming even the slight pain that quickly gave way to growing pleasure.

With the inborn knowledge of Eve, she wrapped her legs around his lean, muscular thighs, undulating her hips, meeting the glory of his male passion with her own. The earth fell away and they were caught in the frozen amber of timeless rapture, locked together as one, until the rapture exploded into a million crystalline stars and drifted slowly back to join with the silence of the snow-covered forest.

Kelt's feather-light kisses on her eyelids and nose brought Ashley back to reality. She opened her eyes and stared full into his. He whispered her name, shifting his arm to cradle her head, and brushed her lips tenderly. "I didna ken," he murmured. "Sweet *ulaidh,* you have given me that which a lass can only give to one mon." He pulled her to him and sighed, burying his face in her hair. "Ye should ha' told me," he reproached her. "Had I known ye were a maiden, I would ha' been more gentle. I'm sorry if I hurt ye."

She snuggled deeper into his arms, tasting his lower lip with the tip of her tongue, then rubbing her cheek against his beard. "The hurt was nothing to the rest," she whispered. "I didn't know it could be like that . . . between a man and a woman." She swallowed and closed her eyes, not wanting to lose the glorious sensations that still coursed through her veins. "Is it always that wonderful?" she asked shyly.

Kelt chuckled. "If it be for other men, I have been missing something." He kissed the end of her nose. "Nay, lass, it isna always like that."

"Thank you, then." She sighed sleepily as thoughts of her mother pressed into her mind. Since she was a child, she had condemned her, even hated her for having had an ill-placed lust. Now . . . perhaps there was more of Cicely in her than she wanted to admit.

"Nay. 'Tis a special thing we shared this night, sweeting. A man gains more pleasure when a woman shares it." Ashley's bare breasts were pressed against his chest and her bottom against his reawakening loins. "It might be wise," he suggested, nuzzling the hollow of her neck and nipping gently at her earlobe, "if we continued this long journey." He chuckled and teased Ashley's swelling nipple with a sensitive thumb. "What say you, lass?"

She squirmed against him as the delicious warmth began to spread upward from her moist core. "You must guide me, sir," she teased. "For this is unfamiliar territory." Their lips met and she caressed his thrusting tongue with her own.

Kelt moaned deep in his throat, letting his hands and mouth begin to work their magic. "Kelpie," he whispered. "You need no guide in this. Ye have your own sorcery to drive a sane mon mad wi' wanting."

The sounds of morning birdsong brought Ashley from her warm nest of darkness into the glittering world of white. She blinked, then inhaled deeply of the cold, spicy fragrance of virgin forest. The snow had stopped falling; already the sun was lacing the snow-covered branches with auras of gold and shimmering silver.

In a cedar tree directly above her head, Ashley

glimpsed a flash of brilliant red as a male cardinal proclaimed the dawn with clear, sharp whistles. Ashley rubbed her eyes and sat up, stretching beneath the bearskin robe, easing the kinks from her back. A soreness in her loins reminded her of what had passed in the darkness, and she felt the flush of heat rise in her cheeks.

"Kelt?" she called hesitantly. A shiver of apprehension cleared her brain and she stiffened, feeling beneath the robe for her shift.

"Aye, lassie, I'm here," he answered, coming from behind the sleigh. "I thought to make a fire for ye, but it seems ye shall go cold as well as hungry this Christmas morn. As ye said, the wood is all too wet to burn." He dropped the squaw wood he had gathered and came to stand beside her. "Ye are a bonny sight," he offered softly, reaching out to touch her cheek. "If you blame me for last night . . ."

Ashley shook her head. "There is no blame. I wanted it." She blushed harder and her mouth went dry. She could no longer meet the clear gray eyes. "Does it shock you, Kelt?"

"Nay. In truth . . ." Color rose in his tanned cheeks. "In truth, it is a relief. I dinna feel like such a thief."

"You took only what was offered."

Concern creased his brow. "The question is, lass, what to do aboot it?"

"What can we do?" Ashley's eyes narrowed, the color darkening to near ebony. She had no regrets about their night of passion together, but she was unwilling to admit to herself that it was anything more than the culmination of an intense physical attraction. The word *love* scurried across her consciousness, but she pushed it ruthlessly away.

"I can make ye my lawful wife."

"Are you asking me?"

Kelt sighed. "Aye, I am. I know I have a great tenderness for ye."

Ashley's head snapped up and pure flame shot from the depths of her soul. "Because you lay with me, you think you have to marry me?"

"Nay!" he roared. "Ye shall hear me out!" He wrenched back the bearskin and ran his gaze over her unflinching body. "Ye are beautiful, woman. A mon could find no fault with your face or form." He dropped the robe. "But I wouldna take a lass to wife for a night's pleasure. I have pleasured wi' many and ye are but the—" He stopped and ran a hand through his hair. "Damn it, wench! Why do ye insist on making this so hard? Stop staring at me as though I have wronged your honor! I have asked ye to be my bride."

"For love?" she lashed back.

"Aye, ye might call it that."

"For love of me or of Morgan's Fancy?"

Kelt's face whitened. With an oath he drew back his hand to strike her, then caught himself and turned away.

Trembling, Ashley yanked the shift over her head and wrapped the wool blanket about her. Tears welled up in her eyes and spilled down her cheeks. "I'm sorry," she whispered. "Kelt, I didn't mean it. I didn't."

Slowly he turned back toward her. "Aye, you meant it," he said. "Damn you to hell." He shook his head. "Never. Never have I struck a woman."

"You didn't do it this time either," she sobbed. "Please, Kelt. It's not you . . . it's me." She wiped her face with the back of her hand. "I told you," she cried. "I warned you I couldn't marry—not now, not ever."

"Then you have led us to this point without reason."

"I didn't plan it, Kelt. It . . . it just happened."

"Aye, such things happen between men and women. But when they do, the people do not turn away from each other." In two strides he was at the sleigh and leaping inside to seize her by the shoulders and pull her against him. Harshly his mouth descended on hers in a kiss of fiery possession. With a muffled cry, Ashley struck at him with her fists.

As swiftly as it had begun, the assault ended. Kelt released her and rolled away. He put a hand to his cheek. "Aye, ye are a kelpie," he uttered softly. "For ye have seeped into my very bone and sinew. I canna hurt ye without tearing my own heart." He reached down to pick up the crumpled velvet gown. "Put this on," he ordered. "I willna harm ye."

Ashley wiped her bruised lips. "You already have," she breathed. "More than you can ever know." She dropped to the seat and buried her hands in her face. "No," she whispered. "We've hurt each other." The tears became a torrent as she turned her face into the fur robe, her shoulders wracked with uncontrolled sobbing.

Kelt's hands were gentle on her shoulders as he pulled her against his chest. "Dinna weep, lassie," he soothed. "Dinna weep. For if we have done each other wrong, it may be that we have found a place to start anew and make it right."

Chapter 11

It was near noon when Ashley, Mari, and Kelt reached Morgan's Fancy. Anxious servants spilled from the kitchen entrance to greet them.

Old Thomas limped forward, his brown face lined with concern. "We were worried about you, Miss Ashley," he said. "That good-fer-nothin' driver got home about dawn, and he said you left way before him."

"Aye, and so we did. We had an accident with the sleigh. I had to carry Mistress Morgan to Mari's cabin."

"We sent out a search party soon as he got here, but nobody thought to look at her place." Thomas glared meaningfully at Joan.

"Well, we're here now," Ashley said. "And in one piece. Has the steer been set to roasting, as I ordered? And the pigs?"

"Aye, mistress," a woman called. "The tables are set and most of the food ready. We were but waitin' your return."

Ashley smiled graciously at them and turned to Kelt. "We make much of Christmas Day here. No cooking to your standards, I'm certain, but all who work on Morgan's Fancy are welcomed into the house for Christmas dinner, and there are gifts for all.'' She led the way into the house, giving orders to Joan and the women as she went.

The rooms smelled of holly and pine. Servants had gathered up the stray saddles and bits of harness and hidden them away. Long tables groaning with food had been set up in the great room. Silver gleamed, and Thomas had put out the finest china on crisp white linen.

''A mon would think ye expected the chief magistrate to Christmas dinner instead of your workers,'' Kelt remarked.

Ashley laughed. ''Christmas is their day. It was always so in my grandfather's time, and I can't let them down. Give me leave to change my clothes.'' She looked down at the hopelessly ruined slippers and water-marked velvet gown. ''And we will show you a time to remember.'' Her eyes sparkled. ''There will be music and games and dancing. We choose a Christmas fool as in days of yore, and there is a great cake.'' She laughed again at Kelt's pained expression. ''No, this one was baked by Cara and some of the other women—not Joan. A bean is hidden in the cake before it's baked. Everyone down to the smallest child must have a taste, and the one who finds the bean will have good luck all next year.''

Ashley put her hand on the walnut banister and for a second, Kelt covered it with his own. ''There is much we must settle between us, lass,'' he said softly.

''I must have time,'' she answered. ''For now, let us remember the day.'' She flashed a brilliant smile. ''I have a small Christmas token for you, but you mustn't expect much. You've already had your big present.''

"Damnable wench," he whispered. "Have ye no shame?"

"None." Laughing, she hiked up her skirts and ran up the stairs two at a time.

As Ashley had promised, the festivities went on until late Christmas night. The merrymakers emptied barrels of ale and wine, devoured baskets of crabs and clams, and enjoyed slabs of beef cooked over an open pit. Ashley presented gifts of shoes and clothing to the workers, along with steel needles and buttons, and new copper pennies for everyone.

At last the rooms were silent. The servants who were unwilling to cease their celebrating had moved the party to the barn. Thomas had banked the fires in the downstairs rooms and gone to bed. Only Ashley remained to lock away the last of the silver plate. Jai lay at her feet, thumping his massive tail against the hardwood floor.

"A pretty scene, mistress," Kelt said. He was leaning against the doorjamb and sipping slowly at a noggin of frothy eggnog. In his other hand he cradled the leather-bound book of sketches of the human body she had given him as a Christmas gift. "I canna accept this, ye know. 'Tis Greek and very old. It is more valuable than you know."

Ashley closed the cupboard and locked the door with a tiny brass key. "My grandfather bought it on a trip to Crete when he was seventeen. He said the drawings were as close as one could come to seeing the real statues." She tucked the key into a velvet bag at her waist and turned to him. "You are an artist. I thought you would like it."

"Like it? O' course I like it. Are ye daft? But I canna take it. There is a name for men who accept such gifts from women."

Ashley looked at him in pure amusement. "You are the one who is daft if your male pride will not let you enjoy such a beautiful gift without worrying what others will think." She shrugged. "It is a Christmas gift. It's yours to do with as you please. Sell it or keep it or give it away, if you like, but do not insult me by refusing it."

"Damn it, woman. Why must you twist everything I say?" His brow wrinkled in a frown. "The price of this book would buy a trained team of oxen and the men to drive them. Why did you not sell it with the others?"

Ashley crossed the room and looked up into his eyes. "Do you think I'm rewarding you for your services last night?"

Kelt's eyes clouded with pain. "Nay, lass. Now you shame me."

She took his hand in hers and turned it over, tracing the lines with a finger. She had waited for him to suggest they be together, but when he didn't, she had to speak. She could not bear the thought of going to her bed alone. "I didn't want to fight with you tonight." She raised his hand and gently placed a kiss on the pulse of his wrist. "I thought perhaps . . ." She blushed prettily. "I thought we might continue that journey tonight . . . while Joan is occupied elsewhere."

Kelt caught her about the waist and lifted her level with his face. Ashley hugged him tightly as their lips met. Would she ever get enough of him? The thought that he might change her life forever crossed her mind and she stilled it. She wasn't ready for such a commitment. She wanted to feel as she had last night—not just the physical pleasure but the security of being in those powerful arms.

"I have a gift for you," he whispered between

kisses. It was not the one he had intended to give her. Ashley's portrait was not coming together as he saw it in his mind's eye. The color of her hair and skin were perfect, the background adequate. But the picture seemed only oil on canvas. It lacked the intense spark that Ashley radiated in life. Twice he had destroyed what he had painted and begun again. Nobody would see it until he had conveyed the exact picture in his mind to canvas.

Instead of the portrait, he would give her a charcoal sketch of the manor house he had done one Sunday afternoon. He had made a frame for it in the plantation carpentry shop. "Shall I bring your Christmas present to your room?" Kelt asked her.

"No." She shook her head. "Go into the far bedchamber. There is a secret passageway between my room and that. No one knows of it, not even Thomas. I will meet you there in half an hour." It would give her time to change the musty bed linen and build a fire in the hearth, she thought, and to change into something very feminine. She brushed his lips once more and pushed him away. "A very Merry Christmas to you, Master Saxon," she teased. "Take the candle when you go up. We want no accidental fires."

She forced herself to climb the stairs in a ladylike manner, walking gracefully down the hall to her bedchamber and closing and locking the door behind her. Jai followed obediently, nudging the back of her knee with his wet nose.

"You shall stay in your usual place," Ashley warned, glancing at the worn rug before the fireplace. There was little chance that Joan or Thomas would seek her out, but if they did, they would expect to hear Jai's usual bark coming from behind her bedroom door.

She threw back her head and chuckled, letting the delicious joy spread through her body. Wrapping her arms around herself, Ashley flung herself laughing onto the bed. He was coming! He hadn't blamed her for what had happened in the sleigh. And in a few minutes, they would be sharing those wonderful sensations again.

Rolling to a sitting position, Ashley began to unbraid her hair. She had washed it just before leaving for Canterbury on Christmas Eve; a few dozen strokes with her brush pulled the curly tresses into some semblance of order. A trace of Mari's red tribal paint on her lips and cheeks added a little color.

Warm bubbles of excitement rose within her as Ashley stripped off her clothes, tossed them over a chair, and pulled a frothy cream-colored dressing gown of Irish lace and sheer linen over her head. She paused long enough to glance into the mirror, wondering if Kelt would like what he saw.

It didn't matter. The beautiful garment had lain too long in her chest, and she had taken it out and held it up to her too many times on lonely nights. At least once in a woman's life, she should wear something like this to make love to a man. Tonight would be that night.

Ashley took a deep breath and hurried to gather fresh linen and pillows for the bed in the far chamber. She twisted the nearly invisible knob, and a wooden panel slid open. It didn't matter that the passageway was dark. She had played here as a child and knew every step. Luckily the floor and windows of the spare room had been scrubbed and the bedhangings cleaned just before Christmas. As particular as Kelt was about cleanliness, he'd have no cause for complaint.

She stepped into the darkened room, dropped the

sheets on the bed, and went to the hearth. Moonlight streamed through the windows, flooding the space between the bed and fireplace with a pool of golden light. Ashley stopped and held out her hand, palm up, letting the soft moonlight illuminate her fingers. When she was a child, Mari had told her that moonlight was magic. If you stood in its glow, it would give you mystical powers.

A rush of wishes filled Ashley's brain and she silenced them with a shake of her head, closing her lips so hard that her teeth snapped. She would ask for nothing. Whatever happened between her and the Scot tonight would be a gift. She would give of herself and take what he offered. But she would not allow herself to wish for more.

Kelt Saxon had no place in her future or the future of Morgan's Fancy. She would not allow it. If she married, she risked losing her independence and her plantation. No matter what promises Kelt might make, if they wed, everything she possessed would become his by law. He could beat her, lock her in a room, or even send her far away from Morgan's Fancy. Men changed after marriage; her stepfather was a perfect example. If she wanted to keep her freedom, she must live alone and unwed.

Cold reason steadied her as she started the fire and made the bed with clean linen. She stuffed the old sheets under the bed and lit the candle, placing it on the table. The doorknob squeaked and Ashley turned with a gasp. Kelt filled the shadowy doorway with his broad shoulders and powerful legs.

"I didna mean to startle ye, lass," he said, coming in and closing the door behind him. Deliberately, he shot the iron bolt, then turned back to her. A smile played across his lips. "Aye," he said. "Aye."

"Aye, what?" Ashley put her hands on her hips.

"Do I amuse you?" She nibbled at her lower lip and tried to keep her trembling from showing. If he was laughing at her . . .

Kelt crossed the empty space between them and took her in his arms, kissing her soundly. "Aye," he murmured as he swept her into his arms and carried her to the poster bed. "I was but thinking I had died and gone to heaven." He kissed the hollow of her neck and the warm spot behind her ear. "And when I saw ye standing there in the moonlight, I knew ye for an angel." Ashley giggled and he stilled her laughter with another kiss as he laid her back against the pillows. "Hush now, woman, this is serious," he said huskily. "If ye are an angel, this must be heaven." He pulled the white linen shirt over his head, then fumbled with the ties of his breeches.

Ashley's eyes grew heavy-lidded with passion as she watched him undress. She moistened her lower lip with the tip of her tongue and held out a hand to him. "I never thought a man could be so beautiful," she said.

Kelt groaned deep in his throat and slid under the sheets. "I never thought to hear a lass speak so," he murmured hoarsely. He put an arm behind her and pulled her close to nestle against him. "Ye must be a kelpie . . . or at least a witch." His lips brushed hers as his hand cupped her full breast. "For I be bewitched if ever a mon was." Clumsily he tugged at her bodice ribbons. "How do ye get into this thing?" he demanded.

Ashley laughed softly, running her hand down his lean thigh. "You're as hairy as an ape," she teased.

"How would ye know? Have ye ever slept with one?" He sighed as the knot loosened, freeing mounds of soft flesh for his caress.

"Umm-mmm," she murmured. "A Scot is wild-enough.'' Her exploring fingers found the swelling of a male nipple. Kelt's gasp of pleasure made her bold and she tantalized the silken nub with her fingernail.

''For an angel, you know many devilish tricks,'' he said, seizing her wrists and pinning her against the pillows in mock accusation.

Ashley laughed up at him, all the while rubbing a knee suggestively against his inner thigh. ''You promised me a Christmas gift,'' she whispered throatily.

''Aye,'' he answered, nuzzling her neck and the curve of her breast. ''And ye shall have one, sweeting . . .''

Ashley reined in the stallion and paused to gaze up at the low-hanging clouds, wondering if it would snow again that day. She hoped not. They had barely enough hay stored to last through the winter, and she'd counted on the cattle being able to forage in the fields part of the time. If it warmed up and the snow melted, they could even turn the horses out to graze for a little while. She had several mares too close to foaling to risk, but most of the stock would be safe enough if she set a few boys to guard them.

Ashley knew that horses would be the last thing pirates would want to bother with. They could butcher her cattle for food and sell her free black workers south as slaves. Raiders came for loot easily carried off. She had little coin on Morgan's Fancy, but there was silver plate and guns as well as casks of wine and brandy.

Prickles of uneasiness ran down her spine as Ashley remembered the young woman who'd been carried off. Jane Briggs had probably been thrown into the sea when they were done with her, God rest her soul. Ashley could not wish that fate on any woman. Unconsciously her hand went to the pistol strapped to her waist. She'd warned her women not to wander from the house. Many of the bondwomen carried weapons with them. Ashley knew it was against the law to allow them guns, but she'd rather see a woman able to protect herself than at the mercy of ruthless scum from the sea.

Kelt had left the house to begin his day's duties before she'd gotten up that morning. She'd found the beautiful sketch that was his Christmas gift to her when she arose. She'd been disappointed not to see Kelt, but perhaps it was the wisest course. What happened between them last night was private—best left in the bedchamber. She wasn't certain she could deal with her passion for Kelt during the full light of day.

She clicked to the bay and nudged him gently with her heel. Obediently he broke into an even, mile-covering trot. Kelt was wrong about Baron; he was a spirited animal, but there wasn't a mean bone in his body. She had no intention of switching to a quieter mount to please Kelt.

She wondered if he could have been wrong about her saddle cinch being cut. Maybe they were just jumping at shadows. Her doubts hadn't kept her from saddling Baron herself and riding out alone that morning.

Baron's ears twitched and he threw up his head. Ashley turned in the saddle to see Short John galloping across the field on a brown workhorse.

"Miss Ashley! Miss Ashley!" he called.

She wheeled the stallion in a tight circle and rode anxiously back to meet him. "What is it, Short John? What's wrong?"

Breathlessly he began to babble of slaughtered cattle discovered near the creek. "Injuns fer certain, Miss Ashley. Moccasin tracks all over the place.

Didn't even take the meat, neither. Jest cut their throats and left em lay. Two cows and a yearling heifer."

"Three quarters of the people in Maryland wear moccasins," she told him. "Are you certain they weren't butchered?" She knew it couldn't be Indians, or anyone hungry for that matter. Indians would have taken the meat once they'd killed the cows. "Not even the liver taken?"

"Hard to say. Wolves been at 'em." He shook his head. "Don't think so. Mighty strange if you ask me. You better come have a look, Miss Ashley."

She nodded. "I will."

"I'll come wi' ye. I kin show ye jest where they's at."

"No, you ride for Master Saxon. He should be with the lumbering crew this morning. Tell him I'm riding out to the creek myself, and I want him to join me there." The chances were that this incident was another of Short John's tall tales to get out of work. Either that or he was merely too stupid to read the signs. Not even pirates would leave good meat on the ground to rot. The chances were that Short John's moccasin tracks were really wolf prints or even tracks of wild dogs.

"Sure you don't want me t' come along? It ain't safe fer a woman, what wi' these pirates on the loose!"

"No, you stay with the lumber crew once you've given Master Saxon my message. You can drive the oxen." She hated to pull Kelt from the lumbering; she knew how pressed for time he was. There'd be a thaw in January and they'd have to get the trees out of the woods while the ground was still frozen.

"Master Saxon, he be mad at me iffen I let ye go alone," Short John protested.

"You do as I say. Get your butt over to the lumbering and fetch Master Saxon. Now!"

Shaking his head, the man rode away to the south. Ashley pulled out her pistol, checked the priming, then urged Baron toward the creek at a gallop. If wolves had killed the cattle, they'd be miles away by now. They posed no danger in the daytime, at least not as long as she was armed and on horseback. Most wolves were shy, avoiding the scent of man like the plague.

Ashley reached the creekbank, stopping long enough to let her stallion drink. Other than a pair of black ducks rising off the water, everything was quiet. She turned the big horse into the sun and rode along the edge of the woods.

Circling buzzards led her to the spot where the slaughtered animals lay. Two of the scavengers were on the ground tearing at the belly of a red and white cow. They flapped their wings clumsily and flew off as Ashley approached.

Baron snorted, flaring his nostrils at the strong stench of blood, and danced sideways, tossing his head and mane. "Whoa, whoa, boy," she soothed. Muscles rippled beneath the walnut-colored hide and the stallion reared, pawing the air nervously. "Whoa," Ashley commanded. "Easy, boy. It's just a dead cow."

Baron reared again and Ashley threw her weight forward, leaning along the powerful neck. Suddenly a musket roared, and Baron screamed and bolted, plunging headlong down the creekbank and soaring over a fallen log in his panic to escape.

Ashley clung to his back, making no effort to rein him in. Whoever had taken a shot at her was far behind them. There wasn't an animal on the Eastern

Shore who could match Baron for speed, especially when he took it into his thick head to run.

It had happened so fast, she hadn't had time to think. If Baron hadn't lunged forward . . . Ashley slowly applied pressure on the reins, unwilling to let herself think about what had just happened. "Whoa, whoa," she murmured. Her hands felt numb. How far had she come? A mile? More?

The bay slackened his pace to a canter and then to a trot. Ashley pulled him to a halt and slid from the saddle; as she leaned against the horse, her knees suddenly turned to molasses. *Someone tried to kill me*. The shot had been no mistake, no accident. *Someone wants me dead*.

She pressed her face against the stallion's neck, letting the fear run its course, letting it turn to anger. The yellow-bellied son of a whoring cockroach! Whoever had tried to kill her had deliberately slaughtered her cattle to lure her out there. They'd known she'd come to investigate. But why? Why in the name of all that was holy would anyone want to kill her?

Strengthened by her anger, Ashley swung back into the saddle and turned Baron away from the creek and into the woods. Alone, she couldn't hope to catch whoever it was. She'd ride back to the house and gather up some men, then go for Mari. If there were any tracks to be found, Mari would be able to read them.

Grimly Ashley rode back through the thick forest, straining for any sound that might be human. How could she have been so stupid? She'd have the skin off Short John's back if he didn't have the right answers as to how he'd found the cows in the first place. Damn! Kelt had warned her. He'd said someone was trying to kill her. She could imagine what he'd have to say about this incident.

The trees thinned and gave way to open meadow. It was low ground, good grazing for sheep and cattle in a dry season but too wet for tobacco or corn. Ashley caught a flicker of movement at the edge of the woods just as Baron whinnied. She reined him up short and pulled out her pistol as a horse and rider came toward them.

"Ashley? What are ye doing here?"

She set her heels into the bay's sides. "Kelt!" He had just ridden out of the same woods she had been in! "What are you . . ." She laughed wryly and pulled Baron next to his dappled-gray. "I wouldn't advise riding out there just now. Somebody took a shot at me over by the creek."

Kelt swore under his breath. "May God rot his greedy bowels! I thought I heard a shot. I was hunting for another stand of white oak that Joshua said was over this way. Are ye certain someone was shooting at you?"

"As certain as I can be and not have a hole in my head to prove my story." Quickly Ashley explained about her investigation of the dead cattle. "I thought you were miles from here, with the lumber crew," she continued. "As jumpy as I am, you're lucky I didn't shoot you when you came out of the woods."

" 'Twas well thought out, this murder scheme." His features hardened. "I've wronged ye by not finding the culprit before this." His gaze rested on her face for a moment. "About last night, lass," he began softly. "I wouldna have ye think—"

"I asked you to come to my room." Her eyes met his without wavering. "Let's not play games with each other, Kelt. If you believe it's what I expect, you don't know me very well." A smile played over her lips. "Thank you for the sketch of the house. It's beautiful. I'll hang it in the hall. You're very talented."

"Ashley, I . . ."

She shook her head. "No, not now, Kelt." She looked back over her shoulder toward the forest. "This shooting has to be settled first. I've got to know who's trying to kill me . . . and why."

"Aye, 'tis fair enough," he agreed. "But ye must face our involvement sooner or later."

She nodded solemnly. "I know."

Chapter 12

Chestertown, Maryland
January 11, 1744

"You have my assurance, Mistress Morgan, that I will use every means at my disposal to bring the perpetrators to justice." The high sheriff laid down his quill pen and regarded Ashley frankly. "Although I must admit that my chances of solving this crime are about as likely as my being appointed to the House of Lords." He spread his hands in a gesture of helplessness. "There are literally thousands of square miles of wilderness to the west of us, swarming with savages, runaway bond servants, thieves, murderers—the refuse of England's prisons, not to mention the French fur traders and army deserters."

Ashley rose and offered him her hand. "You need not tell me, sir," she replied softly. "No one could be more diligent in his duty than you have been. We merely wished to make an official report of the matter so that—"

"So that when we catch and hang him," Kelt said, "there will be no trouble with the law."

The sheriff walked with them to the door. "Would

you like me to ride out that way? I have official business that will keep me in Chestertown until next week, but after that I—''

Ashley shook her head. ''I'm afraid it would be a waste of your time, sir. As we said, our men have combed the area thoroughly. Our scout found the place where the man fired from, as well as the tracks of his horse, but lost them in the forest.''

''We can always hope it was some madman. With luck, he's vanished back into the wilderness.''

''Or gone south to Virginia,'' Ashley added.

The sheriff laughed. ''Same thing.'' He nodded to Kelt. ''I'm glad to see Mistress Morgan has found such a responsible man to manage her plantation. I knew Master Ash Morgan well for many years and I have been concerned about Mistress Morgan's welfare.''

''Thank you for seeing us on such short notice, sir,'' Ashley said. ''Please give my best to your wife and family.''

With a final round of pleasantries, Ashley and Kelt left the sheriff's elegant brick town house and stepped out into the muddy street.

''That was a royal waste of time,'' Ashley said tartly. ''I knew it would be.''

''Aye, but I want no charges of murder when I string the rascal up from the nearest tree. I've had as much of His Majesty's justice as I need for one lifetime, thank you.''

''What the high sheriff says is true. There's no chance of him catching the man.''

''Or men. We have no way of knowing if there be more than one involved.''

Ashley held up the skirt of her riding habit and picked her way carefully through the puddles of water, circling around a pig that wallowed beside the road. "You and your plots. Likely 'tis some madman, as the sheriff suggested, or"—she grinned—"a disgruntled suitor."

"Aye, that I can believe. You must have turned away dozens."

"And you think I haven't?" She sniffed. "If I wished to marry, I could have my choice of a score. Morgan's Fancy more than makes up for my lack of ladylike virtues."

"You'll have to choose a husband someday." He caught her arm to keep her from slipping, then released it when he caught a haughty stare from a passing gentleman in a sedan chair. "You've given running the plantation alone a good try, lass, but ye do need a mon to manage your affairs."

She stopped short and turned hard eyes on him. "You, for instance?"

"I wasna talking of us," he said patiently. "I was speaking of your future. A woman needs a husband."

"This one doesn't." Her shoulders stiffened as she continued toward the inn. "Not now, not ever."

"Are ye so unwomanly that ye would forgo the chance of children? Or is it that you want the children withoot a husband?"

"You bastard," she whispered. It was the one question for which she had no answer. "You've no need to—" Ashley's angry tirade was interrupted by the sight of Joshua hurrying toward them down the street.

"Mistress! You must come to the dock at once. There's a ship's captain there, Captain Fraser. He carries a message for you from your lady mother. He says it's urgent!"

"From my mother?" Ashley's eyes widened in disbelief. "Are you certain?" Cicely never wrote. Her beautiful script was reserved for invitations and for signing the documents Nicholas put before her. "Why would my mother write to me?"

"I know Philip Fraser," Kelt said. "He's an old friend and not likely to make such a mistake. I suggest we go down to the *Merry Kate* and find out what this is all about."

A hill sloped gently downward from the town to the harbor. On the docks, Kelt was able to find a willing fisherman to row them out to where the *Merry Kate* was anchored.

"Captain Fraser's ship seems heavily armed for an honest merchant vessel," Ashley observed as they neared the sloop. "Your friend wouldn't be doing a bit of smuggling on the side, would he?"

"Philip Fraser? God forbid," Kelt exclaimed piously.

The red-haired fisherman grinned at Kelt and threw his weight into the oars.

Ashley pursed her lips and made a sound of disbelief. "She's at least eighty ton and carrying enough cannon to fight off a Spanish armada."

"Ninety ton, miss," the redhead said. "And there's plenty in Chestertown who's glad to see her anchored in the Chester River. Might be she'll keep the Frenchies away." He spat over the side. "Seein' as how good King George 'as forgot there's God-fearin' Englishmen on this side of the Atlantic." He dipped an oar and brought the small boat close to the side of the *Merry Kate*. "Ahoy, there!" he shouted. "Gentlefolk to come aboard!" The man glanced at Kelt. "Shall I wait fer ye, sir?"

Kelt shook his head and reached for the pouch at his waist. "No. Philip will see us safe ashore. Let me pay ye for your—"

"Naw!" The fisherman caught a line thrown from

a seaman and made it fast. "I don't want no coin from a friend o' Philip Fraser. Glad t' help ye out."

"Thank you," Ashley said graciously.

Kelt added his thanks as he caught the end of a rope ladder and helped Ashley get a firm hold on it. "Careful, mistress," he warned. "I'd nae wish to pull ye out o' the drink."

"Or me you," she replied tartly.

Captain Fraser came across the deck toward them. "Ashley." He smiled broadly and took her in his arms, planting a kiss on her cheek. "I'm glad to see this Scootsman hasna got the best of ye."

"So! You two know each other," Kelt said. "I might have guessed." He offered his hand to Philip and they shook vigorously. "Damn your lying eyes, ye knew when ye carried me here from Virginia that old Ash was dead."

Captain Fraser led the way toward his cabin. "I've known Ashley for years. Her grandfather was a good friend."

"And I'm not? Ye might have warned me what I was getting meself into," Kelt grumbled good-naturedly.

"And cost the lass the best overseer in Virginia? Nae likely." He ushered them into his cabin and turned to Ashley, his features suddenly showing strain. " 'Tis evil news I bear ye, child, from your brother Robert."

"Robert?" Ashley sank into a straight-backed chair. "But I was told my mother—"

"Mother, brother, 'tis all the same," Fraser interrupted. "Mistress Randall lies on her deathbed wi' the fever. She calls for ye, lassie, and that . . . gentleman who proclaims himself her hoosband willna let her write to ye."

Ashley shook her head in disbelief. "But Robert—Robert hates me. He wouldn't—"

"Ye be of the same blood," Fraser said. "And he no doubt loves yer mother. I dinna know if 'tis too late, lass, but I would go t' her at once."

"Of course." Ashley's face whitened. "Of course, I'll go." She tried to gather her wits. Cicely dying? She was too young to die, wasn't she? "Are you sailing back to the James, Philip?"

"Nay. I wish I could take ye, but I must wait for a special cargo. I've signed a contract." He motioned to the left. "The *Snow Princess* sails on the next tide. Captain Webb is an able master and he'll carry ye safely. I can arrange passage if ye like."

"For two," Kelt said. "I'm going with her."

"No." Ashley shook her head. "I need you on Morgan's Fancy. I can go alone."

"Two," Kelt repeated. "Ye have no choice in the matter, Mistress Morgan. With people taking shots at ye from every thornbush, I have no intention of letting ye oot o' my sight."

Captain Fraser took a decanter of brandy from a chest and poured a small amount into a pewter noggin for Ashley. "There's other news which may go down a bit easier, lass. I met a brigantine out of Land's End at the mouth of the Chesapeake. He passed your tobacco fleet on his way out, not ten days from Bristol."

"They're safe? They made it through?" Ashley cried. If her tobacco crop was safe . . .

"Four pirate vessels attacked them off the Delaware coast. The tobacco fleet suffered grievous losses. Three ships lost and another had to turn back to New Jersey, but Dayton's *Isobel* came off without a scratch." Fraser poured a second cup of brandy for Kelt. "Even more miraculous, one of the pirate ships closed on her to board, then veered aside, almost as though they were letting the *Isobel* go. They turned on the *Lady Anne* and attacked her instead. God knows what happened to the crew. St. John is ruined and I dinna doubt that more than one plantation will be lost for that ill day's work."

"But the *Isobel* is safe?"

"Aye, lass. There's no missin' her figurehead. The brigantine's master spoke with Captain Dayton himself. If the French or the Spanish didn't catch them on the way in, yer crop is safe in London warehooses by now."

Ashley tried to keep her voice natural and fixed her gaze on the toe of Captain Fraser's boot. "How—how did you know my tobacco was on the *Isobel?*"

"I didna, until I docked here and talked wi' the gentleman I'm carrying cargo for. He knew the ships by heart." Fraser frowned. "Nay, no devil's work here. My client be an honest planter. His tobacco crop went to the bottom, every cask of it. 'Five years work is lost,' he said. With the price of tobacco in London, ye'll make a fortune on the auction block. Ye have the luck o' the angels, lassie."

"The Morgan luck," she said softly, feeling numb. Kelt and Captain Fraser's voices seemed to come from a long way off. I should feel happy, she thought. I should be laughing with joy. My tobacco got through! Why then did her chest feel so tight, her breathing strained? Why did she feel so damned guilty?

The *Snow Princess* was larger than Captain Fraser's *Merry Kate* and carried only a fraction of her bristling arsenal. She was heavily laden with cargo as she fought her way against wind and waves whipping across the open bay, carrying sleet and driving rain.

"A southwest wind," Kelt observed. "You'd be

better off below deck.'' He motioned toward the aft doors. ''Captain Webb has offered the use of his cabin.''

Ashley pulled her cloak tighter. ''I hate it below deck,'' she shouted above the wind. No need to tell him that a choppy sea turned her stomach upside down. On deck with the cold wind in her face she was fine, but down in that dark cabin . . . She shivered just thinking about it. She couldn't bear to be shut in.

Kelt was still talking, insisting that she go below. Scots were supposed to be dour and brooding, but Kelt was as bad as Mari for fussing over her. Ashley braced against the mast and closed her eyes, shutting him out.

It was hard to imagine Cicely deathly ill. She had been radiant the last time Ashley had seen her in Williamsburg. They had spent the better part of an hour together while Nicholas had been occupied elsewhere, their conversation strained as always. That had been . . . Ashley sighed. It had been in April. She had not seen her mother in nearly a year.

At Christmas, she had sent gifts for her mother and half brothers and had received a token from Cicely in return. The corners of Ashley's mouth turned up in amusement. Cicely had sent a pair of dainty primrose gloves woven of silk so fine that Ashley's work-rough hands would have snagged the threads and ruined them at first wearing. The gloves lay in the bottom of her chest with Cicely's other presents.

They had never understood each other—could never be in the same room for more than an hour without arguing. Flickers of regret passed through Ashley's mind. If Cicely died, they would never have time to mend the breach. Perhaps there was nothing to mend.

She tried to push away the bitterness, the memories of nights when she had lain awake weeping, wondering why her mother hadn't wanted her. Mari had soothed the hurt, laughing at the ugly word *bastard* when Ashley had gotten up the nerve to utter it.

"It is more of the English foolishness," Mari had assured her. "Every child is a gift of Wishemenetoo, the Great, Good Spirit, the creator of all things. A man and woman come together and if Wishemenetoo wishes, there will be a child. How can there be shame in a child? To shame the child is to shame the creator. If there is blame, let it be shouldered by the man and woman, never the child."

Mari's words had stopped the tears, but they could never take away the doubt. What kind of woman would deny her own daughter?

Kelt tugged at Ashley's arm. "You're getting soaked," he insisted.

Ashley opened her mouth to protest when suddenly her ears were deafened by the boom of a cannon, followed by the crash of snapping wood and a man's scream. Kelt shoved her down and threw himself across her, shielding her with his body. A second cannonball followed the first, splintering the rail on the starboard side.

Shouts and the sounds of men running echoed along the deck as the crew scrambled to defend the ship. "We've been attacked!" Kelt shouted. "Get below."

The high-pitched keening of the wounded man sent a shiver down Ashley's spine as she made her way down the ladder and along the passageway to the compartment where her belongings had been stowed. A sailor ducked past her clutching a cutlass in one hand and a pistol in the other.

The roar of cannon was louder below. Numb with

fear, Ashley pushed open the door and fumbled in the darkness for her saddlebags. A booming directly overhead told her that the *Snow Princess* was firing back. After gathering up both pistols and the bags of powder and shot, she ran back toward the ladder.

The deck was a welter of twisted canvas and broken wood. Fire smoldered near the bow, and a dead man lay blocking the doorway. Ashley stepped over the body and stared speechless at the pirate schooner bearing down on them. The other ship was so close she could make out the leering face of a bearded buccaneer hanging from a shroud and brandishing a boarding ax.

"For God's sake, lass, have ye no sense?" Kelt grabbed her arm and pushed her back toward the doorway. "I told ye—" His words were lost in the roar of another cannonball. It struck the side of the *Snow Princess* with such force that it knocked Ashley to her knees. Dumbly she handed him a pistol. "This is no place for you!" he shouted. "Get below and lock yourself in the captain's cabin!"

"No! I'll load for you." She held up the powder horn. "I'll not be trapped down there like a rat. What if she sinks?"

Cursing, he opened the door and shoved her inside. "Keep your head down," he ordered, thrusting the pistol into his belt.

A burning torch landed on the deck, and Kelt ran to kick it over the side. For the first time, Ashley saw that he was carrying a musket and a cutlass. Where had he gotten them? He turned and dropped to one knee, taking aim at the man on the shroud. Clouds of black smoke enveloped the deck, making it almost impossible to see. The musket cracked and the pirate fell backward, sliding down the rope like a lifeless doll.

Kelt ran back to the door and thrust the musket at her. "If you're going to load, do it quick!"

Musket balls were flying like hailstones. A deep voice from the stern was singing a hymn amid the curses and cries of pain. Captain Webb ran toward the bow, a smoking pistol in each hand. Ashley winced as wood splintered over her head and something nicked her forehead.

She shoved the loaded musket back at Kelt and brushed at her forehead with the back of her hand. To her surprise, her hand came away streaked with blood.

"Keep your head down!" Kelt shouted.

A man without a face staggered past, then fell backward over the rail into thc bay. Ashley struggled to keep from being sick.

A tremendous shock rocked the deck as the pirate vessel collided with the *Snow Princess*. Ashley caught sight of the schooner's bowsprit looming over the edge of the deck. For a minute or two there was near silence as the cannon ceased firing, then a wave of human voices overwhelmed them as the pirates swarmed aboard the merchant sloop.

Kelt fired the musket into the smoke, then pulled the pistol and fired that also. Before Ashley could get her hands on the musket to reload, a blackamoor leaped across the fallen canvas and slashed at Kelt with a cutlass. Steel clashed against steel as Kelt met the arching blade with his own. Another pirate dashed toward Kelt and Ashley leveled the musket and fired, piercing the man's chest with the ramrod.

The blackamoor delivered a hacking blow at Kelt's hip and the Scot spun away, giving Ashley a clear path. Without a second's hesitation, she fired point-blank, blowing a hole in the man's throat. Spots of black and red whirled in her brain and she fought to retain consciousness, biting the inside of her cheek. The pain brought back sanity and she began to reload the pistol.

A musket ball sliced through the sleeve of Kelt's shirt, turning the dirty white to red. Ashley bit back a cry of terror, covering her mouth with her hand. Kelt circled to the left, deflecting blows from a pirate's cutlass and dodging the jabs of a wicked-looking knife. Suddenly his foot slipped in a pool of blood and he fell to one knee. Ashley raised her pistol, but before she could fire, Kelt whipped a *sgian-dubh* from his right boot. The blade flashed silver in the rain and the pirate fell, clutching his chest.

"Ashley!" he shouted and she threw him her pistol. He fired above her head and a body tumbled down almost on top of her.

The stench of blood and unwashed flesh struck her full force as Ashley instinctively wrenched the wounded man's cutlass from his hand, then scrambled across the deck to retrieve Kelt's fallen pistol. Kelt backed toward the doorway as two buccaneers closed in on him.

"Behind me," Kelt yelled.

Ashley didn't need a second warning. The fight was clearly going against the crew of the *Snow Princess*. All around them, men were throwing down their weapons and crying for quarter.

For agonizing minutes, Kelt kept his two antagonists at bay, blocking first one slashing blow and then another. His smoke-blackened face showed the strain of near-exhaustion. When an opening came, Ashley leveled her pistol at one of the pirates, only to be stopped by Kelt's imperative command. "No! Hold your fire!"

Her eyes streamed water as clouds of thick smoke billowed around them and she struggled to breathe.

The clash of steel filled her brain and she shuddered with each recurring blow. Her mind reeled as the misshapen form of a hunchbacked dwarf wielding a boarding ax materialized from the smoke. "Stop!" she cried, raising the pistol. "Move another step and I'll blow you to hell!"

The dwarf froze, slowly lowered the bloodstained ax to the deck, and began to laugh in high, inhuman shrieks. Spinning around, he vanished off into the smoke as peals of laughter echoed across the bloody deck.

Ashley found her voice. "Kelt!" she cried. "I—" Her words were lost in the scream of the one-eyed buccaneer as Kelt's cutlass slashed through his thigh to the bone. Moaning, the pirate dropped his weapon and clutched at the wounded leg. A second man leaped out of range of Kelt's flashing blade. Trembling with fatigue, Kelt sucked in great gulps of air, holding back the pressing crowd for seconds with the sheer power of his fierce gaze.

Then, with a foul curse, a man pushed through the onlookers and aimed an ancient blunderbuss directly at Kelt's chest.

Ashley screamed and threw herself in front of the Scotsman. "No! Don't shoot!" she begged. "He's—"

"Enough!" The cultured tones of an English gentleman cut through Ashley's plea.

"What the hell?" Kelt's arms closed around her as he moved to shield her with his body, raising the cutlass in a final act of defiance.

"Enough," the man repeated. Twin flintlocks in his hands reinforced his quiet authority. Grumbling, the pirates moved aside to let him pass. "Gavin." The man in the red military jacket slowly lowered the blunderbuss.

Kelt stared in disbelief at the pirate captain. The

man wore an elegant cocked hat trimmed with gold braid over a snowy white bag wig. His azure satin waistcoat was ornamented with embroidered flowers and his matching vest and breeches were of the finest cloth and tailoring. Other than a three-cornered tear in the sleeve of his coat, and a smudge of black on his chin, the captain might have stepped directly from an audience with His Majesty, King George II.

Pulling a silk handkerchief from his vest pocket, the gentleman patted his powdered forehead and smiled apologetically. "I didn't expect to find you aboard, my dear." The brown eyes twinkled. "And I suppose I might say the same of you." The heels of his black Spanish boots clicked together and he bowed slightly to Kelt. "Sir." He chuckled. "Aren't you going to introduce us?" he demanded of Ashley, then laughed again at her stunned silence. "Then you must permit me to introduce myself. Captain Quincy James McCade of the *Scarlet Witch*. Gentleman Jim McCade, at your service, sir. It seems Ashley hasn't seen fit to inform you of our prior connection. I am her father."

Chapter 13

"What madness is this?" Kelt demanded. "Ashley?" He glanced down at her, reading the truth in her eyes. "Nay," he denied. "It canna be."

"Can't?" Captain Quincy McCade shrugged. "Find your tongue, girl, or I'll be forced to send your able protector to his final reward. It seems there'll be a few of my good men waiting in hell to give him a hearty reception." He indicated the scattered bodies with a disdainful sweep of his hand. "I find your silence unnatural, Ashley. You usually have no trouble finding words."

Kelt swore under his breath as Ashley stiffened and stepped free. "Ye be in league with this . . . this murdering pirate?"

She shrugged. "He's my father, that's true enough, but I take no responsibility for his devilment. Believe what you will." She glanced at her father. "This is my overseer. His name is Kelt Saxon and I'll thank you to stop pointing that pistol at him."

McCade laughed. "That's my girl. Drop the cutlass, Saxon. Gently. I won't ask you twice."

"Do it, Kelt," Ashley urged. "He'll kill you if you don't."

"And if I do?"

"Do you have an option?" McCade's finger tightened on the trigger of the flintlock.

With a curse, Kelt tossed down the cutlass.

"Now your pistols, Ashley," McCade insisted. She handed them over, butt first. "Good." He motioned to the muscular man in the red coat. "Gavin, see them safely aboard the *Scarlet Witch*. Put the gentleman in irons until he's had time to cool that Gaelic temper." Folding his arms across his chest, McCade turned fiercely on his crew. "Well, what are you waiting for? Will you stand here like dumb oxen while the sloop sinks under you? Transfer the valuables!"

Two burly seamen seized Kelt's arms and twisted them behind him. The dwarf shuffled forward to clamp handcuffs on the Scot's wrists. Kelt's gray eyes locked with Ashley's accusingly. His features were immobile. Shamed, she looked away, unable to watch as Kelt was shoved toward the gunnel.

"You, too, Mistress Morgan," Gavin ordered. "You heard him. Any trouble from you and I'll slap you in irons myself."

"Well, Gavin." Ashley smiled sweetly at the handsome blond giant. "I heard you were hanged in Lewes on the Delaware."

"And did you shed any tears for me?" he asked caustically.

"I did." Gavin laid a bloodstained hand on her arm and she flung it contemptuously aside. "I was desolate," she continued softly. "I feared Lucifer had come to collect your black soul and I'd not been there to see it."

Kelt shifted his weight, trying to relieve the cramping in his arms, and peered into the Stygian blackness of the hold. The acrid stench of sour bilgewater, sulphur, and tar was thick enough to choke a man. He wiggled his fingers, sending excruciating pain through his hands and elbows.

He had lost all track of them. The sounds that filtered down from the deck above were muffled in the slosh of water and the creaking of wood. Only the boatswain's shrill pipe and the heavy shifting of cargo were audible above the squeak and rustle of the rats and mice that shared his prison.

I've done it again, he thought. I've trusted a woman and she's betrayed me. He'd never have been captured by King George's soldiers in Edinburgh if it wasn't for a lying little whore with the face of an angel. He'd spent the night in her arms, and then she'd laughed when the soldiers captured him still in her bed. The whore had betrayed him for English gold; he wondered what excuse Ashley would give.

An animal ran across his leg and Kelt cursed, kicking at it. Thank God they hadn't chained his ankles. The thoughts of vermin walking over him . . . or worse . . . made the hair rise on his neck.

He was still in a state of shock. No wonder Ashley's tobacco shipments always got through to England. Her father was a swivin' pirate! And not just any pirate, but the infamous Gentleman Jim McCade. Anger rose in his throat so thick that it gagged him. Ashley Morgan an accomplice to piracy? It was beyond belief. How could a man be as intimate with a woman as he had been with Ashley without suspecting?

Kelt had known smugglers—hell, his friend Fraser was a smuggler—but piracy? Despite Gentleman Jim's reputation for his refined manner with the ladies, he was still nothing more than a thief and a murderer. How many men had he killed in the attack on the *Snow Princess* alone?

He closed his eyes and forcibly slowed his breathing. Nothing would be gained by raging like an impotent bull. If they meant to kill him, it was likely they would have done so immediately, he reasoned. That he was a prisoner was a point in his favor. Was he being impressed as a crewman? He'd not be the first man to sail under a skull and crossbones against his will.

The rasp of a hatch cover being pulled aside gave warning seconds before a shaft of light illuminated Kelt's prison. "Captain wants to see ye," a harsh voice called. "Step lively, farmer, and gi' me no trouble or I'll be sendin' ye to the bottom o' Davy Jones's locker wi'out yer head."

Kelt struggled up the ladder to the deck, blinking in the light. Strong hands and cold steel pressed against the back of his neck. It was still raining, but a heavy mist surrounded the schooner. There was no sign of the *Snow Princess* or of any other prisoners and only the fresh gouge made by a cannonball across the deck to show there had been a battle.

Angry murmurs followed Kelt's progress to the stern of the ship. He counted over thirty pirates on deck, some patching injuries and cleaning weapons, others hoisting a sail under the direction of a hard-eyed boatswain. He was shoved through another hatch and down a ladder. At the end of a narrow passageway, the hatch to the captain's cabin stood open. Kelt ducked his head to enter.

The small room was lit by an elegant brass lantern and a stained glass porthole. Ashley was seated at a round mahogany table across from McCade, and the blond-haired man, Gavin, stood by the far wall examining a chart.

"Kelt!" Ashley rose to her feet. "Are you all right?"

"I told you he would be," McCade said. "Have a little faith in your father." He motioned to the seaman. "Remove the cuffs." The man did as he was told, and the captain indicated the empty chair beside him. "Have a seat, Saxon. As soon as we finish this game, we can decide what to do about you."

Kelt moved to the chair, rubbing his wrists to bring back the feeling. For an instant his gaze met Ashley's. There was no mistaking the warning in her eyes. Her face was pale, but she had bathed and arranged her hair and was wearing an elegant blue gown trimmed with thread of silver.

A chessboard lay upon the table, the pieces intricately carved in ivory and jade. McCade rolled an ivory knight between the fingers of his left hand. His right hand remained hidden beneath the table. Kelt would bet a year's wages that it held a loaded pistol.

"Do you play, Scot?" McCade asked. He had traded his torn azure coat for a rich purple one. His white silk stock was knotted and pinned at the throat with a gold filigree brooch, and the lace cuffs of his shirt were starched, pressed, and spotless. "Gavin is an abominable chess player," he declared, smiling at Kelt engagingly. "It would almost be worth your life if you could give me a decent game."

Seeing McCade and Ashley together, Kelt was struck by the resemblance. A stranger meeting them on the streets of Chestertown would take them as father and daughter, if not brother and sister. McCade's features were strong and well defined, his mouth shaped similar to Ashley's, but it was the eyes that gave them away. Ashley Morgan's compelling rust-gold eyes were the mirror image of McCade's.

Kelt had seen laughing men like Quincy McCade

before. A dandy he might be, but he was dangerous nevertheless. The man was lean and sleek, and he moved with grace and purpose. Yes, Kelt was certain the captain held a pistol in his lap, and even more certain that a wrong word or sudden motion would bring an instant and irrevocable response.

"What happened to the *Snow Princess* and her crew?" Kelt asked. "Did you sink her?"

McCade studied the white knight thoughtfully, then reached out to topple a jade bishop. "How many times have I told you, Ashley? You have to plan ahead."

"She was still afloat when we left her," Ashley said. "The fires were out and Captain Webb on his feet. She'll make it to shore."

"Do you take us for barbarians?" McCade asked. "I don't take a man's life without cause. We have the cargo. Why should I sink the sloop?"

"To silence witnesses."

"Ah, Gavin, a man after your own heart!" McCade glanced at his lieutenant. "Did you hear that? He might have the makings of a corsair after all."

Ashley moved her remaining bishop in a diagonal course across the board to capture the ivory castle. "You're slipping, Quincy."

"You think so?" He swept aside her victorious bishop with the white queen. "You play well for a woman. Thank God you inherited my brains instead of your mother's. But women don't have the intellect for chess. Don't you agree, Saxon?"

Kelt gave a grudging assent. "I've never met one who did." Ashley shot him a look of cold disdain. "Chess is a mon's game," Kelt continued, "and few of them ha' the mind for it."

"You have the sound of my grandfather's homeland,'' McCade said. ''But whoever heard of a Scot with such an outlandish name as Kelt Saxon?'' He smiled lazily. ''But perhaps 'tis not your given name, sir. Have you, like many in our brotherhood, adopted another name?''

''Nay.'' Kelt laid both hands flat on the table and leaned back to ease the cramped muscles in his spine. '' 'Tis the name I was christened with. There were Saxons in Scotland before William the Bastard came from Normandy with his armies.''

''Check.'' McCade's smile widened.

Kelt glanced down at the board and frowned. He pointed to the remaining jade knight. ''Move that back and across to defend your king,'' he suggested.

Ashley's lower lip tightened. She leaned forward and nibbled at a knuckle. ''She's sick, Quincy. Maybe dying.'' She looked up into his eyes. ''I want to see her.''

''And you think I don't?'' he answered softly.

''She's my mother, damn it.''

''Ah, yes. Cicely, the loving mother. She's good at holding the affections of those closest to her. It's her intense devotion—her loyalty, don't you think?''

Ashley colored. ''Look, I don't like her very much—I don't even know if I love her. But, damn it, Quincy, I've got to go to her, can't you see that? I don't have time for your stupid games.'' Her hand trembled as she moved a green pawn.

''Temper, Ashley.'' McCade chuckled as he scooped up her pawn. ''You always get careless when you're angry.''

''What am I going to say when Captain Webb reports that we were captured by pirates?'' She gripped the edge of the table. ''I won't have you destroying my life again.''

"Again, is it?" McCade shook his head with mock regret. "You'll think of something. Perhaps your loving stepfather ransomed you." He looked meaningfully from her to Kelt and back again. "Your story would be easier believed if I kept him."

"Give him to me," Gavin said.

"Keep out of this," Ashley snapped. "Kelt's none of your affair."

"No? He killed one of my best men yesterday. A friend."

"You don't have any friends, Gavin."

"Enough," McCade said. "Must you two always squabble like lovers?"

"If you're talking about Horne, I shot the bastard," Ashley boasted. "A pity you didn't cross my sights."

"Check."

"You promised to put me ashore," she reminded her father as she moved another piece to defend her king.

"When have I ever lied to you? I've told Gavin to set a course for the James." He sighed. "I wouldn't hurt you, Ashley. You should know that."

"If you won't hurt me, then keep your hands off what's mine. He's a good overseer. Morgan's Fancy needs him."

"That's the first I've heard o' it," Kelt said.

Ashley glared at him.

"The question is whether this Scot's more a danger to you alive . . . to us all." McCade moved an ivory bishop.

Ashley moved her queen. "Checkmate." She chuckled softly. "My game, Quincy."

Kelt and Ashley stood motionless on the muddy riverbank as the faint splash of oars signaled the departure of the small boat. The rain had stopped, but the overcast sky permitted no moonlight to filter through. The night was so black, it was impossible to see more than a few feet ahead. The pirate vessel was not even a shadow against the James.

Ashley broke their self-imposed silence. "It should be dawn in a few hours. We're not far from a place I know where we can get out of the cold. Rosewood is upriver, that way." She pointed. "We can walk there easily once it's light."

"We're to just continue on to your mother's house, then, as though nothing has happened? Damn you, woman! You deceived me."

"You empty-pated jackass!" she lashed back. "How dare you stand there and accuse me? I got you out of that mess with a whole skin, didn't I?" Ignoring him, Ashley began to walk swiftly past the shadowy outlines of the trees.

"*You* got me oot of it? 'Twas your father who set me free, nae ye!" Kelt protested as he picked up the small wooden sea chest and followed her. "I dinna ken why he did it, but they do say Gentleman Jim is known for his twisted sense of honor."

Ashley walked faster as she felt the ground dip and her feet found the hard-packed trail. She ducked under a low-hanging branch, secretly glad when she heard Kelt stop and curse it.

"Wait for me, damn you," he called.

A solid shape loomed in the blackness ahead. Ashley put out her hand, feeling the weathered siding of the barn, and groped her way around the corner to a door. Her fingers found the wooden latch. It turned easily and she opened the door. The scent of fresh hay and horses filled her nostrils. "Hello," she called. "Anyone here?" A snort and a nervous stamping were the only answer.

"Ashley?" Kelt's voice came faintly through the walls.

"Inside! Watch for the low—" There was a soft thud and an incomprehensible profanity from the doorway. Chuckling, Ashley felt along the wall for a lantern and the tinderbox in the niche below. A few fumbled attempts produced a spark and she was able to light the candle and replace it in the lantern.

A glow of yellow-white light illuminated the small stable. The building was dominated by a sturdy log box stall; a sorrel horse leaned his head curiously over the top rail. On the far side of the room was a bunk built into one wall and a rude cupboard containing crockery jars and a wooden bucket. The lean-to roof was low, slanting down to less than five feet in the back.

"What place is this?" Kelt growled, dropping the sea chest. "A pirate's love nest?"

She gave a wry laugh. "You're not far off. We're on Bantree. It belongs to James Pade, a neighbor of my mother's." Ashley rested her hands lightly on her hips. "Lord Pade is accustomed to making nocturnal visits to certain ladies. He always used to keep a horse and certain necessities here so he could spend the night if it was too late to go home. I used to play here as a child. Quincy told me Pade's habits haven't changed."

"And is this Pade in league with your father and his pirate friends?"

"James Pade?" She laughed. "Good Lord, no! Would a man of forty-five who's so afraid of his mother that he won't admit to having natural urges be involved with pirates?"

Kelt crossed the space between them and caught her arm roughly. "This isna a game! I've witnessed enough to hang the lot of ye!"

"Isn't it a game?" She tried to pull free, but his fingers bit cruelly into her flesh. "Let me go, damn you." She kicked at him and he sidestepped her, pulling her against his chest. Ashley doubled up a fist and tried to swing at his head.

"Nay, we'll ha' none of that," he said, catching her wrist with his other hand. "You'll be giving some answers if ye dinna wish me to turn ye over to His Majesty's justice. I'll be no part o' piracy."

"Let me go! I'll kill you. I swear I'll kill you if you don't let go of me!"

"Why, Ashley? Why did he release me? His lieutenant was fair for cuttin' my throat."

Anger washed over Ashley in crimson waves. Tears burned her eyes as she struggled futilely against him. "I should have let them," she cried. "I'd have been well rid of you."

Pinning both her wrists with one hand, Kelt held her at arm's length and cupped her chin with the other. "Are you party to his black art? Was it because of you that those men aboard the *Snow Princess* died?"

Ashley cursed him until she had used up every expression she had ever heard and invented a few original ones besides. Slowly her rage faded and she began to tremble in the chill night. Her voice dropped to a husky whisper. "It was a game, you witless booby. The chess match." She swayed and would have fallen if he hadn't caught her. "The match," she repeated woodenly. "I played for your life, Kelt."

He shook his head in disbelief. "Nay, 'twas but to pass the time."

"Why should I say anything? When I tell you the truth, you say I lie. Do you want me to give you lies? I can!" she cried.

"But the gown . . . the sea chest there . . . the way he treated you. 'Twas evident you were—"

"His guest?" Ashley gave a bitter snort. "Would you have been happier if I'd been handed over to the crew for their pleasure?" She twisted free and backed away until she felt the log rails on the stall against her shoulder. "Where else on that ship would I have been safe?" she demanded sarcastically. "My clothes were soaked in blood. Was I to keep them on, to forgo washing so as not to offend your fine sense of honor?"

Shaking with rage, he took a step toward her, his fists clenched at his sides. "Were ye a part of it?"

"No! I wasn't . . . at least not the way you mean. Think, man, if you have the brains! Would I shoot down my father's own crewmen if I was part of it? I didn't even know it was he until I saw that devil-spawned dwarf. My father thought to keep you aboard to replace some of his losses. Gavin wanted your head, but Quincy said you were too good with a cutlass to waste."

"And if I'd refused?"

"He'd have given you over to Gavin."

His hands were on her shoulders again, but there was no place for Ashley to run. "Ye ask a lot of a mon, to take what ye say on faith, lass. I wasna born yesterday that I can be—"

"I'm not asking anything of you!" she flung back. "We argued over you and I made him a bet. It amused him enough to accept."

"Were ye telling the truth about the *Snow Princess?* Was she set adrift?"

"That will be easy enough to prove, won't it?"

Kelt dropped his hands to cup her face and met her penetrating gaze. "How long have you known about him?"

Ashley's eyes glazed over in pain. "Since I was a little girl," she choked. "He used to come to the plantation. My grandfather never knew. Quincy said if I told, they might have to kill each other." Shamefully the tears started again as her first memories of her father came rushing back. "It was my grandfather I deceived," she whispered hoarsely. "I never told him about Quincy. Never! I never told anybody but Cicely."

"Hush, hush," Kelt soothed, pulling her against him and wrapping his arms protectively around her. "Dinna take on so. You'll make yourself sick with weeping, lass."

"I hated him," she sobbed. "I did . . . but he was my father. I couldn't let him and my grandfather kill each other. Not on account of me. I couldn't."

"Shush, shush," he murmured into her hair. "I believe you." And, God help him, he *did* want to believe her. He wanted to believe in her innocence. "Ye were but a wee bairn. 'Tis easy to see how ye were caught in his trap. No child would betray her own father."

"Not even if he was a pirate . . . a murderer?"

"Nay, lass. Not even then." Kelt bent his head and pressed his lips against her trembling mouth. She clung to him, molding her body to his. "Did you truly play for my life?" he asked as he swept her easily into his arms.

"Yes." She made a small sound of pleasure as he buried his face in her neck. He was so warm . . . so warm . . . and she needed that warmth, needed his strength and comfort. "I couldn't let him have you," she whispered as his quick fingers found the laces of her gown. There was a rustle of satin as the garment fell to the floor. Then he was kissing her bare shoulders and the rise of her breasts. She moaned and raised her lips. Kelt would shut out the nightmare, if only for the night. She needed him as she had never needed anyone else.

He bent over her, plunging his tongue deep within her mouth, claiming her with his powerful hands and caressing lips.

Somehow, they were on the narrow bunk, her shift gone and his bare chest pressed against her swollen breasts. His legs wrapped about hers as his fingers touched and teased, bringing her to the shuddering precipice of aching desire. There was nothing but Kelt, his touch, his soft words of love.

"I want you," he murmured raggedly. "I want you—now!"

With a cry of passion she pulled him to her, rising to meet the virile thrusts of his body, reaching out to join her soul with his, until both were lost in joined ecstasy.

She wept again in his arms, but the tears were not of sorrow but of joy. The agony of a child's deception, the festering sore of guilt were gone.

Some time in the hours before dawn, the candle sputtered and went out. "See that," Ashley whispered, "it's time for sleeping."

"Nay, woman, there'll be no sleep for ye this night," he teased, catching her bare arm between his teeth and nipping tenderly at the soft flesh. "What need does a mon ha' for light when he can feel this . . . and this . . ."

She gasped, retaliating with teasing fingers. "I'm glad I won," she murmured. "It would not have been the same, to spend my night here alone." She pulled a feather from the ticking beneath her head and brushed it across his face.

With a mock growl he pushed her back and nuzzled against her breast, taking the tip of her nipple between his lips. "And do you always win?" he demanded when he came up for air.

"This was the first time," she answered softly.

"The hell you say!"

"Well," she conceded, moving her legs to take him between her thighs. "I knew I'd have to beat him sooner or later. I've been letting him beat me for ten years."

Chapter 14

Ashley's eyelids flickered and she snuggled deeper into the feather tick, pulling the wool blankets closer about her against the cold Virginia morning. The delicious smells invaded her dreams once more, and she moaned sleepily, reaching out to reassure herself that the man who had shared her passion was real and not some imagined fancy. Her hand felt only the empty space beside her and her eyes opened wide. For a few seconds she stared around the barn, letting all that had happened in the past two days fall into place. Finally she realized that, except for the sorrel horse, she was alone in the barn.

"Kelt!" She sat up, pulling the cloak over her bare breasts. "Kelt, where are you?"

His voice came reassuringly through the open door with the early morning sunlight. "Aye, lassie, I'm here. Are ye to sleep away the day?" His broad shoulders filled the opening; his face was shadowed, but she could imagine his self-satisfied grin.

Once again she was enveloped in the wonderful scent of food. To her embarrassment, her stomach growled. "You needn't look so pleased with yourself," Ashley said lazily.

Kelt chuckled warmly as he sat on the edge of the

bunk and planted a kiss on the tip of her chin. " 'Tis no chin for a woman," he teased. " 'Tis too firm. A woman wi' such a chin is bound for trouble, my grandmother would say. Such a woman probably whistles."

She caught his hand and brought the fingers to her mouth, gently kissing the place between the nails and the knuckles. "And what's wrong with a whistling woman?" she asked throatily.

"Whistling girls and cackling hens always come to bad ends. 'Tis a known fact," he declared smoothly, then kissed her lips in a most satisfying manner.

Ashley slid her arms around his neck, inhaling the strong male scent of him. He had bathed, God knew where, and his hair and beard were still damp. She felt the flush of color rise in her cheeks as she remembered the sensation of that beard against her. "Kelt." She pushed him away. "What is that smell?" She sniffed. It was impossible, but it smelled like sausage—fresh-cooked sausage.

"Hmmmp. It proves you are a kelpie if you can cause a Scotsman to forget his breakfast. Up wi' ye!" He smacked her playfully on a bare thigh. "Since you showed no sign of tending to our bodily needs, I made us some breakfast."

"Breakfast? With what?" She pulled the cloak tighter and rose from the bunk, looking for her discarded shift. Kelt tossed it to her. "Aren't you going to at least turn your back?" she asked.

"Nay."

Laughing, Ashley dropped the cloak and pulled the wrinkled shift over her head. Throwing open the sea chest, she took out a fresh gown of dove gray and quickly dressed, stamping her feet and rubbing her arms against the chill.

"Have ye a maid in there as well?" He opened the

lid a crack and peered inside. "Perhaps a coach and nine?"

Ashley threw a hairbrush at him. "There should be," she agreed. "Somewhere in the bottom." He caught the brush and moved behind her to begin brushing out her long hair in even, gentle strokes. "Mmm," she murmured. "That feels good."

"Nay different than grooming a horse." Before she could turn to smack him, he caught her about the waist. Letting the brush fall to the floor, he caressed her waist and the bottom half of her breasts with his thumbs and fingers. "Perhaps a little different," he conceded. Turning her around, he tilted her chin up to kiss her lips once more.

Hot excitement pulsed through Ashley's veins. What was it about this man that his lightest touch could make her tremble like a willow leaf in a storm? Every hour, every day he became more a part of her, until thinking of life without him was like looking into a yawning void. Her fingers tightened on the back of his neck and she moistened her lips to meet his again.

Both were breathless when the kiss ended. With rough impulsiveness Kelt pushed her to arm's length and gazed into the gold-flecked eyes. "There is a thing I would say t' ye, lass," he said huskily. She blinked, and for a heartbeat Kelt stared into the turmoil of Ashley's naked soul. "Nay, sweeting," he reassured her, " 'tis nothing bad." He cupped her face in his hands. "On the ship, when the pirates came at us . . ." He cleared his throat. "Ye have a way about ye, woman, of making me as awkward as a lad," he admitted with a grin. "What I'm trying to say is that I've fought beside many a mon, but none wi' more courage. Ye can guard my back anytime, anyplace."

Joy replaced the fear in her eyes and she threw herself into his arms. "You're not so bad yourself, for a Virginian," she teased, molding her warm body against his.

"Ye be a bad habit, wench," he murmured into her hair. "A mon can get nothing done for loving ye."

She laughed and wiggled free. "You said breakfast?"

He led the way to a tiny fire outside the barn. Ashley blinked. On a clean slab of wood were sausages and wedges of cornbread with butter. Four eggs, still in their shells, were propped against the slab, and the strong smell of tea came from a kettle balanced over the fire.

"Where did you . . ." She looked at him suspiciously. "You didn't cook this?"

"My lady." He waved gallantly toward a fallen log. "Will you have honey wi' your tea this morning?"

"Kelt!"

"Aye, lass?" Efficiently he swept two of the sausages and a slice of cornbread onto the makeshift plate. He added an egg and deposited the offering in her lap, then began to pour the tea into a tin cup.

"The tea may have come from the barn, but none of the rest. Where did you get this food, Kelt?" she demanded.

"Watch the tea, 'tis hot," he warned. Smugly he served himself and began to devour the remaining food.

Ashley nibbled tentatively at a sausage and found it delicious. Without hesitation, she began to eat, finishing every bite and sipping the heavenly tea. "You're not going to tell me, are you?" she said when she was done.

He grinned. "You may ha' broke bread wi' your

illustrious father, but I didna. I needed something to eat before I died of starvation.'' He motioned to the west where a thin column of smoke rose above the trees. ''I took a few coins from the chest and walked over to the neighbors. The lady of the house was happy to sell me the makings o' a proper meal.''

''And it didn't bother your sense of honor to use a pirate's coin to buy your breakfast?''

''Nay.'' Kelt's eyes twinkled beneath the fallen lock of dark hair. ''A mon must be practical.''

Ashley dusted the crumbs off her hands and shirt. ''If you've filled your stomach, I want you to take a message to Lady Pade. You must have a decent change of clothing.'' Ashley rolled her eyes at his torn and dirty garments. ''And we'll need the loan of a carriage or even a dogcart.''

''You said we were within walking distance of Rosewood. If your mother may be dying, why the delay?''

''I wasn't thinking straight last night. You know these Virginians—each as haughty as Lucifer himself. My stepfather is among the worst. If we arrive looking like gypsies, he might refuse to admit us.'' She shook her head. ''No, we must plan this carefully. Lady Pade is my mother's friend, and she knows I am no danger to her precious son. She will help us for Cicely's sake. You can take the sorrel. The Pade manor is only a mile or so south.''

''And if we are too late at your mother's bedside?''

Ashley's brown furrowed in concern. ''If we are, I'll be sorry. But I'll not be shamed by Nicholas Randall. Not again . . . not ever.''

The wheels of the yellow dogcart spun over the hard-packed dirt as Kelt guided the black mare up the tree-lined lane and through the massive gates of Rosewood. Ashley gripped the side of the cart with one hand; the other was clenched into a fist at her side. Neither had spoken for the last two miles.

When Kelt had returned from the Pade plantation with the horse and cart, he had also brought word that they had arrived too late. "The funeral was yesterday," he'd said gently. "I'm sorry, lass. You would have been on time if . . ."

"If our ship hadn't been captured by the *Scarlet Witch*."

Cicely was dead. Ashley still couldn't believe it. Had she been beautiful in her coffin, or had the fever taken even her loveliness away? She shivered in the late morning air. Why had they buried her so quickly? Did Nicholas hate her so much he'd deny Ashley's presence at her own mother's funeral?

The dirt road curved around a ha-ha wall, giving them a clear view of the magnificent brick house. The original building, a one-and-a-half story manor house, had been augmented by a square center structure rising three full stories, and then duplicated on the far side of the new addition. It was an impressive home, even for the James River aristocracy, and the sight never failed to ignite Ashley's temper.

Kelt reined in the black. "Your stepfather doesn't seem to lack any of the necessities of life," he said dryly.

"You like it?" Ashley's eyes darkened. "My mother's money paid for it all. Two of her plantations were sacrificed to build this—eighteen hundred acres of prime tobacco land." She pursed her lips as though she had tasted something bitter. "Nicholas will have the best," she continued. "The fastest horses, the most beautiful women. He once traded Cicely's favorite maid for a hound, then shot the dog when it lost the scent of a fox during a chase."

"Sounds like a mon with a lack o' common sense."

"He's worse than that. I was terrified of him when I was a child. He beat me once with a riding crop for breaking a saucer." Something cold flickered in the depths of Ashley's dark eyes. "I was four years old. My mother watched without saying a word." She inhaled deeply, letting her gaze drop to a row of boxwood that lined the neatly manicured lawn. "I always wanted to ask her why. I guess now I'll never know."

"Ha' ye thought she may ha' been frightened o' him, too?"

Ashley nodded. "She is . . . was." She clasped her hands together, gripping them tightly. "He used to hit her whenever he was angry . . . and Nicholas is frequently angry."

"Yet she stayed wi' him all these years."

"I think I blamed her for that most. She could have come home to Morgan's Fancy. After my grandfather died, I wrote to her and begged her to come. I would gladly have given her refuge."

Kelt flipped the reins over the mare's back and the cart rolled up to the door. A servant ran to catch the horse's head. Kelt got out of the cart, walked behind it, and assisted Ashley down. Neither had missed the black wreath on the front door.

An unfamiliar maid ushered them into the hall. "Are you expected, ma'am?" she asked shyly. "Master Randall is in mourning."

"Tell your master that Mistress Ashley Morgan of Morgan's Fancy will see him immediately," Kelt said.

"Yes, sir."

The girl hurried away, and Kelt winked at Ashley. "Chin up, lass," he said softly. "Nicholas Randall willna use a riding crop on you today."

A doorknob turned behind them and Ashley turned to stare at the woman in the doorway. "Cicely?" Her face whitened and she took a step back. "Cicely?"

"Ashley."

Even in mourning black, the woman was stunning. The startling blue eyes shone like gems against the canvas of the classical profile and the flawless English complexion.

Kelt bowed. "Mistress Randall." Whatever the explanation, this woman had to be Ashley's mother. There could not be two such beauties on the James. "Your servant, ma'am."

Colored sparks circled before Ashley's eyes and she dug her nails into the palm of her hand. "I thought you were dead," she said slowly. "The wreath."

An expression of sorrow passed over the beautiful face. "The funeral was your . . ." Her voice caught in her throat. "Your brother Robert. He was killed . . . three days ago."

Ashley gazed at her mother in disbelief. "Robert? But how? A riding accident?"

Cicely raised a handkerchief to her lips, shaking her head. "I'm sorry," she said. "It's . . . it's very difficult." She brushed her daughter's cheek with a cool kiss. "I know this is a shock to you." She sighed. "It was to all of us. He was shot in a duel over a woman. Nicholas is taking it hard."

"I don't understand. Robert sent me a message that you were ill—dying. That's why we came." Ashley looked from her mother to Kelt in confusion. "Excuse me, Cicely. This is Master Kelt Saxon, my overseer."

"Pleased to meet you, sir," Cicely said. "There must have been some mistake. I had a touch of fever after Christmas, but nothing serious. I can't imagine Robert writing you such a thing."

"It wasn't a letter. Captain Philip Fraser of the *Merry Kate* brought word. He insisted it was from Robert."

"What are you doing here? I don't remember inviting you to Rosewood, Ashley." A middle-aged gentleman in a dressing gown and turban stepped into the hall.

Ashley whirled to face her stepfather.

"Now, Nicholas, don't make a fuss," Cicely soothed. "It's only natural that Ashley would come. Robert was her brother, too."

"Her half brother," Nicholas said coldly.

Ashley flushed with anger. She had expected as much. When would she learn to ignore the venom of her stepfather's tongue? "I came to see my mother," she retorted. "I'll not impose on your precious hospitality long."

"You've picked a poor time for visiting," Nicholas glanced at Kelt. "And who might you be?"

"This is Ashley's overseer," Cicely explained. "Master Saxon."

"Since when have we begun to receive hired help in the hall of Rosewood?" he demanded scornfully. "Wait outside for your mistress, Saxon. She'll not be long, I assure you."

" 'Tis nae for the likes of you to tell me to come or go." Kelt bristled. His gray eyes narrowed ominously and he moved to stand between Ashley and her stepfather.

Nicholas flushed as the Scot's arrogant gaze swept over him, lingering on his thickening waistline beneath the striped silk banyan, then moving insolently up to the pale, fleshy jowls and bloodshot eyes. "I gave you an order," Nicholas snapped.

"It's all right," Ashley conceded. "You can wait in the cart for me." She turned to her mother. "If we're not welcome here—"

"But you are," Cicely insisted. "Nicholas, please . . ." She laid a hand on his robe. "I want her to stay. It's been months since we've seen each other."

"Come along, mistress," Kelt said.

Ashley was not deceived by the soft burr. Another minute and he'd have the master of Rosewood by the throat—or another infinitely more sensitive part of his anatomy. She shook her head. "No, I'll be all right, Kelt. Just wait for me outside." She threw him a pleading look. With a scowl he turned toward the door. Ashley held her breath until the door closed behind him, then glanced back at her mother. "I would like to talk with you before I leave."

"There is no place for my wife's illegitimate offspring in my house," Nicholas said harshly. "I've just buried my heir! Or have you forgotten?"

"You acrimonious bastard!" Ashley cried. "I should have let Kelt have you!" Her hands knotted into tight fists at her side, and she fought the all-too-familiar waves of hate. Her stomach churned as sickness rose in her throat. She had killed men when she stood beside Kelt on the bloodstained deck of the *Snow Princess*, but she had taken those lives to protect her own. She'd been afraid of the buccaneers, but she'd borne them no hate. This man she hated, and the hate ran so deep it terrified her.

Tears of rage formed in Ashley's eyes and she dashed them away. "I'll go, Cicely," she whispered. "I'm sorry about Robert."

"You won't go!" Cicely turned fiercely on her husband. "You forget whose money bought this house, Nicholas. Ashley will stay until she's ready to leave and you will treat her with respect while she's here. If you don't . . ."

"If I don't? What then, my spitting lynx?" Nicholas shrugged. "Have her here if you must, but I want her out of my way.'' He twisted the heavy gold ring on his right hand unconsciously. ''And, of course, I'll not have her''—he chuckled beneath his breath—''her *man* on Rosewood. She can have all the lovers she wants on her own plantation, but I won't have the Randall name besmirched by her indiscriminate rutting.''

Ashley made a strangled sound as Nicholas dismissed her with a malignant glance and walked stiffly from the room. ''I can't stay here,'' Ashley whispered. ''I can't.''

''Nonsense,'' Cicely replied firmly. ''If you leave, you're just letting him scare you off, and you know what a bully he is. It will only make him worse.'' She motioned for her daughter to follow her. ''Come up to my chambers. I'll have Mona brew a pot of tea and we'll talk in private.'' She paused with one dainty slippered foot on the bottom step of the ornate hanging staircase and smiled. ''But perhaps you'd better send your big Scot away first. He may think we've locked you away in a dungeon and come charging to your rescue.'' Cicely sighed deeply. ''How very like your father you look when you scowl so. Quincy's eyes always darkened to that exact shade when he was in a rage.''

Ashley stared with numb incredibility at her mother. ''How can you speak of him so openly? In this house? With his spies . . .'' She indicated the kitchen wing. ''You know they carry every word you utter to him.''

Cicely gave a brittle laugh. ''I say whatever I like. It doesn't matter. If they have nothing to report, they make up something. He believes what he wants to believe. According to Nicholas, I meet secretly with your father all the time.'' A ripple of regret passed over her flawless countenance. ''Would that it were true," she mused. Moisture glistened in the china-blue eyes and she smiled. "Don't fret yourself about me, Ashley. Come along and tell me all your adventures. Who knows when we will have the chance to visit again?"

Ashley took a long time to answer. "All right," she said finally. "Let me tell Kelt to return for me in a few hours." She threw her mother a beseeching look. "I can't sleep under his roof, but perhaps I can impose upon Lady Pade's hospitality for a few days." Ashley went to the door, then turned to look at Cicely. Beneath the jewels and satin, beneath the impeccable facade of a Virginia lady, was it possible that she might find some trace of the headstrong Cicely who had risked everything for love?

"Why?" Ashley demanded. "Why do you endure it? Why do you stay with Nicholas?"

"Sometimes I ask myself that very question."

Ashley looked about her mother's private chambers. Other than the cherry highboy from the cabinet shop of a new craftsman in Philadelphia and a richly colored Oriental rug before the fireplace, little had changed since she had last been in this room. With its beautiful furniture, charming personal effects, and rare imported fabrics, Cicely's chambers remained a shrine of understated elegance.

Ashley crossed to the familiar mahogany writing desk and reached down to toy idly with the silver inkwell. From where she stood, she had a magnificent view of rolling lawns running down to the James River. Horses grazed in the far paddock and here and there a cloud of white sheep was visible.

"Lovely, isn't it?" Cicely said from her longue by the fireplace. She held out her hands to catch the warmth of the crackling fire. "Sometimes I stand there for hours and I've never seen the same sight twice. Much nicer than a picture. Paintings are so boring. Always the same."

"Cicely . . . Mother." Ashley turned back toward her. "I don't want to talk about the view from your window. We need to talk about us . . . about what's wrong between us. And . . ." She twisted her hands nervously. "I need to know about Robert. Why would he have sent word for me to come here? You know he hated me."

"Nonsense. Robert was too lazy to hate anyone." Cicely sighed deeply and motioned to her daughter. "Come over here and sit where I can see you. You know everything more than ten feet away is a blur. Why must you always be so angry?" A genuine smile spread over her face, illuminating the bright blue eyes. "That's the first time you've called me Mother in years."

Obediently Ashley moved to a straight-backed chair across from her mother. "Someone's been trying to kill me."

"Now I know you have too much of your father in you," Cicely replied calmly. "Why would anyone wish to do away with you—unless it's for your horrible cooking? And that's not a killing offense." She shook her head. "You're imagining things. What you need is to find a nice gentleman and marry him. I could introduce you to several eligible men."

"No matchmaking, Cicely," Ashley snapped. "I should think you'd be the last one to recommend marriage. I'm not taking a husband—ever. I can spend my own money, thank you."

"And I can manage my own life without constant criticisms from my children." A stubbornness settled into Cicely's eyes. "I may not be the best of mothers, but I don't believe I've done badly by you."

Ashley leaned forward. "You sent me away," she accused softly.

"Of course I sent you away, you ninny! Would you have preferred living with Nicholas?" Cicely took up her embroidery hoop and began to stitch at the delicate pattern. "I knew your grandfather would spoil you unmercifully, and up there"—she waved in the general direction of the upper Chesapeake—"who would care if your birth was somewhat . . ." She paused, nibbling at her lower lip. "If your birth was irregular."

"Irregular, hell! I'm a bastard!"

"There's no need to use such vulgar speech, Ashley. That's one improvement I'd have made if you were under my wing." She looked up mildly. "I've never thought of you as being illegitimate. I've simply considered Quincy my first husband. He is the only man I've ever loved. We intended to be wed—we exchanged private vows. I can't believe that God would hold it against me because unfortunate circumstances parted us before the actual legal ceremony."

"You exchanged vows?" Ashley rose to her feet. "You never told me that. Were there any witnesses?"

"Ouch!" Cicely stuck her finger in her mouth. "Don't leap about so, girl. You've made me stick myself." She laid the embroidery on the cushion beside her. "Yes, there were witnesses—my maid and Quincy's friend Harrison Knight."

"Then you were married under the law," Ashley said. "I'm not illegitimate."

"Probably not, but Harrison sailed with Quincy. He drowned off the Carolinas, and my maid died in childhood ten years ago." She shrugged. "No one would believe me then and they certainly won't believe me now."

"But Quincy knows the truth."

Cicely laughed. "You're such an innocent, Ashley. If your father were to appear in court, the authorities would have him clapped in irons and strung up before sunset." The blue eyes twinkled. "Besides, if you're legitimate, your half brother Richard and Henry aren't. Do you want your mother brought to trial for bigamy?"

Ashley dropped back into the chair, letting her hands fall limply in her lap. "Why did you let me believe I was a bastard all my life?"

Cicely shifted uneasily. "I was sixteen, Ashley, no more than a child myself. Your grandfather was so angry, he wanted to kill Quincy. I believe he would have, too, if he'd returned then. Old Ash had a terrible temper. He told me I would be ruined if I persisted in my story that we had exchanged vows; he knew my maid would have lied for me if I'd asked her. Nicholas promised he would give my unborn child his name and protection." She arched an eyebrow. "Should I have told him after we were married? After his son and heir was born?" She shook her head firmly. "No. I believed Quincy was dead. I made the best of a bad situation. And by the time he came back to the Tidewater, I had the boys and a life here. Should I have given up this"—she made a sweeping gesture—"to be a pirate's consort?"

"But all these years . . . you never told me. Why, Mother? Why couldn't you have told me?" Ashley begged.

"Could you have held your tongue? Can you now?" She sniffed and reached for a lace handkerchief. "If you repeat what I've said, I'll deny it. My life with Nicholas is difficult enough already. I don't want him to find out he's been living in sin all these years and that his precious sons are bastards."

"You don't have to stay with him. You can come home to Morgan's Fancy with me."

"That again?" Cicely pursed her lips and reached for the embroidery hoop, bending over it for a long time before she spoke. Finally she said, "I've made my bed, girl, and I'll lie in it. Alone, and that's a blessing. It's been years since Nicholas has demanded his rights. He prefers more earthy women— the younger the better. I rarely see my esteemed husband, except at dinner." Her eyes sought Ashley's. "What you must understand is that I'm making the best of life as it is. I enjoy being the mistress of Rosewood, for what it's worth, and I have no intention of coming to live with you in the wilderness of Maryland and being someone's grandmother."

Ashley went to the window. "Just remember," she said, "if you change your mind, you're always welcome."

"Tell me you're not secretly relieved?"

"I guess I can't," Ashley said frankly. A flush stained her cheeks. "I—"

"Nicholas was right, wasn't he?" her mother interrupted. "That brawny Scotsman is your lover."

Ashley stared out at the muddy river. "I saw Quincy," she riposted. "He doesn't look a day older. He took the *Snow Princess* on the upper Chesapeake."

"Did he ask for me?" Cicely's mouth trembled.

"Doesn't he always?"

Chapter 15

"You are so very kind to offer your hospitality, Lady Pade," Ashley said. Except for the hovering servants, Ashley, Lady Pade, and her son, Lord Pade, were alone at the vast table in the formal dining room of Bantree. "As you know, the relationship between my stepfather and—"

"Tut tut," Lady Pade interrupted. "There's no need for you to say a single word. James and I are all alone in this great house. It's so pleasant to visit with you and hear the news from the Maryland Colony. Winter is so dull."

Lady Pade, a tall, spare woman with gray eyes and an overlong nose, was known up and down the James River for her bountiful hospitality, her forthright speech, and her unwillingness to permit her only son and heir to live his own life.

"Our sincerest regrets on the untimely death of your brother," James offered between bites of the excellent quail and rice dish. "God rest his soul."

Ashley murmured something appropriate and regarded James stealthily from under lowered lashes. The years had been good to him, she decided. He looked as he always had—a thin, balding, scholarly man with his mother's features and a bittersweet smile.

"James tells me he has heard wonderful things about your plantation," Lady Pade said. "A neighbor of ours purchased one of your horses. A work animal, wasn't it?"

"Yes. I expect to have several more for sale by summer. I have a marvelous stallion . . ." Ashley chatted on, speaking easily with the Pades about horses and crops. Lady Pade shared her interest in the details of plantation life. Unlike those who lived off the land without loving it, these two were as much an active part of the James River country as the earliest settlers. Lady Pade was only too willing to discuss the radical theory of crop rotation and of planting corn and beans in the same spot in the Indian manner.

The large room was lit now by candles and heated by a fireplace and charcoal braziers under the table. In good weather, the wide windows would be thrown open to catch the breeze off the river.

A pity Kelt hadn't been invited to share their meal, Ashley thought. He would have appreciated the heavy table and matching chairs, the Irish crystal goblets and candelabra, not to mention the wide array of deliciously prepared food.

Kelt was taking his supper with the overseer of Bantree. On the James, at least at Lady Pade's table, one did not dine with the hired help, even if that hired help was for all intents and purposes a gentleman.

Lady Pade cleared her throat. What was it she had said? Gambling, Ashley shook her head no.

"But you must," the older woman insisted. "You've only just arrived. I won't hear of anything less."

"Now, Mother," James admonished. "I'm certain Ashley feels she has a duty to her people. Her overseer is here. Who is left on Morgan's Fancy with authority?" His pale eyes rested on Ashley, making clear his admiration. "It's not as though she had a husband to share the responsibility."

"Exactly," Ashley smiled gratefully at James. "I would like to visit my brother's grave and see my mother again tomorrow. But we must find a vessel to carry us north as soon after that as possible. I mustn't be away from the plantation a day longer than necessary." She sipped the delicate French wine. "If I could impose on you to make the arrangements . . ." Ashley looked beseechingly at James. "It must be an armed ship. I couldn't bear a repetition of—"

"James will tend to it," Lady Pade assured her. "You're not to trouble yourself about it another moment. You've been through a terrible experience. Thank God you were able to persuade the pirates to set you ashore."

"They robbed us of our money. I believe the captain wanted to hold me for ransom but thought better of it. The murder of innocent ship's passengers in the upper bay would have brought swift and certain retribution." Ashley forced her voice to a faint quaver. "It was an experience I'll carry to my grave."

She had given a complete account of the attack to Lady Pade and again to the sheriff earlier in the day, omitting the name of the ship and its captain. No word had yet arrived on the fate of the *Snow Princess*. She'd been afraid to use Quincy's alibi. No one who knew her stepfather would have believed he would have traded a copper penny for her release.

"Are you certain you didn't hear the pirates call their leader by name? Could it have been Gentleman Jim? He is known for his chivalry toward ladies."

Ashley shook her head. "It was all so terrible, I remember very little. I believe I may have fainted. Master Saxon saved my life," she added smoothly, mixing truth with lies. Despite what her father was, she could not condemn him with her own testimony. If he ever came to trial for the capture of the *Snow Princess,* she would let Captain Webb accuse him. Rising in her place, she laid a crumpled napkin by her plate. "If you will excuse me," she entreated, "I am so very weary. I should like to go up to my room."

"Of course, of course. How thoughtless of us to keep you talking," Lady Pade said. "I admire you, child. A lesser woman would have collapsed. First the attack by pirates, then to learn of Robert's tragic death. You should be in bed." She motioned to a maid. "Ruthie, show Mistress Morgan up to her bedchamber." She smiled at Ashley. "Breakfast is at eight. If you prefer, you may pull the bell and Ruthie will have a tray brought up to you. Sleep well."

"Thank you, Lady Pade. I'm certain I will. Sir." Ashley nodded to James and followed the black girl from the room and up the wide center staircase.

It was after midnight when Ashley was awakened by a tapping at the window. With a start, she sat bolt upright, trying to get her bearings. The tapping came again, and she pushed aside the heavy bed hangings. "Who is it?" she called hesitantly. Her breath caught in her throat as she saw the silhouette of a man outside the window.

"Ashley!" came the harsh whisper. "Open this damned window."

There was no mistaking that voice. Scrambling from the bed, she ran barefoot across the icy floor to release the lock and push open the window. Kelt swung into the room, landing catlike on the balls of his feet. His hands closed around her shoulders and he kissed her full on the lips.

Ashley's astonishment was lost in the delight of his presence. "Are you mad?" she teased when they parted for air. "What if someone saw you? Have you no care for my reputation?"

"If someone saw us, ye might be forced to marry me oot o' shame," he said. One hand slipped down to grasp her lower back. "I was lonely."

"So you climbed the side of the house?"

"I climbed a tree. You sleep like a rock! I've been out there banging on your window like a schoolboy."

"And how did you know which room was mine?"

"I was watching the house. I saw ye by candlelight. Ye should be more modest in your undressing, woman. 'Tis a sight to cause a mon to think lusty thoughts."

"You were spying on me?"

"Aye, I admit it," he said contritely. His hand moved lower to caress the curve of a firm buttock. "Ye have turned me to a satyr." With a wicked laugh, he bent to nibble at her neck and ear.

"My feet are cold," Ashley protested.

"Never let it be said I didna show proper respect for a lady's wishes." Picking her up, he carried her to the bed and tossed her into the center. "Give me but a second, sweeting, and I'll see what I can do about warming the rest of ye."

Ashley lay back against the pillow, watching as he stripped off his coat and vest. God, but he's beautiful, she thought. The golden glow from the hearth formed a hazy aura around Kelt's head and shoulders. He half turned, pulling the shirt over his head, and Ashley caught a glimpse of his sinewy chest and taut, flat stomach. Delicious sensations spread through her as Kelt fumbled with the ties on his breeches. Her pulse quickened and she reached out to him. "I'm still cold," she said raggedly.

He came to her and they snuggled beneath the quilts, entwining arms and legs until they lay breast to breast and lips to lips. The familiar sweet aching returned to haunt her as Kelt's fingers stroked and caressed her body, and her tongue met his in a long, lingering kiss of searing rapture.

"I couldna sleep for thinking o' ye," he murmured into her hair. "And for wanting to hold ye like this."

Boldly Ashley let her own fingers travel through the thick, curling hair on his chest, moving in teasing circles around the hard nubs of his nipples and up across the rock-hard muscles of his shoulder and upper arm. Kelt's moan of pleasure thrilled her and she traced her fingers' path with her mouth, nibbling and nipping, tasting the salt musk of his flesh, breathing in the overwhelming male scent of his mouth and body.

"Kelpie," he accused.

Evidence of his rising desire pressed against her leg and Ashley moved to explore the velvety length of his tumescent manhood. He breathed her name into her ear and she felt a surge of liquid fire spill through her veins. She raised her mouth to join with his, thrilling to the moist, hot thrust of his tongue and the feel of his hands on her breasts.

He had pushed her back upon the pillows and moved to cover her with his body when, without warning, came the clear sound of footsteps and the turn of the doorknob. Ashley pulled away, covering herself with a sheet.

"Mistress Morgan, I must speak with you at once," came the urgent whisper from the door. "Please."

Ashley covered her mouth with her hand to stifle a rising giggle. Sliding from the high bed, she fumbled on the floor for her nightgown. Kelt's hand closed on her arm and he shook his head firmly. "It's Lord Pade. I've got to see what he wants," Ashley whispered.

"Send him away."

The thick folds of the gown fell over her hips and she began to fasten the buttons. "Shhh," she warned. "He'll hear you."

"Damn it, Ashley, don't answer the door. Pretend you're asleep."

"I'm coming," she called. "You be quiet," she ordered Kelt. In a practiced motion she pulled the bed hangings closed. "Just don't say anything. If you make a sound, I'll kill you," she threatened sweetly.

"Mistress Morgan!"

Ashley hurried to the door. "Yes? What is it, Lord Pade? Is something wrong?"

"I must speak to you about a private and urgent matter. Unlock the door."

Kelt made an audible sound of disgust from behind the bed curtains.

"Shhh." Ashley moved closer to the door. "This is not seemly, Lord Pade," she hedged. "What would your mother say?"

"Mother is sleeping off the effects of a strong potion. I have information about your brother. You must let me in."

"All right," Ashley agreed. "Just for a moment." She pulled back the bolt and opened the door.

James Pade ducked inside and shut the door behind him. He was wearing a long silk robe and cap. "My dear Ashley," he began, "you must not let my late night visit alarm you. Let me assure you that you are under my protection."

Ashley forced a modest demeanor and waited. James smelled of brandy and some dreadful sweet scent. He took a hesitant step toward her and she backed up an equal pace. "Lord Pade . . . James . . . you said you had something to tell me about my brother." Ashley pushed a lock of hair off her face and tried not to think of Kelt behind the hangings. "Please state your business, sir. I fear my reputation would be ruined if you are found here."

"My dear Ashley," he repeated, clearing his throat, "you must know in what high esteem Mother and I hold you . . . have always held you . . . in spite of—"

"In spite of my birth? How gracious of you, sir," Ashley replied. "Certainly you must know that I have always considered you both to be among my dearest friends."

"I don't wish to be your friend, Ashley," James cried, seizing her hands and bringing her fingers to his lips. "I want to be more." He covered her hand with damp kisses. "Ashley, say you'll be my wife!"

"James, please!" Ashley's voice was choked. "What has this to do with my brother? Did you shoot him?"

"Me?" James dropped her hand. "Whyever would you think such a thing? I harbored no ill will toward Robert, or Henry either for that matter."

"But you said—"

"A lie born of desperation. Would you have opened your door to me at this hour if I had told the truth?" James moved closer and Ashley backed toward the bed. "I adore you!" he confided. "Your hair . . . your eyes . . ." He exhaled loudly. "Can I compare thee to a summer's day?"

"James, please. I'm deeply honored, but this is too serious a matter to be decided on the spur of the moment. You must give me time to consider your suit." Ashley's back brushed the bed curtain and something hard thumped her between the shoulder blades.

"I know my own shortcomings," he said. "I'm somewhat older than you are, but many people consider that to be an asset in a husband. And certain . . . ah . . . ladies have complimented me on my prowess as a—" He stopped short, stumbling for words. "You'd be the mistress of Bantree after Mother, of course. I have other properties, too. You'll get no better offer, Ashley."

"I'm certain I won't," she agreed, dodging James's sudden lunge and circling toward the door. "I will consider your offer. But you must go. I am a maiden, sir, and your sudden onslaught has frightened me."

"One kiss, sweet Ashley. One kiss, and I promise I shall depart in gentlemanly haste."

"James!" Ashley's voice took on an authoritarian tone. "Out!" She folded her arms across her chest in as near an imitation of Lady Pade as she could manage."

"But, my dear," he stammered, "all I've asked for is a single—"

"Many a maiden has been undone by a single chaste kiss," she reminded him sternly. "And"—her voice softened a little—"as you said yourself, your reputation with the ladies is such that I have every reason to fear your touch, sir." Ashley indicated the door. "I am honored by your proposal, but I would not be worthy of that honor, Lord Pade, if I let you remain a second longer in my chambers. Good night, sir."

"Very well." He sighed sadly. "Until tomorrow." He opened the door, glanced nervously up and down the hallway, then hurried out, vanishing into the shadows.

Ashley locked the door and flung herself across the

room into Kelt's arms, erupting into smothered laughter. "You fiend," she accused as tears of mirth ran down her cheeks. "You nearly shoved me into his arms with that love tap."

"Sweet maiden?" Kelt growled and threw her back against the pillows in mock anger. "One chaste kiss?" Teasingly he nuzzled her neck and breasts, pinning her with his weight and repeating the feigned animal growls.

"Let me up, you beast," she gasped, too weak with laughter to fight back. "Unhand me, I say." In self-defense she began to tickle his ribs. "Villain! Despoiler of innocents!" she accused. Laughing, Kelt rolled away, pulling Ashley on top of him.

"Now who is the despoiler of innocents?" he said huskily as he ran a hand possessively down her hip and bared thigh. "*Uruisg*."

Laughing, she moved provocatively against him, brushing his lips with soft, feathery kisses, running her fingers over his chest and up his throat.

It seemed to Kelt as though her touch turned his blood to pulsing rivers of incandescent heat. With a groan, he arched beneath her, joining his mouth to hers, letting loose the pent-up passion that welled within him and pulling her astride his engorged manhood.

Ashley's muffled cries of desire matched his as they blended flesh and soul in the age-old dance of love, shutting out the world and losing themselves in the sweet joy of shared rapture.

Ashley stood beside her brother's grave in silence. Beyond the cedar grove, Kelt waited with the horse and dogcart. She had wanted a few moments here alone before she said goodbye to her mother.

Only a fresh mound of earth covered with wreaths

of holly and crow's-foot gave evidence of the passing of Rosewood's heir. The tombstone was not finished and the season wrong for flowers. Despite the morning's sunshine, the little graveyard seemed as desolate as Ashley's thoughts.

Why could she feel no remorse, no grief? Robert had been her brother. Even though they had argued frequently, they shared a common parent. Robert was Ash's grandson. What was wrong with her that she could think of nothing but the silent recitation of a rote prayer for his departed soul?

"A pretty picture, sister."

Ashley turned to face the petulant-looking young man entering the gate behind her. "Henry! You startled me."

The resemblance to his father was becoming stronger every day. Both Henry and Robert had favored Nicholas, but no one had ever confused the two brothers. Henry was short, nearly an inch shorter than she was, and had a round face with over-red cheeks and a pouting, girlish mouth. His eyes were blue, like Cicely's, but in Henry's sullen, babyish face they seemed too feminine. A pity, Ashley thought, that her brother had inherited none of their mother's beauty.

Ashley noticed that Henry had grown a sparse mustache since she had seen him last. He was dressed, as always, in the latest London mode and wore a wig over his short-cropped blond hair.

"Your man told me you were down here." He glanced back toward the lane. "He looks vaguely familiar."

"Kelt is my new overseer at Morgan's Fancy. You might have seen him somewhere before. He comes from Virginia."

Henry came within five feet of Robert's grave, then paused, resting one hand on his hip. "A pity about brother Robert, isn't it? I warned him. No matter how good a shot you think you are, there's always someone better." He shook his head. "I know you must be desolate. You and Robert were always so close."

"No closer than the two of you," Ashley said.

"Ah, as sharp as ever." Henry's eyes narrowed. "That's what I always admired about you. You could deliver such stinging comebacks. It drove Robert crazy. That's why he was always playing such nasty tricks on you. And now"—he cleared his throat—"Father is stuck with me as his heir. A fitting—" He began to cough and pulled a lace handkerchief from his sleeve, covering his mouth. Henry turned away, wracked with violent spasms. When it calmed and he turned back, Ashley noticed flecks of scarlet on the balled handkerchief.

"Are you all right?"

"What? Hoping to rid yourself of me, too?" Henry cleared his throat again and fixed her with his intense blue eyes. "Let's have no pretense between us, Ashley. The only thing we share is a fondness for Mother and"—he smiled wickedly—"and our hatred for Nicholas." He dropped his voice and his expression became serious. "Because of that hatred, I'm going to share something with you. Nicholas hired someone to kill you."

"What? I don't believe it!"

"Shut up, you fool!" Henry whispered. "Do you want everyone on the James to hear? Robert told me the morning he was killed. Father is so intent upon having your estates that he's arranged to have you murdered."

Ashley took a step backward, staring at her half brother with numb incredulity. "Someone has been trying to kill me," she admitted, "but I never thought—"

"Thought what? That he didn't hate you enough? That Nicholas was too noble to do such a thing?" Henry scoffed. "Because of you, Father's never been able to forget that our mother slept with someone else first. He imagines that men laugh at him behind his back. You know how he is about money. He honestly believes that Morgan's Fancy should have gone to Mother instead of you."

"And then to you and Robert?"

Henry shrugged. "Probably me, since Robert would have Rosewood and the others. God only knows why Father would imagine I'd go north to live in the wilderness."

Ashley drew a ragged breath. "Does Cicely know?"

"Of course she doesn't know. I didn't know until Robert told me. He said he'd sent a message to you that mother was dying. Since the scheme was going so badly in Maryland, they intended to lure you here."

"And shoot me in my mother's house?"

"Nothing so crude. A riding accident. A fall overboard from the ship, perhaps. No one expected Gentleman Jim to interfere or . . ." Henry chuckled. "No one expected brother Robert to be shot by a jealous husband before the plot could thicken."

"I know Nicholas has always hated me," Ashley said softly, "but murder?" She covered her mouth with her hand and shook her head. "Do you know whom he hired?"

"Not by name, no. But if your new overseer is from Virginia, I'd be very suspicious of him. The price Father set on your head is enough to tempt any man."

Not Kelt, her inner voice screamed. It couldn't be!

Trembling, she raised her eyes to Henry's. "Any man," she repeated. "Any man, but not you?"

A dark flush rose up his neck and face. "I may not like you, big sister, but I draw the line at homicide." He shot her a warning glance. "Don't think to go to the sheriff with this information. I'll forget we ever had this conversation."

"Fair enough, and . . . thank you, Henry." Her mouth tasted of ashes. She had to think. Not Kelt! It couldn't be the man she had made love to just this morning. Maybe Henry was lying. He'd lied to her in the past. She'd be a fool to doubt Kelt on the word of a—

Cold reason flooded her brain. Kelt had appeared the night of the fire in the barn. He had been nearby when she'd taken the fall, when she'd been shot at. Could he have been behind the false message that Cicely was dying—the message carried by his friend, Philip Fraser?

"Go back to your plantation," Henry advised. "And get rid of the big Scot."

"I could tell Cicely," she said. "Mother would never—"

"Mother would never believe a word of it. You know how she is. She lives in her own dream world." He shook his head. "No, say anything to her and you put her life in danger, too. Go home, sister . . . and stay there. And just pray to God you outlive Father."

Chapter 16

Kelt's gaze rested on Ashley as she leaned against the rail of the ship. The hood of her rust-colored wool cape was thrown back and the breeze off the water played with the auburn curls that came loose from the velvet ribbon at the base of her neck. The red-gold of her hair shimmered in the setting sun, sending sharp rills of excitement to his artist's soul. If he had a brush and oils, he would paint her so—with the tumbled Tidewater sky and sparkling waves as a backdrop. She would have made an excellent subject; she had barely moved since they'd sailed out of the mouth of the James River.

Lovingly he caressed Ashley's proud outline with his eyes—the fall of her hair, the lines of her arms and shoulders, the curve of her back. She was a woman such as he had never met before. As hot-tempered and fearless as any Highland warrior, she had fought shoulder to shoulder with him on the deck of the *Snow Princess*. She had saved his life, not once but several times. He had known few men with her courage. Yet beneath that fire lay a loving woman, a woman capable of more passion than he had believed possible.

Kelt drew a long, ragged breath. The feelings he

had tried so hard to suppress were undeniable. He loved her. He loved Ashley Morgan as he had never loved another human being. A rueful smile twisted his lips as pain shot through him. Under other circumstances, in another time and place, he would have traded his immortal soul for the chance to make Ashley his wife. But now . . . He shifted his gaze to the glowing coral and pink of the western sky as the bitter taste of reality filled his mouth.

Ashley was a wealthy woman, a catch for any gentleman. Even with the shadow of her illegitimate birth, Ashley's broad lands and obvious physical attributes made her desirable as a wife. She was young and healthy, fit to bear sons. And more than one man would count her intelligence an asset despite her thorny temperament.

Whoever won her hand would take all. Morgan's Fancy would become his by right of that marriage. The land, bond servants, livestock, and money would pass into her husband's keeping. It was the money that was the problem.

Why in God's name couldn't ye have been a dairymaid? Or why couldn't he have been born with less pride? Most men looked for wealth in a woman. In Scotland, he would have taken his bride-to-be's dowry as a normal part of the joining of two great houses. He would have expected her to add to his estate. But now he had nothing. Nothing but a horse and the few personal belongings in his chest. The savings of ten years in the Colonies would not purchase a single field worker. Even if he could persuade her to accept him, if he took Ashley to wife, men would look askance at him and call him a fortune hunter behind his back. It would be a hard thing to live with—more so because he had no way to deny it.

The British had taken his land, his name, and his

family. They had exiled him from the country of his birth. They had imprisoned him and subjected him to torture. But they had never taken his pride. If he traded that pride now for a woman . . .

His own reluctance to marry wasn't the only barrier to their happiness. "Nay," he murmured silently. "There is more." She was hiding something, he was certain of it.

Ashley's preoccupation with the far horizon made him uneasy. He had no doubt she was watching for the skull and crossbones banner of the *Scarlet Witch*. But whether she watched in anticipation or in dread of another attack, he had no way of knowing.

She had been unnaturally silent since she'd visited her brother's grave. At first he had thought nothing of it. Sorrow at the sudden death of her half brother was easy to understand. But when the meeting with her mother and their return to Bantree had failed to revive her normal high spirits, he became concerned.

They had boarded the northbound merchant vessel at Bantree and Lady Pade had come down to the dock herself to bid them a safe voyage. Her son, James Pade, had been noticeably absent. "He was called away on urgent business," Lady Pade had informed them, explaining graciously that she herself had made the arrangements for their passage. The schooner was laden with cargo and bound for Chestertown. Not only did she carry a larger than normal crew, but she was also well protected with cannon. "You need have no fear for your safety," Lady Pade had said. "She will carry you directly to the dock at Morgan's Fancy."

Kelt could not have chosen a better ship himself. If Ashley watched for a skull and crossbones, did she know something the rest of them did not?

For the hundredth time he cursed himself for his

suspicions. In the months since he'd come to Morgan's Fancy, nothing had given him reason to doubt her honesty. He had come to respect and then to admire her strong character and shrewd business sense. He had pored over Ashley's account books himself and seen the state of her finances. If she were profiting from illicit activities, she had hidden it well. Gentleman Jim's infamy was no proof that Ashley was part of the dark brotherhood. Even the luck of her tobacco shipments could have been purely that—unbelievable luck. He smiled wryly. Was he making excuses for Ashley because of the way he felt about her? Was she innocent, as she said, or a very clever accomplice.

Unbelievable. The word echoed in his mind. If she was involved with her father and his pirate raids, she was flirting with the hangman's noose—and so was he. Her sex wouldn't protect her from a charge of piracy. As for a man who had already received the King's mercy . . . Kelt fingered the old manacle scar on his left wrist. He had been a prisoner of the crown once, a prisoner accused of high treason and murder. He had served time in prison before he was transported as an indentured servant. Another charge, no matter how flimsy the evidence, would see him hang from a gallows.

Kelt stood up and stretched, bracing his legs against the ship's roll. To the west, the sky was streaked with orange and gold as dusk began to settle over the wide expanse of water. To the east, the shoreline faded. Only a vague smudge of dark gave evidence of the thickly wooded shoreline. A smell of frying fish penetrated the strong scent of tar and tobacco. A red-faced sailor ambled past carrying a bucket of water. Kelt stared after him, secretly amused at the man's rolling gait. When his gaze shifted, he and Ashley were alone on the deck.

"Ashley," he called. His voice sounded strange to his ears. She seemed not to hear, and he repeated her name. "Ashley Morgan."

She turned to glance at him over her shoulder and he read the doubt in her eyes as clearly as a written page. "Kelt."

"Aye." He moved to stand beside her. "We must talk, lass."

She sighed, pulling the woolen cloak tighter and nodding. "I think we must," she murmured, her face impassive.

A sea gull circled the ship, swooping low before them and crying in a shrill, raucous tone. Ashley stared at the bird intently as it dipped to skim the blue-green water, then rose abruptly, flying east toward the far shore.

"What troubles ye so?"

Her fingers tightened on the rail and she moistened her lips, tilting her face up to meet his unwavering gaze. The huge cinnamon eyes seemed flecked with emerald as they searched his intently. "I saw my brother Henry at the burial ground," she said.

"And?"

"He told me my stepfather has hired someone to kill me." Her left hand curled into a knot. "He wants Morgan's Fancy. If I'm dead, my mother will inherit it . . . and through her, he'll gain control."

Kelt swore a foul oath as bands of tightness compressed his chest and a haze of anger clouded his brain. "Why the hell are ye staring so at me?" he snapped. "Do ye suppose I'm the mon?"

Ashley didn't blink. "Henry thinks so. You did appear at my plantation the night of the fire and you've been nearby whenever the attempts on my life were made."

"Do ye believe it?"

She swallowed and dropped her gaze to the deck at his feet as bright spots stained her cheeks. "No . . . no, I don't," she answered. "But I'd be a fool if I didn't consider it. With what Nicholas is offering for my life, you wouldn't have to work for anyone else again. You could manage your own place. It would be a great temptation for a landless man."

"By God, woman!" A white-hot fury whipped through him and he clenched his teeth until pain shot up his head. "Do ye think so little of me that you'd believe I'd do such a thing?" he demanded. "That I'd sleep in your bed and then—"

She threw up a hand to ward him off. "Stop being so damned self-righteous!" The dark eyes narrowed. "You doubted me about my connections with my father. You still think I may be a part of their illegal ventures. Can you deny it?"

His hands closed around her shoulders, gripping the wool of her cloak and biting into her flesh and bones until she caught her lower lip between her teeth and winced with pain. "Would ye ha' me go then, lass? Is that what ye want?"

"No, damn it," she flung back. Tears welled in her eyes and he relaxed his fingers.

"I'm sorry, Ashley. I wouldna hurt ye." His voice cracked with emotion and a bitter hollowness rose within him. "Say the word and I'll go."

She sighed and shook her head. "If you are trying to kill me, it would be just as easy to do so even if you aren't living on the plantation."

"Well?" He arched a thick eyebrow wickedly. "Would you expect a murderer to admit his deed to the intended victim? Wouldn't I lie to you, if I was guilty?''

She exhaled loudly, folding her arms across her chest and setting her chin in a stubborn line. ''You would . . . and I would lie to you if I were really working with my father.''

''What's t' be done then?''

''We go on as before,'' she said softly.

''And trust?''

She looked down at her outspread hands. ''I don't know,'' she admitted. ''But I think I'd rather have you put a bullet in my back than risk destroying what we have between us on the word of my brother.''

Even in the final grip of winter, the land was beautiful in Ashley's eyes. The gray of barren trees and fallow fields ran together, melting into the blue-gray sky. The ground beneath her stallion's hooves was rock-hard and the dried grass sparkled with morning frost.

Reining in the prancing animal, she wrapped the leather lines about her wrist and stood in the stirrups, shielding her eyes from the sun as she gazed south across the Chesapeake. Not a single sail broke the expanse of blue. She gave a sigh of relief and patted the bay's neck, speaking softly to him. ''Good boy, good Baron.''

In the weeks since their return to Morgan's Fancy, Ashley had kept a private vigil, riding out before dawn each morning to search the open water for signs of the *Scarlet Witch*. Her fervent hope that Gentleman Jim had taken his hunting elsewhere had been dashed two days ago, when news reached her of a battle that had taken place between the pirate ship and a British patrol boat within sight of the town of Oxford.

The patrol boat had taken a ball just below the waterline and had limped into town for repairs. She'd claimed heavy damage to the *Scarlet Witch,* and ships had combed the coves and creeks of the upper Chesapeake like hounds after a wounded fox.

"Damn you to hell," Ashley cried to the empty sky. "I hope they send you to the bottom." A lump formed in her throat, and she dug her knees into the stallion's side, urging him into a run. *Liar! Liar!* She didn't want Quincy dead. Not really. Despite what he'd done, he was her father.

She leaned low over the bay's neck, welcoming the cold wind that whipped the tears from her eyes. "Faster! Faster!" she shouted. Baron's hooves thundered against the frozen ground, streaking across the open pasture and sailing effortlessly over a narrow ditch. Ashley wrapped her fingers in his mane, letting herself become one with the horse, shutting out everything but the smell of horse and leather. If she could keep on running, maybe they could outrun the danger she felt threatening everything she had worked so hard to achieve.

A three-rail fence loomed up before them. Instinctively she braced herself for the jump, thrilling to the power of the stallion as he flew over it with nearly a hand span to spare. Her cocked hat blew off and she laughed, reining Baron in a wide circle, then leaning from the saddle to scoop up the hat and clamp it down over her forehead.

Foam streaked the animal's chest and legs; his great neck was wet with sweat. Crooning softly, Ashley slowed him to a trot. The run had taken some of the tension out of them both, but it had done nothing about the threat of the *Scarlet Witch*.

There had been enough work on the plantation to keep both her and Kelt busy from sunup to sundown.

The cold, crisp days had been perfect for lumbering. So long as rain or melting snow didn't turn the earth to mire, the men could topple the great white oaks and trim the branches with broadaxes. Patient teams of oxen could drag the logs to the dock to be stacked for sale.

The work was slow and backbreaking, but Ashley took pleasure in the thought that the towering trees were not wasted, as they were in the colonies to the north. Her grandfather had told her of acre after acre of prime timber, girdled and left to rot or piled in mountains to burn. The logs cut from Morgan's Fancy would make masts and hulls for sailing ships. Some cherry and walnut, rough sawn and dried on the plantation, would go to Philadelphia to be planed and dried again, eventually to become fine furniture.

The lumbering was Kelt's responsibility. Ashley supervised the planting of tobacco seed in the woodlots as well as the day-to-day duties of the dozens of workmen and women on the plantation. There were dozens of decisions to be made every day to make certain that all were fed and sheltered and given proper medical care. Food supplies had to be carefully watched over. It would be many months before the gardens produced fresh vegetables and if the women ran out of flour or salt, there would be no more without the expense of a trip to Chestertown to purchase supplies at inflated winter prices. Even with the success of her tobacco crop, Ashley was well aware of the importance of counting every shilling.

Ashley also operated a profitable fur trading business. She met with trappers, counting out the endless bales of beaver and deerskin, the thick wolf pelts and the occasional bearhide from west and north of the Chesapeake. Some of the men were Indians or half-breeds, with sloe-eyed wives and children peering shyly through the doorway of the hide house as Ashley made her purchases. Furs would bring a good price in Europe if they were properly cured and packed. Mari was invaluable, translating for those who spoke no English and advising Ashley with a frown or a wink on the quality or asking price of the pelts.

Ashley leaned forward in her saddle as the ringing of a broadax reached her ears. If she rode down to the lumbering site, would Kelt be swinging that ax? Resolutely she pushed away the desire to find out. She had promised to meet with Joshua and mark the boundaries of a new fence line. She must wait until dinner to see Kelt, or even until night if he took his nooning in the woods with the men, as he often did.

Heat rose in her throat and cheeks as she thought of the night to come. No matter how hard they worked in the daytime, the long hours of dark were theirs alone. Sometimes they played chess or cards, or simply sipped wine and laughed together over the day's successes and failures.

"I never knew how alone I was before he came," Ashley whispered to the big horse. Could she ever face the solitude again if Kelt left her? By the King's bare arse! Why couldn't she be like other women, content to come and go at her man's bidding? Why was she cursed with the desire to rule her own life, to make her own decisions and manage her own lands? "If I don't make a choice soon, I'll lose him," she said softly. It was true. She had read it in his eyes. He would marry her if she asked him, but he wouldn't stay as her lover. They had argued over it just the night before.

"And if you quicken with my child?" Kelt had shouted, throwing down the pad with the charcoal sketch he'd been making of her. "What then?"

"Then I'll have a child," she answered, more calmly than she felt.

"And what name will my son bear?"

"Morgan."

"Damn you to hell for being a stupid bitch!" Kelt's face blackened like a sudden storm cloud over the Chesapeake. "Do you think I'd have a son wi'oot my name? For all men to call bastard?"

"*I* survived it," she reminded him.

"Aye, survived. But tell me it hasna marked ye." He seized her shoulders and pulled her so close she could feel his breath on her lips. "I'll not be your kept man, Ashley. 'Tis unnatural."

"Your contract says overseer. Am I to blame if you come to my bed?"

"Aye." He groaned, bringing his mouth down on hers in a searing kiss of uncontrolled passion. Their angry words had ended, as they always did, in torrid lovemaking that settled nothing between them.

He awakened her in the shadowy darkness before dawn, tucking a coverlet tenderly about her shoulders. "I'm sorry, lass," he whispered. "I do love ye."

"And I love you," she declared, pulling him down to taste his lips, savoring the hard feel of his hands and taut body.

For long moments they lay wrapped in each other's arms, safe from the demands of the world. "Stay with me a little while," she begged him. "Hold me, Kelt . . . just awhile longer."

"Nay, sweeting. I canna," he answered. "For the servants will be about and some might see me coming from this room. I willna give them more to say than they already have." He kissed her lips and the tip of her nose. "A good day to ye, Mistress Morgan. And dinna give too much for your beaver skins today. Mari told me you're getting soft."

"You're welcome to do the job," she offered willingly.

"Nay, not me." He laughed. "A haggling merchant I'm not, nor ever shall be. Gi' it over to Mari, if it's too much for ye. She speaks that wild tongue."

"You see," she said, pushing back the covers and sitting up. "You know nothing about Indians. Mari cares nothing for profit. She would give whatever they asked. You're hopeless, the both of you."

So they'd shared laughter in their last minutes together before the day began. And then she had dressed and gone downstairs to take up her duties as Morgan Fancy's mistress. And with the daylight had come the familiar fears. She loved Kelt, but she couldn't trust him, and he trusted her even less.

Baron turned his head toward the house, but Ashley rained him back firmly. "Not yet," she murmured, more to herself than to the big animal. "There's one more place I want to check."

They followed the woods line for a few hundred yards, then cut into the forest, following an old game trail. Only an occasional crow and the chatter of a squirrel disturbed the solitude of the virgin woodland. Mari said the ground here was sacred. Some of the giant oaks, Ashley guessed, were hundreds of years old. She knew she would never permit lumbering on this section. Sacred Indian land or not, it was too beautiful, too peaceful to disturb.

Ahead the trees thinned to cedar and yellow pine. Beyond that, a meadow ran down to a deep, narrow creek. This was the spot she had to be sure of, the place where she had first met her father.

Tying Baron in a grove of pines, Ashley continued on foot across the meadow to the edge of the water.

Trees lined the banks, broken here and there by patches of reeds and open marshland. Taking care not to soak her boots, Ashley slipped into the reeds, pushing them aside and working her way to the creek bank.

Trembling, she took a deep breath and separated a handful of marsh grass. To the left, the surface of the water was unmarred by any sign of human life. A pair of black ducks paddled only a few feet from her hiding place, unaware of her presence. Relieved, she turned her gaze upstream, already laughing at herself for her foolish fears. Then she froze, catching her lower lip between her teeth and biting down to keep from crying out.

In the sheltered cove, surrounded on three sides by trees, the *Scarlet Witch* rode at anchor. Numbly Ashley stared at her father's ship, taking in the beached rowboat and the crewmen gathered on the far side of the creek. She let the grass fall back into place. Her worst nightmares had been realized. Gentleman Jim had returned to Morgan's Fancy.

Chapter 17

The image of the *Scarlet Witch* haunted Ashley as she mounted Baron and rode back through the forest to meet Joshua. How long would it be before some bondman saw the smoke from a careless fire or came upon the ship while searching for a stray cow? Repairs to the schooner could not be made overnight. Even though the creek was on the farthest corner of the plantation, it was still her land. If Kelt learned that the *Scarlet Witch* was anchored on Morgan's Fancy, it would be his duty to report the pirates to the authorities. Nothing she could say or do would convince him she was not a party to their crimes.

How many times had Quincy hidden there? Usually he would come at least once in the spring and again in late summer or fall. Her grandfather had never known, although Ashley was certain Mari did. The Indian woman knew all too well that if Ash Morgan and Gentleman Jim had met, it would have been over the crossed steel of dueling rapiers. Old Ash had never forgiven her father for seducing Cicely and had sworn to kill him on sight. If he had ever guessed that Quincy was using Morgan's Fancy to hide from the British navy . . . Ashley shuddered. Once aroused, her grandfather's temper would have put the fear of God into Blackbeard himself! Nothing would have prevented a battle to the death between the two men.

Joshua pulled her firmly back to the present with a repeated question. Patiently Ashley stooped and drew an outline of the new pasture fence. "I want no holes dug until well after the thaw, but you can put two men to cutting cedar and thorn trees for the posts. I mean to raise work horses, mules, and milk cows for sale, as well as oronookoes."

Joshua spat on the ground and rolled his knit cap into a ball. "It's a waste o' good cleared ground, mistress. What wi' the high price o' tobaccy, ye'd do better t' put the lot in that."

"Tobacco's high because of the war in Europe. When King George signs a peace treaty with France and Spain, the price will drop again. Tobacco's our cash crop, but I don't want it to be ten years from now."

Joshua vented his disapproval on a tuft of dry weed, grinding it into the ground with the heel of his shoe. "Old Master Ash put his land in tobacco."

"He's dead." Ashley turned and motioned for her horse, taking the reins in hand and swinging into the saddle in a single, smooth action. "And he left Morgan's Fancy in my care. Right or wrong, I'll make the decisions now." Dismissing the man with a nod, she turned Baron's head toward the manor house. Thank God her grandfather was safely in his grave. He and Quincy slicing each other to pieces before her eyes was the one thing she *didn't* have to worry about.

That consolation carried her through the rest of the day's duties, making it possible for her to settle an argument between Short John's wife and the weaver, Sarah Reid, without wholesale bloodshed. The fracas had come on the heels of an afternoon of crisis.

First, there had been no dinner. When Ashley had gone to the kitchen to find out why, she'd nearly been suffocated by the thick smoke of burning corn mush. Joan's reply to Ashley's mild admonishments had been to tear at her clothes and shriek like a slaughtered shoat. She was with child, she admitted, pregnant by either Martin Hopkins's blacksmith or Daniel the stableman. And if one of them wasn't forced to marry her, Joan would throw herself down the well!

They had barely opened the doors and windows to let the smoke out when Dickon came crying to the back door. He'd slipped and fallen through the hayloft opening. A nasty gash above his temple dripped blood and his left arm had a suspicious crook in it.

Setting the arm and stitching the boy's head had taken the better part of an hour. The break seemed clean and the skin hadn't been broken. "You'll be right as rain," Ashley had promised him. A copper penny and a handful of molasses candy had brought back his usual smile.

"Master Saxon will be proud o' ye when I tell him how brave ye were," Joan said. "Jest like a wild Injun."

An Indian attack would have caused less screaming than what came from the dairy only minutes later. Ashley had run across the yard, along with a half dozen others, to find out who had been murdered. Two girls ran out of the log building, each shouting and wailing more loudly than the other.

Ashley grabbed the closest one by the arm and gave her a shake. "What's wrong?" she demanded. "Is someone hurt?"

The bondwoman stared at her mistress with wide blue eyes, threw her apron over her face, and began to wail in German.

"Meta don't speak no English," Joan reminded Ashley smugly. "She ain't too smart."

The second dairymaid found her voice. "A rat, mistress! Big as a dog, 'e were, wi' teeth like—"

"A rat! All this commotion over a rat?" Ashley yanked open the door and looked at the destruction the hysterical girls had created. The normally spotless floor was awash in milk and spilled curds; a large mound of butter lay by the door sill and an uncured cheese was visible on the plank floor under the worktable. Nothing moved.

The room was small, whitewashed, and spotless, with a sound floor and ceiling. If a rat had gotten in through an open door, it must still be there. Ashley whistled for Jai and the big dog came running. "Find the rat, boy," she ordered. "Go get him."

As the shaggy tail disappeared through the door, Ashley shut it firmly behind him and turned to her people. "What are you all standing around for? Have you nothing to do?" She put her hands on her hips and glared in an unconscious imitation of her grandfather. "Is all work to stop for an overgrown mouse?" she demanded.

Quickly the men and women scattered to their various tasks, leaving only Ashley and the two flustered maids. " 'Twere a big 'un," the freckle-faced Irish girl insisted. "This big." She held out her hands to measure a space as wide as her own shoulders. "It run up Meta's leg!"

"Ja! Ja!" The German girl nodded vigorously, obviously understanding the fervent gestures more than the words.

A snarl from inside the dairy was followed immediately by a high-pitched squeal. Ashley opened the door cautiously and Jai trotted out with a large rat between his teeth. He dropped it before his mistress's feet. The rat's face was smeared with cream.

The restoration of the dairy took the remainder of the afternoon. Patiently Ashley watched as the open tubs of butter and cream, and the morning's milk, were carried to the pigpens and poultry yard, and the floor and tables were scrubbed clean. Only the sealed containers and cheeses hanging from the rafters were safe. It was maddening for Ashley to have to oversee such routine tasks, but she knew that if she didn't personally watch to see that her orders were carried out, the contaminated milk and butter would show up on the plantation table. To the two bondwomen, a small matter such as rodent hair or tracks would seem no reason to throw out good food. Ashley had few illusions about the behavior of fifteen-year-old bondmaids.

The fight between Sarah Reid and Short John's wife was not so easily settled. Ashley had just begun to count the measures of seed corn for the coming spring planting when a little girl burst into the barn. "Mistress! Come quick!" the child panted. "They're gonna kill each other!"

Ashley threw a bridle over Scarlet's head and rode bareback to the line of houses just beyond the orchard. A knot of screaming women had gathered around two figures rolling on the ground. Sarah Reid had Short John's wife by the hair and was beating her head against the hard-packed earth. Sarah's dress was ripped to the waist and one shriveled breast hung bare. Her lip was split and an eye swollen closed. Still, the older woman clung to Short John's wife with the tenacity of a terrier.

The air rang with profanity as the black-haired slattern on the bottom spewed filth with the virulent imagination of a dockside harpy. Ashley slid from the mare's back and pushed through the crowd to see Sarah tightening her fingers around the younger woman's throat.

"Stop it!" Ashley commanded. Neither woman seemed to hear. Short John's wife continued to pound Sarah Reid about the head and face, raking her with dirty fingernails and lashing out with knees and feet. Sarah held on and tightened her grip. "Separate them!" Ashley cried to the onlookers. Shaking their heads, the women and children moved back, widening the circle. Short John's wife was beginning to choke.

"Fetch water!" Ashley ordered. "From the well! All of you!"

The younger woman's face had begun to blacken when the first bucket of cold water splashed over the two. Sarah Reid screamed and fell backward. Three more buckets soaked clothes and hair, and Short John's wife began to sob.

Ashley signaled a halt. "That's enough." She turned a hard face on Sarah. "What's this about?"

"She's been sniffin' around my boy!" Sarah's teeth chattered as she pointed an accusing finger at the sobbing woman on the ground. "He's only fourteen. He's a good boy! I won't have him ruined by trash like her!"

"Liar," Short John's wife said. Her voice was a strangled whisper. "She's crazy! What would I want wi' her horse-face son when I kin get any man on this place t' warm my bed?"

"Whore!" Sarah flung back.

"Halfwit!"

"Slut!"

"Slattern!"

"Bumpbacon!"

"Poxbox!"

"Enough! Both of you!" Ashley shouted. "Get back to your cabins and make yourselves decent. Another word and I'll have the skin off your backs." The women hurried to obey, each followed by her own band of sympathizers.

Scarlet whinnied and Ashley turned to face Kelt riding up behind her. ''Why didn't you get here five minutes earlier?'' she asked.

He rolled his eyes heavenward. ''It seems I make a practice of arriving too late to break up your fights.'' He glanced at Sarah Reid's departing back. ''And this one may even have been enjoyable.''

''You're welcome to them,'' she said, catching Scarlet's mane and leaping up on her back. ''But you don't seem to have had much luck taming Short John's wife. She's behind this fracas, as usual.'' Ashley brought the mare up beside Kelt's dappled-gray and looked up into his face. ''Are you certain you've not fallen for her charms? She insinuated as much.''

He chuckled. ''I like my lassies clean, thank you.'' His features turned serious. ''One of the men found the black mare up to her belly in mud. We've spent most of the afternoon digging her out. I've had her brought back to the barn, but I fear she'll drop her colt early.''

Ashley swore under her breath. ''Not today. I can't take another thing today.'' She shook her head. ''I was counting on this colt. The mare's close to twenty years old. We'll not get many more from her. Damn!'' Ashley pulled off her cocked hat and ran a hand through her hair. ''My grandfather brought Dulcinea by ship from Normandy when she was a yearling. She's descended from the old warhorses and he thought he'd get a good strain of work animals out of her. Last year she dropped a dead horse colt. I wanted at least one more filly out of her to take her place. She's bred to Baron.''

''She was exhausted, but still on her feet. I thought it best to have her led up to the barn. We can do more for her there than we can in the field. She's nae gone into labor yet.'' Kelt's eyebrows raised in mock recrimination. ''Ye should ha' taken my place in the woods this morning. Then ye could ha' complained about a bad day. Your day's chores were nae oot of the ordinary, as I recall. A lass tends to exaggerate.'' He held up his hands to show the fresh blisters across the palms. ''My hands will be a week in healing. I'll nae be able to wield a paintbrush properly until they do.''

''Have you finished my picture?'' Ashley asked innocently.

''Nay.'' Kelt's head snapped up. ''And what do you know of that? Have you been poking where you ha' no business?''

''It's very good, but . . .''

''But?''

''But it doesn't look much like me.''

''Aye.''

''I've seen the sketches you've done of Joan and Thomas, and even little Dickon. They're so real they could come alive.''

Kelt's lips compressed tightly.

''Mine looks like a portrait.''

''Aye.'' A curious yearning flickered behind the gray eyes. ''She's beautiful, is she nae?''

Ashley nodded. ''It's very flattering.'' Her gaze met his and held as a spark of white-hot desire arced between them. ''Almost as though you'd painted my mother instead of me—but I don't look anything like her.'' Ashley felt a familiar excitement throb within her. Her breathing suddenly quickened and she turned her face away to prevent him from reading the message in her eyes.

''There is a resemblance, elusive but it's there,'' Kelt said. ''No man would deny your mother's beauty, but ye have something more.''

Ashley laughed. "Calluses?"

"Nay, lass. 'Tis a flame that glows within ye. A flame I canna catch wi' brush and oil. But I will." He grinned. "Calluses and all—I will."

Ashley felt the heat rise in her throat and cheeks. He would come to her tonight; she knew it. Unconsciously she arched her back and softened her expression. She tried to force her voice to normal tones. "There'll be no decent meal for supper unless you make it."

Wordlessly Kelt held up a wild duck tied to the far side of his saddle.

"Roast duck?"

"Wi' sweet potatoes and berry tarts. Can you find us a decent bottle of wine?"

"If you'll make scones."

"Ha' ye learned nothing? Scones are nae for a supper."

"No scones, no wine," she threatened. "The little ones, shaped like triangles."

" 'Twould be more natural if you would learn to cook, woman," he teased.

"You may be right, but I'll not have the time to learn until you've grown a gray beard to your knees. If you want to eat now, you cook."

Grumbling good-naturedly, Kelt began to relate his morning's experiences with the lumbering crew. Ashley gave him her full attention, glad for the easy laughter and the sharing of mundane affairs. It was a companionship she hadn't known before. Even with her grandfather, it hadn't been the same. He had been the teacher, she the student. With Kelt she felt equal and the quiet contentment of companionship was spiced with the thrill of what would come in the night.

Ashley tensed, startling the mare and causing her

to dance sideways. What was she thinking of? There could be no equality between men and women. What she and Kelt shared now could never be if they were husband and wife. If she married . . . Her knees tightened at Scarlet's sides. If Kelt became her husband, he would be master of Morgan's Fancy. He would control the money and the land. He could sell the plantation or gamble it away if it pleased him. He could even send her back to England as Charles Wright had done with his wife.

Mary Wright had inherited her plantation from her first husband. But after two years of marriage, Charles had ordered her to his family's home in Lincoln. He had separated her from her small son, keeping the boy with him. Now he kept company with a former indentured criminal—a woman he called his housekeeper, but who had given him two children in three years.

Ash Morgan had gone to great lengths to leave Morgan's Fancy to Ashley, and he had warned her against foolishly giving her trust and fortune to a man. Even a man like Kelt might change after they were married. Ashley drew in a deep breath and urged the sorrel mare into a canter. She was as close to happy as she had ever been since she was a child. To risk it all would be madness.

Supper was all Kelt had promised it would be. Later, after spending a reasonable time going over the plantation ledgers, Ashley ordered hot water for a bath to be carried up to her chamber. She bid Kelt a polite good-night and went upstairs alone, trying to banish the worry that nagged her—the thorny problem of the *Scarlet Witch* anchored on her land. If Kelt found out before she told him, he would be furious. He would surely believe she knew about the ship and had given her permission for it to hide there.

Resolutely Ashley pushed her problems to the far corners of her mind and slid into the bath. The warm water and soap felt wonderful, but she didn't linger in the wooden tub. She quickly washed her hair and wrapped it in a thick towel, drying her body before the fire. After donning a clean dressing gown and soft leather moccasins, she poured wine into two silver goblets and set them on the table next to her bed. Tonight Kelt would be coming to her chambers. The thought was wickedly exciting and she laughed to herself. He could enjoy the luxury of a leisurely tub bath and she would have the pleasure of watching him.

For once they were alone in the house. Thomas was in Chestertown buying supplies for his school and Joan was spending the night with the blacksmith, presumably to inform him of his status as future father. The kitchen maid had gone back to her mother's house and no one had seen her for several days. Ashley meant to make the most of the privacy, even to shutting Jai in the kitchen.

Perhaps tonight, after they had made love, she could tell Kelt about the *Scarlet Witch*. Perhaps she could make him understand that she hated Quincy and all he stood for, but loved him too much to turn him in. Telling Kelt would be better than having him find out on his own.

She heard Kelt's hurried steps in the hall and turned toward the door. "I thought—"

His big form filled the doorway. "The bath will ha' to wait. Your mare's gone into labor. Ye'd better dress and come doon. 'Tis nae a normal birth."

In minutes she joined him in the barn. The black mare lay on her side in the corner box stall. An anxious groom tugged at her halter.

"I heard her holler, mistress. It ain't natural fer her to be down so soon."

Ashley waved the man away and approached the massive animal. Dulcinea's neck was damp to the touch and a sheen of sweat covered her swollen belly. The mare raised her head and nickered plaintively as Ashley stroked the silken hide. "Easy girl, good girl," she soothed. She ran her hands down the thick legs and over the shaggy fetlocks, clean now of the black mud that had held her prisoner for so many hours that afternoon.

The mare groaned, grinding her teeth and rolling her eyes as spasms of excruciating pain gripped her body in an iron vise. She lashed out with a hind leg and Kelt dragged Ashley out of the way.

"Watch yourself!" he warned. "One of those hooves could crush your skull."

"Do you think we can get her on her feet?" Ashley asked, moving toward Ducinea's head. "She needs to walk."

"Aye, but I doubt she has the strength. She's old, lass, and tired. Listen to her breathing." The mare's harsh rasping in the quiet of the barn was impossible to miss.

"She was all right before supper," Ashley said. "I checked her myself." She motioned to the groom to bring a bucket of water and knelt by the mare's head, lifting handfuls to the graying muzzle. Gratefully the horse took a little, then dropped her head to the hay and closed her eyes. Ashley patted her neck and head, whispering endearments.

Daniel moved to the horse's hindquarters and lifted her tail. "No sign of the colt," he said, frowning.

"We'll stay wi' her," Kelt said. "You can go to your bed."

"You certain ye won't need me, mistress?" Daniel asked.

Ashley shook her head. "No. You've put in a long

day. We'll wait. It may be hours before anything happens."

"Thank'ee, Mistress Ashley. I'll do that." With a tug of his forelock, he left the barn.

Minutes slipped into hours as the two crouched beside the laboring mare. Kelt hung two lanterns at the corners of the box stall; the rest of the barn lay in shadow. The other horses were quiet for the most part; Ashley was certain they were aware of the black mare's critical condition.

Kelt lay back against a pile of hay and stared up at the massive beams overhead. Outside a storm was rising, but the barn was snug and tight. Nothing swayed in the wind and the heat of the animals kept it warm. He was proud of the structure. The design was a good one and with luck it would stand for two hundred years.

Ashley shivered as the first rumblings of thunder penetrated the thick walls. "Did you hear that?" Her voice echoed in the stillness.

"Aye, thunder." Kelt leaned forward and stretched his arms, rubbing the cramps from shoulders that had swung a broadax for hours that morning.

"It's early in the year for a thunderstorm," Ashley said.

She'd always been terrified of thunderstorms. When she was a small child, she had been taken to visit her mother in Virginia and woke crying in the night, afraid of the thunder and lightning. Nicholas had called her a crybaby and refused to let her get into her mother's bed, and when she continued crying, he'd thrown her kicking and screaming out of the house into the rain. She'd beat against the door until her hands were bloody, but no one had come to let her in until the storm passed. Lightning had struck a tree in the yard, bringing a branch down only feet from where she'd crouched.

Strange, she couldn't remember being let in. In the morning, her mother's face had been bruised and swollen. When she asked what had happened, Cicely had shushed her. She'd even tried to convince Ashley that she'd never been out in the storm, that it had been a bad dream—but Ashley knew better. It had been another secret she'd kept from her grandfather. She'd been—

Kelt laid a hand on her shoulder and she jumped. "Oh, you frightened me," Ashley admitted. "I guess I was half asleep."

"You're trembling, lass. Be ye cold?" He knelt beside the mare and laid his hand on the horse's neck. "She's growing weaker."

Ashley shook her head. "No, I'm not cold." A lightning bolt struck so close that the horse quivered with fear. Ashley tried to cover her own terror by concentrating on the mare. Whispering to the animal in soft, soothing tones, she ran her hands along the animal's belly to try and locate the colt. "It must be stuck," she said to Kelt. "If we can't turn it, they'll both die."

"Ha' ye done it before?"

"No." Ashley shook her head. "I've watched my grandfather, but I've never turned one. He said you just reach for all the parts and straighten them out."

Kelt looked unconvinced as he unfastened his cloak and pushed back his shirt sleeves. "I'll have to wash up. Do you think you can hold her or should I call some of the grooms?"

Another pain caught the mare and she moaned, thrashing with her forelegs. "There's no time," Ashley cried. "Do it now if you can."

Cautiously Kelt moved to the mare's hindquarters and waited until the pains had ceased. Ashley took firm hold of the halter and began to murmur to the exhausted animal as Kelt inserted his hand into the birth channel and felt for the colt's legs.

Sweat ran down Ashley's face as she tried to quiet the mare. "Good Dulcinea," she whispered. "Easy . . . easy, girl."

Kelt's face was taut with concentration. "I've got one leg, but I can't tell if it's front or back. The colt may be breech. I'm going to pull with the next pain. Steady her if you can."

The mare heaved herself up on her front legs as a great gush of blood and fluid ran down her hind legs. "Now, push!" Kelt cried. He gave a tug and a pair of tiny hooves appeared. "Once more now!" When the spasms came again, he pulled hard and a bay foul slid out onto the damp hay.

Ashley knelt beside it and cleaned out the little mouth. The baby sneezed and gave a high squeak. "She's alive!" Ashley cried. "It's a filly and she's alive!"

The mother gathered her hind legs under her and got to her feet, pushing at the foal with gentle eagerness. The bay filly kicked her spindly legs and squealed, staggering to her feet and nuzzling at the big mare's belly. Dulcinea began to lick at the foal's hindquarters, then she stopped, stiffened, and moaned again. Almost immediately, the forefeet and nose of a second foal appeared.

"No wonder she had all the trouble," Kelt said, easing the second baby into the world. "This one's a black." He laid it gently on the straw. "You got yourself a second filly, lass. Two for the price of one."

Ashley laughed out loud, wiping away tears of joy. Outside, thunder rolled across the heavens, drowning out the patter of rain on the roof, but her fear was lost in the delight of the newborn foals. Kelt plunged his hands into a bucket of water, washing away the worst of the blood and birth fluids, as she began to dry off the second filly with handfuls of hay.

"I think I need that bath now, lass," he said, shaking his hands dry. "The mother should have warm mash and plenty of warm water with molasses and vinegar in it." He reached down to pat the rump of the firstborn. The minute bay filly was making soft little grunts as she nursed greedily at the mare's teats. "I'll wake the grooms. Someone should watch over them for the rest of the night."

"It's all right, I can stay," Ashley offered.

Kelt grinned wickedly at her. "Nay, woman. I ha' more important things for ye to do between now and daybreak. Didna ye promise we would ha' the house to ourselves this night?"

Ashley blushed. "Yes, but—"

"Nay buts. Yond mare is content and I mean to be the same." He chuckled deep in his throat as his eyes devoured her. "Is there no reward for a starving mon?"

"You can't be hungry," Ashley protested teasingly. "Not after you ate most of that duck at supper."

"Aye, but I am. I've a mind to taste a bit of sweet"—Kelt's eyes twinkled—"and perhaps a tasty bit o' breast and thigh."

Chapter 18

Kelt gazed down at the red-gold mass of Ashley's unbound hair spread across his naked chest and smiled. They'd had little sleep that night, but he'd gladly work the coming day tired for such a reward. The hairs at the base of her neck were soft and curling; he couldn't resist brushing the intimate spot with the tips of his fingers. Ashley sighed sleepily, nestling even closer and bringing her bare leg provocatively close to the source of his growing agitation. Tenderly he caressed the curve of her spine, lingering at the hollow of her back, then spanning her hip with exploring fingers.

"Ashley." He cupped a round buttock playfully. "The sun is well up, Mistress Morgan. Your kingdom awaits."

She groaned and burrowed her face under his arm. "Go away," she murmured. "I've paid my taxes."

"What? Do ye think me a tax collector?" Rolling her onto her back, he pinned her to the bed and kissed her full on the mouth. Saucy eyes laughed up at him as her arms wrapped around his neck and she gave as good as she got.

"Do you make a habit of ravishing sleeping maids?" she whispered.

Ashley's tongue flicked against his lower lip and then darted out to touch his. A shaft of fire shot through him and he joined his mouth to hers, savoring the sweet sensation of her breasts pressed against his chest and her undulating hips that fanned a white-hot desire in his loins.

"If not . . . you should." Her voice was strained and husky as her nails dug furrows of pleasure down his back.

"Witch." His breath came hard and ragged as he brought his lips down to taste the tantalizing bud of a satin-skinned breast. Ashley moaned with delight, parting her legs to receive the full power of his thrusting manhood.

With a cry he plunged inside her, unable to hold back the primitive instinct to possess her fully, to spill his seed in her womb and make her irrevocably his—forever. To his joy, she met him thrust for thrust, mingling her passion with his own, blending flesh and spirit until he reached an earth-shattering release, a rapture greater than he had ever known.

They drifted off to sleep wrapped tightly in each other's embrace, and when he woke, it was to find her staring at him intently. "Whist, lass," he murmured. "Did I leave ye behind? I wouldna—"

She laughed and shook her head. "No, no, I wanted you," she admitted. "I still do."

"Atchh, ye'll be the death of a mon," he protested. "Even a Scot has his limits." Kelt ran his hands through his rumpled hair and sat up. "What time is it? There's an auction of bondmen in Chestertown today and I mean to be there."

Ashley slid from the bed and caught up her wrapper from the floor. From the window she could look out across the greening fields. A shiver of happiness passed through her and she hugged herself. Spring was the time of rebirth, of renewal. Somehow she would find a way to make thing work out. She couldn't lose Kelt or Morgan's Fancy. They both meant more to her than life itself.

She turned and looked at him, forcing her thoughts away from their lovemaking and to what Kelt had just said about going to Chestertown. "You'd best take the sloop then," she replied softly. "I'll come, too. I have financial matters to see to." She leaned forward at the waist, brushing out her hair with long, even strokes. "Do you think we can afford more workers? Even with the tobacco—"

"We canna afford not to ha' them. And if I can find a likely woman, I'll buy us a cook. There's no excuse for putting up wi' Joan's nonsense. I canna be coming in from the fields ever' morning to make the day's dinner for the rest of my life!"

"And what makes you think you'll be here the rest of your life?" She paused in the act of drawing on a stocking and glanced back at him, not quite hiding the thread of steel in the teasing question.

Kelt dropped his feet to the floor and stood up. "I ha' decided, lass. We canna continue to go on like this. I know your wealth and my lack o' it will be a problem between us, but I want ye for my wife. I want us to be married—now. As soon as the banns can be cried."

Ashley's face darkened and he seized her roughly by the shoulders. "Nay!" he insisted. "Ye must hear me oot for once! If ye wed, then your stepfather would ha' nothing to gain by your death."

"Let me go!" She jerked free. "I won't marry you, Kelt. I told you that before."

"Then this"—he motioned toward the bed—"means nothing more to you than a roll in the hay wi' your hired man."

Ashley's hand lashed out and slapped him across the cheek. "You bastard!"

Kelt threw up an arm to block a second blow, then seized her wrists and pinned them behind her. She kicked him sharply in the shin and he shoved her backward onto the bed. A trickle of blood ran down his chin where a tooth had cut his lip. Kelt's hands knotted into fists as he stood over her, daring her to move, then he turned away, nearly speechless with rage.

"I'm . . . sorry," she stammered, covering her mouth with her hand. "I didn't mean—"

"Damn ye for a wave-tossed kelpie!" he swore. "Can you nae see that this way lies only heartbreak and sorrow for us both?" He grabbed for his clothes, thrusting his legs into the doeskin breeches. "It's over between us. I'll see ye through the planting," he said, "but then ye must find another overseer. I willna live like this."

"Kelt, please . . ."

He picked up his boots and vest and put his hand on the brass doorknob. "Ye ha' my notice, Ashley. I'll not tell ye again . . . and I'll never ask ye to be my wife again, either." A curious moisture clouded his vision. "The pity is, I believe ye love me as much as I love ye."

"I do love you," she said. "I just don't want to marry. Not you—not anyone."

Kelt closed the door firmly behind him.

Chestertown bustled with the air of a growing metropolis. The town square was crowded with farmers and merchants come to view the afternoon's auction. Uniformed soldiers made their way down the dusty street in groups of twos and threes, occasionally calling out to passing maids or unaccompanied townswomen. The taverns were packed, and smells of roasting pork and beef wafted through the air to mingle with the strong scents of passing livestock and the ever-present tobacco leaf.

Children and dogs darted in and out of the throng, shouting and laughing. Babies wailed. Respectable mothers called for their offspring, mistresses for their wayward servants. At the edge of the square, a group of half-grown boys tossed eggs at the drunken occupant of the newly erected stocks and two Dutch sailors tossed pennies beneath a lightning-scarred cedar tree. Women had erected booths to sell hot meat pies and gingerbread. Sweet cider could be had at a price within the reach of the barefoot boys.

A woman was sitting on a wooden crate of chickens, holding up a fat hen by the legs for all to see. A circle of feathers surrounded her modest establishment. "Plump birds!" she cried. "Plump birds! Tender as a baby's bottom!"

Kelt stood near the chicken woman, talking quietly with Ashley's neighbor, Martin Hopkins. "It's tempting," he said, "but ye must know how she feels aboot the issue o' slavery."

Hopkins nodded. "I know. That's why I bring the matter up with you, instead of Ashley. I'd not part with them if I'd not lost the whole of last year's crop. Damn me, but your mistress has the devil's own luck." Martin reached up to scratch beneath his dusty wig. "I don't need to tell you, Saxon, that I'm hurting. You can't imagine the expenses a family man has. And my wife—a good woman, mind you—will hear nothing of cutting household expenses." He sighed sorrowfully. "They go on the block right after the bondmen. It's nothing to me if you buy them or another. But Abe is a skilled carpenter, and George and Tom can cut timber with the best. Abe has a wife, and I'm hoping that whoever buys him will buy Elvy and her daughter. The girl's fourteen and a hard worker, but I won't lie to you. She's got a clubfoot. She's been trained in the house, but she's slow."

Kelt let out a low whistle. "Five slaves?" He laughed. "Ye mean to see me in yond' stocks." He looked pensive. "I'd want to look at them myself, but I take your word that Elvy's a good cook. I came looking for woodsmen and a woman. I just didn't think to buy slaves."

"One or all," Martin said. "I could give you a good deal on the lot. I'm saving the commission if I don't put them up for auction and I'd know they'd be getting a good home." He scratched the back of his neck. "It's bad business, selling slaves. I don't like it. They're the last of what I have. I'll tell you the truth, I'll buy no more. But I don't have the money to salve my conscience by setting them free." Martin wiped his damp hands on his breeches. "In the fall, you let me know what ship is carrying Ashley's tobacco. I'll put mine nowhere else." He paused. "There's some say she's got the seventh sight, but that's all right by me. I only wish I'd shipped with her this year. If I lose this year's crop, my land's in danger."

"You're nae alone in that. If this cursed war doesn't end soon, England may expect little profit from her colonies."

"Would you like to go and see them, or do you want to talk to Ashley first?"

"Let's talk wi' your people, sir." Kelt grinned. "We both know what Mistress Morgan would say. But I have the authority to make the purchase. If we make a bargain, ye need ha' no fear that I'll go back on it."

* * *

"You did *what?*" Ashley stared at Kelt in disbelief, unaware that the fork had slipped from her fingers to clatter across the inn's table. She half rose in her seat, her eyes narrowing in anger. "You bought slaves for Morgan's Fancy?"

Kelt slid into the chair across from her. "Sit down, woman, and close your mouth. People are staring at ye."

"Are they now?" Her tones dropped to a cold, precise pattern. She glanced about the small private room reserved for the gentlefolk. Most of the tables were occupied by men and women, not a few of which were staring at her. "I would think they would attend to their own affairs and let me tend to mine." Ashley glared fiercely at a bewigged gentleman sipping tea across from them. The man flushed a deep shade of purple and turned his face away.

"Hear me oot before ye—"

"There's nothing you could say that would make it right," she flung back. "Martin will have to take them back." Ashley's hands knotted under the table and she forced herself to quell the trembling. "I won't have it, Kelt. You knew it all along!"

The innkeeper appeared beside them. "What would you like, sir? We've some very nice roast goose, or perhaps a clam pie."

"The goose," Kelt said, "and bread and cheese."

"Very good, sir. And to drink with your meal?"

"Ale."

Ashley waited until the man had gone back to the kitchen, then pushed her own plate away. "You had no right!"

"You know better."

She swore softly under her breath. "They're going back, Kelt. And you're going to straighten it all out with Martin."

"On a cold day in hell." His voice was a soft burr, the Scots lilt so heavy she could hardly make out the words. He reached for the thick slice of brown bread and butter on her plate. "If you're going to let this go to waste—"

"Not a chance!" she said, giving the plate a vicious shove across the table.

Kelt caught the edge of the plate, narrowly avoiding having her meal dumped into his lap. "Ashley."

She heard the threat, but was too caught up in her own anger to heed it. "Bastard." Deliberately she picked up her pewter goblet. His hand closed over her wrist and squeezed until she thought her bones would crack.

"No scenes, Mistress Morgan. Put it down."

She flexed her fingers, but her wrist might have been caught in solid rock. "Let me go," she whispered. She could feel curious eyes on her back and she blinked back tears of rage. "I'll kill you."

"The wine, m'lady."

Defeated, she set the wine goblet back on the table. He released her wrist immediately. "If I was a man—"

"If you were a mon, we'd nae ha' this problem, would we?"

A maidservant came toward them with a platter of food. Ashley stood up. "Enjoy your goose, sir," she said coldly, "and tend to the matter we spoke of as soon as you are finished." She threw a coin on the table. "I'll pay for Master Saxon's meal. He works for me—at least for the time being."

Kelt's parting sarcastic chuckle burned in her ears as she made her way down the hill to the dock. Damn his arrogant disregard for her feelings! She called for a boatman to row her out to the sloop. Kelt could find his own way home or he could go to hell!

Every time she thought about the slaves she got angry all over again. Martin knew she would never agree to such a thing. They both knew. An inner voice reminded her that this was what could be expected of letting a man take control of her life.

"No more." Ashley stepped into the rowboat as it touched the dock.

"What did ye say, mistress?" the boatman asked.

"Nothing . . . nothing at all." Ashley stared into the swirling water. Her confusion over her feelings for Kelt these past months had made her as indecisive as men accused women of being. No more. She would return to the plantation and do what she should have done yesterday. She'd confront Quincy and demand that he remove himself and his crew from Morgan's Fancy once and for all. Once Quincy was gone, she would find the strength to deal with Kelt. She needed no men to complicate her life—not now . . . and not ever.

It was dark when Ashley stepped into the captain's cabin aboard the *Scarlet Witch*. Her father was seated at the table with Gavin; Quincy rose to greet her.

"Ashley, what a pleasant surprise! Although I must say you took your own good time about it. We were expecting you two days ago." He crossed the room to embrace her. "Sit down. Will you join us in a glass of wine? I have a marvelous Bordeaux . . ."

She stiffened and stepped back, taking a deep breath. "Why are you here?"

Gavin laughed, slamming shut the small iron-bound box on the table. "Same questions, Quince. She's consistent, you've got to give her that." He leaned back in his chair and stared insolently at her. "Did you think we could make repairs in the port of Chestertown?"

"They're searching for you everywhere," Ashley said. "It's only a matter of time before you're found here. Don't you care anything about me? About what would happen if the authorities—"

A smile played at the corner of Gentleman Jim's finely drawn lips. "Ah, the recriminations. Is this daughterly concern? Surely you've heard of our narrow escape by now? Would you rather we'd lowered our colors and placed ourselves at the mercy of King George?" McCade chuckled, extending a slim hand toward an empty place at the table. He was dressed, as usual, in spotless satins and velvet. His coat was dove gray, the breeches a shade lighter. The silk stockings were stitched with a pattern of silver hummingbirds and the square-toed shoes bore jeweled buckles. McCade's sparkling white periwig was as tidy and sweet smelling as his cabin.

"Damn you, Quincy," she cried. "You can't do this to me! I've put my life into this plantation."

"Do you think I'd endanger you if it wasn't necessary? Tut tut, girl." He pulled out the chair for her. "Sit down and have a little wine. Tell me about your mother. I have a little gift for her . . . something I picked up in the islands. She'll love it."

Ashley tightened her hands into fists. It was always the same. She had known he would be like this. Charm. He thought he could talk her out of her anger with charm. "No! I mean it, Quincy! I want you and your scum off Morgan's Fancy on the next tide."

Firm hands pushed her into the chair. Beneath the satin, Quincy was all muscle. Although he wasn't more than medium height, Ashley had seen him pick up a huge, surly crewman and throw him over the rail of the ship.

"We'll go when it's safe—and when we've finished our repairs." His eyes met hers and for an instant she saw a flicker of distress. "We lost the sloop in that fracas off the coast. Twenty men went to the bottom with her."

Ashley smiled coldly at Gavin. "I guess that demotes you to mate again, doesn't it?" Gavin had captained the sloop. It was immensely useful for sailing into shallow water; the *Scarlet Witch* and the *Cazadora* made a deadly team, even if the sloop carried fewer men and fewer cannon. "Isn't the captain supposed to go down with the ship, Gavin? How did you avoid the fate of your brave men?"

"Fortuna."

Ashley shivered under his malignant stare. Gavin frightened her. He always had and her fear had made her determined never to give him an opening to hurt her. She knew why her father kept him by his side—kept him despite the underlying current of insidious malevolence. Gavin was the dark side of Quincy. He could carry out the distasteful requirements of their trade without blinking an eye. Gavin was a man without conscience, an ambitious man—the perfect foil for Gentleman Jim, the courtly buccaneer.

She had asked her father once about his handsome lieutenant. Ashley had been fourteen and Gavin still young enough that they referred to him as "the boy." "Why do you keep him with you?" she demanded, angry that Gavin had watched her with the heavy-lidded glare of a viper. "You can't trust him. He'll betray you one day, Quincy. I can see it in his face."

Quincy had laughed. "On the last day of his life he'll betray me."

"He's not like the others," she protested. Ashley hated Cato the dwarf, but she wasn't afraid of him. There was an odor of evil about Gavin, despite the fair, even features and the laughing manner. Gavin had the look of a killer.

"Has he insulted you? Laid a hand on you?"

"No, but—"

"He won't. He's smart, Ashley. That's what you see. He has a Machiavellian mind. I couldn't pick a better second in command." Quincy had smiled coldly. "We use each other, child."

"Where is your trusty Scot?" Quincy said, snapping Ashley back to the present. "Your . . . overseer?" He poured wine into a priceless Venetian goblet and offered it to her. "He's not hiding in the forest spying on us, is he?"

"Not likely. If Kelt knew you were here, he'd send for the high sheriff. He knows I'm not a part of your foul dealings."

"You came alone, then?"

"Don't I always?"

Gavin swore softly under his breath. "Listen to her, would you? As pure as an angel." He leaned toward her and Ashley caught the odor of stale rum. "Are you a fool, woman?"

"That's enough!" Quincy snapped.

"No! Not enough!" Gavin's fingers tightened cruelly over hers. "If we hang, she hangs with us."

She struggled to pull her hand free. "What's he talking about?" she demanded. "I didn't ask you here. I'm no part of it!"

Quincy shrugged. "Not quite, my dear. Did you really think your tobacco shipments were getting through by sheer chance? I've been protecting your grandfather's tobacco for years. And then when you gained control of the plantation . . ." He arched an eyebrow cynically and sighed. "You have to grow up sometime, Ashley. The reality is that you're an accomplice. You always were."

"No!" She rose to her feet. "No. I don't believe it!" She looked from her father's smooth face to the smirking one of his lieutenant. "You couldn't have—"

"Of course we could have." Quincy's eyes narrowed. "I let your ship go. Hell, I rescued it. What did you make on that shipment alone? Considering how many vessels we've taken this year, the price of tobacco in London should be astronomical."

The room seemed to spin as Ashley fought for control. All these years . . . all these years and she'd never guessed. She bit her lip, welcoming the pain. She'd sworn to Kelt that she wasn't a part of it. The Morgan luck. The Morgan luck had been no more than a pirate's fancy. "Why?" she whispered. "Why did you do it?"

Quincy blinked. "You're my daughter. Why shouldn't I improve your fortunes?"

"I never asked for it."

"Do you think it will save you from the gallows?" Gavin asked. "You're a part of it—you've always been."

"You never told," her father reminded her. "You never told the old man."

She shook her head. Her mouth was dry. "I . . . I couldn't," she murmured. "If I—"

"Enough of this womanly protest," Gavin said. "You've profited from our venture, with damned little risk, I say. Now you can repay our efforts. We need supplies and powder. Musket and cannonball if you can get them. Powder and bandages."

"Do you really believe I'd help you?" Anger rose within her. "Do you think I'd bring powder and shot to aid in the murder of my friends and neighbors?"

"You'll do as I bid you." Quincy's voice was hard. "You've been cosseted and protected long enough. You owe me, daughter . . . and I'm calling in my debts."

Chapter 19

Ashley was halfway to the door when Gavin seized her by the shoulders and spun her around. She tried to twist free, but his fingers pinched into her flesh.

"You're going nowhere!" he snapped.

With a cry Ashley lashed out at him with her boot, clipping him in the ankle as she threw up an arm to block the blow she knew was coming. Gavin's fist halted in midair and he stepped back. Light from the gently swaying ship's lantern shone on his white face.

Ashley's gaze dropped to the shining blade that rested against the base of Gavin's spine. Quincy flicked his wrist and the repair sliced through the big man's shirt to draw blood. She froze.

"You're a fool, Quincy," Gavin said. He winced as the rapier tip pierced his skin again. Fear filled his eyes. "She'll betray us."

Quincy glanced at his daughter and then the doorway. "As long as I'm captain of the *Scarlet Witch,* I'll give the commands, Gavin. If you'd like to try and alter that . . ."

Ashley backed slowly toward the doorway, keeping her eyes on Gavin. "I can't do what you ask," she protested. "I can't." Her ears caught the faint scrape of leather against the deck and she whirled to face the leering dwarf, Cato. Choking back a cry of alarm, she stood her ground, trying to ignore the cutlass in his hand.

"Ye need sump'in, cap'n?" he asked. His eyes were like round bits of glass that seemed to mock her.

"Show Mistress Morgan off the ship," Quincy ordered. "Have someone row her across the creek." He turned his cool gaze on Ashley again. "I presume you've left your mount somewhere nearby?"

She nodded.

"You have two days to acquire the things I asked for," he said. "Don't make me come looking for you." He stepped back and sliced a three-inch scratch across Gavin's right cheek with the point of his rapier. Blood welled up in the cut and dripped down the front of his ruffled shirt. Cursing, the pirate lieutenant slumped into a chair, cupping his wounded face.

Ashley fled from the cabin, scrambling up the ladder and out onto the moonlit deck. An ominous form moved to block her escape, but a word from Cato the dwarf, cleared the way. His nasty laugh followed her as she descended the ladder to the rowboat.

What am I going to do? Her mind was numb with disbelief. She barely noticed when the boat nudged the bank. Cato mumbled something obscene.

"Go to hell," she flung back, running into the darkness. She must find Baron, mount up, and ride. But ride where? A strangled cry rose in her throat. She wouldn't cry. She wouldn't. She had to think of something . . . some way out of this.

Ashley stumbled over something and fell headlong into the dirt. A branch scratched her face and she bit her lip. "Damn." Breathing in ragged gasps, she got up and dusted herself off as best she could. She felt sick. "What am I going to do?"

The bay stallion's answering whinny was reassuring. Quickly she made her way to where he was tied and swung up on his back. The familiar smell of the big horse and the feel of his body moving under her brought a return to reason. "I'll go to Mari," she whispered. "She'll help me."

Far off a wolf howled and the lonely cry sent a shiver up Ashley's spine. She hated the dark. Pushing back her fears, she turned Baron's head toward the Indian woman's cabin. If anyone could make sense of this mess, it would be Mari.

Mari's cabin stood in a small clearing beside a creek. Ashley dismounted and led her horse the last hundred feet toward the house, pausing to tie him to the hitching post. A warm glow of light shone through the window of the main room. Ashley paused and called Mari's name. She was certain the woman knew she was there; she'd never been able to approach Mari's cabin without the woman being aware of it.

"Mari! It's me."

A doleful wail filled the air. *"Du-wit-doo-wooo."* Ashley started as a ghostly shape dislodged itself from the trees and floated toward the house. The mournful trill gave way to a muffled flap of wings and the click of sharp claws as an owl landed on the carved perch an arm's length in front of her.

"Anequo!" Ashley lunged for Baron's reins as her childish fright gave way to a nervous chuckle and her heart slowed to a near-normal beat. "Whoa . . . whoa," she soothed the stallion. "It's only a little screech owl. Easy boy."

The door opened and a woman's form was outlined in the firelight. Mari chuckled softly and beckoned. "Must you ride that beast? You know he's terrified of Anequo." The dark form hopped to her shoulder and pointed ear tufts became visible above the round head. She led the way inside and pushed the door shut behind them.

The main room was almost square and dominated by a huge brick fireplace with a wide hearth. Baskets, tools, and various objects hung from the beams; the walls were covered with animal skins. A scarred wooden table and two chairs filled one corner.

The heart-pine floor was swept spotlessly clean, and the cabin smelled of herbs and evergreens. A deerskin curtain divided the main room of the cabin from the sleeping annex. Niches between the wall beams held bowls, birchbark boxes, and jars. Ashley smiled wordlessly, turning around once, then twice. Mari's home was always the same—a combination Indian-white world of magic and mystery. She sighed contentedly, letting Mari's peace calm the whirling turmoil in her brain.

A cold nose pressed into her hand and she reached down absently to pet the yearling fawn. "She's growing."

Mari nodded. "I'd hoped to set her loose this spring, but the leg will never be strong enough to keep her from danger. She must be content to be a lodge deer."

Ashley scratched the soft chin and the deer rolled her big eyes and moaned happily. "Is she still at war with Ethepate?" Hearing his name, the raccoon uncurled from his spot before the fire and strolled lazily over to sit on the visitor's boot. "You want to be petted, too? No biting," she warned, "or I'll make you into raccoon mittens."

Mari clapped her hands. "Leave her be now," she scolded in Algonquin. "Behave." Kneeling on a deerskin before the fire, she motioned Ashley to join her. "You are troubled," she murmured. The firelight danced on the side of Mari's face as she worked the little owl's claws loose from her shirt and tossed him into the air. The owl squeaked and fluttered across the room to land on the edge of the table.

Ashley lowered herself to the rug beside the Indian woman. "Quincy's back, Mari. The *Scarlet Witch* is anchored in the far creek."

The older woman sighed and reached to stroke Ashley's hair. "I know. I have watched them."

"I went to see him tonight." Quickly, without emotion, Ashley related what had transpired between them. "I can't do what he wants," she said finally. "Half of me wants to run away and hide, and the other half says I should ride to Chestertown and tell the authorities where he is."

A stick snapped in the flames, sending sparks spinning against the back of the hearth like falling stars. Slowly Ashley unknotted her clenched fists, letting them fall loosely in her lap. The fierce pounding in her head began to recede and her breathing slowed. Hopefully, she raised her eyes to meet Mari's.

For long minutes the two women regarded each other without speaking. Mari broke the silence at last. "What he does now is a greater wrong than he has done before," she said in precise, lyrical English. "It may be that his spirit trail has led him to a life of bloodshed and raiding. But to force you to become like him is a great evil. He must be driven by unseen demons." Sighing, she took Ashley's hand in hers and began to rock imperceptibly. "This is a heavy burden to lay on your shoulders, child of my heart. No matter which path you choose, you may forfeit all that you hold dear."

"He is a pirate, a murderer, no matter how he tries to hide it behind his powdered wigs and satin coats. Men die because he desires their belongings." Ashley swallowed, trying to rid herself of the lump in her throat. "I know it wasn't like that in the beginning, but year by year he gets worse. He's becoming more like Gavin and the others."

"But he is your father."

"He's my father."

"And the tie of blood between you cannot be lightly disregarded."

Ashley shook her head, picking idly at the deerskin rug. Ethepate wiggled under her elbow and turned round and round in her lap, settling himself comfortably. "If he were dead, I'd weep for him, but—"

"Accepting what must be is not the same as causing it."

Ashley's face twisted in pain. "What shall I do?"

"Will you bring him what he wants—powder, shot, cannonballs?"

"No."

"Will you betray him to the English soldiers?"

"No," she whispered. "Not if I hang for it. I can't."

Mari poked at the coals with a piece of kindling. "And if you do nothing?"

"Quincy will still think it's a betrayal."

"What would your grandfather say?"

"That a man . . . or a woman . . . always pays their debts."

"Are you not repaying that debt by allowing your father the chance to repair his ship?"

Ashley rose and paced the room. "If I'd told my grandfather about Quincy years ago . . ."

"The fault is not yours," Mari said firmly. "And if you did wrong, I did the same. Quincy placed his life on the shoulders of a child. He knew you would not betray him then, and he knows it now. If you refuse to help him, he will go without harming you. And no matter what he says, his heart will be glad that you did not weaken."

Tears welled up in Ashley's eyes. "I've felt so guilty over it," she admitted. "First with my grandfather and then with Kelt."

"Truth is a double-edged blade," Mari said softly. "A wise person is cautious about whom they hand it to. You acted out of love—first for Ash and then for this man. I cannot believe that Inu-msi-ila-fe-wanu, the Great Spirit, will judge you harshly."

Ashley wiped away her tears and sniffed. "Why do you always make me feel like I'm twelve years old?"

Mari laughed. "It is a failing of mothers." She rose gracefully. "Are you hungry? I have fresh corn cakes with blueberries. You are welcome to spend the night with me."

"Thanks, but I'm not really hungry. I've got to ride back to the house and see what Kelt did about . . ." She trailed off, not wanting to have to explain the Scot's purchase of slaves and their public argument. She took a gourd dipper from its hook on the wall and scooped water from a covered crock, drinking thirstily.

"Would you like me to ride back with you?"

"No," Ashley said. "I'll be fine. Baron knows the way, and besides, there's plenty of moonlight." If the time came when she was afraid to ride her own land alone, she would truly be unfit to be the master of Morgan's Fancy.

"Are you armed?" The Indian woman folded her arms across her chest. "I would feel better if you stayed here until the sun comes up. I have a bad feeling."

"You always have a bad feeling. I'll be careful." Ashley moved toward the door. "Thanks for the advice."

"I told you nothing."

"And everything."

"Ride easy, my child." The small brown fingers moved quickly, making a sign of protection in the air.

"I will."

Mari's concern echoed in her thoughts as Ashley rode back along the path in the chill night. The moonlight was pale, the shadows deep and menacing. Even the big bay seemed nervous, tossing his head and snorting at the ordinary noises of nocturnal creatures beside the trail. The forest path twisted and turned, crossing a marshy spot, then rising to an open meadow.

A herd of grazing deer threw up their tails and fled, plunging into the thick woods on the far side of the clearing. Ashley hesitated only a moment before riding out into the meadow. She clicked softly to Baron, relieved to be out of the closeness of the trees. The stallion had gone no more than two lengths when the first shot rang out.

Baron screamed and reared, pawing the air with his front hooves. Ashley struggled to hold her seat, fighting the animal's head for control. The second bullet struck the horse in the neck and he fell backward. Ashley kicked free of her stirrups and flung herself away from the thrashing stallion. She hit the ground hard and rolled.

Another musket shot shattered the night as Baron moaned and tried to stagger to his feet. Dirt flew up, spraying Ashley's cheek. Instinct overcame terror. Desperately she ran toward the shelter of the trees, cursing the moonlight that made her a perfect target against the open meadow. A bullet whistled over her head and made a hollow thud as it buried itself harmlessly in a tree trunk. Another heartbeat and she was safe behind a big oak.

For long minutes Ashley pressed her face against the rough bark and tried to shut out the sound of Baron's cries of pain. Her pistol lay somewhere on the grass near the fallen horse. Her only chance was to outrun her assassin and hide in the forest. Her shoulder ached from where she had landed on the ground and one knee was numb. Her nose was bleeding, but she barely noticed it. She tried to slow her breathing and listen intently for any sound.

Ashley's mouth was dry and her palms sweaty. She couldn't keep her eyes off Baron. He was down again, lying full length on the grass, his harsh breathing clearly audible. Was he dying? She wanted to run to him, to hold his head in her lap and stroke the soft nose. Baron needed her, but she knew that if she went into the meadow again, she went to a swift and certain death.

Damn you! Damn you! she screamed silently. It tore at her insides to know that Baron was suffering and she couldn't help him. There were no tears. The hurt went too deep. "You'll pay for this," Ashley promised. "So help me, God!"

Trembling, she wiped the blood and dirt from her mouth. The acrid taste of fear was beginning to recede and she became aware of the musty smells of molding leaves and earth. A squirrel chattered angrily on a branch above her and a nighthawk screeched. Cautiously she dropped to her knees and began to inch backward into the woods. She was too close to the meadow for safety. Whoever was shooting at her would look here first.

Ashley had moved about fifty feet from the edge

of the clearing when the clear, plaintive call of a whippoorwill echoed through the trees. Startled, she dropped facedown in the leaves and lay still. Minutes passed. Then the sweet notes came again from the same direction. Ashley puckered her lips to return the whistling cry, but her mouth was so dry, only a useless puff of air came out. She licked her lips and tried again. Nothing. When the whippoorwill called a third time, from a much closer location, Ashley managed to give a respectable imitation of an owl's hoot.

"Mari! I'm here!" Ashley scrambled to her feet and moved toward the sound of Mari's voice. On the far side of the meadow a shadow detached itself from the trees and waved.

"It's safe, daughter," Mari cried. "He was alone."

Ashley ran across the grass to the place where Baron lay. The big horse raised his head and whinnied. Trembling, she knelt beside him and tried to determine the extent of the animal's injuries. His neck and chest seemed a sea of blood. He flinched as her fingers found the hole; blood was still flowing.

Tears blinded her as she moved to the far side of the stallion and rubbed his neck, trying to find the exit wound. There wasn't any. "Easy, boy, easy," she murmured. "I know you're hurting. Good boy, good Baron." She tried to guess how much blood he had lost, but it was impossible to tell. She'd have to examine the injury in good light and see if it was possible to remove the slug, or at least to stop the bleeding.

"Ashley!" Mari's voice was insistent. "Come quickly. Leave the horse!"

Reluctantly she obeyed, running across the meadow to the spot where the Indian woman waited, bow in hand. "He's hurt bad," Ashley said. "We've got to stop the bleeding or he'll die."

Mari shook her head. "You must see this first." She motioned toward the trees.

"How did you get here?" Ashley asked. "I thought—"

"You thought I would let you go alone when I had a bad feeling?" Mari gave a short laugh. "I could not face your grandfather beyond the river if I did. No!" She laughed again. "I followed you. I could not stop him from shooting at you, but once he fired, it was an easy thing to circle around behind him." She made a face. "You make a sorry owl cry, daughter. Not even an Iroquois would be fooled. Not even your Kelt Saxon, I think."

"Did you catch him?"

Mari nodded. "You know this man who tries to kill you," she said softly. "He will go nowhere, but I think he follows the orders of another. We must find out who while he still can speak." She grasped Ashley's arm and squeezed it tightly. "You are all right? Good. Now let me have my way with this man. Death hovers over him. We must be quick." Ashley nodded again and followed Mari into the shadows.

A white man lay on his side gasping for breath. An arrow protruded from his chest. Ignoring Ashley's strangled cry, Mari knelt beside him. "You are hurt bad," Mari said, "but I do not think you will die."

The man opened his eyes, moaned, and stretched out a hand to Ashley. "Mistress . . . help me," he begged. "You've got to help me."

"Short John?"

"Yeh . . . it's me," he whispered hoarsely. On the ground beside him lay two muskets.

"You're the one," Ashley said. "You tried to kill me before, didn't you?"

"I'm sorry. I swear to God, I'm sorry! Please! You can't let me die here like an animal."

"You cut my cinch?"

"He made me do it. It's his fault. He paid me." Short John began to cough, and a dark ribbon of blood trailed down the corner of his mouth.

"Who?" Mari demanded. "Who paid you?"

A spasm of coughing wracked the twisted body on the ground. "Please," he begged. "It hurts. Get it out." His fingers clutched at the arrow shaft.

"Tell us who paid you and we will take out the arrow," Mari promised. "It is not too late to save your life. Do you want to live, Short John?" Mari's voice took on a strange tone. "Was it the overseer? Did he pay you to kill Ashley?"

"Yeh. Yeh," the wounded man agreed. "It were the Scot." He choked again. "I don't wanna die. Please, mistress . . . help me. Get this arrow out o' me before it's too late."

"You're lying," Ashley said. "It's not Kelt. Who paid you?"

Mari got to her feet. "Your death is on your own head, Short John. Even when the ghosts hover over you, your tongue cannot speak the truth. You deserve to die here." She took a step back. "But I do not think you will die so easily. Did you hear the wolves before, Ashley? I think the smell of the horse's blood will draw them. And when they finish with the horse . . ."

"It was Randall!" Short John screamed. "Nicholas Randall of Rosewood! He tempted me, mistress!"

"What am I worth, Short John? How much was he going to give you for murdering me?"

The man began to sob, mumbling a string of broken pleas. Ashley turned away. "Help him, Mari," she said.

Mari went to her knees and seized the arrow shaft, snapping it off just below the iron head. In a single quick motion, she yanked the remaining shaft free from the man's chest. Short John screamed once and was silent.

Shaken, Ashley turned back to look at the still form. "You said he would live," she whispered. "You said it wasn't too late."

Mari shrugged. "I lied."

The two women kept vigil through the long hours of the night, changing the bandages on Baron's wound and talking softly to him. Twice Mari returned to her cabin to bring water, medicine, and supplies for the suffering animal. Short John lay where he had fallen. Ashley suggested dragging the body near their campfire to keep the wolves from disturbing it, but Mari protested in a rare show of anger.

"If the wolves come for carrion, then let them have it," the Indian woman said in her own tongue. "Daylight will be soon enough to carry him back to his woman. She knew of his plan to kill you, of that you can be certain. That one"—Mari motioned toward the body—"would never have dared murder without her urging."

Ashley nodded. "You're probably right, but we'll never prove it. No matter what she is, I'll not bring her husband's body back in pieces."

Mari shrugged. "You always had a soft heart. Bring the body by our fire if you wish, but do not ask my help. He would have shot you down without pity, and you are all I have left."

Chapter 20

It was midafternoon by the time Ashley returned to the manor house. Baron was still alive; the bleeding had stopped and Mari was treating him for fever and infection. Ashley hated to leave the animal, but she knew Mari would do everything in her power to save him.

Joshua and Edgar had listened in astonishment as Ashley had told them of the attempted murder and John's death. She did not tell them who had hired Short John. "Send men to bring his body back," she ordered. "Give it to his wife and make the arrangements for his funeral. Tell her that her indenture will be torn up, but I want her off Morgan's Fancy as soon as Short John is buried."

"Aye, miss," Edgar said. "We'll take care o' it right away."

Ashley dismounted and handed the reins of Mari's horse to Joshua. "I'll contact the sheriff about Short John tomorrow. Right now, all I can think about is a bath and some sleep."

Joshua frowned and scuffed the ground with a worn shoe. "They's somethin' you oughta know, mistress. *He* come back yesterday."

"Who? Master Saxon?"

"Yep." Joshua spat out a wad of tobacco. "Master Saxon come back and brought slaves wi' him."

"Slaves? Are you certain?"

"Yep. Got some women up t' the house, cleanin' like it was Judgment Day."

Ashley's face whitened in anger. "Do you know where Master Saxon is?"

"Down by the dock."

"Tell him I'd like to speak with him, at once." Her shoulders stiffened as she strode toward the house. Kelt had brought the slaves here in spite of everything she'd said, had he? She'd soon see about that!

A scratching noise caught Ashley's attention as she passed the woodshed and she stopped to listen. A dog whined and then barked loudly. Ashley unlatched the heavy door and Jai bounded out wagging his tail. "What are you doing in there?" she demanded. She patted his head and then turned back toward the house.

"You wanted to see me?" Kelt asked as he entered the great hall of Morgan's Fancy an hour later.

Ashley turned from the window and glared at him. "Who do you think you are?" Her fingers tightened around the handle of her whip as she glared at him. "Knowing how I despise slavery, you bought those slaves anyway? You brought them to my plantation? How dare you!" She threw the whip on the floor as her smoldering gaze traversed the room.

Nothing in the room was the same as it had been twenty-four hours ago. The half-mended bridle was missing from the cherry table; the books she'd been reading had vanished as well. The window glass sparkled. The floor had been swept clean of dustballs and sand. The silver candlesticks and brass andirons shone. Even the furniture had been moved.

"I come back to find strange women cleaning my kitchen—slaves! And my dog . . ." Ashley paused for breath. "My Jai locked in the woodshed!" She kicked at the whip furiously. "I told you I wouldn't have slaves on this plantation! I told you—but you just don't listen."

Kelt bristled. "Enough of your damnable temper, woman. I'll explain about the new servants later. I've more important things to discuss wi' ye at this moment." He extended a hand toward her and she slapped it away.

"By God, we will!" she cried. Her brown eyes hardened to shards of jasper. "Since I left you in Chestertown I've been roughed up, threatened, had my horse shot out from under me—" She broke off and choked back an onslaught of tears. "Baron . . . he was shot in the neck. I still don't know if Mari can save him or not. A man I trusted—a man who worked for me—tried to murder me. And I come home to find you . . ." Ashley couldn't keep her voice from shaking. "To find you demanding answers to your questions."

"Aye," he said flatly. "I'm demanding answers. And I'll ha' them now. No more o' your tricks and no more lies."

Ashley bent to retrieve her whip from the floor. "Get off my plantation. Now. Today. You—" Kelt's hand shot out and grabbed her arm. "Bastard! I'll—" His free hand clamped over her mouth. Furiously she lashed out at him, kicking and punching.

"Stop it!" Kelt yanked her against him, pressing her head into his chest, holding her so tight he nearly cut off her breath. "Don't make me hurt you. This is no game, woman," he insisted. "You'll listen to what I ha' to say."

"Say it then." Her angry words were muffled in his shirt.

"Upstairs. Where they'll be no ears to hear." His fingers tightened on her back. "Gi' me your word you'll come wi'oot a fuss, or so help me God, I'll knock ye cold and carry ye o'er my shoulder like a sack o' wheat."

"Let me go."

"Your word!" She nodded and he released her cautiously. "Damn your hellish temper, woman! There's no need t' stare at me like I was some slavering beast. I'd nae wish to lay hands on ye like that. I've not hurt ye and you've tried me sore." He motioned toward the doorway. "Please, Ashley."

Spine rigid, she spun and stalked from the room and up the staircase to his chambers. Kelt closed the door behind them and took a deep breath. Ashley sat on the bed and folded her arms across her chest. "Well? I'm waiting."

"The *Scarlet Witch* is anchored on Morgan's Fancy."

"How did you find out?"

Kelt swore under his breath and sent a canvas and tripod flying across the room with a backhanded blow. "Ye knew it." It was an accusation.

Ashley flushed and dropped her eyes. "Not until yesterday," she lied.

"Aye. And I'm Bonnie Prince Charlie." Kelt moved to the bed, towering over her, his face dark with rage. "I'm nae fool, Ashley. If ye speak the truth, ye'll go wi' me to Chestertown to report it to the authorities. They can send ships to block the creek. He'll be trapped."

Ashley knotted her fingers in the woven bedspread.

"You don't understand," she pleaded. The anger was gone from her voice. "Kelt . . ."

"Once and for all, ye must decide." Kelt's brow furrowed in frustration. "He's a killer. If you're innocent, you've got to declare that innocence by helping to capture him." He laid his hand on Ashley's cheek and tilted her face up to his. "They'll hang ye wi' him if ye don't."

Ashley pushed his hand away and tried to put her tortured emotions into words. "He's not . . . not all bad."

He took her shoulders and shook her roughly. "Stop looking at it like a child! Quincy is a pirate—a murderer. I'd have to stop him . . . if he were my own father."

"Are you asking me to betray Quincy because you're angry with me?" she cried. "I thought you loved me."

"Love ye?" He released her and turned away. "And that's the hell o' it, lass." Kelt covered his face with his hands. "I do."

"So much that you're leaving?" She laughed bitterly. "It's a strange love you offer a woman, Kelt Saxon."

"Nay." His head snapped up and he turned back. "Nay. The fault is yours. I offered ye marriage an' my name." He reached down to pick up the unfinished canvas. "Do ye see this?" He held it up for her to look at. It was a portrait of a woman on horseback. The horse was clearly Baron; he had captured the proud animal, with his flowing mane and tail, to perfection. The young woman had Ashley's hair and posture, but the face was blank. "Look," Kelt insisted. "I'm an artist, but I canna paint you." He let the canvas drop from his fingers. "There's a wall between us, Ashley . . . a wall of your making. I dinna know you. You willna let me.''

''Short John was the one who cut my cinch, who shot at me the first time. Hell, he probably set the fire in the barn the night you came,'' Ashley said. ''He tried to kill me again last night, but Mari killed him instead. No, wait!'' She threw up her hand. ''Now you listen to me! Before he died, we asked him who put him up to it—why he wanted to kill me. You know what he said? He said you paid him to do it.''

Kelt's face whitened to marble. ''And you believed it?''

Ashley sighed in disgust. ''Of course I didn't believe it. Mari persuaded him to tell the truth, that it was my stepfather. Just like my brother said. Nicholas has been trying to get rid of me all along.''

''What's your point?''

''The point is, you thickheaded Scot, that I didn't believe him. Not even for a minute. I knew you couldn't hurt me. If I can trust you when the evidence says otherwise, why can't you believe me?''

''A pirate ship hidden in your creek—your father's ship—is pretty hard evidence. Better than the word o' scum like Short John.''

''I didn't—'' Ashley was cut off by an urgent knocking at the door.

''Miss Ashley? Are you all right?'' Thomas called.

''Thomas?''

The door swung open and the old black man stood there, an ancient wheel lock musket cradled in the crook of his arm. ''Jane said she heard shoutin' up here.'' He glared fiercely at Kelt.

''No, Thomas, I'm not all right,'' Ashley said. ''Train your gun on him and shoot him if he moves.''

''What the hell?'' Kelt checked his sudden movement as Thomas brought the musket barrel to rest on his midsection.

"Best you do what the mistress says," Thomas advised. "Best you find a place on that floor and sit. I don't wanna hurt you, Master Saxon, but I will."

"Keep him here until the hall clock strikes ten," Ashley ordered. She threw Kelt a last glance. "I'm sorry," she whispered, "but I can't let you do it. He's my father."

"Dinna go out that door," Kelt said. But she was already halfway to the stairs.

The accusation in Kelt's eyes haunted Ashley as she galloped across the open fields toward the far corner of Morgan's Fancy. He would never forgive her now. Any hope she had harbored of saving their relationship was lost. And when Thomas released him at ten o'clock and he went for the high sheriff, they would come with a warrant for her arrest as well. Perhaps Kelt was right. She had to choose. And she had chosen to warn Quincy, which made her one of them. But she wouldn't run. Once she'd given warning, she'd return to the manor house and wait to face the sheriff.

A hollow emptiness dried her tears. She'd lose Morgan's Fancy, to her stepfather if not to the crown, but it wouldn't matter. The penalty for piracy was death. She didn't want to die, but she wasn't certain she wanted to live without Kelt.

"Damn you to hell, Kelt Saxon," she cried in the wind. But she knew she'd damned herself.

It was dusk when Ashley entered the woods. The mare was streaked with sweat despite the cool evening air. Ashley was glad she'd taken precious seconds to change out of Mari's buckskins into her own clothes. It was important that she face her father, even now, as the mistress of Morgan's Fancy.

She'd give them warning, precious hours to sail out of the creek and lose themselves somewhere on the sprawling shoreline of the Chesapeake. Quincy would have to take this as payment in full for her debt. If they met again, it would be as enemies.

The smell of smoke wafted on the wind. Ashley reined in the mare and stood in her stirrups, peering through the trees. A flicker of light showed a campfire built on her side of the creek. Resolutely she pulled her musket from the saddle holster and eased back the hammer. The gun was no idle threat; it was loaded with a deadly charge of chain and split shot. She'd not be bullied by Gavin tonight.

She rode a few hundred yards closer, then dismounted and tied the mare. Something warm nudged the back of her legs and she stifled a cry of alarm as she whirled on the intruder. "Jai!" Laughter bubbled up in her throat as she dropped to her knees and hugged the big dog. "How did you find me?" It was a foolish question. She knew he had tracked her by smell. She'd deliberately left him in the house to keep him from following. Obviously he'd found a way out.

"You stay here," she whispered. "Stay, Jai."

Leaving the animals, she moved forward until she had a clear view of the firelit circle. Several heavily armed men sat around it. Ashley stepped behind a massive beech tree and called out. "It's Ashley Morgan! I must see Captain McCade at once! It's urgent!"

A figure dashed to throw something on the fire; there was a loud sizzle and the flames were extinguished. Men dove for cover and one cursed. There was murmur of voices and then a familiar one. "Ashley? Are you alone?"

"Yes! I'm alone!" It was Gavin. "I have to see Quincy."

"Drop your weapons and come in with your hands in the air!"

"In a pig's eye, Gavin! Call my . . . call Quincy!"

"He's not here! You'll have to talk to me! Have you got the stuff?" Several figures detached themselves from the area near the drowned campfire and moved into the darker shadows of the woods.

Ashley caught her breath. Where could he be? She'd counted on giving him her warning so the ship could sail immediately. With an easterly wind, the *Scarlet Witch* could manage a decent speed, even with the damages to the ship they'd not had time to repair. "This is important, Gavin!"

"How can we be sure you're alone?"

Ashley laid her head against the cool bark of the beech tree and let her eyes close for just a second. She was exhausted and her head was aching again. When had she slept last? Two nights ago? "For God's sake, Gavin! If I'd wanted to bring men against you, we'd have fired first and saved the talking!" Ashley's throat felt sore. All this yelling back and forth wasn't helping.

"All right," he answered. "Come on in. But keep your hands where we can see them."

The hairs rose on the back of her neck as she moved out from behind the tree and walked cautiously toward the clearing. "No tricks, Gavin."

She stopped ten feet away from the shadowy form. There was no mistaking the pirate lieutenant; he was a head taller than most of the crew and as broad across the shoulders as Kelt. Distaste curled in the back of her mind. If it wasn't for Quincy, the crown could have the lot of them and good riddance. Slowly she raised the barrel of the musket until it was aimed at the center of his chest. "I have to speak to Quincy now," she said. "It's a matter of life and death."

"Whose?" The taunting voice flicked at her like the tip of a whip.

"Where is he?" Ashley's finger tightened on the trigger. Something was wrong. She'd never known Quincy to leave the ship when they were anchored here.

"He's gone with that devil-spawned dwarf to bury his treasure."

"When will he be back?"

"When he gets here." Gavin spread his legs and rested his hands on his hips. "Your message will have to go to me. If you have a message."

Ashley glanced around the clearing. The few faces she could make out were strangers, probably Gavin's men from the sunken sloop. "He still doesn't trust you enough to take you with him?" she said, stalling. "Maybe the dwarf should be second in command."

The blond giant erupted into laughter. "You've got spirit, Ashley. I like that in a woman . . . in the beginning, at least." He unfolded his long limbs and took a lazy step toward her. "He trusts Cato because Cato knows he wouldn't live ten minutes on my watch. The little bastard makes my skin crawl. Besides"—he chuckled wryly—"what use would a dwarf have for a fortune? If he tried to spend a gold crusado, he'd end up floating under the dock with his throat cut from ear to ear. No honest man would believe a hunchback dwarf could come by gold or silver unless he stole it and no thief would let him keep it." Gavin shook his head. "Cato's better than a priest for keeping secrets."

"Is that envy I hear? You spend your share readily enough." Ashley tried to hold down the prickling fear that made the mild spring night seem raw. "What makes you certain he even has a buried treasure?"

"He has one, all right. He's been coming here for twenty years or more. When he leaves the ship, he carries a heavy burden. When he comes back, he comes empty-handed." Gavin took another step closer. "We've taken ships from Newfoundland to Barbados. Spanish gold idols from Peru and silver bars from Mexico. Crusadoes and guineas, shillings and pieces of eight. Rubies as red as blood, and once . . ." Gavin's whisky voice grew soft. "Once an emerald as big as a peacock's egg." He cleared his throat and spat. "What do you think the captain's share of such booty might be?"

"It cannot be cheap to maintain the ship and crew," Ashley suggested. "Or to wear the finest clothes. Quincy has expensive tastes."

"Oh, he dresses like a lord, does our noble captain. And he likes the best in wine . . . and in women. But he's spent no twenty years' take in Persian rugs or satin waistcoats. Most of it he's hoarded away like an old miser. Some might think more than his share." Gavin took another step.

"If you think he's cheating you, it's your right to demand an accounting before the crew." Ashley's breathing quickened. She could smell the sharp odor of rum on his breath. Gavin was always more dangerous when he drank. "What you're saying is close to mutiny." She stepped back and trained the barrel on Gavin's face. "Don't make me shoot you, Gavin," she said. "I came here to warn you. The authorities know you're here. Even now, they may be sailing to block the mouth of the creek. You've got to get the *Witch* out of here or you're all dead men."

"So you betrayed us after all."

"You're such a fool. If I'd betrayed you, would I

come to—" A twig snapped behind her and Ashley half turned toward the sound. Gavin lunged toward her. With a cry, she raised the musket to her shoulder to fire, but as her finger tightened on the cold steel of the trigger, a snarling fury leaped out of the darkness and pounced on Gavin. "Jai!" Ashley screamed.

Man and dog rolled over and over on the ground. Ashley stood frozen to the spot, unable to fire for fear of hitting the animal. Men ran toward them, yelling. In desperation, Ashley dropped the gun and grabbed Jai's collar, trying to drag him off.

"Jai! Jai!" Her hands on his collar yanked with all her might. Both she and the dog fell backward. Scrambling up, she saw a sailor advancing on them with a drawn cutlass. "Go!" she screamed at the dog. "Go to Mari! Jai, go!"

Jai shook his wolflike head and crouched, hackles raised, eyes gleaming. A low growl issued from his throat. Ashley slammed her hand down across his back. "Bad dog!" she cried. "Bad dog. Go to Mari!" She snapped her fingers sharply and let out a low whistle. With a last look of bewilderment Jai turned and loped away into the forest.

Gavin's face twisted in demonic wrath as he swayed before her. His shirt was ripped to the waist and one hand bore long gashes from Jai's attack. "Hold her," he commanded.

Rough hands closed on Ashley and a bloody fist descended. Ashley's world exploded in pinwheels of shimmering, multicolored light that faded slowly to soft, timeless black.

Kelt threatened, pleaded, and bargained until his voice cracked with exhaustion. Nothing would sway the stubborn old man with the deadly wheel lock musket.

''Mistress Ashley said to hold you here until ten, and I hold you,'' Thomas said flatly. ''You might jest as well save yer breath, Master Saxon, 'cause the fear of Judgment Day wouldn't sway me from pullin' this trigger if you get out of the chair before the clock strikes ten.''

''You're no murderer, Thomas. You couldna' shoot me in cold blood.''

''No, sir, no, sir, I couldn't. But I could blow away one of your knees and you'd be walkin' on a tree stump the rest of your days.''

''She could die if I dinna stop her.''

''Maybe she dies if you do.'' Thomas shook his gray head and frowned. ''I like you, sir, I like you a lot. But I been watchin' over that girl since she was a babe. You do whatever you want to me at ten o'clock, but 'til then, you stay put.''

Kelt's apprehension grew as the hours ticked away and the old man held firm. The day had faded to dusk and then night. Ashley had gone to warn her father, of that he was certain. But why hadn't she come back? Despite his harsh words, he really hadn't believed she was part of their piracy. Sweat broke out on his forehead. If she sailed with them, it would mean her death.

The clock had struck nine-thirty when the sound of running footsteps on the stairs brought them both upright. But the voice that called out was not Ashley's but the Indian woman's.

''Kelt Saxon!'' She threw open the chamber door. ''Thomas! What do you do?'' Firmly she pushed the barrel toward the floor. ''Ashley's in bad trouble,'' she said to Kelt. ''You must come.''

Thomas let the gun slide to the floor. ''I'm sorry, sir, but you see how I had to do it.''

''Where is she?'' Kelt demanded, ignoring Thomas's apology. "Has she been arrested?" His fear for Ashley's safety was so real he could taste it. Damn her reckless ways!

Mari shook her head. "Jai came to my cabin. I followed him back to the creek." Knowing looks passed between them. "Her horse was tied to a tree, but she was gone. I found the evidence of a struggle on the ground, but whether Ashley was involved I do not know."

Kelt swore a foul Gaelic oath. It mattered not a tinker's damn if she had gone willingly or been taken forcibly by her father. Aboard the ship, she would suffer the same fate as the pirates. "You're certain she's not there somewhere? Hurt or . . ." He could not put voice to his greatest fear, that she might already be dead. McCade seemed to have a twisted fondness for her, but it was no assurance that he might not have killed her in a fit of rage, or that another of the cutthroats might have ravished her and thrown her body overboard.

"You must bring her home, Kelt Saxon," Mari said. "She would not leave Morgan's Fancy. She would not leave you."

Kelt shrugged. "She cares nothing for me."

"Your lips speak the words, but your heart knows it is not so." Mari's dark eyes held his. "There is a bond between you that only death can break."

Kelt glanced back at the unfinished painting of Ashley. How could his world have come to center on such a willful, obstinate, unwomanly wench? He had given her an ultimatum and she had thrown it back in his teeth. She deserved to hang for her shrewish tongue alone. "Gi' me a reason, Mari," he said in a low burr, "why I canna leave her to reap the harvest o' her own sowing?"

"*Dahoola.*" Mari smiled with her eyes. "Love."

She reached out to touch his cheek with one slim finger. "You must follow your heart, Kelt Saxon. Bring her home safely . . . or the sun will have no warmth for you, and the rain no joy. Without her, you will find no peace in this life or the next."

"And how the hell am I supposed to get her back?"

The smile spread to her lips and Mari chuckled. "You are the warrior, are you not? You must find a way or make one." She turned to go, then looked back, her smooth brow creased with worry. "But you must hurry. The cord which binds her to the earth is thin tonight. I feel she is in great danger." Mari let her eyes drift shut and her head rested against the door frame. "I see blood and fire." She took a deep breath. "And death wears the face of . . ."

"Of what?" Kelt felt the chill of her unseen premonition like an icy hand on the back of his neck.

"Of a man with hair the color of a hunter's moon."

Chapter 21

Ashley raised her head and blinked, trying to adjust her eyes to the morning light pouring through the open hatch above her. Something hard struck her leg and she cried out, struggling to sit up.

"Have a nice night's sleep?" Gavin asked sarcastically. He struck her again with the toe of his shoe and ripped the filthy gag from her mouth.

"He'll kill you for this," Ashley whispered hoarsely. Her jaw felt as if she'd been kicked by a horse. She breathed in a little of the fresh air, ridding her mouth and lungs of the fetid stench of the hold where she'd lain since she'd been carried aboard the ship the previous night. Gavin's face came into focus before her and she wasn't certain if reality was worse than the nightmares. Her inbred terror of the dark, the rustling and squealing of rats, the fumes of pitch and bilge water, had driven her to the brink of madness.

Sweet reason flooded Ashley's mind like a cold bay wind. She could tell by the motion of the deck that the *Scarlet Witch* was under way; she also knew that the water was rough. Some time during the long hours of darkness she'd been sick. Her stomach was empty and her brain clouded by fear. What if Quincy was dead? What then? What did Gavin want with her?

Gavin grabbed a handful of her hair and dragged her to her feet. "You disappoint me, Ashley. I expected something original from you at least."

"Why?" she demanded. He twisted her hair and the pain brought tears to her eyes.

"That should be obvious." He untangled his hand and stepped back, running the tip of his tongue suggestively across his full upper lip.

Ashley blushed as she felt his eyes travel over her, lingering on the curve of her breasts and hips. Gavin laughed and whipped a knife from the sheath at his waist. For a long heartbeat, he laid the cold blade along her cheek. The point was dangerously close to her right eye and she held her breath, afraid to move.

"Are you frightened?"

"Yes."

"Good." He laughed again. "I'll give you even more reason to fear me, Ashley . . . before I'm through." With one swift motion, he dropped to his knee and slashed the ropes that held her ankles. "Up the ladder with you!" he ordered. "We can play later. I know lots of games. But now it's time we had that talk with Gentleman Jim."

Ashley stumbled toward the ladder, seizing on the fact that her father was alive. Nothing would make her believe Quincy would hold her prisoner, or allow Gavin to threaten her. This was all Gavin's doing. "Tell me one thing," she said, mentally grasping for something solid to cling to. "Who led the raid on that plantation on the Eastern Shore last fall?"

"What makes you think I'd know?"

"A place called Swan Point. Four slaves and a white woman were taken. It wasn't Quincy, was it,

Gavin?'' Please God, don't let it be Quincy, she begged silently. If my father did it . . .

''Are you certain?'' He grabbed her wrists and sawed at the ropes behind her back. ''You know he has an eye for the ladies. He always did like the pretty ones with yellow hair.''

''What happened to the woman?''

Gavin shoved her roughly toward the ladder. ''What's it to you?''

Ashley whirled fiercely on him. ''Is Jane Briggs alive?''

''Hell, no,'' he said. ''She went to the bottom with the *Cazadora.*'' Gavin made an obscene motion and grinned. ''But she was fine while she lasted.'' He touched Ashley's chin with the tip of his finger, trailing it down the line of her throat. ''She liked to play rough.''

''You bastard!'' Quickly she turned and started up the ladder. Gavin had commanded the sloop, *Cazadora.* The murder of the Briggses had been his doing, not her father's. She'd known all along it wasn't Quincy's style. ''Quincy never tried to stop you?'' she dared, looking down at the white-blond mop of hair below her.

''He's getting old and soft. There's a lot goes on he doesn't know about.'' He grabbed her ankle and squeezed until she winced with pain. ''Now, when you get on deck, you be nice. Just walk real quiet-like to his cabin. You try anything, and I'll run this blade through you and dump you into the bay before you can scream twice. *Comprende?''*

Ashley murmured her assent as she climbed onto the deck. Poor little Jane. It had been foolish to hope that she might be alive after all these months—and maybe after what had happened, after being a prisoner of Gavin and his crew, maybe she was better off. Pray God she hadn't known of the baby's death in the fire.

Several of her father's old crewmen glanced up curiously as she walked toward the stern of the ship with Gavin, but most of the men were engaged in adding canvas to the fore-and-aft rigging to give the *Witch* extra speed. It was a cloudy day with poor visibility and the wind was from the northeast, promising foul weather. Obviously the captain wanted the ship to make as great a distance from Morgan's Fancy as possible before the full force of the storm hit. Ashley could just make out a faint line of trees on the port side and was certain they were still on the Chesapeake, but she didn't know where. It was possible that Quincy was headed for the mouth of the bay and the Atlantic.

Ashley caught sight of the dwarf clinging to the bowsprit, freeing a jammed pulley on the billowing spritsail. Spray from the waves soaked him each time the *Witch* dove into the next trough, threatening to pull him into the churning blue-gray water.

"Move it!" Gavin said, giving her a shove.

"You're headed out to sea."

"Aye. If you're lucky, I'll show you Madagascar. It's time the *Scarlet Witch* anchored in richer waters." Gavin's hand tightened on her arm. "And if you please me enough, I may not kill you when I tire of you." He chuckled unpleasantly. "That red hair of yours would bring me a sultan's ransom in the slave markets of Mozambique or Marrakesh." He brought his lips close to her ear. "Would you like to end your days in a Muslim seraglio? You could wear pants there to your heart's delight."

Ashley checked the curse that rose in her throat. Why waste her time with threats? Gavin was dangerous and unpredictable. He might stab her or knock her senseless again. It was better to wait and watch for an opening than to give him the satisfaction of knowing he was terrifying her.

Quincy was shaving when Gavin pushed open the cabin door and shoved Ashley inside. He turned to face them, an ivory-handled poniard in his right hand and one cheek still lathered with soap.

"Ashley? What in God's name are you doing here?"

"I found a stowaway," Gavin said.

"He's lying!" Ashley cried. "Watch—"

Gavin pulled his cutlass free. "It's over, Quince. I'm taking the *Witch*."

"Are you now?" Quincy smiled lazily. The dark eyes narrowed, urgently conveying a warning to Ashley on the floor.

She froze, mentally calculating the distance between her hand and her father's rapier hanging beside his bunk. "I came to the creek to warn you, but you weren't there," she said. "He hit me and carried me aboard."

"Gavin likes his little jokes, don't you, Gavin?"

"This is no joke. You've had your day, old man. Now, it's mine." Keeping the cutlass ready, Gavin reached behind him and slid the iron bolt across the cabin door. "Look for no reinforcements. My men have their orders."

"This is between us. Why did you bring Ashley on board? This has nothing to do with her."

He's strong, Ashley thought. In spite of everything Quincy had done to her, she couldn't suppress the overwhelming pride that washed through her. No wonder Cicely loved him all these years.

When Quincy moved, it was too fast for her to see. There was a flash of steel and the poniard quivered to the hilt in Gavin's upper arm. Two inches to the left and it would have pierced his heart. With a curse, Gavin yanked the knife from his flesh and lunged across the room toward Ashley. He swung the cutlass in an arc that would have taken off her head if she hadn't scrambled aside, seized her father's sword, and thrown it to him.

"On guard!" Quincy shouted, dropping into a fighting stance. Ashley put the table between her and Gavin. Quincy's poniard lay on the floor near the doorway, but she would have to pass Gavin to reach it. Frantically she looked around the room for a pistol.

Steel clashed against steel as the two men circled each other, slashing and blocking. Quincy's rapier was a gentleman's weapon, fragile, almost delicate-looking compared to the massive cutlass. A few seconds, however, and Ashley was assured that her father had learned the art of fencing from a master. Again and again the narrow blade of the rapier proved true as Quincy executed a series of breathtaking attacks and ripostes.

Gavin's size and longer reach gave him tremendous advantage as he drove Quincy back with the sheer force of his powerful swings. The blows were almost too quick to follow. Then, like a silver bolt of lightning, the slender rapier cut a furrow across Gavin's neck. He spun and slashed at Quincy's midsection with the cutlass, slicing the white lawn shirt like butter.

"You're good," Quincy gasped, dancing back out of reach of the deadly weapon. "Very good."

"I should be," Gavin answered. "You taught me."

Warily they circled each other, seemingly unaware of the gunshots and cries of fighting above deck. It was all Ashley could do to keep out of their way as they battled back and forth in the cabin. Once she nearly reached the fallen knife, but Gavin caught a glimpse of her from the corner of his eye and nearly took off her arm.

"Give it up, Quince," Gavin said. "You know you're licked. You're breathing hard."

It was true. Both men were wet with sweat, but Quincy's breath was coming in ragged gasps. Gavin's youth and superior strength were beginning to show as he drove Quincy unmercifully. Slash and parry, circle and swing, both blades moved as though they were alive. Blood ran freely from both men; their clothes were cut to ribbons.

The cutlass blade struck with enough force to drive Quincy to his knees. The rapier slid down along the steel edge of the cutlass until the hand guards caught. Quincy and Gavin stared into each other's eyes, close enough to feel the heat of each other's breath. "Why did you bring Ashley into this?" Quincy demanded.

"I want everything that's yours." Gavin laughed and stepped back. "Your ship, your fortune, and your daughter. She's mine, Quince, just like the *Witch,* and I'll use them both as I see fit." Gavin slashed at Quincy's legs. "Besides, I think you'll tell me where the treasure's buried . . . or she will."

"She doesn't know."

"So you say." Gavin charged again, hacking at Quincy's head and shoulders, pushing him back toward the bunk. Ashley ran and seized the poniard from the floor, lifting it by the point to throw at Gavin's back, when Quincy let out a cry and fell back against the wall, clutching his side. Gavin withdrew the bloody cutlass, picked up Quincy's rapier, and turned toward Ashley. "I wouldn't, if I were you," he threatened.

Ashley ran to her father. Blood was seeping through his fingers and his face was the color of milk. "Quincy!"

He grimaced in pain and slid down the wall to the

deck. "I guess I was a good teacher," he said to Gavin. Ashley pushed aside his fingers to look at the gaping wound. "No fuss, girl," he said. "Give us a spot of rum, will you."

Ashley glanced at Gavin questioningly.

"Whatever he wants . . . except this." He flipped open a sea chest and removed a brace of pistols. "If you'll excuse me, I'll see to putting the ship to order. Don't leave the cabin, Ashley, or I won't be responsible for your safety." The door slammed shut behind him.

"Let me help you into the bunk," Ashley said, putting her shoulder under Quincy's arm. "You need a surgeon. I'll get something to stop the bleeding, but this wound is beyond my skill."

Quincy coughed and sweat broke out on his forehead as they managed the few steps to the bunk. "Don't worry yourself. St. Peter himself couldn't sew this up. No." He raised a hand to stop her protests. "I've sewn more cutlass wounds than you have years. I may linger a few days, but this one is mortal."

"Quincy, please."

"Would you have me lie to you now, Ashley?" He bit his lower lip and shifted onto one shoulder. "Pour a little rum into it. It can't hurt any more and it may halt the infection for a few hours. If I'm to get you out of this mess, I'll need all the time I can borrow."

Tears ran down Ashley's cheeks, making it hard for her to see as she ripped strips of linen into bandages. "Damn him to everlasting hellfire!" she swore.

"Don't waste your energy on him," her father advised. "I've things I want to tell you. Things I should have told you a long time ago."

She pressed a rum-soaked pad against the bloody wound, and Quincy moaned and shut his eyes, clenching his fingers into tight fists. "Bring me a drink," he ordered weakly. He downed the goblet of fiery liquid and held it out for another. Ashley refilled it, taking time to swallow a few mouthfuls herself.

"Ah, that's better," Quincy said between clenched teeth. He sighed, reaching for her hand. "I've wasted my life, Ashley. I've done things that will see me in hell if there is such a place. I've hurt you without meaning to. But I love you . . . and I'd not have put you in danger this way." He squeezed her fingers. "You must believe that."

"I do," she whispered.

"I've buried a fortune in Spanish booty on Morgan's Fancy over the years," he said painfully. "If I'd lived long enough, I meant to offer Governor Bladen a large enough bribe that he would give me a full pardon. I've never stopped loving Cicely, girl." He chuckled and the strangled sound became a choking.

"Don't try to talk," Ashley said. "Save your strength." She raised the pad, then clamped it down when fresh blood began to flow from the wound.

"For what?" Amusement filtered through the pain-filled eyes. "I wanted to be a tobacco planter, Ashley. I wanted brick walls around me at night and a lawn with grass and flowers where your mother and I could watch our grandchildren play." He forced a crooked smile. "Gentleman Jim. I'm a farce, girl. I always was. As much a failure as a buccaneer captain as I was as a father."

"Did Cicely know?"

He shook his head and frowned. "I saw no need to disturb her life until I had something to offer her.

Your mother was always a delicate flower, Ashley. In the wrong setting, she would wither and die."

"Maybe." Ashley brought a fresh bandage and exchanged it for the soaked one. The bleeding seemed to be slowing, but still Quincy had lost a lot of blood.

"The treasure is yours now. I want you to have it all."

"Not Cicely?"

"No. Do for your mother what you think right. But Cicely's not strong enough to manage it."

"And you think I am?" Ashley's eyes darkened. "Do you think me willing to take the rewards of my neighbors' harvests? I don't want your blood money, Quincy."

"Spoken like old Ash Morgan himself." Quincy chuckled. "Even old Ash would approve of you taking it. It's all Spanish, girl. Pieces of eight, gold doubloons, and heathen treasure from the Spanish colonies in Mexico and South America. They stole it from the poor red savages, didn't they? And took their land and souls besides." He grinned. "Oh, I'm not so noble as all that. I've taken my share of silk, and tobacco, and good English guineas. But I knew I'd bribe no Maryland governor with English gold. What's buried on Morgan's Fancy is as honest as any privateer's booty. Besides, we're at war with Spain, aren't we?"

"If England's not, she soon will be," Ashley agreed. She shrugged. "You're right. Even grandfather would take Spanish gold. Where is it buried?"

Quincy beckoned her closer, whispering the location into her ear. "Only Cato knows besides me, and he'll go to his grave with the secret," he said. "Gavin mustn't learn you know where it is. He's not above torturing you to find out."

Another shot rang out above deck and Ashley flinched. The sounds of clashing steel and men's angry voices became louder. "Can he take the ship?" she asked. "How many men can you count on to remain loyal?"

"If they know I'm dying?" Quincy grimaced. "Only Cato. But Gavin hates him. He may already be dead." He swallowed and motioned for another cup of rum. "Cato was never much in a fight anyway."

"I don't—" Ashley whirled around as the door banged open. Two evil-looking men glared back at her, both carrying cutlasses stained red with blood.

"What do you want?" Quincy demanded, struggling up on one elbow. "How dare you force your way into my cabin!"

The red-bearded man laughed harshly. "Captain wants ye and the wench on deck."

"He's hurt," Ashley cried. "I'll go, but leave him be."

Ignoring her protests, they crossed the room and dragged Quincy from his bunk.

"You'll kill him!" she shouted. "It's bad luck to move a dying captain from his cabin. Do you want to—" The roar of a cannon drowned her words. "We're under attack!"

The men let go of Quincy's shoulders and Ashley helped him back onto the bunk. Red-Beard glanced at the smaller man questioningly. Then the ship vibrated with the shock of answering cannon fire. "Leave him and bring the wench," Red-Beard said.

"No!" Quincy cried.

The bearded pirate shoved Ashley toward the doorway. "Move!" he ordered. With a parting glance at her father, Ashley obeyed.

When she reached the open deck, she stopped short, stunned by the scene of utter chaos. Dead and wounded men lay scattered on the deck, and the air hung thick with smoke and the stench of powder. But there was no fighting among the pirates now. All hands were at their stations as the *Scarlet Witch* bore down upon a square-rigged brigantine off the starboard side. The crew had obviously broken off their private squabble to attack a passing merchant vessel.

Frantically Ashley looked to the port side, trying to gauge the distance to land. If she dove over the side, could she make it to shore? Deciding any chance was better than what she had aboard the *Witch*, she made a sudden dash for the port rail, only to run into the solid bulk of a man's chest.

"No, you don't," Gavin said, grabbing her and twisting her arm behind her back. "I promised you a good time, Ashley . . . and we haven't even started to play."

It had taken Kelt precious hours to get to Chestertown and convince Philip Fraser to take the *Merry Kate* in search of the pirate vessel. The heavily armed sloop was built for speed and her crew were all tough, seasoned men. They slipped out of the Chester River in the early hours of dawn, using the wind from the coming northeaster to make up for lost time.

Beside the crew of the *Merry Kate*, Kelt had brought along a band of men from the plantation, priming them for battle against the pirates with promises of a rich reward.

" 'Tis a chance you're takin', Kelt," Captain Fraser said as he scanned the compass. Rain beat against his lined face and ran in rivulets down his foul-weather gear. "There are a thousand places a schooner can hide along the Chesapeake. What makes ye think she's nae gone to ground again somewhere else?"

"If I were Gentleman Jim McCade," Kelt answered slowly, "I'd make for the open sea. If a Royal Navy ship did find his hiding spot, he'd be caught like a fox in a hole. If he gets out of the Chesapeake, where do I hunt for him? New Providence? Guayaquil? Jamaica? We both know I'd never see Ashley again. And I'm not going to let that happen."

"And if you do find her, and if we take the ship—I say *if*, mind you—what will you do with her? You can't force her to wed you. She may have gone with her father willingly."

"Nay!" Kelt shook his head. "I know she dinna." It had been a risk to tell Philip of the relationship between Ashley Morgan and the pirate, Gentleman Jim McCade, but if he was asking his friend to chance his ship and his life, he felt Philip should know the whole truth. Kelt put his hands behind his back and paced the small section of deck where they stood. "But I canna, for the life of me, figure why McCade would take her wi' him. It makes no sense and he's a wily one. He'd do naught from whim or fancy. I believe he has an affection for Ashley."

"If he did take her against her will, he'll fight to keep her. You may ha' to kill him."

"Aye. The thought has crossed my mind."

"And ha' do ye ken what the lass will do if ye kill her father?"

Kelt stared out across the water. "Aye, Philip," he said softly. "She wouldna take it lightly. But we must cross that bridge when we come to it. I'll ha' her back, Philip, by fair means or foul. And once I ha' her, I'll ne'er let her go again."

"Well, then, you've made up your mind." Captain Fraser turned to motion to his first officer. "Keep a sharp watch for sail," he ordered. "A prize of silver coin to the man who sights the *Scarlet Witch* first.''

''Yes, sir.'' The man hesitated as though waiting to say something.

''What is it, Isaac?''

''One of the seamen, Cap'n. John Voshel. He's asked to speak with you on an important matter.''

''Do you know what he wants?''

''No, sir, I don't. But the word is, before he signed on with us he—''

''Oot wi' it! He what?'' Captain Fraser demanded.

''It's only rumor, but the scuttlebutt in the foc'sle is that Voshel used to be a pirate. And they say he sailed with Gentleman Jim McCade.''

Chapter 22

Cannon roared as bar and chain shot whirred through the air to cut the merchant vessel's rigging. Forward, Ashley saw the dwarf, Cato, manning a swivel gun with the aid of a half-grown boy. Cannon fire from the square-rigged brigantine had dwindled to a sporadic volley as the deck became a morass of tangled line and canvas.

The shrill pitch of an officer's whistle mingled with the screams of fallen men and the crack of a breaking mast. The merchant ship shuddered as she took the full shock of a broadside, bringing a rousing cheer from the crew of the *Scarlet Witch*. Before the shouts subsided, a second swivel gun on the elevated poop raked the deck of the brigantine with musket balls. The sounds were deafening. Ashley shut her eyes and put her hands over her ears.

Gavin grabbed Ashley and shook her. "Coward!" he taunted. "Where's all that bravado now?" Letting go of her shoulders, he wound her single braid around his fist until her head was bent back at an unnatural angle. "Get below with your father, then," he growled. "I wouldn't want anything to happen to you—not just yet." He shoved her aft toward the quarterdeck. "Prepare to board!" he shouted to his men. "No quarter!"

Ashley ducked through the wooden doors and down the steps. Her heart was racing and her breath coming in frightened gasps. Gavin was a madman! She'd be better off dead than in his hands. To be touched by him . . . violated . . . No, by God! She'd see him in hell first. If she had to die in the process, so be it. Anger began to replace the numbing fear she had felt on deck. Why should she be afraid of dying? She had seen hell, smelled the fire and brimstone, and stood in the arms of Satan himself.

Quincy's eyes were closed when she entered the master's cabin. His breathing was faint but regular. The bandage was bloodstained, but no worse than before. Ashley sank into a chair beside her father and tried to block out the sounds of battle above. There seemed to be nothing to do now but wait—and waiting was never a thing she did well.

She had lost all track of time when suddenly there was a tremendous shock and a grinding noise. She jumped to her feet, realizing that the cannon fire had ceased.

"We're boarding," Quincy murmured.

Ashley looked up, unable to suppress a shudder. "He's going to murder them all. I heard him give the order. No quarter."

"Try not to think of it." Quincy grimaced in pain and shifted his hip. "Water."

Ashley poured him some and held the cup to his lips. "Is the pain bad?"

"Ahhh," he sighed. "I've felt better . . . and worse." He forced a thin smile. "You're a good chess player, Ashley. You can beat him if you use your head."

"We've got to get you to a doctor."

"Stop it." Quincy's eyes darkened with anger. "No games between us. Not now." He took a deep breath and pulled himself up on an elbow. "If I haven't bled to death by now, I probably won't. That's means I may have a little longer." He motioned toward the sea chest. "Look in the bottom. There's a little rosewood box with ivory elephants on the top." Ashley went to the chest. "Beneath the clothing. Yes, that's it. Inside is a gift for your mother. I want you to give it to her if you can."

Ashley opened the rosewood box. Wrapped in dark blue velvet was a shimmering gold necklace bearing a single square-cut emerald mounted against a frame of tiny diamonds. "Oh," Ashley said. "It's beautiful."

"Gavin doesn't know I have it. He thinks I lost it in a card game in St. Mary's. Otherwise it wouldn't still be in the chest. Hide it somewhere. No, wait," Quincy said. "Give it here." He took the necklace and shoved it down into his breeches. "If I don't run too far, it shouldn't fall out. There's more jewelry in the bottom. Put something else in the box in case he gets curious in the next twenty-four hours."

Quickly she replaced the box and closed the lid of the chest. A woman's scream filtered down from the deck above and Ashley paled. "Was it always like this?" she asked her father bitterly.

"Hold your tongue, girl. I'll not be judged by you. What debts I have accumulated will soon come due in a higher court." Quincy's voice softened. "The penalty for rape among my crew was death—delivered by my own hand. Gavin must answer for his own crimes." He raised an eyebrow. "What of your Scotsman? Has he asked for your hand in marriage?"

Ashley nodded. "I refused him."

"You don't love him?"

"What right have you to ask me these questions?" she demanded. "You can't start playing father after all these years."

"Do you love him?"

"Yes. I love him," she snapped. "I love him. Are you satisfied?"

"It's not me who has to be satisfied, Ashley, but you. Marry him, if he'll have you. Try and make a normal life for yourself while you can. It's no good alone. I know . . . I've tried it."

"He'll not have me now, so there's no sense worrying about it, is there?" Ashley went to the porthole and stared out at the churning water. When she had left Kelt in his room under Thomas's gun, she had lost any chance of their working things out. And without Kelt, even Morgan's Fancy didn't seem to matter.

She turned back toward Quincy with steel in her eyes. "I can't stay down here like a rat in a hole," she said. "I've got to try and help them." Ignoring his protests, she hurried topside again.

Crewmen were just cutting away the lines that held the merchant vessel fast to the *Witch*. The deck of the captured ship was still. Bodies lay where they had fallen and there was no sign of life. On the quarter deck she saw an elderly woman, arms flung out, head lolling to one side like a broken doll.

"You shouldn't be here," a high, distorted voice rasped. Cato took hold of Ashley's arm and began to pull her back toward the quarterdeck. "They got the bloodlust on 'em," he warned. "And she"—he motioned toward the sinking ship—"she were carryin' rum."

Ashley recoiled from the dwarf's touch. His hands were black with powder and something wet and sticky.

"Yer just like the other women, ain't ye?" He laughed. "But they's others worse than Cato." He lowered his massive head and peered at her through bloodshot pig-eyes. "Be he still alive? Cap'n McCade?"

She nodded. "He's hurt bad."

"That's why Mister Gavin took on the brigantine, ye know. Some was fer him and some still fer Gentleman Jim. We all fight t'gether fer booty. We don' fight each other." He cackled deep in his throat. "Not yet, we don'." He brought his face so close to Ashley's that she could smell his foul breath. "When the cap'n dies, you and me, we ain't worth that." He snapped his fingers. "Now, you get below, girl, lest you want to die like that old woman, wi' yer legs in the air." He hefted his battle ax. "I'll foller t' watch yer back and do what I kin fer Gentleman Jim."

Ashley looked back at the brigantine. She was floundering in the waves as water poured through the holes blasted by cannonballs. The coming storm would soon sink her. For a long moment she stared at the ship, offering a prayer for the souls she would carry to the bottom with her. Then Cato's impatient tugging at her arm drew her back to her own danger. The sounds of drunken revelry from the crew gave proof to his warning. Resolutely she stiffened her shoulders and hurried back to her dying father.

Darkness had wrapped the *Scarlet Witch* in a mantle of driving rain and howling wind when Ashley felt the motion of the ship alter abruptly. Quincy raised his head and looked at the dwarf slumped against the cabin hatch. Cato nodded. Both had caught the sound of the anchor line feeding out. Ashley went to the brass-bound window, but nothing except driving rain was visible through the thick panes of bull's-eye glass.

"What's happening?" she asked.

"We're anchored," Quincy said. "I wondered how long he'd try to run before the storm." He glanced at the dwarf for confirmation. "Blind Man's Creek?"

Cato nodded. "I heard him gi' the order."

Quincy sighed. " 'Twas a neat bit of sailing to bring her into the creek in this wind. I'm glad Gavin learned something I tried to teach him in all these years."

"Where are we?" Ashley asked. "I've not heard the name."

"On the Eastern Shore." Quincy motioned toward the desk. "There's a chart in the drawer. It should be on top. Yes, that's it, girl. Bring it here." He pointed to a spot on the map. "There. Blind Man's Creek lies between this point and this spot here."

"But there's no creek on the map," Ashley said.

Cato laughed and spit on the blade of his ax, polishing it with the corner of his shirt.

Quincy grinned. "Would it be likely that it would be? The creek mouth opens thusly." He drew an imaginary line in the air with his index finger. "You must bring the ship in toward the beach, toward what looks like a wooded beach, then cut hard to the starboard. The channel is deep, but leaves no more than a fathom on either side of the ship. The creek makes a sharp dogleg, then widens out beyond the trees."

"Hiding the ship from any passing vessels on the bay," Ashley said.

"Exactly. I wouldn't bring the *Witch* here in winter." Quincy took another sip of rum. A flush had replaced the ashen hue of his skin, and his eyes glowed with unnatural brightness. "The creek's not wide enough to sail her far inland. But any season you have foliage on the trees, a ship's invisible from the water."

"And what of the land?" she demanded. Her hands were gentle as she changed the dressing on his wound. That, too, had reddened around the edges. The bleeding had almost stopped, but she knew that what Quincy had said was true. A man could not live long with such damage to his vitals. She tried to keep her voice from betraying the awful sense of hopelessness that threatened to drain her will. "What's to say you wouldn't be sighted by a hunter or a farmer searching for a lost cow?"

"Not flamin' likely," the dwarf said. "There's a thick wood an' marsh a'hind thet. Sand that'll suck a man down and leave nary a trace." He shook his ponderous head. "A safe harbor t' ride out a storm, or lay low 'til the sea is clear."

"I don't know if—"

The door swung open and Ashley twisted about to meet Gavin's rapacious scrutiny. "Still above water, are you, Quincy?"

Ashley glanced back at her father and a chill passed through her as she witnessed the transformation of Quincy's face from the features of a courtly gentleman to the granite mask of a stranger.

"Have you come to finish it, Gavin?" Quincy's low voice was edged with steel.

Gavin braced his muscular legs against the roll of the ship and laid his huge right hand over the butt of the flintlock pistol jammed under his wide leather belt. In his left hand he carried a cutlass, and the spotted cowhide strap that ran diagonally across his bare chest bore a second pistol and an ivory-handled dagger. Two days' beard marred the classic square chin and the full, curving lips. His white-blond hair was held back from his face with a strip of red and white cloth, and a gold earring dangled from one ear.

"Only a coward would harm a helpless man," Ashley cried, stepping between Gavin and her father.

"Who said anything about harming a man?" Gavin's blue-green eyes reflected the gleam of the light from the whale-oil lamp. His slightly slurred speech gave evidence of his lack of sobriety. "I'll not harm a hair on Quince's head—not if he tells me what I want to know." He smiled with his lips. "And even if he doesn't . . ."

"Leave her out of this," Quincy warned. "No one knows where the treasure lies but me and Cato. And you know he'll tell you nothing."

"A man can be persuaded to talk," Gavin suggested. "Even you, Quince, if offered the right reward."

"Abuse my daughter and I'll feed your guts to the crabs before your living eyes." Quincy fought to a sitting position. "By God, I will, Gavin! If I have to come back from hell to do it."

"You can try, old man."

"Leave 'im be," Cato growled. "There's men topside who won't stand for that kind of talk," the dwarf reminded them. "They followed Gentleman Jim too many years to see what belongs to him boarded." He blocked Gavin's path with his hulkish body and raised the ax. "It goes against the grain, Mr. Gavin. You kin see thet, can't ya? Even the brotherhood has laws. We don't feed on our own."

"No?" Gavin's eyes narrowed. "What if I give you seconds? How long has it been since you've had a woman free of the runnin' pox? Or any woman at all?"

Cato's mouth hung open and his eyes widened. Hesitantly he took a step toward Gavin.

Bile rose in Ashley's throat. "Stop it," she shouted. Black spots danced before her eyes as fear turned her muscles to water and her sanity wavered. This couldn't be happening to her! "Hold your filthy tongue," she said. "What kind of man are you?"

"A man who's waited too many years for what's rightly his," he answered bitterly. "And one who's hungry for a tender bit of woman."

Ashley leaned over her father. "To hell with the treasure," she whispered. "Tell him where it is, Quincy." She glanced back at Gavin. "Maybe he'll take it and go."

"She's talkin' sense," Gavin said. "Make up your mind before we drag you out of that bunk and throw her in it."

"Ye'd let me hav' a bit?" Cato asked, running his tongue over his lips. "Yer not lyin' t' me?" The dwarf moved closer. "Yaaaa!" Giving a wild cry, he swung the ax at the blond corsair's midsection.

Gavin sidestepped the blow, tossed the cutlass from one hand to the other, and brought the cutlass down with such force that it severed Cato's head from his shoulders. Ashley let out a sob and turned away, covering her eyes with her hands. There was a dull thud as the dwarf's lifeless body fell to the deck.

Gavin looked down at the growing pool of gore. "A pity," he said. "I'd planned to drown him in a keg of rum. The men were taking bets on how long he'd kick." He nudged Cato's body with the toe of his shoe. "Damned abomination. I should have done it long ago."

"Let her go free and I'll lead you to the treasure," Quincy offered. "You don't need her."

Gavin shook his head and grinned. "I don't let go of what's mine 'til I'm done with it. You'll tell me what I want to know or every man jack on this ship will have the use of her—including the boatswain's pretty boy. And I'll make certain you get to watch."

With a curse, Quincy struggled to his feet and forced himself erect. Sweat broke out on his face and the bandage turned to red. "Stay away from her," he said. "Ashley, behind me, girl." From the sleeve of his shirt a small dagger appeared. Swaying slightly, Quincy dropped into a fighting stance, the knife in his hand.

Gavin whipped the pistol from his belt and leveled it at Quincy. "You son of a bitch! I'll blow you to hell," he swore.

Quincy jabbed at him with the knife and the lieutenant brought the barrel of the flintlock down across the captain's temple. Quincy dropped like a stone. Gavin reached for Ashley and she fled to the far corner of the room, seizing an inkwell and heaving it at his head. Gavin ducked the inkwell, then caught a wine goblet full in the face. He grabbed Ashley's arm, slammed her up against the wall, and ground his mouth against hers.

She struck at his face with her free hand and tried to bring her knee up to strike him in the groin. Ignoring her blows, Gavin ran his hand over her breasts and squeezed her viciously. She cried out and went limp in a feigned faint. Cursing, he shook her by the shoulders, then picked her up and carried her toward the bunk. From the corner of her eye she glimpsed the empty rum bottle. The instant he laid her down on the bed, her hand shot out, seized the bottle, and slammed it against his head.

Ashley clenched her eyes shut as a shower of glass

rained around her. Gavin groaned and fell forward on top of her. Shoving him aside, she scrambled off the bunk and ran toward the door. For a heartbeat she hesitated and looked back at her father's prone body on the floor. He hadn't moved. Was he dead? Gavin groaned again, compelling her to action. Ashley snatched the pistol from the floor and fled from the cabin, running so swiftly down the passageway that the bearded guard in front of the powder magazine door was unable to stop her.

Up the ladder and out onto the deck she ran, almost into the arms of a drunken buccaneer. He threw out his arms to seize her, but she kicked him as hard as she could in the knee, dodged sideways, and ran for the railing. Wind shook the masts and rain beat against Ashley, soaking her to the skin. A shadowy figure loomed ahead of her in the darkness and she turned and ran back the other way.

"Don't let her get away!"

"Stop her!"

Gavin's command rang above the wind as Ashley scrambled over the rail. She couldn't make out the shore, but it didn't matter. Even drowning was better than staying aboard the *Witch*. A hand closed over her shoulder and dragged her back, lifting her into the air. Instinctively she raised the pistol and pulled the trigger point-blank. The only sound was the click of the trigger. Misfire. Desperately she squeezed again just before something slammed her down against the deck.

Gavin's face hovered over hers. "You bitch!" he shouted. "I'll—" His words were drowned in the roar of a cannon. Suddenly the air was thick with falling canvas and rope. Something heavy hit the deck only inches from her head. Ashley curled into a ball and covered her head with her hands.

The clang of metal against wood and shrill whistles sounded from both starboard and port sides of the ship. Ashley lifted her head cautiously to peer through the falling rain and saw a man's head appear over the rail of the ship. Screams of fallen men and musket shots filtered back from the bow of the ship. Within seconds it was evident to Ashley that the *Scarlet Witch* was under attack from all sides. She had barely gotten to her feet when the shock of a collision between the schooner and what must be another vessel threw her to the deck again.

A grappling hook flew over the side and two more men climbed over the rail. One was struck almost at once with a pike, screamed, and tumbled back into the water. The second man dropped to one knee and fired a pistol into the darkness. A scream testified to the accuracy of his blind aim.

Ashley began to crawl toward the quarterdeck, keeping her head low. Between the driving rain, the tangle of canvas and fallen yards, and the fighting men, it was almost impossible to go more than a few feet at a time. When she was close enough to make out the wooden doors that led to the passageway below, she got to her feet and made a dash for the opening.

"Ashley Morgan!"

Kelt's voice pierced her terror and she froze, turning toward the source. "Kelt! Where are you?" she cried.

"Here!"

"Kelt! I—" Something grabbed her by the hair and yanked her back. A man's hand closed around her throat, followed by the cold edge of a steel blade.

"Move a muscle," Gavin whispered harshly, "and I'll cut your throat from ear to ear!"

"Ashley? What—" Kelt lunged toward them, then stopped short when he saw that Gavin held her captive. "Let her go," he ordered.

"Drop your weapons. Order your men to retreat, or I'll kill her," Gavin shouted.

"No. Don't trust him," Ashley said. "He'll—" Her breath was cut off as Gavin tightened his fingers on her throat.

"You've got five seconds," Gavin threatened. "After that, she's fish bait. One . . . two . . . three . . ."

Chapter 23

Kelt peered through the driving rain at the shadowy forms of Ashley and the pirate who held her prisoner. He gauged the distance between them to be twice a man's height, too far to rush him. Slowly he raised his pistol, extending his right arm to its full length. "Let her go," he ordered. Blind rage warred with fear within him. The man would kill her, no matter what. He knew it as surely as if it had been written in her blood. If he could just get a shot off before . . .

"Four," Gavin said. "I mean it. I'll cut her like a Christmas goose. Fi—"

A muffled explosion checked Kelt's fire. He lunged forward as the corsair's hand holding the knife slowly fell away from Ashley's throat. Ashley let out a scream and tore free, throwing herself out of the line of fire. Gavin stared wide-eyed at Kelt, his face a mask of surprise. He clutched the front of his belly. His mouth moved, but his sounds were incomprehensible. Then his knees folded under him and he pitched forward onto the deck, twitched, and lay still.

A second figure stood behind Gavin, leaning against the double doors leading below deck, a smoking pistol clutched in his hand. Kelt dropped to one knee and raised his own weapon.

"No!" Ashley screamed, blocking his aim. "Don't shoot! It's my father." She turned and caught the sagging man in her arms. "Quincy! Quincy," she cried.

"Are there any of the crew left below?" Kelt demanded.

Quincy shook his head, unable to speak.

Kelt thrust his loaded pistol into her hand. "I'll deal wi' ye later, woman. Get ye below and lock yourself in the master's cabin. Shoot any son of a bitch who tries to get in! Quick!" He gave her a shove as two men crashed to the deck beside him, locked in mortal combat. Seizing Gavin's cutlass, Kelt made short work of the pirate on top, dragged the fallen sailor to his feet, and threw himself back into the fray.

Ashley put her arm under Quincy's shoulder and together they retreated back down the ladder. "You're bleeding again," she said, as the swinging ship's lantern showed the gush of red down his shirt and breeches. "Where'd you get the pistol?"

Quincy took a deep breath and motioned to the bearded man sprawled ahead of them in the passageway. The ivory handle of a knife protruded from the middle of his back. "His," Quincy gasped. "He had no need . . . of it."

It was nearly an hour before Ashley heard Kelt's deep voice demanding entry to the cabin. Her father lay on the bunk once more, his face as deathly white as a shroud. Quincy's eyes were shut and his breathing uneven and shallow. He hadn't spoken a single word since they had reached the comparative safety of the master's cabin.

"The ship is secure," Kelt assured her. "Unbar the door."

Ashley crossed the room to stand by the door, pistol primed and ready. "How do I know someone isn't making you say that?" she called. True, the screams and clash of battle had faded minutes before, but he had told her to open for no one. Past fear, Ashley was acting on instinct alone, knowing that if she allowed herself the slightest bit of hysteria, she would go completely to pieces.

The flood of obscenities that poured through the heavy wooden door were proof enough. With nervous fingers, she fumbled with the bolt, then stood back as the big Scotsman crashed into the room.

Gray eyes scanned the area, taking in Quincy's still form on the bunk and the blanket-swathed bundle on the deck. Nothing could hide the wash of drying blood that stained the white oak planks beneath his feet. Kelt lowered his cutlass and glared at her. "What ha' ye to say for yourself, woman? Shall we bind you along wi' the rest for delivery to the governor at Williamsburg? There's a reward on the head of every freebooter, dead or alive."

Ashley's stomach churned. "Speak not to me of heads!" she snapped. The image of Cato's horrible death lingered in her mind. By the King's gout! She had witnessed enough of blood and gore to last a lifetime. She'd not now be badgered over trifles by the man she loved.

"Will ye say nothing in your own defense?" Kelt roared. His clothes were shredded and bloodstained, and one arm dripped blood, but from the way he moved, she could tell he had taken no serious hurt.

"Why should I have to?" The Morgan chin firmed as Ashley's eyes took on a gleam of pure defiance. "I was hit over the head, kidnapped, nearly raped, and almost had my throat cut! What kind of man comes to rescue a woman and tries to blame her for being a victim?'' Her balled fists rested lightly on her hips as she advanced on him. ''If you are captain here, do as you will! Hand me over to the Virginians. Hang me, if it gives you pleasure. But you'll not have him!'' She motioned toward the man on the bed. ''He's dying, and I shall see him given decent Christian burial. Do what you will with me, but . . . but . . .''

Ashley drew in a shuddering breath and then another as a cascade of tears tumbled down her scratched and swollen cheeks. ''Oh, Kelt,'' she wailed. ''Please . . . don't let them take him. He saved . . . he saved my life and maybe yours. Don't let them make a mock of his corpse, or of his friends.'' She pointed to the blanket covering Cato. ''They've earned better. Let God in his mercy judge them.''

''It doesn't matter,'' Quincy rasped. ''Cato might like . . . the idea of being worth something . . . dead. Crows or worms—what difference does it make?''

Kelt and Ashley moved close to the bed and Ashley caught her father's cold hand. ''It matters to me,'' Ashley said. ''I won't let them.''

Quincy forced a laugh that became a hacking cough. He fell back against the pillow and Ashley brought him a sip of brandy.

''I'm afraid I used the rum,'' she said, indicating the broken green shards on the floor. ''But then, I never was much for housekeeping.''

Quincy's lips moved and he beckoned Kelt closer. ''She's innocent of . . . the game . . . Scot,'' Quincy murmured. ''On her immortal soul . . . I . . . swear. Gavin . . . Gavin took her. I knew . . . nothing of it.''

"I did go to warn Quincy," Ashley admitted. "So if you'll hang me for that, you're welcome. I couldn't let them take him if I could help it." She looked up at Kelt with frightened eyes. "He's my father, no matter what."

"And it didn't mean anything to you that Thomas could have killed me?" Kelt asked.

Ashley looked sheepish. "Thomas is always threatening someone with that old wheel lock. So much so that my grandfather altered the firing mechanism years ago. He could hardly kill you with that gun unless he beat you over the head with it. It won't fire."

"You bedeviled kelpie! By all that's holy, I should strangle ye wi' my own hands!"

"Would you rather I had shot you? Or hit you over the head with a rum bottle like I did Gavin?"

Quincy laughed weakly. " 'Twas a mistake not to finish the job once he was down, girl. You would have . . ." He began to cough again. ". . . saved me the trouble of coming topside to kill him myself." His eyes met Kelt's. "But I suppose one can expect such poor logic . . . from a woman."

"Enough." Ashley's brow furrowed. "Must you taunt me on your deathbed? You must be serious. Prepare to meet your maker." She lifted his fingers to her lips and kissed them. "Is there anything you want?"

"Only that you give this to Cicely." Quincy dug the necklace from his inside breeches' pocket. The green stone caught the light from the swaying lantern. "It shimmers like the sea off Cape Henlopen on a summer day," he said softly. "I promised her an emerald and I've never kept that promise."

Ashley accepted the golden chain and closed her fist around it. "You'll give it to her yourself, Quincy," she said. Her eyes flew to Kelt's. "Please. Rosewood is near to Williamsburg. If he lives that long, can't we—''

"Aye,'' Kelt agreed. "If he breathes, we will stop long enough for him to gi' his goodbyes to your mother. If she will see him.''

Quincy nodded his thanks, letting his eyes flutter shut then snap open. "How did you find us?'' he demanded fiercely. "In this storm, 'twould be like searching for a shilling on the beach.''

"A sailor aboard the *Merry Kate,* John Voshel, told us where you might shelter from the storm. He said he used to sail wi' you under the skull and crossbones.'' Kelt turned away from the bed. "A mon will do almost anything for money—even betray his friends.''

Footsteps came down the passageway and Kelt turned to face two men. "Aye, what is it?''

"Cap'n Fraser's askin' fer ye, sir. He sent us to find ye.'' The sailor snatched off his cap as he noticed the presence of a woman. "Be ye all right, sir?''

The second man wound a bit of cloth around his left forearm and used his teeth to pull the knot tight. "Thirty-two dead, Master Saxon. Four knocking at the gates o' hell and the rest in irons.''

Kelt reached out and picked up Ashley's pistol. "I've business topside,'' he said gruffly. "Consider yourself under my protection, both of ye. I'll leave these men to be certain no one tries to harm ye. Like as not, we'll lie low until the storm passes, but if Quincy lives, I'll do my best to see him to Rosewood.''

"And me?'' Ashley asked.

"I canna deal wi' ye now, woman. There's much I must sort oot in my brain. I dinna ken if you be a victim, but 'tis plain you are no ootright pirate. No mon will hand ye o'er to the courts.'' Kelt compressed his lips into a thin line. "If we go to Rosewood, there may be danger for you. Your stepfather may try to do away wi' ye again. Ha' ye thought o' it?"

"Yes, but it's not Nicholas's way to do things in the open. He's a coward and a sneak. I should be safe enough."

"Will ye tell your mother that he hired a mon to murder ye?"

She shook her head sadly. "What use would there be? She wouldn't believe me any more than the authorities would. Short John is dead, and there is my word and that of an Indian that he was hired by Nicholas."

"Your brother might back you up. You said he warned ye before."

"He told me he wouldn't." Ashley rubbed her aching eyes. "Henry will stick by his father out of fear of being disowned. It's useless."

"Nay, 'tis not useless. I intend to present the matter to the court when I hand over the pirates. Even if nothing can be proved, it may prevent your stepfather from ever trying such a thing again."

"Do what you will, but I think it's a waste of time."

"My time is my own. And I am a mon who believes in the law, whatever others may think."

Ashley turned back to her father, wincing at the pain that cut through her with bittersweet reality. There was a real chance that Kelt would never forgive what she had done to him. If he left her, she knew she would spend a lifetime regretting what might have been between them.

The following hours blurred one into another as Ashley ate and slept and tried to do what she could for Quincy. Captain Fraser ordered warm water for her to wash and she did so gratefully. She was totally exhausted, hardly able to keep her eyes open or to pull on the clean women's clothing from her father's wardrobe.

When the rain finally slackened, Kelt came to inform them that they would be transferred to the *Merry Kate*. "The little man has been given a burial on the beach," he added. "I said a prayer o'er him, if it means anything to ye." He raised one dark eyebrow. "Such a wee pirate wouldna bring much in the way o' reward."

Ashley looked around the cabin of the *Scarlet Witch* one final time as she prepared to follow Quincy's litter, wondering if the deck could ever be scrubbed clean of blood. "What will happen to the ship?" she asked wearily. "Will the courts claim her?"

"Nae likely," Kelt proclaimed. " 'Twas a toss-up as to whether Philip Fraser or I should ha' her as prize. Being gentlemen, we decided to roll dice to see who should ha' the master's share."

"And?" Ashley curbed her impatience. Kelt had promised to take Quincy to Rosewood, something few men would have done. She owed him respect and good manners in return. If only she weren't so tired. If she let her eyelids drop, she would fall asleep here on her feet.

"I won." Kelt grinned. "Am I too old to take up the sea as a trade, do ye suppose?"

She shook her head. "No. Go and be a privateer, if it please you. Just take me to Rosewood first."

"Philip will stay here with some of his men to watch over the *Witch* while I take the pirate crew to Williamsburg." He hesitated. "Philip's men have cut the ears from the dead men and dropped them into a barrel of pickles. They would be certain of collecting all their reward.''

Ashley waited. There was more he was not saying; she could read it in his eyes. ''Yes?''

''Except for Gavin. The master of the *Cazadora* is well known on the Chesapeake. They have taken his head as indisputable proof of his passing.''

She blinked, taking hold of the door frame for support. ''And am I supposed to be horrified?''

''You are a most unwomanly female,'' Kelt declared loudly. ''Have you no bit of gentleness? No proper softness?''

'' 'Tis a mother's touch compared to what I would have done to Gavin, had I the chance,'' she said flatly. ''He murdered that family on the Eastern Shore last fall. When I am done praying for that helpless infant, perhaps I will have tears for such scum as Gavin.''

Kelt shrugged. ''At least no one's eating the pickles.''

Ashley paled and swayed. She would have fallen if he hadn't caught her, sweeping her up against his chest and carrying her swiftly topside. ''Are you ill?'' he asked as he put her down.

She shook her head. ''No. Just weary unto death.'' She paused and looked around her at the hidden creek. It was daylight and the rain had dwindled to a slow, steady rhythm. Gray clouds swirled overhead and Ashley glimpsed a brighter light that might be the sun trying to break through. The thickly wooded shoreline curved around them, strange surroundings for two seagoing ships. Even knowing the secret, she couldn't see where the ships had entered. The wide part of the creek was scarce larger than the farmyard at Morgan's Fancy. To the south, reeds grew down to the water's edge and several ducks had just pitched down to shelter there.

"Shall I carry you onto the *Merry Kate?*"

Kelt's voice was strained. He's weary, too, Ashley thought. "No," she answered. "I'll be all right." Oh, to be home again, to ride the green fields of her plantation and have the last days be a nightmare.

Already order was being made of the schooner's deck. Crewmen from the smaller sloop were sawing through fallen spars and cutting free tangled canvas sails. There was no sign of the prisoners and Ashley supposed they were tied up in the hold of the *Merry Kate*. A plank had been stretched across the water between the two vessels. Kelt's big hand steadied her as she walked gingerly over the narrow bridge.

"I'll not forget your kindness," she said to him when he left her at the door of the master's cabin.

"Aye, ye willna forget," he agreed. "For our business isna yet settled."

On seeing that Quincy had been made as comfortable as possible on a pallet, Ashley lay down on the captain's bunk and fell instantly asleep.

Cicely stood up and dropped her napkin onto the dining table, her blue eyes sparkling with pleasure at the unexpected sight of her daughter. "Ashley!" she cried. "Why didn't you tell us you were coming? And where did you find that gown? It's hopelessly out of date." Ignoring Nicholas's scowl, she ran to Ashley and hugged her.

"You're looking wonderful, as usual," Ashley murmured. She glanced about the elegant dining room. Except for the servants, they were alone with Nicholas and her brother.

"Henry, don't you have a word of welcome for your sister? You missed her last time she was at

Rosewood. Where are your manners?'' Cicely took hold of Ashley's arm and pulled her toward the table. ''Have you eaten? Of course not. Gabby, set another place for Mistress Ashley.''

Cicely's wig was arranged in elaborate curls that hung over one shoulder. Her satin gown was a deep rose with a tiny waist and plunging neckline that showed off her flawless figure. Around her slender neck she wore a simple string of pearls, the last gift Ash Morgan had given his daughter before he died. Ashley had never favored pearls, not since Captain Fraser had told her that young men and women often lost their lives diving for them in the far-off South Seas. But she had to admit they suited her mother. Would the raw beauty of Quincy's emerald necklace look as well? she wondered.

''I need to talk to you in private,'' Ashley said hesitantly. ''It's urgent.''

''Nonsense,'' Cicely said. ''We're family. You can speak freely in front of Nicholas and your brother.'' She motioned to a chair beside hers. ''Come, eat with us. We have a delicious veal pie and—''

''There's no time. A friend of yours is on the *Merry Kate*. He's been badly hurt and he's asking to see you.''

Henry kept his eyes on his plate and continued chewing his buttered biscuit as though he were alone in the room.

Nicholas's face flushed angry red as he got to his feet and exchanged a few whispered words with his manservant. ''What friend?'' he demanded. ''What's all this about? Really, Ashley, this habit of descending on us without warning has gotten out of hand.'' He folded his arms across his chest. ''You will kindly explain why two common seamen armed with muskets and cutlasses are standing in my hall.''

"They're my escort," Ashley replied smoothly. "To make certain *nothing* happens to me while I'm here. I've been prone to accidents lately."

"An accident? You've had an accident? Oh, dear," Cicely fussed. "You are all right, aren't you? I've asked you time and time again to stop careening about the countryside on that terrible horse."

"Pity," Henry said, taking a sip of white wine. "Now that someone's finally asked for her hand in holy matrimony." He glanced at Ashley through heavy-lidded eyes. "And they do say—" He cleared his throat and began to cough. The hacking became a spasm and he struggled for breath.

Cicely jumped up and hovered over him. "Henry, are you all right?"

He waved her away and wiped at his mouth and eyes with a linen handkerchief—a handkerchief, Ashley noticed, that was flecked with red. He gulped another mouthful of wine. "Excuse me," he said. "That was quite unforgivable. What I started to say was that, once someone starts to have accidents, they usually continue. Wouldn't you say that's true, Father?"

Nicholas swore under his breath. "Damn it, Ashley, this sport has gone on long enough. Who is here to see your mother and why?"

"Why, Father, I'd think Ashley would rather hear who is foolish enough to want to marry her. You thought it was amusing enough when he came calling the other night." Henry leaned back in his chair and began to pick his teeth with a gold pick.

"Stop it, both of you," Cicely said. "It's no laughing matter. James Pade is a respectable gentleman with a title and no small fortune. Lady Pade has assured me she will not stand in your way if you wish to accept her son's proposal, Ashley. You should certainly give it some thought."

"Are you certain you want her outranking you, Mother? And living so close by?" Henry chuckled, reminding Ashley just why she had despised him when they were children.

"Why Lord Pade would want to link his family with a bastard is more than I can say." Nicholas came to stand behind Cicely's chair. "Now, what is all this secrecy?"

"Yes, darling, who on earth are you talking about?" Cicely asked.

Ashley swallowed hard, looking from one face to another. "I would rather have talked with you privately," she said, "but it's Quincy McCade. He wants to see you. And . . . he's dying."

"Quincy?" Cicely recoiled as though she had been slapped and the blood drained from her face. "Quincy dying?" She shook her head. "No . . . it's not true. It's a lie."

"You dare to bring him here?" Nicholas roared. "You filthy little trollop!" He drew back a clenched fist. "Get out of my house!"

"Quincy?" Cicely rose unsteadily to her feet. "He's here?"

"At the dock," Ashley said, ignoring Nicholas. "I'll take you to him."

"The hell you will!" Nicholas bellowed. He grabbed Cicely by the shoulder and spun her halfway across the room. "You'll go to your pirate lover over my dead body!"

"Let her go," Henry said, getting up. "It can hardly mar your honor any further."

"Keep out of this." Nicholas whirled on Ashley, but she had put a chair between them. "Get out!" he shouted again. "Before I have you whipped off Rosewood like the bitch you are!"

"Better a bitch than a murderer," Ashley said softly.

Cicely stiffened. "I'm going to him, Nicholas. It will do you no good to make an ugly scene in front of the children." She took a few steps toward the doorway. The servants exchanged knowing glances and fled through the other door.

Nicholas moved to block her way. "I said no!" he repeated.

"And I said I will," Cicely insisted. "Get out of my way, Nicholas. I won't be bullied by you any longer."

"You won't, won't you?" Nicholas seized her by the arm and slapped her twice across the face. She fell back against the wall, blood seeping from a cut on her lip.

"I will," she sobbed. Before she could get her feet under her, Nicholas hit her again.

"No!" Ashley cried. She ran toward her mother, but before she could reach her, Henry stepped between Cicely and Nicholas and gave his father a rough shove.

"Leave her alone," Henry threatened.

"You ungrateful pup. I told you to stay out of this." Nicholas took a swing at his son. Henry ducked out of reach.

Ashley helped Cicely up, pulling her away from the two circling men.

"Go to your pirate, Mother," Henry said, throwing up his own fists. "I think it's high time I taught your husband a lesson in manners."

There was a sound of flesh striking flesh and someone groaned. Cicely stopped short. "Ashley? What shall I do?"

"Go to him if you want to see him alive."

"He's really dying?"

Ashley nodded. "He wants you with him."

"Then I have no choice." With a last frantic look at her husband and son, Cicely hurried out into the hallway.

Henry shouted something and Ashley turned back in time to see her brother's fist connect with Nicholas's jaw. Nicholas fell backward, striking his head sharply against the inside corner of the brick fireplace. With a groan, he slid down to lie full length on the floor, his head lolling sideways on the blackened hearth. For an instant, Henry's startled gaze met hers, then she turned and followed Cicely out of the house and down the hill toward Rosewood's dock.

Chapter 24

Captain Quincy James McCade, Gentleman Jim, lay propped up on a pillow in the master's cabin of the *Merry Kate*. He had been shaved, and his shoulder-length auburn hair was drawn back neatly and fastened at the nape of his neck with a black velvet ribbon. Ashley had insisted that her father's own clothing be brought from the *Scarlet Witch*, and Kelt had helped him dress in a spotless white linen shirt with a fall of Dutch lace at the neck and azure blue breeches and vest. The vest served to cover most of the bandages at his midsection.

Even with the skin drawn taut across his cheekbones and his ashen countenance, he was still a striking man, Ashley thought as Cicely ran across the room to his side. The mortal wound had added years to the lines of Quincy's face, but the aging had brought a softness that made him even more attractive. His eyes had darkened to glowing obsidian, radiating a power no dying man should possess.

Ashley had wanted to leave them alone, but Quincy had asked her to stay.

"No," he'd whispered. "I . . . want you both . . . by me. I need . . . you both."

Cicely was weeping softly, raining tears and kisses

on his face and hair. "Oh, Quincy," she sobbed. "Quincy."

He raised a trembling hand to stroke her cheek and guide her face down to meet his kiss. "I love you," he murmured silently. "My Cicely."

"Shhh," she soothed. "Don't try to talk, darling. I know. I've always known." Her fingers entwined in his hair. "What sons we would have had," she whispered.

Quincy exhaled sharply and turned his gaze on Ashley. "No . . ." he managed. "That . . . one girl is . . . worth all . . . the boys that ever . . . that ever . . ."

Overcome with emotion, Ashley ran from the room. Her eyes blinded by tears, she rushed down the passageway and crashed head-on into an immovable object. The force of her collision would have thrown her backward off balance, but strong arms caught her and pulled her against a hard masculine chest. "Kelt!"

"Aye."

For long seconds he held her prisoner, so close that she could feel the beat of his heart, could feel the rock-hard sinews of his thighs pressed against hers as his familiar clean smell assaulted her senses. Her knees felt weak and her head spun. Even a token protest was beyond her strength as she tried to recover her breath. "I'm sorry," she murmured. "Please . . ."

He released her, stepping back yet still supporting her with one arm. "Are ye all right, lass?"

She nodded. "I need some air." Taking a deep breath, she wiped her eyes with the back of her hand. "I'm sorry. You must think I'm a fool. Please, could we go up on deck?"

Wordlessly he led the way, assisting her up the steep ladder, then leading her to a spot on the bow of the ship where they could be alone. Ashley sank down on a coil of rope and buried her face in her hands. "I can't bear it," she said. "All these years I've hated them both and now . . ." She chewed her bottom lip and looked up at Kelt. "Now it's too late."

"We each ha' our own devils to face." He crouched down to look her full in the eyes. "Ye were but a bairn. If ye ha' forgiven them now, then ye canna blame yourself for what lies in the past." A scowl passed across his craggy face. "And ye had plenty o' cause for anger. They ha' both wronged ye and I think your lady mother more than McCade."

"Oh!" Ashley jumped up. "I should have warned you. Nicholas tried to stop her from coming down to the boat. He hit her, and my brother fought with him. Nicholas fell back and struck his head on the hearth. When he comes around, he's going to be in a rage. You'd better prepare the men for trouble. He'll probably come with guns and he won't come alone."

"We'll be certain we have a proper reception for the master of Rosewood if he comes." Kelt stood up. "Let me inform the first officer. Will ye be all right?"

Ashley nodded, watching as Kelt went aft to speak with Isaac Kahn, the man Captain Fraser had assigned to sail the *Merry Kate* while he remained with the *Scarlet Witch*. She glanced up the hill toward the house. How strange that Nicholas hadn't come after Cicely by now. Could he have been seriously injured by the fall? Fancy Henry having the nerve to stand up for Cicely. She wouldn't have thought he had it in him.

More than an hour passed before Ashley gathered her courage enough to return to the captain's cabin. When she did, she found that Quincy had ceased to breathe. Cicely sat beside the body, holding his hand and crying softly.

"He's gone, Ashley," she said. The emerald necklace lay on the floor at her feet. "He's really left me this time. What am I going to do?"

Ashley crossed the room and put her arms around her mother, hugging her tightly in the first real embrace she had ever given her. There were no words between them, but each woman took a little comfort from the other's touch.

When Ashley finally let Cicely go, her mother gathered up the necklace from the floor. "He said he wanted me to have this," she murmured. "Is it right, do you think . . . to wear it?"

Ashley nodded wearily, feeling old herself. "He stayed alive just to give it to you. But don't let Nicholas find out where you got it."

Cicely sniffed and wiped her eyes. "I have my ways of dealing with Nicholas." Her mouth puckered into a pout and she leaned over Quincy's body, stroking his hair. "He's the only one I ever loved more than myself, Ashley. Can you understand that?"

"I think so."

"I want him buried on Rosewood with full honors. I don't care how much it costs or who we have to bribe. There'll be no pauper's grave for Gentleman Jim. Couldn't we say he gave his life for . . . oh, I don't know, Ashley. You think of something. I don't want people saying nasty things about him."

"I'll talk to Kelt. If Nicholas will let you, I'm certain he'll release the body. Kelt's a good man, Cicely."

"Yes, he is. I thought so when I first met him. But don't get any ideas. He's far below you. Just be certain he doesn't try to take advantage of his position in your bedchamber."

"His what?" Ashley felt a blush creeping up her throat.

Cicely sniffed. "You think I've lived to be my age without being able to recognize a pair of lovers when I see them?"

"You're wrong, Cicely. There's nothing between Kelt and me."

"Liar." She kissed Quincy's palm and laid his hand on the blanket. "You'd do well to accept James Pade's proposal. He doesn't know about your relationship with your overseer and he probably wouldn't know a virgin if he fell over one."

"I have no intentions of—"

A sharp rap on the cabin door caught their attention. Ashley turned to see Kelt and her brother standing in the doorway. Henry's face was a mask of anguish.

"Henry has something to tell you." Kelt stepped into the room and Ashley knew from his expression that something was terribly wrong.

"He's dead," Henry blurted out.

Cicely let out an exasperated sound. "I know he's dead, Henry. What are you doing here?"

"No," Ashley said. "Not Quincy. Nicholas." She took her brother's arm. "Nicholas is dead, isn't he?"

Henry broke into tears. "Yes," he sobbed. "He's dead and Nate has gone for the sheriff, and Gabby says they'll hang me for murder!"

Cicely took a step backward and sank into the chair. "Nicholas is dead?" she asked softly. "Dead? You're certain?"

Henry fell to his knees and buried his head in his mother's lap. "Yes," he moaned. "He's . . . dead . . . and I killed him. I didn't mean to ki-kill him. I only meant to stop him from . . . from hitting you." His wailing became a series of hacking coughs. "Don't let them . . . hang me," he begged.

Cicely looked up at Ashley. "Go up to the house and see if Nicholas is really dead. If he is, take control of the servants. I'll be along as soon as I can calm Henry. All this excitement is terrible for his condition."

Ashley stared at her mother in astonishment, unable to believe the sudden change in her demeanor.

"Well? Are you deaf? Master Saxon, go with her. See that the servants speak to no one until I've talked to them. We'll have no scandal connected with Rosewood because of an unfortunate accident." Cicely nodded firmly. "If Nicholas has taken too much brandy and had a fall, that's certainly a family matter." She patted Henry on the back. "For God's sake, stop that choking, Henry. No one is going to hang you. Well, what are you two waiting for? Go and do as I've instructed. And if the high sheriff comes, I'll deal with him. His wife is a personal friend of mine."

"You heard the lady," Kelt said with unconcealed amusement. "Mistress Ashley, we had best get up to the house and see about your poor stepfather."

Apprehensively Ashley entered the room. Nicholas lay on the floor where he had fallen. Only a small pool of blood on the rug beside his head gave evidence of his fatal injury. A mahogany Windsor chair lay on its side near his feet. The house was hushed and still, seemingly empty of servants.

"He looks dead enough to me," Kelt said. "And good riddance. 'Twill save the crown the expense of a trial."

"It wasn't Henry's fault," Ashley defended.

Kelt went to a sideboard and picked up a decanter of brandy and a glass. He filled the glass and dropped it on the brick hearth. Ashley winced as the glass shattered. Kelt walked over to the dead man and poured a little brandy on his shirtfront and face. "Poor mon," he said. "Your lady mother was right. He did ha' an accident." He replaced the decanter on the sideboard. "Were there any servants present when he hit his head?"

"No. Only Henry. And me. I was there." She pointed. "Cicely was already in the hall."

"Then you and Henry are witnesses. Nicholas was drunk. He fell." Kelt shrugged and spread his hands palms up. "A tragic loss for your mother."

Ashley sat down in the nearest chair. "You mean we lie to the sheriff?"

"Nay, lass. Who said anything about lying? We just don't tell him everything."

"I thought you were the one who believed so strongly in the law."

"I do, but it's the spirit o' the law that's important, nae the letter. I would say that justice was done here today. Would ye not?"

The *Merry Kate* sailed on the next tide to deliver her prisoners to the authorities at Williamsburg for trial and subsequent hanging. Ashley remained behind at Rosewood with her mother and brother for the funerals of Quincy McCade and Nicholas Randall, and for the inquiry into her stepfather's accident. Cicely Randall conducted herself with grace and decorum through all three ordeals.

The name Gentleman Jim was never mentioned by the minister who conducted the services for Quincy James McCade and Cicely let it be known about confidentially that Master McCade had lost his life in the battle against the pirates. He was given a place of honor in the private cemetery at Rosewood beside Nicholas Randall, with a space left for Cicely when she should reach the end of her days.

"Don't you think you could have buried him somewhere else, Cicely?" Ashley asked as they walked up the hill from the graveyard. "Instead of side by side?"

"Hush, Ashley, the reverend might hear you. Why shouldn't a hero like Captain McCade have a nice resting spot? After all, I'm mistress of Rosewood. It's my place to make such decisions now."

"Henry wasn't too happy about it." Ashley glanced at her brother trudging steadily behind them. "Some would say he is master here now."

"Oh, poo. Henry is Henry and there's no sense in us pretending anything else. Robert would have thrown a fuss, that's certain. Robert was the best of Nicholas and me." She sighed. "But Robert's dead, too." Cicely's blue eyes suddenly became fierce. "I hate all this dying!" The blue eyes clouded as tears welled up. "I shall never marry again, not with Quincy gone. Stay with me, Ashley. I shall be so lonely."

Ashley picked up the skirt of her borrowed satin gown and hurried ahead. "You know I can't do that. I've got to get back to Morgan's Fancy."

"Nonsense. That man of yours hasn't returned from Williamsburg yet, but when he does, you can send him to tend to your plantation. James is coming back to the house later. I want you two to have time alone together. I think you and James would make a good match, Ashley."

"No. I will not consider marrying James."

"Shhh. Do you want the reverend to hear you?" Cicely quickened her step. Even in black, she looked like an exquisite china doll.

"I don't care who hears me. I am not marrying James Pade." Suddenly everything seemed to be closing in on her. She couldn't wait for Kelt any longer. She had to be away where she could think. She had to get back to Morgan's Fancy.

In the house, Ashley hurried up the grand staircase to her room. Water would be the quickest way to get home, but she couldn't stand the thought of setting foot on a boat again just now. There were too many fresh memories. Hastily she began to pack a few articles of clothing as a plan formed in her mind.

"Going somewhere, sister?"

She spun around to face Henry. "Yes. Don't tell her. I can't stay here any longer. I'm going home."

"I know the feeling," he said. "But where do I run to?"

Ashley's face softened. "You'll be all right, Henry. You're master here now."

"I am?" He brightened. "I could go to London if I wanted, couldn't I? Or even Italy. They say the weather there is good for consumption. Do you think she'll let me go? God knows there's enough money." He nervously twisted the lace on the cuff of his sleeve. "She liked Robert the best of all of us, you know. Sometimes I used to wonder what I would have been like if I'd been McCade's son. Would she have loved me then?"

Ashley shrugged. "I don't know, Henry. It didn't do much for me." She smiled at him. "I need to borrow a few things from you. Some clothing and a good horse."

"You're going to ride back to Maryland?"

She nodded. "I've got a lot of thinking to do."

"You'll want Robert's roan gelding and you might as well have my gray. I haven't been in the saddle in months. Take what you will . . . and Godspeed." Henry's face reddened. "You're not so bad . . . for a sister."

Dusk was falling when Ashley tied the roan's reins to a tree by the cemetery wall and went to say her last goodbyes to Quincy. Heaps of flowers covered the raw earth of the new graves; in a few weeks grass would spring up and blanket the mounds in soft green. Ashley dropped to her knees beside her father's resting place, but once again she found no words.

The scent of honeysuckle and lilacs filled the air. The sounds from the manor house were muted and far away. She was alone in the warm Virginia night with a solitary mockingbird and the ever-present litany of spring peepers. "Goodbye, Papa," she whispered. "Rest now. You've earned it."

Chin up, she returned to where she had tied the horse and swung up into the saddle. She turned his head north and dug her heels into his sides. "Get up," she murmured. "Let's go home."

"Wait, Ashley! Wait!" A horse and rider galloped down the dirt lane toward her. "It's me! James!"

Reluctantly she pulled up the gelding, turning him to face the oncoming rider. Damn, she thought. A few minutes more and I would have made my escape.

"Ashley! Henry told me what you were up to. How could you think of riding off like this with matters not settled between us?" He reined in his horse beside her and pulled off his cocked hat. "Didn't Cicely tell you I was coming?"

The two animals sniffed one another, nickering amiably. Lord Pade's horse was nearly sixteen hands, with good lines and a noble head. Ashley reached over and patted the animal's neck. "You always did have good taste in horseflesh, James. And you ride as well as any man in Virginia."

He grinned, tucking the feathered hat under his left elbow. "That's a compliment, coming from you."

"I'd not say it if it wasn't true. Cicely said Nicholas always envied you your hands. You have a way with horses."

"I came to offer my condolences to your mother, but I'd be a liar if I said I regretted Nicholas's passing. He was no gentleman and Cicely deserves better." He cleared his throat. "I'd have been at the funeral, but I had urgent business elsewhere."

"You witnessed the hangings."

"I did." He stared off into the darkness. "I'm not a vengeful man, Ashley, but I believe in justice. We must make the Chesapeake safe for honest citizens." The bay danced sideways and James soothed the animal with a firm hand, maintaining his erect posture in the saddle without visible effort. "I believe you'll think no less of me if I tell you I took no pleasure in watching them die."

"I have known you all my life, James. Nothing could make me think less of you."

"Ashley, you must stop this wild manner of living. You could have been murdered by these people . . . or worse." He broke off, plainly embarrassed. "I want you to be my wife. I asked Nicholas for your hand, but he gave me no answer. However, now that he's gone, I'm certain Cicely would give us her blessing." He cleared his throat again. "Mother has given her approval. I need only your agreement."

Ashley leaned forward in the saddle and scratched the roan's neck. How could she turn this good man down without offending him? "James . . . Lord Pade," she began softly, "you do me great honor. But have you fully considered this match?"

"I know I'm considerably older than you, Ashley, but that is often an asset in marriage. I would like an heir, children. And despite your extraordinary upbringing, I think we would suit each other."

"You have said nothing of love, James."

He coughed. "That would come after marriage. Where there is friendship and respect, love follows.

Who should a woman love if not her husband?'' He brought the bay closer. ''Damn me, girl! I'm not a milksop boy. You'll get no fancy talk. But I will treat you well and share my name and all that is mine with you.''

''That's the trouble. I like you too much to become your wife,'' Ashley explained. ''You are a leader in the colony, a lord, a person men come to for advice. Who knows what advancement might come your way in the future? With my . . . background, I'm not the wife for you. I might become an embarrassment in years to come. No.'' She threw up a hand. ''I mean it, James. We would not suit each other. I am far too used to having my own way. You need a wife of a more gentle and pliable nature. Do you want to spend the rest of your life with a woman cut in the same mold as your mother?''

''God forbid!''

''Exactly. You would do far better to wait a few months and then court Cicely.''

''Your mother?''

''Why not? She's beautiful, isn't she? And rich. And she has always admired you.'' Ashley smiled up at him. ''She's young enough to give you an heir and wise enough to support you against Lady Pade.''

''I had not thought of Cicely.''

''Then it's time you did. She is the perfect hostess and her land joins yours. If you do not wed her, who knows what other man you might have for a neighbor.''

''But Henry is master now. Surely—''

Ashley sighed loudly. ''My brother is not long for this world, James. He told me just this evening of his plans to go to England. Henry would not be an obstacle to your suit.''

''You are a most unusual young woman, Ashley Morgan.''

"Thank you, sir. I will take that as a compliment. And now"— she pulled up the roan's head—"I will be about my business. You are on your honor as a gentleman not to tell my mother I am leaving. You may, however, say that I declined your offer of marriage. Or perhaps it would be better to say that you had had second thoughts."

"You're certain you will not have me?"

She laughed. "As a stepfather, gladly."

"Cicely may turn me down, too."

"I doubt it. I do not think my mother is a woman who cares to be too long without a man."

"Do not be too hard on her, Ashley. If there are things in your childhood that . . ." He trailed off, uncertain.

"I would not have suggested her for you if I held any bitterness against her, James. I think the two of you could find happiness together."

"And us?"

"We will remain friends, no matter what." Ashley raised her hand in a salute and nudged the roan's side with her heels. "Remember, not a word," she warned.

"You'll not do anything reckless?" James called after her.

"Not if I can help it," she shouted back over her shoulder.

Chapter 25

It was early May and the dogwood was in bloom when Ashley crossed the northern boundaries of Morgan's Fancy. The days of solitude had given her an opportunity to think, and though she'd found little peace of mind, at least she'd recovered most of her inner strength. Her sorrow at Quincy's death was tempered by the knowledge that with the loss of her father, she had truly found him. Old fears and guilt could be put to rest. She had even come to accept Cicely for what she was. There was little love between them, but at least she could think of her mother with some affection.

Kelt was gone. Ashley knew in her heart that she had lost him. She had deliberately made a leisurely trip from Virginia to Morgan's Fancy, stalling until the spring planting was finished on the plantation. Kelt had told her he was leaving after the planting and she had no doubt he would keep his word. If she had been there when he left, it would have been too painful to bear. The dark Scot had offered her a love she'd never expected to receive from a man, and out of stubborn willfulness and lack of trust, she had thrown it back into his face.

A hundred times on the trip north from Rosewood she had seen his face. He haunted her dreams with his soft burr and magnetic gray eyes. She'd shed enough foolish tears to float a cask of tobacco, but it all came back to the same thing. A man like Kelt Saxon came to a woman once in a lifetime and she'd not had the sense to recognize him for what he was before it was too late.

At least Kelt was not leaving empty-handed. His share of the reward money offered by the Virginia authorities would be substantial. The *Scarlet Witch* alone would make him a man of means. With the sale of the pirate schooner, he could buy his own plantation and till his own fields instead of another man's.

For the first time since Quincy's death, Ashley thought of the buried treasure and laughed. Beneath her, the horse gave a snort and flicked his ears. She patted the roan's neck. "Just a little farther, and you'll have a nice stall and some grain," she promised. The animal quickened his step and Ashley chuckled again. "Just like a man," she observed. "Mention food and you're all ears."

She decided to wait a few weeks or even months before she went to check out the location of Quincy's fortune. She guessed she and Mari would have to move it to a new location. Several spots would be better than one. It was surprising how little the thought of being rich meant to her. After all the struggle to keep Morgan's Fancy solvent, her worries on that account were over.

"I suppose I could even buy my own ship to carry my tobacco to England. What do you think of that, Shawnee?" The horse ignored her. She'd not thought to ask her brother the animal's name, so she'd been forced to give him a new one. So far, the gelding didn't seem to respond to it one way or another. Ashley sighed. "It shows just how batty I'm getting when I try to talk financial matters with a Virginian."

The sound of axes and falling timber drifted toward them from the creek. Ashley turned the horse's head toward Mari's cabin. She wasn't ready to speak with her lumbermen yet, wasn't ready for the mountain of problems she knew they would have for her to solve. She wanted to see Mari and find out if Baron had survived the gunshot wound. The roan was a fine blooded animal with heart and staying power, but he wasn't a lifelong friend. Her bay stallion was more than a horse, and if he was dead, she doubted she would ever find another animal that suited her as well.

The forest was a canopy of lush green in every shade from cedar to the pale new green of sprouting grass. From every tree came choruses of lilting bird song; on the ground, she spotted fresh deer and rabbit tracks, and even glimpsed a bushy russet tail as a red fox dove for the protective cover of a green briar thicket.

To Ashley's keen disappointment, Mari's cabin stood quiet. Even the corral was empty. Ashley dismounted and checked the ashes in the fireplace. There had been no cooking fire there for days and there was no sign of any of the Indian woman's assorted pets. Mari was undoubtedly off on another visit to her relatives. Slowly Ashley swung up into the roan's saddle and turned toward the manor house.

As she reached the dirt road, she urged the horse into a canter. Suddenly she was tired of being alone. She wanted to see familiar faces, to have a hot bath and wear her own clothes again. After all these days of camping out, the thought of sleeping in a feather bed was pure luxury.

At first the farmyard at Morgan's Fancy seemed as deserted as Mari's pound. A few horses and a spotted cow stood with their heads hanging amiably over the split-rail fence. A long-eared hound bitch lay with her eyes shut in the shade of the barn well house, nursing a half dozen multicolored pups. There was no sound but the *perk-perk* of a turkey hen scratching for worms in the dirt beside the fence. Then a groom sauntered lazily out of the barn, breaking into a run when he saw who the visitor was.

"Mistress Morgan! Welcome home!"

Her attention was caught by an urgent whinny from the barn and the sound of a horse's hooves hitting the side of a box stall. Ashley dropped the roan's reins into the groom's hands and ran into the barn. "Baron!"

The big stallion reared, striking the top rail of the door with his front feet, and let out a welcome nicker.

"Baron!" Ashley threw her arms around the massive head. "Good boy! Good horse." Entering the stall, she anxiously examined the pink scar, stroking the animal's neck and withers. "Good boy," she soothed. "Good old boy." He'd lost a lot of weight, but it was plain that the wound was almost healed. "Mari must have spent a lot of nights with you," she murmured. "Yes, but you're worth it."

"Glad to have you home, mistress. That horse is hard to handle. He's had this barn on its end since Mari brought him up here."

"Do you know where she is? When she'll be back?" Baron pushed at her with his nose and she scratched him behind the ears. She couldn't quite keep her eyes from wandering to the stall where Kelt had kept his dappled-gray. It was empty, as she had known it would be.

"Nope. I wouldn't know nuthin' 'bout that, mistress. You know how Injuns is. She didn't say nuthin' to me, jest put the stallion in his stall and said take care o' him. She looked at me wi' snake eyes like she does. Gives a body the creeps."

"You haven't seen Jai, have you?" Even her dog seemed to have deserted her. She missed the shaggy head and rumbling bark he always gave when she came home.

"Yes'm. The Injun woman, she had the dog wi' her. Said to tell you somethin' 'bout takin' him swimmin' in the big salt water."

"All right, thank you. See that the roan gets a good rubdown and some warm mash. He's had quite a workout."

A little girl with a cat under her arm paused to call hello to Ashley as she crossed the yard to the kitchen door. It stood open, with a boy swinging a pine bough to keep out flies. Ashley nodded to him and paused to take a deep whiff of the delicious odors coming from the kitchen. The smell of bread baking was enough to make her ravenous. Trail cooking, and especially hers, was never the best, and she hadn't stopped to eat since daybreak.

"Good day, Mistress Morgan."

"Good day, mistress."

"Miss Morgan."

Three woman echoed greetings as she entered the kitchen. The older white woman was wife to one of the indentured servants, but the two blacks were strangers. One was a tall, broad woman with tribal tattoos on her cheekbones, and the other, a small copy, looked about fifteen. The girl braced one hand against the plank table for support, half hiding a crippled leg behind her.

Ashley glanced around the shining kitchen. Every cobweb had been dusted from the rafters and the walls glistened with fresh whitewash. The pine floor was scrubbed clean enough to see her face in it, and the baskets, hooks, bowls, and pots all hung in orderly rows. Fresh bundles of spices and herbs dangled from the beams, and a crock of butter in the center of the table, set into a bowl of water to keep it cool, was topped by a clean linen cover to keep out insects.

"Good day," Ashley replied. "Samantha, are you working in the kitchen now?"

"Yes, Miss Ashley, I am. Master Saxon said I could. My daughter, Mary, helps out, too, but she's fetchin' some fresh fish from the dock."

Ashley turned to the older black woman. "And you are?"

"Elvy, mistress, an' this my girl Rose-lind. We pleased to have ye home."

Ashley nodded. "Rose-lind." She ran a finger over the scrubbed tabletop. "The kitchen is . . . It looks wonderful, Elvy. I hope you will like living on Morgan's Fancy." She swallowed hard. "I think we must have a talk soon about your papers."

Elvy blanched. "What's wrong wi' my papers, mistress? Master Saxon say it all done legal. Roselind here, she got seven-year bond, jest like Abe and d'others." She twisted large, muscular hands in the folds of her apron. "Master Saxon say I a free woman, mistress. He say I work fourteen year in Maryland for white folks an' that's all anybody can ask."

"Master Saxon said you were free?" Ashley let

out a sigh of relief. "That's wonderful, Elvy. Of course, you're free. I didn't know if he'd told you or not," she lied quickly. "There are no slaves on Morgan's Fancy." Ashley's heart began to pound. *He freed her. He did listen. He freed the slaves.*

Elvy, Rose-lind, and Samantha all began to laugh and chatter at once. "You go on up, Miss Ashley," Samantha said. "We'll heat you some water. I know you want a bath after all that ridin'."

"Rose-lind been straight'nin' up some upstairs, mistress," Elvy explained. "Your clothes is all nice an' ready fo ye. Everythin's there. You need somethin', you jest holler."

"And Master Saxon? Is he here?" Ashley asked.

"Oh, no, ma'am," Samantha said. "He left two, three days ago. Him and old Thomas. Nobody here but us."

Nodding, Ashley left the kitchen and climbed the stairs to the second floor. She had known he was gone. Why hadn't she let it be? Numbly she went down the hall and pushed open the door to Kelt's chambers.

His things were gone, as she had known they would be. Her unfinished portrait leaned against the cold fireplace. "Oh, Kelt," she whispered into the empty room. "Why?"

In the orchard Ashley sat on the soft grass with her knees drawn up to her chest and her arms wrapped round them, leaning back against a tree trunk amid the gentle showers of fragrant apple blossoms. Twilight had come and gone, melting into the warm spring night like new-spun honey, and the mockingbird had ceased his chirping song, giving over to the whippoorwill and other birds of the night. Still Ashley sat there, lost in her own thoughts and treasured memories.

At last, when the moon's pale light had turned the rows of trees into a fairyland of shimmering other-world beauty, Ashley sighed, unfolded her stiffening legs, and rose to her feet. She had not taken a dozen steps in the semidarkness when a man's voice startled her from her reverie.

"Stop there, woman."

She whirled toward the source of the voice, peering into the shadows. "What do you want?" she demanded huskily. A rivulet of fear ran through her and she trembled.

"Come here." It was an order.

Ashley licked her dry lips. "Who do you think you are?"

"I'll brook no sass from you, girl!"

"I'm mistress of this plantation!"

"Aye, ye may be that, but I think we both know who is master here." The tall form stepped from the shadows and Ashley hurled herself into his arms.

"Kelt! Kelt!" she cried, wrapping her arms around his neck and covering his chin with kisses. "Kelt," she murmured as he lifted her and his name was lost in the depths of their kiss.

"Darlin' *mna,*" he whispered, intertwining his fingers in her hair and loosening the silken ribbon to let it flow like a dark curtain around them. "Kelpie, mine. I ha' missed ye so . . . like a parched field misses the rain."

"I thought you were gone," she murmured.

"The fires o' hell wouldna keep me from ye, lass."

"They told me you were gone," she insisted between kisses. "I asked and they said—" She pushed his face away. "Your beard! What have you done with your beard?"

"I shaved it. Do you see any need to cover such a handsome face as my own?"

She stared at him and ran a finger down his bare cheek. "I'm not sure I like it," she teased.

"Well ye'd best learn to like it."

"But why? Why did you shave it off?"

His mouth covered hers as he knelt on the grass, pulling her down beside him. " 'Twas a Scotsman's face, nae that o' a Maryland planter," he said huskily.

Trusting, she lay back in his arms, caressing his craggy features with her eyes, leaving her heart free to welcome the flood of joy that brought tears to her eyes.

"Are you so sad to ha' me here that ye must weep?" he teased, stroking her throat and hair, and pressing his lips to the opening at the neck of her shirt. "I would ha' thought ye would be glad to see me after so long apart."

"I am," she whispered, running her hands over his shoulders, squeezing and touching the sinewy hardness to be certain he was real and not some dream. "Oh, Kelt, I am. I don't care about the beard. You can shave your head like a Turkish pirate for all I care! But those damned women lied to me. They said—"

"Like a dog wi' a bone ye are," he teased. "Taking on Richard Chadwick's suspicious ways. No one lied to you. I was gone—to Chestertown on business." He kissed her again and she parted her moist lips, letting their tongues touch and caress.

"You said you were leaving Morgan's Fancy," she breathed softly. "At the end of spring planting."

"Did no one e'er tell you nae to remind a mon o'

what he ha' said?'' Kelt's hand slipped under her shirt to cup a love-swollen breast.

''I told you to go,'' she dared, ''but I want you to stay. Please stay with me, Kelt. I want to be your wife.''

''Aye, that may be,'' he said after a long silence. ''But what o' the problems between us? Ye are still a lass o' great land and property.'' He propped himself on one elbow and leaned over her. ''What will the Chestertown folk say if Mistress Morgan marries her hired overseer, a mon who was once a bond servant?''

''To hell with what they say, Kelt,'' she whispered. ''I love you and I want you for my husband.''

''And I suppose if I agree t' this, I'll be asked to sign a marriage contract?''

Ashley shook her head as a lump rose in her throat. ''No. No contract . . . unless''—mischief gleamed in her moonlit eyes—''unless you want one. With the *Witch,* you are a man of substance now.''

''Aye, so I am.'' He curled a lock of her hair around his finger. ''But as a mon o' substance, should I not take care in arranging a hasty marriage?''

''Hasty?'' Ashley balled her hand into an angry fist and slammed it into his shoulder. ''This wedding was your idea in the first place, not mine!''

Kelt captured her hand in his and chuckled deep in his throat. ''Why would any sane mon wish to gift his sons and daughters wi' such a shrew's disposition?'' He pursed his lips. ''And how do I know ye are not barren? Ye have not quickened wi' my seed and I have given ye every opportunity.''

''Am I a brood mare that I must produce a child before we wed to prove my worth?''

''Aye,'' he agreed. ''It may not be a bad idea.''

"Beast! Let me up!" Ashley insisted. "I'd not have you to husband if you were the royal governor himself!"

"Hist, lassie," he soothed. "Bide awhile here and smooth your pretty feathers. I didna say I wouldna wed. I only said we shouldna be hasty."

A curse rose to her lips to be smothered with his kiss. Her struggles weakened and then became an embrace as she pulled him down to her. "Don't tease me," she begged. "I don't want to fight with you. I— Where are your things? Your paints, your canvases, your clothes—everything was gone. If you didn't leave, where are they?"

He chuckled again. "In the master's room, where else? We've met and loved there so often, I didna wish ye to lose the way in the dark."

"In the master's room?" Ashley caught her breath. "Then you knew I would—"

"I was certain enough o' it that I stopped in Chestertown on the way home and had your solicitor draw up a marriage agreement. Nay! Dinna fuss. It's better this way. Morgan's Fancy is yours, lass, and we shall pass it to our children and they to theirs. But all we make together, that belongs to us both."

Ashley knotted her fingers in his hair and pulled his head down to brush her lips with his. "I love you," she whispered. "More than life itself. And I don't want to fight with you. I want to make love to you."

"A sensible woman," he murmured, letting his hand run provocatively down her hip and thigh. "But if I agree to this match, when will ye say the words?"

"As soon as the banns are cried," she answered softly, molding her body to his.

"Then our wait will be short," he replied. "I had

the banns cried in Chestertown before I sailed in search o' ye. You'll find I am a mon who always gets what he sets his heart on."

"Kelt Saxon!"

He pushed her full length in the soft new grass, cradling her against his pulsing body. "There is but one thing that still bothers me," he said in a deep burr.

"Aye, laddie?" she answered huskily.

"Do ye think I'll e'er teach ye to wear skirts like a proper lass? These breeches are the devil's own curse to contend wi'."

JUDITH E. FRENCH

JUDITH E. FRENCH and her husband of twenty-seven years make their home on a small farm in Kent County, Delaware. They are the proud parents of four children, and the grandparents of four grandchildren. Coincidentally, one of their daughters is also a published romance author. Judith has been writing professionally since 1959 and is known locally for her collection of authentic folk tales and ghost stories. She and her husband are presently restoring an 18th-century farmhouse that has been in the author's family since 1743. Judith E. French's other interests include caring for her dairy goats and Siamese cats, collecting Indian artifacts and antiques, and participating as a member of Romance Writers of America. She is also the author of two previous Avon Romances, *By Love Alone* and *Starfire*.